DARKNESS REBORN

DARK SPELL SERIES BOOK 8

ISRA SRAVENHEART

CONTENTS

To the superior know-it-all of the universe himself.
This one's for you.
I know you always wanted a bigger role in the Dark Spell Series.
Well, now my dear, you have one!
You are finally getting to unravel the mystery that has always been trapped
inside you.

To the glowing, vibrant sun...
My truth. My spirituality. The other half of my soul.
The person who makes me question every single facet of myself, and for
some reason, I always end up back to you once I find myself again.
It was always going to be you. There is no other.

1

Lady Isra laid completely still on her bed with her eyes half-open. She was not asleep, but not totally awake either. It was almost as if she was in a meditative state, travelling to another land from the comfort of her warm, safe bed. This was ironic considering she had been in another desolate realm of darkness and death while her body lay sleeping for aeons in the golden field.

But Isra felt over-rested. Lying awake would suffice her needs for now. Time away from Astrid was wholly needed, though she hadn't come to the bedroom to sleep. She had already slept away an eternity.

When Isra returned to Shambre Fell with Astrid, the atmosphere could have been cracked into with a knife. He had kissed and awoken her from Ronald's spell, but she had already been informed of his betrayal by both Everilda and Kane.

Isra and Astrid went their separate ways. She retired to the bedroom while he sought solace in their grand throne room, probably brooding over everything he'd done. And it wasn't that their relationship was over. Their love had not shrivelled up and died. And no—Isra didn't hate him, but after Everilda's revelation and hearing the truth from two ghosts from her near distant past, things between them felt awfully strained.

She needed quiet time to mull over. Finding out someone you love had been hiding something from you for two whole years was not something terribly easy to sweep under the rug.

Isra needed the sanctuary of her space to figure things out. How she hadn't picked up on the signs was inconceivable. How was it possible she hadn't noticed Astrid's fiery anxiety that peaked whenever she was near him? Especially when Onyx crashed into the grand throne room, wailing like a banshee. Isra wondered if she was under Astrid's spell... or more precisely, was she so in love with him —his magnetic, heroic presence coated in deep-seated brooding— that she'd let her guard down, allowing him to deceive her the way he had?

Either way, it didn't matter. She knew the truth now, the whole sordid truth. And as grotesque as it was, Isra understood Astrid's reasoning. She wasn't about to run out on him. She got him on a spiritual level, and in turn, he did her. Astrid got into the places of Isra that no man had ever been able to touch.

Isra delved into all the aspects of how it had panned out. It wasn't that hard to fathom why Astrid took over Kane in that manner. He felt that by doing away with the boy, transforming him into a kitten, Kane would be unable to harm them. And he was right; Kane was totally helpless.

However, Isra loved that sweet kitten Onyx from the moment she'd laid eyes on him. His death was something that shook her to near rock bottom, causing her to flee from Astrid for the first time. But now that she knew Onyx was Kane? It wouldn't be easy to simply slink away from that, knowing all she knew now.

I mean, she'd petted that sweet, furry head, totally unaware it was the slithering, whimpering man hidden away in a furry suit. It was sickening! All that time, it had been Kane... When she'd fed him and kissed him. Oh god, that was irksome to think about, for she'd spent many sweet moments gushing over Onyx, cooing at him.

It didn't even bear thinking about. Just the mere idea of it made her stomach turn inside out.

It's absolutely vile at best, Isra thought to herself. *But no matter; we must move on.*

Isra let her head fall against the soft, white pillow. It was a warm, yet breezy December day. The window was open just enough to let some icy air in.

It was hard for Isra to believe winter had already arrived. From her bedside, she watched the snow gently fall, her eyes closing as she began drifting off, remembering how Astrid had awakened her only twelve hours ago.

Astrid couldn't believe it. He was like an excited child. Those brown eyes were warm and full of glee. He was unable to contain his happy tears. They tumbled down his face like avalanches of joy.

"Isra!" He gasped. "I can't believe it. I thought I had lost you. Again!" Astrid emphasised.

He remembered how she had died in his arms on that all too painful rainy night. It was only a year ago, but the memory still stabbed him right in his humanised heart.

"You won't ever lose me," Isra muttered.

She attempted to lift herself, although it was a strain to even rise from the position she was in.

"No, don't try moving too quickly," Astrid warned while also smiling.

He was practically beaming at her, just watching as Isra slowly adjusted to the world around her. Isra was not smiling back at him. For the first time, she seemed stiff and uncomfortable in his company. He had never witnessed her like this. She seemed cold and irrational.

"I want to go home," she announced. "Back to Shambre Fell. Now."

"Okay," Astrid replied, taken aback. *I was hoping we could continue where we left off without this stuff surfacing out,* he thought to himself. *I know I messed up. I know I played one hell of a masquerade here, but believe me, I did it for you.*

"I know many things have happened in my absence." She breathed softly, eyeing him as if feeling her way through him, examining every facet of his being. "I am not trying to be awkward, but after resting an eternity while being taken down to a subliminal hell-like place, I am not one for small talk at this time."

Astrid hung his head. Guilt crept up on him, sweeping over him like a tidal wave, soaking into every part of his soul. It was inevitable Isra would react like this when she finally discovered the truth, and it was clear in her tone of voice that she knew.

"I understand, but I hope you don't hate me," Astrid admitted, reaching for her hand, clutching it in his own cold palm like it was a lump of hot coal full of heat and smouldering passion. "I cannot lose you," he whispered, looking up at her.

Isra smiled for the first time since awakening. "I know. You won't lose me. I just need time," she said with a solemn expression. "Just... let's go home, Astrid."

Astrid climbed onto her, taking care not to allow his weight to submerge her before pressing his lips onto hers in a passionate embrace.

"I am so lucky to have ever laid eyes on you," he gushed, his eyes beaming while his heart jumped inside his chest, gently slowing as he met her eyes with his own. A moment of pure happiness emitted from him as he twirled one of his fingers through her luscious, golden hair. "I never regretted my decision to come after you when I was warned not to, but even with the prophecy of the black rose, I still came crashing in like the knight I always wanted to be, just with feathers."

IsRA was deep in sleep as a memory swept over her in her dream state. Smiling to herself as it unfolded, she was suddenly jerked awake by something landing on her bed with a thump. Anxious, she threw the covers off with a start, only to find a black raven looking up at her with a cheeky, crooked smile. A half-eaten worm dangled from his mouth as if he had been recently enjoying the slimy offering. Isra felt relief, relaxing a little by setting herself up.

"Silas!" she exclaimed. "I thought you were an intruder."

Silas bent his head apologetically. "I am sorry. I should have made myself more known. Anyway, enough of the formalities. I wanted to ask how you were?"

The raven looked guilt-ridden. He was the one that had not assisted Astrid in finding her sooner.

"I am afraid the blame lies with me for Astrid not getting to you quicker than he did. I refused to help him," Silas explained, lifting his left wing as if in mid-stretch. "You see, my brother has done some terrible things in his time, always getting into one scrape or another, and I've always been the one that helped him out of it. Finally, I told him it was time he corrected his mistakes. I know it was harsh of me, but if I had known better, I would have sought to find you myself."

"It is all right, Silas," Isra comforted him. "You only did what you deemed right."

Silas seemed grateful for her understanding, but still, something inside him felt off. He hated making a choice and then finding out something much more ghastly could have commenced as a result of him making that choice. Silas lowered his wing once more before moving toward Isra. He found a spot just below her thighs and perched on her legs.

"Yes, but I still regret it and the issues my wrongdoing caused. I do wholeheartedly apologise," he affirmed.

Isra smiled at him, patting his head. Her fingers glided down his soft black feathers, gently stroking him. "You are a good soul, Silas. You cannot fix everything in Astrid's life. You just simply cannot be that for him. Even he knows that, deep down."

"Yes, well, I do agree with that, but I still feel badly about how it went down, you know? One minute I hear you've been taken by that mortal... and the next? Well, it doesn't bear thinking about. Here you are, a powerful witch in possession of powers most couldn't dream of, and you were carefully lured away by a treacherous trick from someone who wanted to place their blood-soaked wrath upon you," Silas explained in a serious tone.

"And worse so, this man enacted a deed much worse than your own and still couldn't see the light of what was right and good!" he added solemnly.

There was a pause in the air. Nothing was said for a moment. Silas and Isra looked at each other with plain, emotionless expressions. Both seemed to read into the other's thoughts as their eyes twitched at the same time, an acknowledgement of the existence of one good friend to another. Minds meeting in the aftermath of chaos and bloodshed, merging into one. Warm smiles in reciprocation indicated mutual heartfelt feelings as both souls connected, fleeting as they shifted their eyes away, unable to stop the need to blink.

"You know, don't you?" Silas realised without hesitation.

His eyes narrowed at Isra. Those warm black holes of mysticism and wonder seemed to go on for aeons as he stared into her ones of bold, magnificent emerald-green.

Oh, she knows, all right. This is a woman that isn't afraid to delve into the dark. She knows every gritty, terrifying aspect of him. Isra isn't a fool. She was bound to uncover the deceit sooner or later, Silas thought to himself.

Isra lowered her gaze with a furrowed brow. "Oh, yes. I know. Having the man I mentally mind-fucked reveal Astrid's sordid little secret while being held hostage in another realm was not on my to-do list," she muttered sarcastically.

"But still, I'm here to tell the tale, which is more than I can say for Kane," Isra added with rapturous humour.

Silas nodded. He had to admit, looking at Isra, after all she had been through, she looked mighty fine. Maybe some weakness showed when she moved her legs or shifted her upper body to become more comfortable, but otherwise, she had come through almost untouched.

"You are a fine woman, Isra. How you tolerate my brother is beyond me, but at least I can see the devotion you have for him.

That's enough to tell me you won't cast him aside if he crosses the line..."

Silas trailed off, quickly realising Astrid had already done that and here Isra was standing by him.

Wow, she has some gusto, Silas thought to himself with a chuckle. *But I do secretly wonder whether she will dish out her own form of punishment? Still, it's not my business.*

He finished his train of thought, glancing back to Isra with a cheeky smile. Silas's smile was enough to make Isra fall for his wayward charms and warped sense of humour that normally had them in hysterics with uncontrollable laughter.

Isra lowered her gaze a little, those piercing green eyes of hers just about reaching the same level as Silas's head and with a fixated grin, she replied, "Because I love him."

"I know. Anyway, I just hope things are back to normal around here," Silas hinted, giving Isra a wink. "I must depart, I am afraid. I can't stay here for too long. Astrid relies on me too much, and it's time he stood on his own claws; well, feet," he corrected himself at the end. "Still, I am so pleased you are well, Isra. I do hope you wouldn't mind me dropping in on occasion as I do miss our chats, as few as they were."

"Of course. You are always welcome," Isra replied, extending her arm to Silas.

"Well, I must bid you *adieu,*" Silas remarked, lifting his wings in anticipation.

"Yes, as must I," Isra whispered, watching Silas fly out of the open window. "I have an old friend to pay homage to," she recited, smiling to herself once again.

But unbeknownst to Isra, someone was lurking behind her bedroom door, keeping themselves hidden and quiet, while being an eavesdropper on the conversation Isra and Silas shared. The familiar face resisted the urge to cough, sneakily backing away a few paces, knowing Isra was about to step out at any moment.

It was then that the person revealed themselves, that short black hair now showing strands of grey as the stress had weathered him over the past few days. Their muscular frame showed way too much caffeine consumption, and warm, brown eyes with a yellow sheen displayed a tinge of hurt resounding inside.

It was none other than Astrid, hurriedly moving down the cold stone steps to avoid being spotted by her, or anyone, for that matter.

"I wonder who she is paying homage to," he said to himself as he reached the bottom of the stairs, dashing across the hallway as he disappeared out of sight.

2

Quickly fleeing the scene, Astrid skedaddled. He had someone to pay a visit to. His destination wasn't that far away whereas Isra's... well, he wasn't too sure.

Astrid racked his brain, trying to figure out who Isra might be showing her adoration toward, because the last time he had checked, her number of close companions had severely diminished. Apart from him, of course. There was none, so who the hell could it have been?

She has no close friends but me. I'm not even her friend. I'm her everything. I'm trying to fathom who on earth it could be, Astrid conferred with himself.

The thought plagued him, even as he walked far and wide to get to his chosen destination. Finally, amongst all the greenery and wondrous nature, stood that tall, grey castle he had always fondly remembered as home for a while.

Astrid hadn't set foot in Spirisity for fourteen years. He couldn't help but marvel at the yellow crocuses and sweet violets that still grew wildly in between the soft, tall grass blades that dominated Samuel's gardens. Even more miraculous was the fact the warm yellow flowers were covered in ice and still thriving so wonderfully.

Still, Astrid wasn't here to admire the scenery; he was here to hold true to his word.

Samuel had given Astrid the exact whereabouts of Isra, and in return, Astrid had given Samuel permission to take the vengeful Ronald O'Kutte as an animal familiar. Honestly, Astrid wanted to end Ronald and likely do far worse to him, but Samuel held the power in that situation since he was the only one with the insight regarding Isra's whereabouts, so Astrid had relented.

Ronald was now an amusing parting gift of sorts from Astrid to Samuel.

It would only have been presumed rude if Astrid didn't check in on his old employer and how he was getting on with his new house pet, as entertaining as that idea sounded in Astrid's head. And so, Astrid trod all the way here to endear Samuel with his welcoming, witty presence and perhaps offer Samuel some compensation in the form of dry humour.

Since Astrid had been preoccupied with getting Isra safely home, he hadn't given much thought to what Ronald might have been transformed into; however, the idea that Ronald might be rolling around in manure gave Astrid a sinister chuckle, one he wasn't about to admit now that he was only seconds away from the door.

Normally, Astrid wouldn't knock. In days gone by, he'd have pushed his way through with his claw, using the rest of his body to make the door fly open; however, times had changed. Astrid no longer inhabited a raven body, so he was going to adopt the human way of doing things. And just like a humanised being, Astrid pounded upon the wooden door so loudly that some poor servant would have dropped their pail in sheer horror of such an impounding noise disturbing them.

It was only a few seconds of Astrid announcing his arrival before a familiar face stood peering at him with silver framed moon spectacles as they waited in the doorway with queer excitement.

A mass of jet-black hair that had been meticulously slicked back could only match Samuel's pristine and highly precise appearance. There he was, in a black overcoat with shiny black suit trousers to finish off the ensemble. Anyone would have thought Samuel was someone with a lot of material wealth or powerful prowess, but really, he was just someone highly refined.

Samuel smiled at Astrid, clearly happy that the old boy had done well on his promise in making an esteemed visit. It might have seemed like a small favour to some, but Samuel regarded acts like this as truly immeasurable in quality.

"Ah, well done, old chap. You made it then! Oh, come in. Come in. I have the finest coffee readily prepared for us upstairs. It's a rich caramel. Sweet and salty in all the right places. A bit like me, really. Oh, don't stand there like a statue, boy, come on in!" Samuel addressed Astrid warmly as he held the door open for his grandest and oldest of companions and went on to pardon himself as he led Astrid up the steps. "You must excuse the mess of my hovel upstairs. I've been rearranging things."

These were the same steps that led to that famous royal blue curtain Astrid had pushed his way through hundreds of times when he lived here long ago.

"Spring cleaning?" Astrid asked.

It was light conversation, but Astrid felt familiar here, so he was able to engage well enough without fear.

"Something like that. I've felt I needed a change for a while now," Samuel affirmed. "I've always felt something was missing, but I have yet to discover the answer. And so I must plod on despite the confusion that happens to be in my midst."

Samuel and Astrid reached the blue curtain that Astrid knew so well from his days here. Astrid knew the way, so he went on ahead, pushing through the curtain only to be stopped by Samuel, who was, in fact, turning left much to Astrid's surprise.

"We're not going in there. I thought we'd occupy my living area. As I said, I am making some changes and this includes my home, too," Samuel explained as he held a door open for Astrid.

Of course, nobody had ever been in Samuel's living area, so this was a total surprise when Astrid walked in and saw brightly lit white walls with a large four-seater settee in black, perfectly contrasting against a hot pink throw draped across the back of it. Among the snow-white walls were endless amounts of books slotted neatly onto pine shelves. At last, in the middle of the room, was a large bay window overlooking the land of Spirisity.

Just when you thought there was nothing else to admire, there to the side of the window was an ornate gold-gilded fireplace. It had real coals that were lit and sizzling furiously as grey smoke wafted up into the air.

Astrid could easily picture Samuel standing by the window whilst also warming himself next to the fireplace, but never in his wildest dreams did Astrid imagine that Samuel would have a taste for the colour pink.

My goodness, he has gone through some changes, Astrid mused to himself. *If I didn't know any better, I'd say he's going through a crisis of some sort. Maybe one of those mid-life things that people deny experiencing when it happens but yet when it does, they seem to be frantic, pulling apart every aspect of their life and analysing every sordid thing they've ever executed and then trying to make it all fit in some sort of way. And if it doesn't, they go and rehash everything, just like Samuel has been of late.*

Astrid waited for Samuel to ask him to sit; however, he was distracted by the rich, pungent smell of strong caramel stuck in his lungs. Samuel presented two mugs of steaming hot coffee. Presumably, it was the scrumptious caramel flavour Samuel had been so enthusiastic about only moments ago.

Samuel placed the black mugs on the oak coffee table sitting in front of the refined black couch before grabbing his mug and presenting Astrid with his.

Astrid sat nearer to the window since he felt more drawn to that area of the room. Everything else was dressed in this sodden black colour and since Astrid was trying to get his head around Samuel's changes and strange taste in décor, he needed some space between himself and Samuel.

Samuel sat on his settee, crossing his legs in a relaxed fashion. It was something Astrid had never witnessed Samuel do before, and he couldn't help but comment on it because it was so unreal.

"Nice couch," Astrid remarked as he wrapped his fingers around his steaming mug of coffee. Pausing before taking a sip, he pondered the notion that this was a spiritual awakening of sorts. *Yes, but if that is the case, why is everything black? Apart from the glaring pink throw that stares back at us whilst we sit against a slithery leather throne also dressed in the finest black Samuel could muster. It is unorthodox for him, to say the least.*

Astrid didn't want to come across as rude so he took a swig of the rich beverage. Much to his surprise, the rich caramel flavour was sweet but with just the right amount of saltiness as Samuel had described. It wasn't something that Astrid's dignified palette would appease but in this case, he made the exception.

Samuel lifted his eyebrows in response while aimlessly drinking his coffee. He hadn't had anyone in here to take note of his interior antiquities, making Astrid the first, strange as that was to comprehend. Samuel didn't have much in the way of company that often came around these parts.

"Why thank you, Astrid. It was a rather splendid find at some old castle that had been long forgotten. The salacious pink throw came with it, though I never knew I had a liking for anything in pink. But stranger things have happened," Samuel chortled as he slipped his coffee mug back onto the table in front of him.

"Interestingly, you're suddenly changing things up," Astrid cajoled with a grin as though he found the situation somewhat amusing, like Samuel going through this only added to his comedic character.

"I'm having a spring cleaning, if you will. Just more with myself than the actual chateau," Samuel replied as he straightened himself against the settee.

He arched his back as though something was bothering him, or perhaps some*one*. Although with Samuel, he normally expressed his distaste in any matter.

"Spring cleaning in December?" Astrid joked with a snigger.

Again, he found it immensely entertaining that Samuel was

reshaping every part of his home, even his life, just as winter was in full swing.

"You know, I never even noticed it was winter until that boring old soul Ronald pointed it out. I'm afraid I'm not that connected with things these days. I seldom pay any attention to the changing of the seasons," Samuel explained as he reached for his coffee again, gulping its entire contents down in a matter of seconds.

Astrid stared, but didn't say anything.

"That's the point," Samuel said at once. He remembered the most important reason he'd invited Astrid out here in the first place. *Of course! How silly of me to let it slip my mind about Ronald. I've been so abuzz with my own life that I forgot to mention the mortal was still part of the equation. In a manner of speaking, anyway,* Samuel conversed to himself, scolding himself for his poor memory.

"Ah..." Astrid responded curtly.

He guzzled the rest of his caramel coffee in an instant before slapping the mug onto the coffee table. Astrid smiled triumphantly as though he had accomplished something spectacular. He showed no emotion at the mention of that name. It didn't seem to interest him much, although his eyes and ears perked up.

Perhaps Astrid was trying to show some restraint since he didn't want to make a show of himself in front of Samuel, or maybe he was making an unduly effort to keep the matter hidden since it was due to Ronald that Isra was trapped in some ethereal dimension. Also, it was due to Ronald that Isra managed to learn of Astrid's transgression in which Astrid had not only taken Kane out of the picture by changing him into their family pet, but he had gone on for almost two years not telling Isra what had really happened.

There was also the slight hint of bitterness in Astrid since Isra had gone off into an isolation of sorts since hearing of Astrid's betrayal. Maybe in Astrid's mind, he was thinking if Ronald had never gone after Isra, perhaps she would never have discovered the truth. This would have possibly led to the idea that Astrid would have got away clean without saying anything to her.

Of course, there was no such thing when you lived under the

same roof as a witch. They are metaphysically inclined creatures. They are instinctively drawn to the hidden realms of this physical world and pick up on all the little nasties tucked away between delicately weaved webs supposedly concealed from everyone. However, witches and those that walk among the night have always had the gift of tapping into things that people would rather they didn't.

Astrid should have known better, that Isra would eventually seek out that which he was so desperately trying to hide from her. But he had his reasoning in doing so, and for that alone, Isra had not deserted him. She knew deep in her heart that he had good intentions for his actions, and so this was why she chose not to toss him out into the wilderness.

Samuel immediately picked up on Astrid's lack of feeling toward Ronald. Samuel was not one for tact. He would be the only one to bring up the subject as he pried further into the debacle.

"Old wounds still cut deep, eh?" he inquired, although it wasn't a question.

Samuel knew the truth lurking within Astrid. Astrid just didn't have the gusto to admit it as of yet. However, Samuel was rarely defeated and so he was going to get down to the nitty-gritty truth, no matter what it took.

"I'm sorry?" Astrid replied.

He was cleverly brushing the matter aside, but it was clear to Samuel that Astrid was wholly defensive. His brown eyes were narrowed, almost staring into space, making the yellow sheen in them a little brighter than usual. Astrid blinked uncontrollably as though he was frantically trying to conceal something he'd much rather keep buried, the type of burial where you would only be able to obtain knowledge of it if you dug at least six feet into the ground.

Samuel sighed. He had predicted this would be how Astrid would react to being questioned, to deny all knowledge and act as though everything was rosy while still yearning for revenge... or the chance to gloat at Ronald's misfortune.

It was true. Astrid always believed those who wronged others without just cause should be mercilessly punished. I mean, he'd said it himself, so there was no disputing that.

"I mean, Ronald. He took your Isra to that dreaded hell-like place, after all. You can't possibly say you don't hear his name and not secretly wish something ghastly on the boy," Samuel concurred bluntly without a second glance.

Samuel was sincere but yet also careful with his eye contact. He sensed Astrid was riled with this area of conversation, and they hadn't been discussing it for that long.

"Oh, that pitiful human. I don't have much care for it, to be honest," Astrid retorted, shrugging it off as though it meant nothing when in reality, it was the complete opposite.

Yes, well, Samuel wasn't fooled by that statement as he pressed eagerly, "Oh, so you're telling me that you have no interest whatsoever in hearing what became of him? You can honestly say that you do not care? My boy, don't delude yourself. Or me."

Astrid's eyebrows rose as though Samuel touched a nerve, but again, he maintained his resilience throughout as he stated, "Yes, well. I am intrigued to learn what horrific thing you've turned him into."

Samuel smiled, only being too careful not to show just how pleased he was. *Finally, we are getting somewhere. I knew that old Astrid was in there. This new pompous one that acts as if he's cool with the whole thing is getting rather irritating. Just be yourself, boy, for goodness sake. Nobody cares if you hate Ronald so much that you'd want to split him in two. Honestly, not a soul would bat an eyelid,* Samuel thought.

He was satisfied Astrid was starting to admit the truth of the matter at hand because Samuel knew Astrid better than anyone and so he knew that Astrid couldn't hide under a facade for long.

Samuel chortled at the thought of Astrid expressing his curiosity at what form Ronald was now melded into. He had a sneaking feeling it would delight and also amuse the former raven, especially since it wasn't something that Astrid would expect. It was a lot worse than that.

Oh, just you wait, boy. Even the most hellish things come to those who wait. Samuel chuckled to himself while thinking that Astrid really would find it hilarious, to say the least, when he revealed Ronald's new guise.

As Samuel was a man of his word, he wasn't kidding when he said Ronald would be punished. Samuel strongly believed in redemption. And so with Ronald's new form as his right-hand man, so to speak, Samuel had a feeling the new Ronald would be a great shock to many.

"Now now, Astrid, we don't deal in theatrical horrors here, but I do find you may well be impressed when you learn exactly what form Ronald now possesses," Samuel reprimanded in a stern tone but he was also being comedic as there was an element of light-heartedness.

"So what is he then?" Astrid pressed.

Obviously, his curiosity was getting the better of him since he seemed more eager in knowing exactly what physical form Ronald now held.

"I thought you might ask that. Just hold on a moment," Samuel replied, turning away from Astrid.

This only bemused Astrid, who wondered just what the hell was going to come bounding through that door at any second. *Well, it won't be a man, Samuel assures me of that, but what will it be? A nice, timid little mouse or something more suited to Ronald's character? Hmm.*

Samuel gave his full attention to the door that opened into his living area. His eyes focused on it as he suddenly called out, "Oh, Ronald. Come, come. We have guests!" in the loudest, shrill voice he could muster.

The irony of it amused Astrid; Samuel calling Ronald in such a commanding voice only added weight to how much Samuel called the shots around here. Ronald didn't get a say in any of it, apparently.

And justly so, too. That man manipulated Isra, using grieving over Onyx as a way in and thus capturing her under his spell, but it didn't last. That kind of magical trickery never ever lasts, Astrid retorted smugly to himself in sardonic thought.

And then the strangest thing occurred, one that interrupted Astrid's train of thought. He suddenly found himself lost for words as his gaze fell to the floor. He was completely dumbstruck at the sight set before him.

The most endearing purple spider walked in on all eight legs. Each leg was a bright violet and had a lilac boot on it to match as though it was making a statement of some kind.

Well, my goodness. I never saw that coming. A dainty little spider, and purple of all things! Samuel must be having the time of his life playing dress-up with the boy, or should I say, former.

Astrid laughed away merrily to himself, unable to contain just how hilarious he found Ronald's revealing new look.

Of course, Astrid's reaction didn't go unnoticed since his amused face said it all. The highly entertained grin ensured Astrid showed all of his white shining teeth as he flashed a smile that could only display his glee even further. However, Spider Ronald wasn't enjoying this. It also had the most perplexed look on its face as though it didn't understand why it was being summoned.

It gave Astrid and Samuel the impression that perhaps even after a few days under Samuel's roof, Ronald wasn't quite adjusted to his newfound lack of freedom. And neither was he used to his new eight-legged form.

And just when Astrid thought things couldn't get any more baffling, it was then that he heard the purple spider speak fluently in Ronald's voice. And yes, it was indeed him; Astrid remembered that sour-toned, overly prolonged cocky manner in Ronald as though it were yesterday.

"Yes, Master. What do you want?" Ronald asked in a pressing tone, like he was preoccupied with something far more important than coming conversing with Samuel and Astrid.

I was busy draining the blood from a wickedly sweet little fly that landed in my trap, and so you are interrupting my lunch right now, Ronald mused to himself, hoping the fly had not got away.

Since becoming an insect, he was finding it difficult to capture his meals. They always seemed to have a way out if he wasn't efficient enough in his process of weaving the silvery threads around his chosen victim.

And Astrid's face was not one Ronald wanted to see, as it was thanks to Astrid he was stuck like this for all eternity, or unless something terribly dire occurred and Ronald was somehow magically set free. But the likelihood of that was near impossible at best.

Ronald flashed Astrid a sneering glare as though Astrid was some vile creature trespassing upon his web. The look upon the creature's face was that of sheer annoyance as though he would like to ensnare Astrid while wrapping him with layers of carefully spun silk before slowly and surely draining the life from him.

Oh, how I'd like to suck you dry before moving on to your sweet lady friend, taking her in before suffocating her so that no more rancid remains, Ronald cajoled in thought, taking care because he knew Samuel could read minds extremely well.

Samuel had been fully in the moment and saw the glowering look he'd flashed Astrid. And believe me, the light-bringer was not impressed in the slightest. Samuel didn't take kindly to any kind of attitude and waved a finger at the arachnid version of Ronald, sternly warning him to refrain from such behaviour in the future.

Samuel's eyebrows were raised to a considerable height as he formally addressed Ronald, "Now, now Ronald. You know I will not tolerate that. Remember, I own you, so do not beseech my order when I make the call."

"Yes, Master," Ronald answered sharply. But the question remained in the spider's mind: *Why did you disturb my luncheon? Hmm.*

"Now you remember Astrid, don't you, boy? He's come to visit us. Or more precisely, me," the light-bringer added quickly, recalling that Ronald wasn't exactly Astrid's favourite soul in the realm. But Samuel wanted to showcase something prominent to Astrid, a lesson of sorts.

Yes, nobody escapes karma. We are all one of the same, even those drawn to the dark ways. Not a soul can escape that fate they have deliberately created for themselves. I want to show Astrid that even someone like Ronald has to pay the piper for his wicked crimes. And yes, Lady Isra is on the darker side of life, but just the same, the man who tried to harm her does not get to go away unpunished for his crimes, Samuel conferred to himself as he imagined how he'd bring the matter up with Astrid to convey exactly what was happening here.

"Yes," Ronald answered promptly before retorting, "He is the very same man who protects that vile creature, Lady Isra of the Dark. Okay, so she didn't kill my brother but she's hardly innocent. I mean, you must have known what she did to Lillian?"

Samuel softened his stance a little, relaxing against the couch as he recited, "Yes. I am aware of Lady Isra's murder of Lillian, but please do remember that Lady Isra fell prey to your little spell and thus ended up in some devilish dimension, and therefore met both Kane and Lillian as she faced her dark deeds in the most despicable way."

Ronald seemed dumbstruck at such a revelation, stepping back a couple of paces before admitting, "Well, I did not know that. How could I? He had me tied down in some old cottage. I was not even aware of Kane's receding eventuality until he informed me of it."

Ronald seemed angry and irritated, having to contend with the notion that Astrid protected the woman who infiltrated Kane's family in such a way that could only be described as horrific. And not only that, but Astrid was the reason Ronald was now eating flies and other delectable tiny treats because he had made a pact with Samuel not to kill Ronald.

Samuel had not wanted Astrid to go to such extreme lengths as unfortunately, it would have fallen upon Samuel to deal with Astrid's transgression and Samuel much rather preferred they remained on good terms. And so, he persuaded Astrid that there were better ways of handling it. He'd bartered with Astrid that if he spared Ronald, Samuel would reveal exactly where Isra was, paving the way for Astrid to awaken Isra in the blessed golden fields.

"Yes, well. She didn't get away lightly. And so what I am trying to say is that everyone meets the forces of the universe in the end. No matter who or what they are. By bringing you and Astrid here together, you can observe that neither you nor Isra escaped anything as a result of actions you committed in the name of darkness," Samuel articulated in an earnest tone.

"Sounds reasonable, I guess," Ronald muttered, although it wasn't evident whether he was being sincere or not. He could have just been agreeing to get out of the conversation.

Apparently, Ronald wasn't the only one getting uncomfortable; Astrid shifted awkwardly against the couch, lifting himself from his seat before looking at Samuel as he motioned, "I should go. Isra will be awaiting me."

Samuel met Astrid's eyes in a forewarning glance but he saw through Astrid's formal exterior and quizzed, "Ah, things still not back to normal yet at the homestead, eh?"

"She's distant with me," Astrid replied swiftly, making his way towards the door, not even proceeding to say goodbye to Samuel.

Astrid didn't acknowledge Ronald as he made his way across, a move which probably made the spidery Ronald feel ignored and unaccepted, but Astrid gave no fucks about that. As far as Astrid was concerned, he had overstayed his tenure here and was anxious to get home. There was also the bizarre conspiracy of whom Isra was paying her respects to, since Astrid had overheard Isra and Silas's conversation earlier this morning.

Samuel responded promptly as he summarised his exact feelings on the situation. The light-bringer nodded, knowing this was the eventuality that many in a relationship dynamic faced when the subject of betrayal arose.

"She will come around. And if not, there is always the chance to begin anew. You don't have to keep treading the same path, Astrid."

Samuel spoke fluently and clearly, although his advice was not welcomed.

Astrid gave Samuel a stern stare. "I don't wish to start anew," he snapped.

He rested his fingers on the door handle, willing for it to be right for him to twist it. Astrid felt increasingly irritated because someone always had to stick their oar in when it came to his union with Isra. Astrid felt like even Samuel was against them now, although he always had been, from the very same day that Astrid laid eyes upon

Isra. Samuel had given the raven a stern warning that it was best for him to steer clear.

However, Astrid paid Samuel no mind and continued his relentless cause to see Isra. He even went to great lengths to be with her later on by calling upon an old friend, who transformed Astrid into a human. And it was Astrid that persuaded Isra to unleash her own darkness unto the world. But alas, they'd never got that chance; Samuel got there just in time to nip it sorely in the bud.

Isra had no recollection of that day or any other featuring Astrid. Samuel used the greatest magics he had access to and wiped her memory clean. Even to this very day, Isra had no memory of meeting Astrid, James, or even Samuel because Samuel's technique to disarm her from creating further havoc worked perfectly. Samuel had even set Isra up in the iconic Shambre Fell location shortly afterwards, which Astrid later discovered when he viewed her from her bedroom window as she slept.

But, of course, all of this was fourteen years ago.

Astrid was just as devoted to Isra now as he was then. He didn't care for the guarded secret that threatened to drive a wedge between them as that was not his doing. However, he was cautious, fearing that one day either Samuel or James might strike back at him by revealing the truth to Isra.

No, of course, he didn't want to begin again with somebody else. That was obvious to anyone who knew Astrid in the slightest. If they had any idea of his character, he was not going to leave Isra without putting up one heck of a fight, even if it happened to be her that made him do it.

"No, of course you don't, but sometimes we cannot control the people around us," Samuel replied in a drawn-out tone, seeming like he was annoyed.

This succeeded in completely knocking Astrid out of his mind reverie. Astrid realised he had stood by the door the entire time as he had reached into the darkest depths of his mind, mulling over many of his interactions with Isra that he had during the time he had come to know her.

"I better go," Astrid mouthed, not apologising for his rudeness in leaving so abruptly.

He twisted the handle on that door and before you knew what was happening, Astrid shot down those steps until he made it to the front door. Surfacing amongst all the green, his head bobbed up and down, and he strode on, heading straight for home.

3

Isra took care to ensure she wasn't seen as she approached the scorched land of Rainfur.

She had been careful to sneak away while Astrid was not around, for things between them were still strained. She suspected that if he knew where she was going, he might not have fully understood. After all, as far as Isra was led to believe, Astrid had no knowledge of her friendship with Everilda.

Of course, we know Astrid fully knew because he was there from the start, but alas, Isra was still under Samuel Reynaldi's elaborate magics that kept her memory imprinted with a very different outcome, one where she never met Astrid and had no knowledge of who he was.

Rainfur was a rather picturesque place. Quaint and with its own amount of charm, especially when you considered it was a Wiccan village, it was also the same place where she and Everilda stood facing each other when she'd vanquished her former foe with one simple entity. It was that of love. It eliminated Everilda, reducing her to a large pile of red glittery dust in moments. And that was it; it was done.

It didn't matter because it had been two years since Everilda and

Isra had that final standoff. Isra recalled telling her former friend that she had acquired love, a simple thing which Everilda would never attain, and thus Isra used that same energy to destroy Everilda. It wasn't exactly a brutal killing like the one she exacted upon dear Lillian. However, it was all rather bittersweet since the repercussions, seconds later, resulted in Isra being stabbed through her chest with three shards of ice.

Isra perished as a result of that avalanche and the mysterious circumstances surrounding it. But beyond the grave, Isra's dear friend Romeo had brought her back to life only hours later, in front of Astrid who was mourning by Isra's graveside.

All of this seemed so trivial now. Since the incident with the black rose only a few days ago, whereby Isra found herself in a hellish dimension beyond her comprehension, it seemed pitiful to be angry about. You see, when Isra was in that realm, she was reunited with Everilda, who had come to greet Isra upon her arrival.

Everilda saw that Isra was still mighty stubborn, but Isra, in time, relented. It was much easier for Isra to let go of things in recent times whereas years ago, she would have held onto them as if her life depended on it. But Isra finally came to her senses, albeit fifteen years later, and dropped that grudge. It happened to be an occasion where she and Everilda conversed quite politely. They even talked about Jonathan, and although that was a touchy subject, it was apparent both women were long over it and could put it aside.

Isra was reluctant, as one might have expected, but if it hadn't been for her hellish nightmare featuring Kane O'Kutte and his bride Lillian, the situation may not have commenced the way it did. Isra viewed this event as a karmic situation in which she got to revisit her past and at long last put those teenage horrors to bed.

Now Isra stood in that very same spot where she had taken Everilda's life. Isra found herself staring at something peeking out amongst the burnt grass. Her eyes were affixed to it, and before she knew what was going on, she felt herself going into a trance-like state.

Isra felt emotional. All that pain, anger, hatred, and resentment surfaced out of nowhere. And sadness to boot! Oh yes, there was plenty of that. Isra felt regret at the notion that she hadn't made up with Everilda while they were still living. It was with this deep sentimental sense of inconsolable loss that Isra couldn't help but shed a tiny tear, which trickled from Isra's duct onto the gravesite where she stood.

It didn't seem like much, but it was enough to generate a red mass of sparkles that appeared out of nowhere in a circular shape. The beautiful ruby-red coloured energy danced around the scene where Isra's tear fell until it formed a robust globe that was nearly translucent.

Isra could almost make out an image inside it. The image was barely visible but it was almost like a moving picture. Isra could just about decipher there were eyes staring back at her from inside the globe, but to whom they belonged was anybody's guess.

Anyhow, the mysterious effect was becoming more and more blurry as though Isra was losing her perception, her ability to see things clearly. You can imagine the irony of it since when it came to sight, Isra had it in the bag.

Before Isra knew what was happening, she found herself looking at an old recollection of herself. She was standing with Everilda, taunting her as though Everilda was nothing. Yes, that was a painful memory to have unleashed right in front of her.

And just before you think it couldn't get any worse, there was Isra, hurling the unkind truth at Everilda that she'd never discover the love of another. Yes, that was horrid even for Isra's standards, but it was the past, and alas, she could not do anything to change it. Even if she wanted to, which she felt inclined towards, Isra did not have that kind of power.

Every action in life has a karmic consequence. It is only when we take ourselves out of the equation, realising just how horrific you once were, that we stand back and take in the silence around us, Isra thought.

And then everything stopped. The memory vanished, completely gone, leaving Isra confused and bewildered. Then she noticed the glowing red orb of magic that had transfixed her was also gone. Perhaps it was an earthly reminder from the universe that Isra had to be humble because what's had today can quite easily be snatched away tomorrow.

Maybe I am being too hard on Astrid. Perhaps I am blowing this out of proportion. I should just look inside my heart and see where it lies, came to Isra thoughts immediately.

How baffling that Isra being reminded of her dire situation with Everilda would cause her to suddenly have a change of heart in regards to Astrid. Of course, one must make it known, Isra was not leaving Astrid. She was simply having a tough time with the revelation of his betrayal surfacing since she had trusted this man for a near whopping three years.

It was crushing to her, knowing he'd kept a most dastardly secret from her, although it was evident he'd done it out of protecting Isra. But honestly, she would have much preferred to have heard it from him instead of finding out secondhand, from the man she tortured, no less.

It was going to be very hard for Isra to trust him again, but she was just taking some time to herself as she didn't want to make a big show of things. Overreacting was one of her classic trademarks, and she certainly didn't want to showcase this with her eternal counterpart, Astrid.

I should get along home and just hear him out. After all, what's the worst that could happen? Isra pondered as she took one last look at Everilda's gravesite before turning her head and walking away.

Isra had just got back from her little outing to see Everilda, in a manner of speaking.

She gently pushed past the great ornate oak door and glanced up at the stone staircase. Her eyes dazed for a moment as she pondered what kind of reception she would get. Astrid was likely sitting and brooding in Isra's armchair. I mean, it was her chair, but he often sat upon it when Isra was off on one of her many solitary walks.

He's probably sat up there; waiting for my arrival for hours, Isra predicted.

She had a smile on her face as if the thought amused her. Just the notion of seeing Astrid all moody and worn down with those warm brown eyes of his narrowed at her as if he was about to scold her for something sent shivers down her spine. When Astrid was annoyed with her, he could also be very sensual. This kept the romantic side of their relationship like cinnamon... hot but yet also incredibly sweet.

Still staring at the staircase, Isra began climbing the many steps leading to her main area of the house. Isra took due care to be quiet, ensuring that not even an idle dormouse would hear her approach. She began slowly treading upon each step, doing her utmost to ensure she was light-footed until she got to the top.

At last, she came face to face with yet another ornate oak door. This led into her grand throne room; well, it was more a quintessential living area these days.

In the early days when Isra first came to Shambre Fell, her throne room was more elaborate; plain white walls with hints of grey and gold. And standing in the middle was the beautiful red velvet armchair saturated with gold gilding on the back of the seat and fine gold details on the arms of the chair.

But these times were when Samuel Reynaldi created Shambre Fell out of nothing. He designed it to be like a fortress in many ways, but there was a grand element to it, which reminded Isra of a palace found in some prestigious land. Although when Isra had first laid eyes on Shambre Fell, she found there was a remarkable charm about it, which influenced her choice to dwell there.

Isra wasn't royalty, and while there was a red velvet armchair covered in gold gilding, she much preferred the ambience of the white couch sitting just across from the window, overlooking her elegant kitchenette. It was the place where she and Astrid indulged in conjuring up fascinating beverages such as his favourite, which happened to be coffee. However, this was also a place where Isra weaved her most vile enchantments and cooked up the most ghastly potions and other trickery most wouldn't dare to delve in.

Feeling nervous, Isra pushed the oak door open and let her piercing green eyes guide her as she softly walked inside.

Oh, isn't this just darling? Isra remarked to herself in thought as she glanced upon the sight she only mused about seeing a few moments ago.

There he was. The king of broodiness sat bolt upright in Isra's beloved red armchair. His darkened hazel eyes fell upon her immediately, giving her a cold, hardened stare, one that showed no emotion as he allowed himself to drown in her presence. Anyone would think Astrid was mad at Isra, but in reality, he was in a deep state of contemplation. He suddenly shifted in the chair, causing his position to change.

This startled Isra, but she maintained her silence. It was almost awkward; the two lovers gave brazen stares to one another, neither knowing what to say or do, and so penetrating looks were good enough.

Astrid didn't say anything for a few seconds. He flashed Isra another bold, transfixing stare. Only now, he tapped his fingers across the arm of the chair in a repetitive motion. All that could be heard was Astrid's extraneous tapping as he refused to take his eyes off Isra.

After what seemed like several moments of eternity, Isra found herself practically gasping in shock as at last, Astrid found his voice.

"Oh, so you are back then? Nice walk?" he inquired.

His tone was questionable but she knew Astrid was grilling her in a sense. He hated this strained atmosphere between them, but he felt if he kept it somewhat amicable, maybe they could get to the nicer parts later.

If I go all out and ask her where she's been, I'll be tempted to bring up the subject of whether she is going to leave me. So let's just start small and have idle conversation, for the time being, Astrid thought. He felt like having too much too soon was going to be disastrous at best.

He had no idea if Isra was going to issue him her forgiveness or whether he'd be walking on crushed glass for the rest of his days, knowing he'd made one terrible mistake in the name of protecting his love. And to be clear, Astrid's misdeed was trying to conceal the truth from Isra.

"It was somewhat pleasant. I find the December chill rather pleasing," Isra muttered. "I find I can tolerate it more than I used to," she added as if referring to having the ability to stomach things even if they grated on her.

"Good," Astrid concurred.

He seemed abrupt. Again, he wasn't taking his eyes off her but he had trouble finding the words he wanted to say. For some reason, they just were not coming to mind. It irritated him. He was normally so good at knowing what to say. But now, he was inexplicably stricken with doubts, impending fears that Isra was about to walk out of his life for the rest of his years. Astrid had no possible way of communicating that to her, and he had been sitting here for an awfully long time, trying to figure out how he'd express his concerns.

"So perhaps we should talk," Astrid said, still glancing across at her.

Isra didn't say anything in response, so Astrid decided to elaborate, making his meaning crystal clear. "I mean properly. About us. About our future in this ethereal world… " He trailed off, realising that perhaps a departure was inevitable. Soberly he divulged in a low voice, "If we have one."

Isra was a little perturbed, but she remained dignified and responded, "I second that."

Astrid did his utmost to stay calm because honestly, it was becoming harder for him to read Isra's mind; she wasn't giving him any access into what may be occurring inside there.

I would have assumed that if she wanted me to depart from her life, she would have instilled that feeling by now, but maybe she's just being courteous. Or trying to catch me out or something, Astrid worried while conversing to himself in thought. He had never really had trouble reading Isra, and this was the first time he was coming unstuck in regards to knowing what she was thinking.

Isra was a stubborn and sometimes reckless creature that ultimately did what she wanted despite what others thought. Isra rarely had a care for what other souls thought about her or her life choices, but Astrid knew better than anyone that if someone told Isra specifically not to do a certain action, it would be certain that Isra would do it just to rub them the wrong way.

"So let's get down to it," Astrid began. "I know I made some bad decisions and the worst one was not being authentic with you about them, but I'm hoping this is not the end for us."

He spoke quietly, hitting Isra directly in the eyes with another flashing, burning stare—one that told her even if she wanted him to go, he'd never leave. Astrid was possessive. He was almost obsessed with her, having been since the moment he learned of her existence. But there was a bit of intensity as he refused to take those brown eyes with yellow sheen off of her. That stare was enough to make someone tremble... Astrid could be powerful in his masculinity when he wanted to be.

Isra sighed before turning towards the window. She pressed her back against the warm glass, sitting on the sill as she gave him her full attention. Those piercing lime green eyes of her dazzled more than usual as though she was amped up about something.

But she was assertive when she uttered her truth on where she was at in her heart, confirming, "Astrid, I do not expect you to leave and neither do I ask for it. But of all the silly things you manage to enthral yourself with inside that head of yours, I have to say that this is the worst one of the lot."

Astrid didn't say anything. He was dumbfounded, but again, she had given him a harsh reprimand by calling him out on his not so pleasant thoughts, the entities living inside him that were no doubt created as a by-product of anxiety. Not that Astrid would even dare confess to that, but nonetheless, Isra's summary was accurate as to what was playing out.

"Our future in this darkened hell-hole of a realm is set in the stars. It always has been, but I was so worried that this time I had gone too far and you would not accept me for who I am despite everything I have done in the cause to protect you," Astrid mumbled.

There was a strong sense of anxiousness coming through with a worried look that he shot at Isra that spoke of untold tales he had yet to unleash.

There was a likelihood that the memory magic performed on Isra in the early days was at the forefront of Astrid's mind. He was so nervous now about her finding anything out that she might see as a betrayal, whether it was direct or otherwise. Astrid had great concerns that Isra's patience was wearing thin, but he had a sheer determination to prove he was worthy of her trust.

I will do whatever it takes. Whatever she asks of me in order to prove myself, I'll do it. Even if she does not request it, Astrid thought. With the knowledge that the road ahead would indeed be a treacherous and tricky one, he knew he'd do whatever was needed to restore harmony and balance to their connection.

"And so it shall forever be, Astrid," Isra answered with a confident stance.

It was almost as if she had heard his thoughts because let's face it, she could read Astrid's mind very well. Their endearing link went beyond anything metaphysical. It wasn't magic; it was a profound kindred that went between his heart and hers. Neither Isra nor Astrid knew anything like it before, but still, it surprised Astrid when Isra practically told him what he already knew deep inside his mind.

Astrid was just about to say something when he heard a loud rapping coming from downstairs.

Their heart-to-heart conversation had been well and truly interrupted. Whoever it was at the door was not taking being ignored well as another loud rapping sounded out. This time, the knock was even more vociferous than the first.

It had Isra's attention now as well. Her head almost spun around as she peered out of the window to get a good look at who or what the intruder may be. Of course, her head didn't literally spin around, otherwise, there could have been some fatality involved there somewhere. However, Isra was immortal, even if she possessed such gifts.

Astrid lifted himself out of his armchair, looking and feeling rather awkward as he had an inkling that this visitor would not be a welcome one. How he knew he wasn't sure, but Astrid knew better than anyone to always trust his gut.

I better go down there, but what if she follows? Damn. I need to find out who it is. And why do I feel like I am not going to like what I discover? Fuck. Astrid cursed in his thoughts, busying himself with making out a practical plan on just how to deal with this.

As always, Isra managed to put the kywash in his reveries when she retorted, "Just who in the devil is making their presence known at our front door?!" More a question than a statement, but she pulled herself away from the window with her eyes on Astrid once again.

"Damn good question," was all Astrid mustered as he ran out of the living room, taking care not to trip himself up as he spun down that stone staircase at rapid speed, thus ensuring he would get there before Isra.

One would think that Astrid had something to hide from his beloved. He left Isra wondering just what was eating him, bemused as to his swift exit.

4

Astrid was moments from opening that damn front door when the rapping sounded again. The racket caused him to get even more annoyed as he was behind the door, trying to unlock it from his end.

Yes, Astrid had made sure that Shambre Fell was always secure, especially since the incident where the gnome Klinq had infiltrated their home when he was knowingly a spy for Everilda. And other incidents forced Astrid to rethink the security of his and Isra's home.

"Hold the hell on, will you! I'm coming," Astrid called out as he fidgeted with the lock and bolt protecting the entrance to Shambre Fell. Clearly, whoever would be greeting Astrid outside heard him as they failed to make any more noise.

After what seemed like a troubling few seconds of frustration building inside him, Astrid finally slid the bolt off the door before pushing it wide open. Astrid stepped up to show his face to whoever might be standing on his doorstep, and he honestly could not believe what he was seeing.

The mass of mousy brown hair that had evidently darkened in recent times along with a furrowed brow that matched his sword could only belong to one soul. And Astrid was right; he was not amused at this onlooker making their very inconvenient emergence before him.

You have got to be kidding me. No—not him. Not at this time when I am just fragments away from saving my union. This is the worst possible occurrence that could have arrived in my domain. Shitting hell universe, what gives! Astrid chortled away to himself as he remembered he was standing in front of the one person he hadn't expected to ever see again.

Astrid presumed Isra would be heading down here at any second now. And there was no telling what she'd say, because, shit! Astrid would have a lot of explaining to do pertaining to this not-so-charming visitor, one that was patiently awaiting Astrid to acknowledge him. This person, being what they were, bit the bullet before Astrid got the chance to be hospitable.

"It really is nice to know that you are still such a most welcoming person," James quipped in a snarky tone as he stood waiting. Nonetheless, James was still smiling, which Astrid found off-putting as he expected James to be more annoyed with him.

This is the real test now. Will I be welcomed inside and we can put the past behind us? Or is he still resentful? I mean, I haven't even got to the part about Samuel yet... but we must get past this issue first, James thought.

Resolving the situation between himself and Astrid was at the forefront of his mind. The truth of it was that James was not entirely sure if he was going to be let into the doors of the iconic Shambre Fell or whether Astrid would abruptly tell him to fuck off, shutting the door on James's face. Really, only time would tell. James wasn't at all clear on how Astrid was going to handle this.

Honestly, Astrid and James had not laid eyes on each other for almost fifteen years. James's appearance was unsettling to Astrid. It was even more awkward since Astrid was now officially in a commitment with Isra and back then, James was totally against it, labelling it as an obsession.

And of course, it was because of James that Samuel took action and got there just in the nick of time to thwart Astrid's plans to unleash Isra's inner darkness and bestow it onto the world.

Samuel collaborated with James to have Isra's memory wiped by "on high," with Samuel performing the metaphysical enchantment on Isra while he was right beside her. Within seconds, she had no idea who Samuel or Astrid were.

It was worth noting that James played a significant part in it since James was the one who petitioned the plan to "on high" when they gave Samuel the go-ahead to stop both Isra and Astrid. And it was important that they did so before they caused serious damage to themselves and others. Although Isra was considered the more dangerous of the two, she was still nursing a wounded heart and Astrid had been the first man to befriend her since that tragic heartbreak.

So, is he going to open the damn door so that we can enjoy a nice little chat in peace or what? James wondered with sheer impatience, still waiting on Astrid to make his move.

He had already stood here for over ten minutes and time was getting on. James had journeyed from Spirisity to make this most important visit to Astrid, and he felt as though he had come at a most torrential time.

All was not lost though, because at last something finally escaped Astrid's mouth. However, it was not what either of them expected.

"I guess time has weathered my soul impetuously so much that I am too tired to care for most of that crap," Astrid replied with a sharp glare in James's direction, which would have made James question a few things. However, James knew better than to believe Astrid's hard man front, so he relented.

"I don't see how that can be true, but I'm not here to boost your ego, old sport. I'm here with a message about the future for all of us. Not just you and me, but the realm in general. Times are changing for the better," James announced with great enthusiasm, pleased with himself.

Astrid seemed wildly curious as to what this intriguing and yet subliminally vague statement referred to. For once, Astrid changed his tact and was almost polite to James as he pressed, "Oh, yes; and what just might that enlightening bulletin be?"

James smiled. He felt like he and Astrid were finding common ground, a solid footing in which to placate an infrastructure where the two might finally have a meeting of minds in which there would be no indifference or conflict. But perhaps the latter was too good to be true although, at this point, James was remaining positive.

As you can never know what something will bring unto you unless you take the small steps by first of all asking. Only then will you know whether you are greeted by success or confronted by rejection, James thought to himself, pondering this wonderfully inspirational piece of know-how that had just miraculously come to him on a whim.

James arched an eyebrow at Astrid as though he couldn't quite believe what he was hearing. But in any case, the best method to solve any conflict between two souls was always going to be communication. There was no other way to begin other than expressing their deepest thoughts and fears to another, finding answers along the way to all of the most pressing questions.

"That cautionary tale doesn't have a tragic ending. At last, there is light at the end of the long tunnel that has led to nothing but bitterness and disappointment because darkness has always been thy faithful friend to many," James recited cryptically.

It was as if James was expounding on a great revelation of some kind. Or maybe he was talking about a prophecy that hadn't been fulfilled due to entities blocking the way, but now there was a glimmer of hope. There was a strong indication in his words that something finally could come into the light and bring change unto all that sought it... if they wanted it, that is.

"Perhaps we should go inside so I can talk more freely," James suggested.

Astrid appeared nonchalant all of a sudden. The mere idea of letting James into Astrid's home wasn't really on the former raven's to-do list, but there was a much greater matter. And that was how Astrid would explain who James was to Isra, especially since she had no memory of James, courtesy of the esteemed light bringer Samuel Reynaldi who had worked his brand of magic on Isra.

"We have a problem," Astrid muttered slowly. He was careful not to show any disdain, but there was a real issue poking its head out of the water.

James didn't seem to recognise Astrid's need for caution at all. James eyed Astrid sternly. As far as James could see, it was all about Astrid showing off his more rebellious side but then again James had not been around Astrid or Isra for that matter for a timely fifteen years. And a lot could happen in a quarter of a century, believe you me.

"And what might that be?" James piped up in an eager tone, bringing up the subject Astrid did not want to talk about, much to Astrid's disapproval.

"Isra!" Astrid replied sharply.

Astrid folded his arms across his chest, irritated with James. Perhaps in Astrid's peripheral vision, James was the unwanted guest, like the fruit fly that had been caught haphazardly in a widow spider's web. He sighed, showing much annoyance at James's mere presence in his vicinity.

He has no fucking idea of what will be unleashed if Isra gets wind of what occurred back then. A turbulent tornado could be classed as mild compared to our formidable Isra. Just add in seemingly toxic explosions of fiery anger and we'll have a most memorable explosion, Astrid guffawed in a serious train of thought.

However, James didn't seem to catch on as he recited, "Ah, yes. You are on a solid foundation with her now. How interesting, I must say."

It sounded a bit sarcastic, but Astrid couldn't tell. James had always been sardonic in his manner to a certain extent with Astrid.

But this statement was patronising, to say the least. James deemed the union with Isra to be impossible. That such a thing could not have ever been attained because it was doomed from the very beginning. Perhaps it was James's perception of the whole relationship dynamic between Isra and Astrid that assumed this, or maybe there was more to it James was not revealing.

"Yes. I am, but..." Astrid trailed off, trying to figure out how he was going to unleash this tasty detail that had obviously been neglected by James.

Astrid paused, stopping to think. He put his finger to his lips as he pondered the situation carefully.

I can't lie. Isra will have no recollection of him or the me she laid eyes on back then. But how to get that across? Hmm, Astrid questioned carefully as he weighed out his options.

It didn't take much before he suddenly blurted, "But she has no idea who you are!"

James was deeply surprised. His face became tinged with red as his cheeks burned with shock at this revelation that was not at all expertly delivered. Oh, in all honesty, James should have known since he was the one that had actually given "on high" the go-ahead to seal the deal in regards to wiping Isra's memory. Samuel did the physical work required to activate it.

"Oh. That could be difficult at best," James replied, but there was a small pause as if something wonderfully insightful had come to him, like lightning striking out amongst the darkness.

"But I wonder if there is some small way of changing things. Not dramatically, you understand, but there might be some kind of loophole," James suggested as he put his fingers to his lips in a quizzical motion. "Why don't you invite me inside and we can talk this over. Maybe an agreement could be made. Who knows? Efforts might be doubled and some energies could be broken down once and for all." James pestered Astrid with an eager tone in his voice.

Just invite me in. Damn you, man. Hurry up and drop this relentless pride of yours. It doesn't serve a purpose other than to royally piss me off. So off with you. Let's have at it already, James scolded Astrid in thought.

James hadn't come for pure shits and giggles. Neither had he arrived in Shambre Fell to cause a ruckus between Isra and Astrid. No, there was a far greater matter on the forefront of James's mind, one that could potentially impact Astrid if he wasn't made aware of all the facts. And that was where James came in, literally.

Astrid felt a pang of anxiety hit him in the head, right in the middle of his temples. He resisted the urge to rub a finger across his forehead for the fear it would make him seem unmanly. Appearing as if he was a moron in front of James was not on the top of Astrid's agenda. However, James was still standing there like a woodpecker that wouldn't quit nibbling away at an already battered tree, so Astrid needed to think of how to handle what was brewing here. With a migraine pounding on his skull, that wouldn't be the most straightforward of tasks. But needs must, right?

He's not going anywhere. I daren't try and tell him to piss off because I already know what his answer will be, but how the hell am I going to explain this to Isra? Oh, for the love of heavenly sanctification, think of something, Astrid. Because if I can't be plucky and summon the courage to find a reasonable explanation for this, Isra is going to get suspicious. She's not exactly a stranger to magical trickery. She would be able to sniff it out even if it was coming from the weary stank pits of hell. That's just how adept she is at her vocation, Astrid thought.

He knew Isra far too well than to try and justify hiding something like this from her. She'd find out eventually. Isra always found out the most inconspicuous things that anyone, even Astrid, attempted to keep from her. Isra was just incredibly perceptive. Her credentials on the metaphysical realm alone were enough to know that the wool could not be pulled over her sharp piercing green eyes without her getting wise over it! That was a fact.

"I guess that could be acceptable," Astrid muttered. He was probably trying to be clever to ensure no unsuspecting ears heard him, but honestly, Astrid should have known better.

"Excellent," James mustered excitedly.

He sounded extremely pleased and it was obvious just how happy he was that Astrid finally dropped his guard. He could have at least toned down his enthusiasm.

"Good. Hurry now. Isra is upstairs," Astrid interjected without any feeling.

You could almost detect the animosity in his voice as he scampered as quickly he could away from James.

Astrid proceeded to lead the way inside the passageway, not uttering a sound as he glided up the grey stone staircase. Astrid was as swift as he could be. You couldn't help but notice Astrid was not bothering to instil any hospitality towards James as he was feeling as though he was about to walk into some rapturous impending doom, one where Astrid would inevitably find out just how much of a good liar he really was and James also when Isra would meet James for the first time.

Only it wasn't, but Isra was not *yet* aware... though she may later discover the truth. Astrid would do his utmost to frantically cover that up.

5

strid did not hesitate in running over to the kitchenette. A bemused Isra stared at him intently as he filled a large pan with fresh water from the cold tap.

However, Astrid was so preoccupied with what he was doing he failed to notice that James went on ahead, walking into the living room without being given permission. Not that James was an uninvited guest or anything, but Astrid wanted to undertake this very meticulously while also exercising caution, something he failed in doing since James was already opening his trap more than necessary.

"Nice place you have here, old boy! A bit too fine for my liking, you understand, but nonetheless fine for your impeccable tastes!" James enthused wildly as though he was suddenly an expert on the art of finely detailed interior decorating.

"Thank you, but you know it's not mine," Astrid retorted in a sharp tone.

His eyes caught sight of something he'd much preferred not to be happening in his home. Isra stood right by the back of the room with her arms folded and pressed against her chest and those lime-green eyes of hers were all over James as if he was something most unwelcome.

The only problem was Isra was giving James a death stare and as Astrid dared to look up from taking his attention off the hot stove, he saw it for himself. Astrid resisted the urge to take an idle glance at James. His reaction would be a likely clue of how he was handling it. Instead, Astrid retrieved the boiling pan of water from the stove and began fumbling around the kitchenette, trying to look busy when really he was listening with all ears.

And since Astrid was making a rich, bitter coffee for all of them to delight in, it was certain the atmosphere generated between Isra and James couldn't be any more perfectly fitting for that beverage in question. You'll have to remember Isra had no clue who James was, so finding herself face to face with someone in her home, that could have been anybody, was not pleasing to her in the slightest.

It gave Astrid the sincerest impression that Isra was acting cold because not only did she feel the need to be on defence, her privacy was being greatly intruded upon. Isra didn't take kindly to that.

Of course, James gave little to no fucks for that. Being the bold individual he was, he took great pleasure in wholeheartedly embarrassing Astrid right in front of Isra, especially when the opportunity to do just that was staring James in the face. And let's face it, James couldn't resist watching Astrid squirm in the presence of his not-so-divine counterpart.

"Oh boy, did it just get cold in here or what?!" James elaborated in a sardonic tone that only made Astrid quiver as he hastily produced three hot mugs of steaming coffee, handing one to Isra before practically slamming another into the palm of James's hand.

Did he honestly have to say that? Damn, where are that boy's manners? Etiquette or none at all, that was not an appropriate thing to comment. And now Isra is mad as hell because of it, Astrid blundered away to himself, beginning to wonder just how intense things could get. *What will Isra say in response? She must be able to decipher his wayward attitude is sarcastic as hell. She's not stupid or immune to the idea, but my goodness did he press the wrong button there!*

Astrid summarised the situation carefully in his head, not

wanting to say anything just yet. The mood was already sour. He didn't want to add to it if at all possible.

He didn't have to wait long; Isra only sneered in James's direction as she probed the subject of her inquiry with yet another fierce stare. That penetrating rubberneck Isra threw at James was enough to turn anybody's blood stone-cold. Just the way her piercing lime-green eyes burned ever so gracefully in James's direction without even blinking was a most immaculate poise that Isra had down well.

It was safer for all concerned if Astrid didn't try and make too much of an approach with Isra for the time being, so he placed her coffee on the window ledge, taking a minute to give Isra a raised eyebrow so that she knew it was there.

There was no way on this green glorious earth that Astrid was going to risk walking over to Isra, handing the bitter-tasting beverage to her while she was exhibiting this vile torrent of a vagary. Because honestly, who knew what she would do next while in this frame of mind.

It was obvious for anyone who was not feeble-minded that Isra was not best pleased. Her thoughts detailed just how violated she felt by this intruder, whose name she did not happen to know, but no doubt there would be time for that minor detail later.

Oh, to hell with this and whoever you are. You're in my home now. So you play by my rules! Isra thought to herself. *If Astrid won't cough up and admit who you are, I'll find out for myself. You can pretty much guarantee it.*

She finished her thoughts with confidence as she waited before making her bold move that would only make Astrid want to recoil from the inside out. He'd witnessed just how brassy and determined his femme fatale really was. That girl sure as hell didn't take any shit. Didn't matter who it was.

Isra was not kidding around; she intended to intimidate James as much as she'd have to in order to discover just what in damnation he was doing in Shambre Fell. As for her beloved beau Astrid, Isra suspected he had some kind of an inkling as to what and whom this individual was. But as usual, Astrid was maintaining his silent pliancy, much to Isra's disapproval. Nevertheless, she'd handle that debacle later.

"Hmm. And just who the hell are you? What are you doing in my home at such a defining time?" Isra quizzed James in a fierce voice as though she was emitting anger, but instead showed nothing but defiance.

There was nothing worse than someone who was about to blow but instead of erupting as you'd expect, they portrayed a demeanour where you had no clue just where you stood with them. Oddly enough, Astrid suddenly found himself in a position where he had no inclination just what was about to happen next.

Astrid could tell that Isra's questions were justified, of course; it was natural that Isra viewed James as an unwelcome visitor, but there was an edge of curiosity piquing within Astrid. It showed when Astrid viewed Isra so intently like he was drowning in her. While doing his utmost to hold down some integrity, Astrid analysed every last detail. Isra was a watercolour needing special attention.

A defining time? What is that supposed to mean? Astrid thought as he pondered Isra's cryptic flavour. Her words had always baffled him since she spoke with such elegance, but this time, Astrid was truly puzzled by Isra's vagueness.

It was as though Isra knew a tiny bit more than she let on, but she was never one to drop her guard. Not even if she knew you well enough. If Isra believed if there was just one shred of misleading intentions, she'd grill the crap out of you until you coughed up the truth she sought.

James bowed his head apologetically before rising again and announcing himself in a low voice that only made Astrid cringe at how terribly dire James's imitation was.

"Oh, how presumptuous of me. I assumed you knew! I am a friend of Astrid's. I am James," he finished. He was seeming mighty pleased with himself as though he had conquered something empirically impossible.

Goddamn it, can this actually get any more fucked up? Now he's gone and said I am a friend of his. Yeah, maybe in some alternate fucking universe. You gotta be kidding me! Astrid blasted James internally in his most fiendish of thoughts.

"How wonderfully quaint for you. So, why is it that we have never made acquaintances before?" Isra questioned with a fiery glare, one of which could only be described as robust flames simmering gently for a while and then suddenly and violently sizzling before heading into a searing climax. And you sure didn't want to be caught in the midst of that flame when push came to shove.

"Oh, he didn't? Damn. Well, I'm sure he meant to," James cajoled to Isra in a jokey sort of tone, almost friendly, but you could tell he was slightly enjoying the way this conversation was working itself out. And apparently, the idea of one-upmanship had not lost its impeccable charm.

This action only resulted in James being on the receiving end of a seriously stern eye roll from Astrid. It was the kind of look that said, "Oh, I can't believe you actually said that, you dumb imbecile." But nevertheless, Astrid would have to maintain his composure because he had a most profound notion that he'd have a lot of explaining to do.

I shall deal with you later, boy, whereas now, more important matters are at stake, such as my relationship, which, thanks to you, may be hanging on its legs, Astrid moaned to himself in thought. Evidently, he was very annoyed by James, only adding more salt to an already fragile and open wound.

"I bet," was all Isra muttered in response to James. "Well, good day to you, sir. I shall leave you and Astrid to your..." Isra stopped midway with that before she slipped back into her focus and added, "delegations."

What she meant by that, neither of them knew. Astrid and James were dumbstruck, but it wasn't a moment where anybody was able to claim clarity on the predicament. Isra skedaddled out of the room in a second, leaving both Astrid and James bemused, but more so Astrid as he was expecting to have to make a compromise of sorts with Isra.

Astrid ventured back over to his comfortable red velvet chair. Or Isra's, more accurately, but since she had taken her leave by scampering away without so much as a goodbye, it was very much vacant. And perhaps an old and most reliable friend would be helpful to Astrid at this point since he had been left on his lonesome to contend with James and whatever delightful expose he'd soon be hearing all about from the man himself.

James, however, noted the vile reaction he'd just received from Isra despite her being almost civil with him earlier. It wasn't exactly difficult to notice she had a sheer dislike for him, or perhaps she just spoke in that manner with everyone who entered her home unannounced. But ultimately, James got his wish. He and Astrid were alone, and James could speak freely about the real reason he had come all this way.

Since the living area was fairly sparse apart from that majestic throne-type chair that sat at the back of the room, James perched himself on the beige couch a few feet away from Astrid, a nice, healthy distance some might say since it wasn't just Isra who was irked by James's appearance in their domain, but James knew better than to take Astrid's wordless huffs seriously.

"I can see I have not made the best impression where Isra is concerned," James earnestly began.

He was hoping that his sincerity would help regain some trust between himself and Astrid because all matters of sardonic torture regarding Astrid aside, James wasn't here to play piggy in the middle between Astrid and Isra.

"No, she doesn't seem very amused," Astrid affirmed.

He was allegedly agreeing with James but Astrid didn't give much away. He took a long gulp of his coffee before resting the mug on his knee. Not giving James a second glance, Astrid looked downward at the grey stone floor.

"Yes, well, I didn't anticipate that, but I wanted to assure you it was not my intention. I came here to inform you of a period of great change. To be precise, stagnation will come to a timely demise when I take over the reins at what is to be my biggest role I have ever found myself in," James announced with great zealousness.

"And what role is that?" Astrid pressed with sudden interest, waiting to hear some vastly intriguing detail at any moment now.

"I am soon to be taking over the vicinity in Spirisity. The wonders of 'on high' and the light and darkened shadows in our realm will be completely in my domain," James firmly answered.

"Ah, and what about our old friend, Samuel?" Astrid quizzed in astonishment.

Astrid would never have imagined the day someone else would take the reins as far as the fight with light versus dark was concerned. I mean, when you think about it logically, Samuel was born for that role. He snapped everybody who fell from the good graces in shape and eliminated anything that even remotely resounded darkness in any form. Samuel had always taken care of business in reference to the dark souls of the eternal cosmos and maintained a strong relationship with those behind the scenes that were ever so fondly named "on high."

So, it really did beg the question of why on earth Samuel's tenure would come to an end? Surely he was the only one able to handle such a demanding devoir. When it came down to it, Samuel was firm and intimidating when he saw fit. And quite honestly, no one else could fit the bill since Samuel had his own unique brand of communication brimming with sarcasm and vulgar references that many wouldn't dare to comprehend the meaning of.

However, James brought severe mental clarity to Astrid's disbelief when he uttered profoundly, "Samuel is hanging up his hat."

"Oh, my!" was all Astrid could articulate in response. He had to be honest, he was truly lost for words.

"Yes, it's a shocker, I know, but the old boy is retiring. It's a shame really, as folk saw this coming many moons ago. In fact, some would even go as far to say that *you* brought this delicate collapse of power in a way," James confirmed, adding far more detail than Astrid expected.

"So he's really going then! Wow, I knew when I saw him the other day that he was out of sorts, but I never expected this!" Astrid concurred in amazement, still blown away by this lightning bolt of a leak that had hit him so fortuitously.

"It's something he didn't really want to admit to anyone. Especially himself," James elaborated, half expecting to be praised for filling in the holes in this story.

"So, in spite of it all, I have one question," Astrid started in a stern manner, one that suggested he was not completely convinced by this convenient transition occurring in his midst.

"Go on," James urged.

Of course, James didn't have any idea of where this was going, but he presumed Astrid would give him headway.

"Please, tell me why Samuel maintained that all was fine and dandy, telling me how delighted he is to have Ronald O'Kutte for a villainous tarantula?" Astrid probed, nervously eyeing James up as he waited for a straight answer.

James could only look Astrid dead in the eye as he divulged his insight carefully. "It has been known for aeons now that Samuel isn't really happy with anything. Being involved in such dire circumstances has only led to more unhappiness within himself. You could say he is a danger to the cause because of his hatred for the work."

Astrid was speechless. He barely paid any attention as the mug of coffee rolled right off his knee, tumbling to the floor in an instant. Climaxing against the veracity of the stone floor, the mug shattered into tiny pieces and yet Astrid still could not utter a single word.

Samuel had fed him a load of bologna with the great inner knowing that all was not well inside himself. In a nutshell, Samuel misguided Astrid, but the only pressing question was... why?

6

While this revelation pertaining to Samuel was shocking, to say the least, Astrid was far more concerned about the "he is a danger to the cause" factor.

I mean, honestly, Samuel upheld the position of light bringer for aeons, maybe even longer, and not once had there been any suspicions. It was also accurate to say not one soul had given any thought to the idea that Samuel might be wrongly suited for the strenuous mission due to some perturbed notion that Samuel may well be precarious to the cause itself.

Of course, such a statement was hair-brained to Astrid, but then again, when did James come along spewing out falsifications? The last time Astrid paid heed to it, there had been none whatsoever but sometimes people in certain organisations liked to chatter about things they had no comprehension about. It wasn't graspable to Astrid whether this was one of those scenarios. However, he was going to ask questions and with James sitting in front of him, there was no more perfect opportunity for Astrid to take it upon himself to find out the truth.

"What do you mean, Samuel has a hatred for the work? He has a passion, yes, that goes without saying, but hatred? That has to be hearsay, surely?" Astrid probed with a stern glance.

"I wish I could say it was," James answered, not caring much for the arrogance Astrid emitted in his tone.

Let it be known that James had been dropped in at the deep end with this one, having only recently unearthed the news that he was to be the one taking Samuel's place. It had been a proclamation of sorts whereby James had accidentally stumbled upon this unknown knowledge that Samuel was finally saying goodbye to the life he had built his entire foundation upon. Even James wasn't completely clear on all the fine details, but nevertheless, Samuel would be vacating Spirisity and James would be moving in. The rest was to be revealed at a later date, but James wasn't overly preoccupied with the latter.

I don't even know where I am headed. Am I destined to fail? Will I manage to bring down the most torrential forces of evil? Who actually knows. Samuel was my master. My mentor. And now he's distancing himself altogether from the antecedent he doted upon his entire existence, James thought, still not knowing what was ahead for him and his impending role. Being the guardian of Spirisity alone was going to be a challenge, but overruling darkness was going to be a much more onerous one.

"I see," Astrid muttered without warning, which totally interrupted James's train of thought. "This is most peculiar, I have to say, James. Especially since I saw the man myself only a day or so ago, and he mentioned nothing of this... development." He was careful to pause as yet again his suspicions were heightened.

"Well, it is true," James retorted, sounding a little defensive, but Astrid decided to shrug it off for the time being he wanted to get to the real pressing questions.

"Aha, that is how it appears, but what is really behind his rash yet bold transition? Samuel is a proud man, is he not? I mean, how can he subject himself to such judgment as surely 'on high' will roast him for his lack of integrity? It has to be said that Samuel is soon to be a matter of public enquiry considering you stated he actually 'hates' the work, James?" Astrid questioned, still regarding him with a high amount of distrust.

Nevertheless, something wasn't quite right here. While Astrid had never seen James as someone dependable for the absolute truth, even James seemed to be in the dark about what was really going on.

As far as Astrid was concerned, James gave him the impression that he was just creating a vast concoction he was adding to as he went along. Not one single shred of adeptness or planning had been brought into James's not-so-elaborate delivery, and this only added more weight to Astrid's misgiving of James. Astrid expected James to be more professional, especially since he had come all this way to unleash this exciting news. But yet again, there were kinks in James's conveyance.

However, you have to remember Astrid was a worldly man. He had the most esteemed intelligence and a conniving nature to boot that gave him precedence to discover the most well-concealed facets of information. So, Astrid decoded it quite easily enough by the mere fact that James was hesitant in answering Astrid's very well put together questions. The man was almost acting in defiance before he mumbled something that sounded remotely like anything that made any kind of sense amongst all this nonsensical speculation.

"I'm not in the loop as to everything, Astrid, but I can promise you, I do plan on doing better than Samuel ever did," James responded with a slight grumble as though he felt like he had been on trial and Astrid was his judge, jury, and executioner.

Astrid let out a huge, drawn-out sigh. This fiery exhaling of emotions revealed much impatience and hostile energy towards James. He emitted in a cross voice, "I am very much aware of that, boy. The question that I must ask is are you even aware of just what you've been placed into?"

James turned his back to Astrid in a swift movement, turning his focus to the glorious view that showcased Shambre Fell and all the precious acres around it in all its glory. Just beyond the stunning, green, glossy hills and up a little, if he looked hard enough, James could see the grandeur of Spirisity, the place he would soon occupy.

"I feel like we are getting nowhere with this. I've told you what I know. I cannot divulge any more than that," James answered bluntly.

"Hmm, and yet I feel we are only just starting our journey in uncovering the treachery going on behind closed doors, namely those doors inside that melancholic institute better known as Spirisity!" Astrid concurred with his arms folded firmly across his chest whilst giving James an icy stare.

"Oh, for goodness sakes, Astrid. I've told you all I know. Don't start jumping down my throat because you don't happen to like what you've heard! Samuel is retiring from the lightworker business. He's out. That's it. Game over! Take it as it is. Don't try and mould it into something it is not," James snapped before he stormed out of the living room in a huff, leaving Astrid completely bemused, his suspicions aroused even more so.

Well, boy, I only asked the relevant questions, but your tense reaction to my prodding is only further indication that something is amiss. But don't worry, I'll find out what's really going on underneath that delicate exterior of yours. You can guarantee it, Astrid thought to himself.

He realised there was yet another predicament floating around in his domain. Isra... and her unknowingness of the truth, to be exact.

7

Apparently, the matter concerning James had long been forgotten by Isra the following morning as she strode hand in hand with Astrid, walking along the cold cobblestone road. It was a rare outing; needless to say, Isra often went for joyous walks alone with Astrid pacing around their home, anxiously awaiting her return.

However, Isra had invited him out with her on this wondrously sunny day, despite some lingering grey clouds hovering amongst the beaming cerulean-blue skies.

Astrid was greatly relieved from all the pressure resting upon his shoulders. Isra didn't seem cross with him at all, but maybe it was just a smoke screen. Nonetheless, it was bright and cheery outside, so Astrid saw no reason to be overly concerned since Isra was carelessly walking alongside him without any visible downturn in her mood.

Isra was in remarkably high spirits on this intriguing visit to the quiet village of Bitterquel, a charming little place just outside the neighbouring palace, which was home to royalty.

Now, Astrid was left bemused as to why Isra suggested they come here. It wasn't anything to marvel over. All of it consisted of was a narrow pathway made up of rough cobblestones with quaint stall-

"

fronts scattered all over the area that sold a range of things, from freshly grown fruits to sweet little trinkets and even handcrafted jewellery fit for a king.

On the other hand, Bitterquel was also the home of a mighty fine prince. Apparently, this fellow had once lost claim to his throne, but something most miraculous happened. The heir the king had chosen to succeed him unexpectedly succumbed to a most untimely and tragic death, and the once rejected prince finally rose to greatness. At least, that was according to what the legend said, anyway.

Isra's attention, however, was not on the finery of this so-called bitter land. Amongst all the drudgery of this sweet yet homely little village, something had the witch's attention. A young girl dressed in white linen rags, which Isra presumed was supposed to be a dress, was walking on the other side of the road. The girl dragged a chestnut horse behind her. The interesting thing about the girl was her dull mocha hair that reached just below her shoulders, contrasting with her warm hazel-brown eyes.

Isra couldn't help but stare at the girl, for there was a strong stench of horse manure coming off her clothes in waves. It was enough to make Isra want to hurl; the smell was so vile. However, Isra resisted the temptation because of yet another thing that caught her attention. The horse's saddle had a royal crest with a crown emblazoned onto it. This gave Isra the distinct impression that this girl was private property to the prince or hereof.

How intriguing that she was allowed to wander the village so carefree, as though she wasn't a servant!

Isra mocked the girl to herself in most callous thought. *How is it she can go around the town like that, stinking of excrement? It really is riveting to me. The poor girl could use a decent bath... or a hundred of them.*

Astrid noted that Isra was staring at the girl with the dreary muck-coloured hair, and he couldn't help but chuckle since his counterpart was thoroughly distracted. He squeezed her hand a little tighter as they walked to jolt her trance before remarking candidly, "Is something amusing you, my love? This is a most ridiculously sunny day for a stroll. I must say, I am greatly pleased to get out of our château, even if it is to come to a scum pit filled with peasants like this one."

Isra didn't pay much heed to Astrid's comment; her eyes were fully on this girl, as baffling as that was to Astrid, who couldn't understand just why Isra was so fascinated with the young little thing. As bizarre as it was, Astrid couldn't help but smile wickedly to himself; he admired Isra's child-like piquancy. It was a most remarkable quality of hers that he'd always found extremely attractive from the moment he laid his beady eyes on her.

"Yes, well, I thought it would be good for us to go elsewhere for a change," Isra muttered.

Isra had finally taken her eyes off the girl with the shoulder-length brown hair, but there was something rather familiar about that crest on the horse's saddle. Isra wasn't exactly sure what it was, but she remembered seeing that crown on something before. Although she found it odd she hadn't encountered anyone even remotely close to being royalty, there was something so distinct about that crest. Maybe it would come to her later.

Perhaps it is just a coincidence, Isra conferred with herself in her head. "Maybe we should head off?" she suggested to Astrid.

She pulled her long midnight-blue cloak towards her neck as though trying to distract herself from something that was most pressing.

Astrid gave Isra a sceptical look as if he found something indescribably off with her behaviour. For a start, her body language was all wrong. She was nervous, and Isra was rarely found to be in that manner about anything. Not only that, but when did Isra ever want to leave a place?

"Oh? I thought you wanted us to come here," Astrid quizzed with a wide-eyed stare. He didn't believe there was some simple explanation that she'd just had her fill and it was time to peruse the delights awaiting them at home. *No, something isn't right. She's not telling me everything. Something's stirred within her and she's not sharing with me the glorious details. But whatever it is, she wants to run,* he mused to himself.

"I think I've seen all I need to see," Isra recited cryptically, although there was very little meaning behind her words. She was doing her utmost to conceal something from him... and maybe even from herself, too.

"All right then. Let's go," Astrid agreed. He squeezed her hand again whilst in the grip of his own. They veered around, back towards the path that would lead back to Shambre Fell. *Something is amok, but maybe later on she will let me in on it. I don't have any inclination as to what it could be, but it's sure got her on her heels,* he thought.

He resisted the urge to put his index finger to his lips and continued pondering the situation, steadily walking alongside Isra. Knowing they'd be home before sunset, Astrid decided he could finally bring forth what he'd been keeping locked inside of himself for such a long time.

ASTRID WAS STILL hand in hand with Isra as they trudged upon the glimmering green hills that would soon reveal the majestic tower that stood out amongst the wilderness that was Shambre Fell.

"You know an old friend came to me today?" Astrid began his conversation with Isra, keeping her hand in his as he eyed her seriously for a moment. "And it's made me think very seriously about a few things. Us. The things that have occurred of late... Ronald coming along and sucking you into his trap, you finding out about my secret of what became of Kane. It made me consider the future because it's true what my friend said; change is afoot."

Astrid suddenly let go of Isra's hand. Isra didn't utter a single word. She eyed him cautiously, not quite sure exactly what he was doing, but instead of being suspicious, she decided she would simply listen to him.

"I don't want to spend my entire existence not making the changes I should have aeons ago. I want to be the transformation that lives inside of myself. I have no time for the petty and the mundane any longer. I know exactly who I am and what I want to become, and so to get right to the heart of the matter…"

Astrid crouched on the thick grass, looking straight up into Isra's shimmery green eyes that, for some reason, glowed a little brighter as he viewed them from this position.

"Samuel, my friend and old employer, is retiring from the love and light business. This means he will no longer be part of the war of light versus the dark. It means all the things that he tried to keep me away from where I desired to be all those years ago have found themselves in a tailspin. James won't have half the determination as Samuel did, and so I see that there is no longer anything standing in my way."

Astrid realised that this needed to get somewhere fast, but he was taking due care to give Isra the absolute truth. Not just that, but the truth of his heart.

"Samuel has opened my eyes to a variety of misdemeanours that went down in my wake. The vile, gory truth of what went on back then has finally emerged for what it is. I have no reason to fear it or anyone that tried to stop us."

He reached for Isra's left hand, holding onto it tightly as he erupted, "I'm done with the treachery and the constant demands. I will do what I deem right, even if that happens to be something that these souls do not approve of…"

Astrid took a breath, feeling the warm sun shining down upon his back. It was a remarkably hot day considering it was in the middle of December, but no matter; Astrid could just about adjust to any type of temperature. It was bemusing and somewhat nerve-wracking to him that Isra was still completely silent. She didn't show the slightest sign of any emotion either, and he wasn't sure if that should give him reason to be apprehensive, but it wasn't going to sway him.

I'm not held to any regime. They might have been able to call the shots back then, but this is a brand new dawn. A fantastical paradigm has been unleashed for the first time in centuries, a change of tactical beliefs, and now I can finally enact what I have been yearning for, Astrid confidently thought.

However, Isra decided to break her silence. Her lime-green eyes were all over Astrid now. They were luminous in their colouring with a slight tinge that reminded Astrid of that familiar sap-green hue of when he had given Isra the glowing green orb all those years ago. There was something strong and intangible about the magic the orb possessed. It had shone like a beacon that would guide the lost back to their rightful destinations, and that was what he'd intended to do with Isra if Samuel hadn't come at the most impeccable time to throw his plans into chaos.

Isra's eyes reminded Astrid of that meticulously vibrant sphere. Isra had once been lost, needing assistance. She had been secretly craving someone or something to bring her back to salvation. Astrid believed that he had come at exactly the right time, just when Isra needed him the most.

"I don't quite comprehend what it is you are trying to say," Isra mouthed.

Her tone was stiff and a little wary. It was as though she was still fighting something within herself to protect her heart. She felt she needed to keep that fiery, wailing surge of betrayal at bay, for she knew it had battered her more times than she cared to acknowledge.

Of course, Astrid knew Isra better than most. It would be fair to say he even knew her more than she did. He knew she had reservations over many people, and maybe even one or two over him, but Astrid didn't let this deter him. He had always known she would be a tough cookie to crack.

"Just listen to what I have to say," Astrid commanded in a low voice.

"I don't care about our past. I have no concern over the things you and I have done to those that have forsaken us. The only thing I care about is what we bestow unto each other, and so I have a proposition for you. For us to never endanger the other's sacred burning heart, Lady Isra of the Dark... you, the sorceress that many dare to fear, will you marry me?" Astrid asked without hesitation.

~

MEANWHILE, in the neighbouring land of Spirisity, a charming fellow looked taken aback as he examined the scene closely in his magnificent selenite crystal sphere. He had both of his hands affixed to the translucent ball of wonder and was in sheer shock at what he had just witnessed. There was no time to waste.

The man tapped his fingers ferociously upon the shimmery sphere, apparently very annoyed at the situation playing itself out before him. He sighed as he noticed a stray hair had come undone from his perfectly combed, slicked-back hair. Making haste, he quickly smoothed it into place. Now it resembled the rest of his jet-black hair.

"Oh, no. This won't do at all. Astrid has taken it way too far this time. He's gone and proposed marriage to the most immoral enchantress this land has ever had the pleasure of knowing. I think it's time I announced my presence in Shambre Fell," Samuel Reynaldi announced through gritted teeth.

He would once and for all be showing the villainous side he kept locked away for some time now. And most importantly, nobody. Not Astrid and definitely not Isra. None of them would ever see it coming.

8

Isra stood, taken aback. She was unable to accept the reality and remained shell-shocked at Astrid's revelation and marriage proposal. If it wasn't for the fact she remained solid in her stance, then she might have lost her footing, but Isra had great composure for someone so reckless.

Isra suddenly remembered she was still positioned on the green glossy hills that tumbled down below to reveal the majesty that was her home, that tower she had occupied for as long as she could remember.

She had always dwelled here, and many didn't care for it. But for some reason, as Isra glanced at the striking tower that shot straight up into the sunlit skies, she found she was unable to recollect how she had come to be here. It was most peculiar, as she had always had it in the back of her mind.

Before her arrival, there was a tale of a witch that lived in the vicinity that met an untimely death, although it wasn't totally clear as to why that was. Isra recalled the memory of being told, but for the life of her, she could not hang onto whom or what had told her. It was just an inner knowing she carried with her since the first moment she had eyes on Shambre Fell.

Isra stared into Astrid's brown eyes, their golden sparkle reflecting at her. She was not at all fully grasping what he requested of her. It was unthinkable for her to even conceive of the idea that another soul would desire companionship with her for all eternity.

Alas, Astrid was different from all of the other suitors Isra crossed paths with during her tenure on this earth. He showed her that she was worthy of such a love and that more importantly, it was safe for her to be vulnerable. She could expose that sacred entity to another being when she had spent many years hiding it from the world by encasing it in a protective shell. Of course, that precious being was Isra's heart.

And although there was still a chance it could break, Astrid had done what so many had failed to do. He had taken immense care of it in showing Isra trust and friendship, two commodities that were paramount if one is to gain back the ability to open up their heart to love again after it had been so carelessly shattered.

Never in the wildest dreams or the most violent nightmares had Lady Isra of the Dark envisioned this, and so this was why she struggled to answer Astrid. But as usual, he had her sussed.

The raven-turned-man had the inkling that something within Isra had been stirred up and yet again, it had made her go deep inside herself, curling among the broken bric-a-brac and debris that laid in the murkiest depths of her soul. And no doubt, it was an enormous mass of heartache, betrayal, and deceit from those she had most fondly come to know.

Of course, Astrid knew Isra better than she knew herself. This was why he was the most immaculately fitting piece to her because he had what all those others had failed to truly attain from her, and that most remarkable thing was the trust of her heart.

"Why do I get the feeling you're about to run from me?" Astrid quizzed with wide eyes.

He was a little scared but more so about her reaction. Love was tragically a slippery slope at best for Isra, but love turning out to not be the fiery, shattering of hope and dreams was far more frightening than anything else.

Isra gasped in bewilderment. She clasped her hand over her mouth in shock; Astrid called her out on her fear. Never had anyone before had the audacity and sheer bravery to tell her outright that she was about to skedaddle. Nevertheless, Astrid was a complete breath of fresh air when he was put against the suitors Isra had encountered before him.

Alas, even when Astrid first departed, he still found ways and means to keep watch as she engaged in romantic liaisons with fellows that were not him. It was fair to state that no man survived being with Isra long enough for it to be a memorable affair, though there was one of whom Astrid remembered being particularly brutal.

This reckless philanderer tossed Isra's heart like it was some plaything and thought nothing of it when she came shrieking and begging to be released from his callous claws. At the time, Isra had only been the pure age of nineteen, and this short but brief infatuation had devastated her, leaving her with even more resentment when the man returned a year later, wishing to start anew. That didn't end well since he did the same thing again but with even less care the second time around.

And thus, Isra came to be even more cut off from human life than ever before. Still sheltered in the idealistic Shambre Fell, when young Kane O'Kutte came to Isra many years later, it was no surprise she took her chance to take her vengeance upon the male species. However, as far as Isra was concerned, Astrid knew nothing of her past before he had made his "first" appearance at the window of Lillian Blackwell's cottage. She had been led to believe that was the location of their first meeting, yes, but Samuel Reynaldi's swift spell upon her memory left her recollection of anything prior in tatters.

But now was a much more surreal experience for Isra. She had been with Astrid in a solid and stable union for three whole years. Isra had no idea of the circumstances that surrounded their relationship from before as already stated; she was under Samuel's spell, which ultimately blocked her from remembering her and Astrid's past back when she lodged at Wingdom's Academy.

"I'm sorry. I didn't mean to go quiet on you. It's just..." Isra trailed off.

Her words seemed to dissipate. It was as though she knew what she wanted to say but wasn't sure how to unleash it. This was a tough call for her to make. And there were only two choices as far as her warped vision could see. She could run and find some delightful excuse to not accept Astrid's proposal, or she could take a chance and find eternal happiness. There was no in-between or finding a middle ground for Isra. It was do or die.

Why does he always make me question myself so wildly that I feel my head might spin if I speculated more? He always goes for the heart of the matter. And yet I feel I may well explode into some unknown territory just by standing in his presence when he's being so inviting to move our connection to the next level. Figuratively speaking, anyhow.

Isra immersed herself intensely in a bucket load of thoughts, as she didn't have one shred of clarity on what choice she was going to enact upon. It was evident that Astrid was a man in his prime. He was more than prepared to take care of Isra emotionally and give her the stability she needed. So, it did beg the question as to why she found this to be such a stumbling block of a decision to make?

"It's just what?" Astrid questioned. His feet were tapping on the grassy bank before him and he seemed impatient. However, he was making haste not to show that disposition to Isra.

She always does this. She gallivants around the garden wall, not remembering that it's much easier to jump across and get to the solution without driving yourself up some narrow bend that is going nowhere. Life is problematic, I agree, but I also state that it's much more beneficial to communicate to your counterpart how you feel. It would save a lot of heartache and disarray if only she would speak to me about it without going all around the issue itself, Astrid thought.

He knew this was a delicate matter, but still, it always stunned him how Isra would do her utmost to avoid conversation about deep-rooted issues. She'd much rather shoot out a few well-timed bolts of fiery lightning out of herself than amicably deal with whatever was troubling her. And perhaps literally, since she often felt comforted by the fierce hellish fire that illuminated the entire night sky, no matter how dark it was up there. But Astrid was not one to give up easily. Oh, he'd get to the bottom of this, and they'd find resolution. He could guarantee it.

His character wasn't easily broken down by someone that launched as many obstacles as physically possible in order to avoid handling things. The motivation in him was something to be admired because no matter what the universe threw at him, Astrid always came back fighting even harder than before he had been knocked down. It was a rare feat indeed to see this man thrown to the wolves but he ensured that he clung on as tightly as he could, for survival was his birthright. Giving up was not an option. It just simply wasn't built in his vocabulary.

"I am not openly sure, really," Isra spluttered out of nowhere, sending Astrid sauntering out of his train of thought. "It's just that romance is normally futile with me. Somewhere along the line, it comes to a close. It's inevitable. And I don't often consider it to be any other way."

She tried to explain carefully, noting that she was wary of the connection she and Astrid shared before coming to a grand halt.

"Maybe it's time for a new perspective," Astrid eagerly suggested. "Not everything in life is destined to fail. Have a little faith in me. Place your trust in me as I place my trust with your heart."

Astrid wasn't able to control himself any longer. It was so clear. His never-ending passion for her was undeniable as he reached for Isra, pressing his lips onto her forehead. He clung to her in such a manner that he was refusing to let go.

"Please, allow me this one honour. Be my eternal life partner. Let's make it official. We can scream it to the stars, and who cares about those who don't celebrate with us. I have no time to waste on the pathetic undesirables in this almighty forsaken realm. I just want to be with you," he announced with such fierceness that his brown eyes sparkled with a hint of that bright golden sparkle that always mesmerised Isra.

Astrid took his lips away from Isra in a delicate but sweet

moment, but he only moved to press them against her succulent lips. He savoured them slowly and softly as though they were their brand of beautifully delectable candy that had just enough sweetness to satisfy him. Gently putting pressure as he kissed her, only further displaying his enthusiasm for her, she couldn't help but give in to his soft, light touch.

Glazing over Astrid, lost in awe of him, Isra marvelled over him with such magnificence in her bright, emerald-green eyes. Having been astounded by such spectacles of beauty, Isra mouthed so quietly that it was almost inaudible, "All right, let's take the risk."

Astrid only held her even tighter, not letting another word pass his lips as he was only focused on her, deeply engrossed in her entrancing light.

9

Isra and Astrid were arm in arm as they skipped merrily down the gravel pathway that led to their grand establishment, Shambre Fell.

If it wasn't for the happiness beyond reprieve Isra was experiencing, she might have glanced sideways when she noted her beloved oak door had been left ajar. However, Astrid's sharp eyeballs hadn't missed a trick, and without warning, he let go of Isra's hand. If she wasn't so blissful, she might have been offended; but alas, she knew the raven-turned-man had his reasoning for everything, so she didn't question him. She did give him an inquisitive stare as she folded her arms across her chest, almost as though she too had sensed something from within the ether.

Astrid approached the situation with caution, edging towards the door with a certain finesse. He carefully inspected it, turning his head and peering through the doorway. Isra was about to head in when Astrid halted her at once, placing his hand mid-air in front of her and blocking her from entering.

"No. Someone has been here," he muttered with a wary tone.

Astrid sniffed the air with impatience, yet again thoroughly examining the door. The detection with his nose wasn't a necessary means of tracing whoever gained entry, but Astrid wanted to leave no stone unturned as he carried out his search.

"I think we might find ourselves a little human up in here! Judging by the foul smell, is that the faint whiff of stables I sense with my highly refined system of knowing?" Astrid cajoled as he threw a snide wink at Isra.

"Yes, that is evident, but the question is whom?" Isra asked out loud, although she was merely conversing with herself. She didn't need the validation of an answer from Astrid, but judging by the look on his face, he was going to find who or what was causing so much trouble.

Astrid surveyed the hallway before turning his attention to the cold stone steps. He planted his index finger to his lips in thought and perused the complexities of the situation befalling him. *I bet whoever was up there is STILL there, and perhaps we shall catch them in their sordid act of breaking and entering. And if they aren't so lucky, I might get to unleash my true feelings on just how I stand with regards to someone infiltrating my sanctuary with my beloved.*

"There is only one way to find that out," Astrid returned in an unforgiving tone. Whoever ensconced their delicate self into his fortress was endangering themselves for sure, because he was not one to be trifled with.

Having been satisfied that he had done all he could, Astrid signalled for his counterpart to come in. Just with a wave of his finger, Astrid beckoned Isra to come forth but he also exhibited the need for silence as he hushed her by pressing his finger to her lips.

"Quiet, now. I don't want any wretched being to be alarmed as I feast my eyes on their guilty conscience," Astrid ordered in a serious voice, taking his focus back to the matter at hand.

Astrid took the lead as he veered slowly towards the stairs, turning to face Isra with a commanding look. Yes, Astrid liked taking control in every facet of his life, especially when it featured Isra. He had only just gained her acceptance of his hand in marriage, after all. He wasn't going to let it fall flat by the wayside just because of some miscreant squatter.

Astrid wasted no time in making a strong resilience. He climbed the grey stone steps one by one, making a mental note that Isra was still behind him at an equally slow pace. However, Astrid was the one taking the initiative. He came to the door of their living room, being extra quiet as he pushed the door open; he didn't want to cause any alarm. You know, just in case a certain intruder was still inside their humble abode.

And his action proved to be rightly so, as despite being ever so careful not to make a sound, he couldn't help himself when he spotted what closely resembled a young girl with mousy brown hair helping herself to herbal concoctions from the shelf positioned above the kitchenette.

"Aha! A stowaway!" Astrid pointed and jeered as he ran over to the girl.

He grabbed her by her earlobe, pulling her tightly. She appeared to be both distressed and shocked that she had been found out. The sad thing was she couldn't have been any older than nineteen but yet had that disdainful look upon her face as if the world owed her something. She gave the impression that she was one of those particular girls that had a lot of wealth, but it was just a desire, for the only richness in such a person's life was not having stained their linen.

Astrid called to Isra in an astringent tone of voice, "Isra. Come, see what I have discovered. A delightful human making merry with your potions!"

"Oh, how sweet. A thief that knows what magic she is searching for!" Isra responded, eyeing the girl with fierce scrutiny.

Isra noted the girl had dark brown hair down to her shoulders that didn't match her white cotton sundress at all, other than that there was nothing remotely intriguing about this child as far as she could see.

However, the girl broke her silence to plead with Isra. The girl flashed her warm brown eyes with hues of red on the outside in a complacent manner that was designed to win someone over, no doubt.

She entered her pleas in a low voice. "Oh, if you please, I'm not a thief. I was just hungry. The prince is so vile when it comes to sharing his meaningless edibles."

"If that is so, then why did you come here, into someone's home? You know it is awfully rude to enter a place which you do not reside, dear. Someone may regard you as an intruder," Isra countered in a harsh voice, but she also heard the girl when she said she was hungry and remembered to grace the child with her pity.

"I didn't mean that in the way you perceived it at all. I was just so ravenous. I didn't mean to cause any harm," she advocated before bowing before Isra.

Of course, such an act didn't impress Isra. That was astoundingly true as she wasn't moved by it at all. Even worse, Astrid was far from pleased and regarded this insignificant soul as someone that was under much suspicion from his watchful eye.

"Hmm, so you serve for a prince and yet despite being among royalty, you think it is acceptable to commit injustices whereby you enter someone's domain without their permission. Why, for the life of me, do I not believe you?" Astrid quizzed, still maintaining his grip on her ear.

He wasn't going to let her go until she told him the truth, and if that meant she'd be coughing and spluttering, then so be it, in his view.

"Please! I beg you. Let me go. Prince Jonathan, my employer, will have my head for sure if he finds out about this folly I have made."

The girl petitioned Astrid for release as not only was her ear stinging from the harsh grip he had on it, but she was also incredibly nervous being around these "people." This wasn't something she did every day; sneaking into a lonely, stately home, which she presumed was empty, but she was desperate. The man she worked for was a ruthless brute, a foul-tempered being that did nothing but criticise her no matter how much hard graft she put in.

But this young lady, despite working among a most privileged citizen of the realm, was greatly troubled because her accommodation was under threat. It was clear in the way she stumbled upon her words that this sweet yet quaint girl would do anything in order to better her situation, even absconding from her job and breaking into someone else's property. All right, so the door had been unlocked, but that didn't justify her actions.

Isra was beginning to see some rationalisation, understanding that this child was a most wretched soul who simply needed to find nourishment and that perhaps scolding her was not the correct way to handle her. If there was some serious wrongdoing that had occurred here, Isra would handle it later. For now, she was being diplomatic as she hadn't heard the full story yet.

"Oh, hush now, Astrid. Don't berate the child. She's just a helpless peasant who wanted to find herself food and shelter. It's not her fault; our place was the one she decided to recklessly ransack."

Isra cajoled him but there was some warning in her tone as though she wasn't completely on the girl's side since her tone was purely sarcastic, if nothing else, but Isra was not letting on so the girl had no inclination of that.

Astrid smirked, releasing the girl's ear. "Hmm, if you say so, dear."

The girl reached out to comfort herself. She found her ear to be incredibly hot to the touch. It was painful, too. If she had been able to examine herself in a mirror, she would have seen that her skin was incredibly angry as a result, with it almost matching the colour of blood, most red and raw.

"Thank you," the girl extended in not so gracious gratitude. "My name is Ava. Prince Jonathan has no understanding of me leaving, and so if I don't return to the palace soon, he will scold me for sure. I already have the strenuous task of mucking out his stables."

Ava was stricken with a look of pure disgust and disdain as if she hated equine culture and all it stood for.

"So your employer is a prince, and he is named Jonathan? Perhaps if an issue does arise as a result of your transgression, I can intervene on your behalf," Isra suggested with a poignant gaze, though again, her voice sounded very sardonic.

However, it was clear as Astrid watched Isra engage with the naive

Ava that this wouldn't be an endeavour in which the little peasant would have herself some assistance without Isra wanting something in return.

"Yes, he is," Ava answered without hesitation.

It didn't occur to Ava as to why Isra was broaching the subject with her in the first instance, but then again, Ava never considered things on a serious notion.

I don't understand why this woman wants to help me without some gratification for herself. Perhaps I should take her up on her gracious offer to mediate with that grouch, Jonathan. After all, what's the worst that could commence from her intervening? Ava chortled to herself wildly in thought.

"Aha. Well, if you kindly tell me where I might find his kingdom, I shall see to it that you are not punished," Isra pronounced with sharp fervour, as if she was being authentic, but Astrid smelt a rat as he watched from afar.

This can't be right. Isra is never nice to someone just for the sake of being kind. There must be something enticing to be so deeply enthused with this Ava. I don't feel Isra had something slipped into her morning beverage. And honestly, the whole thing sounds awry. Why Isra would go out of her way to assist some young juvenile is anyone's guess, but I am more interested in this Jonathan big wig and why he's having little Miss Steals-a-lot, practically foaming at the mouth in sheer terror of him? Astrid thought, concerned over this new personage Ava and just exactly why Isra was so drawn to her.

Baffling, some would say, but there must be some reasoning for it or else Isra would not feel inclined to involve herself with such a low-level minor. And it was soon to become clear as to whom and what Ava was when she opened her mouth, fully detailing exactly where she stood on the food chain between herself and the hierarchy she served.

Ava looked at Isra with a furrowed brow, expecting some kind of impending doom to come at her at any moment. It was clear that Ava was ridden with anxiety as she blundered haplessly, "Oh, but I am sure to be punished. I am with child!"

This revelation left Astrid gob smacked. His eyes lit up as he quickly caught on to exactly what that meant for Ava and her current employment. And there was a strong emphasis on "current." No prospective king would ever allow a young protege to contaminate herself in such a way that she would be unsuitable for the job at hand.

However, Isra remained calm. She didn't flinch as she processed the words carefully; Ava was in more hot water than Isra first estimated. Evidently, Isra was also unaware of the concept as she had no comprehension of the definition behind the statement Ava had made.

"With child, dear? Oh goodness, you're not sick or impaled, are you?" Isra questioned with menacing intrigue, so much so that Astrid resisted the urge to open his smart mouth and say something that would ultimately compel Ava to be even more intimidated by him. Ava was already almost squealing at him reprimanding her. She didn't need any more excuses to be in fear of what the terrible Astrid might enact next for her.

"No. I am soon to be a mother," Ava said clearly.

She then demonstrated further by patting a large, rounded lump on her abdomen with an honest look of sincerity and affection. This was something that only mystified Isra as she had no real understanding of what Ava was detailing. Isra stood taken aback, staring at Ava with wild inquisition, only to find herself staring at the young girl with sheer fascination as to why she'd get herself into such an abhorrent state of physicality.

It must have been desperation that pushed her to engage in such an act that she would be found carrying an insolent child, and goodness only knows if Ava happened to know who the paternal donor was. But needless to say, Isra agreed to speak with Prince Jonathan, and, of course, she would keep her word, no matter what she thought about Ava and her vile predicament.

I will talk with this unsightly prince and perhaps some arrangement can be made in regards to Ava. She is still an adolescent herself, and so she doesn't need the worry of being made redundant because of her poorly made life choices. Mother or not, she is incapable of raising herself, let alone a poor changeling child, Isra murmured to herself, carefully placing a well-designated finger to her lips as she pondered the situation.

"So where does he herald, child? This darling prince which you are situated with?" Isra questioned Ava again.

This time, Isra had a more warning voice. She expected Ava to tell her where Jonathan resided, and she had very little time for childish games.

"Bitterquel," Ava answered abruptly. "It's a neighbouring kingdom, not far from here."

"Yes, I know where it is. I've heard of it," Isra replied sharply. "I will go and have a little chat with this Jonathan, and perhaps efforts can be made," she finished, not bothering to elaborate her meaning.

10

Isra stood impatiently at the entrance to Bitterquel castle. Her black lacy dress swished back and forth in the late December wind while her long golden tresses wandered away from her face as she awaited her arrival to be acknowledged.

Finally, a face appeared at the door. A woman completely clad in white linen, although evidently, it wasn't silk as the material was thin and paper-like, had a headscarf covering her head so Isra couldn't make out anything. But the woman's powdery blue eyes flitted back and forth, as, apparently, the woman was in a world of her own.

"Yes, can I help you?" she probed with a frown as she stood anxiously at the door's edge.

Perhaps they don't get visitors often. How odd, since it is a castle with a prince that claims to be of finery and grace. You'd expect the service staff to be a little more acquainted with their manners, Isra articulated to herself in profound thought.

You'd think with this esteemed Jonathan being a ruler of his kingdom, he'd at least have something to marvel over when people came by, but apparently, this was not the forefront of his focus.

"Yes, I am here to see Prince Jonathan," Isra retorted to the cold, evasive woman, who still lacked little in the way of people skills.

"Ah. Is he expecting you?" the woman questioned with a perplexed glance, as if she didn't know exactly how to handle this.

"He is not." Isra motioned abruptly. "But perhaps if you allowed me in to see the man, I could say what I have to say and then we could both get on with our day, rather than standing here like fools!"

"Right you are," the woman agreed, dropping her guard a little. It was crystal clear she felt less apprehensive now as she opened the door, allowing Isra to walk right in. "He's on the left of the first floor. Just go straight in. Although I warn you, the man isn't easily appeased to people barging in on his privacy," she advised in a worrisome tone of voice.

"Be that as it may. However, I am not a person, so hopefully, my presence will not irk him," Isra countered in a firm tone.

"Oh, and what are you, dear?" the woman asked with sheer fascination.

Her eyes would have turned on in their insides if she realised just what she had let herself in for when Isra happily gave her the knowledge she was seeking.

"Why, I'm a witch! We simply do not need this mortal coil," Isra commented proudly, proceeding to glide up a pristine golden staircase that presumably led to the prince's throne room.

"Oh, my!" the woman gasped.

She placed her hand across her mouth. Her eyes told stories of unbearable fear and exasperation. The poor dear looked as though she was about to vomit at any second.

Poor thing. She looks like she's going to have a haemorrhage at any moment. The girl needs some ice water or something to calm her nerves. But oh well, this is not what I came here for, so I shall pay it no attention, Isra thought as she began to ascend the stairs.

Isra was used to ordinary people, more precisely humans, reacting in this manner. And honestly, this servant wasn't the first courtier Isra had witnessed cower in terror at the notion of knowing exactly who and what she was. But no matter; she had a handsome prince to see.

Isra finally reached the top of the staircase after she climbed what seemed like a hundred steps. It was baffling, as she was then greeted with golden walls that had a tinge of brown ochre. There wasn't anything typically royal about the place in Bitterquel, which made Isra wonder if it was really as stately as it had been made out to be.

You'd think they'd at least invest in some red velvet drapes or something that showcased their wide range of luxury. But perhaps this prince isn't quite as privileged as Ava made him seem. Maybe he is sodden. Lacks glamour of anything closely resembling taste, Isra thought as she came across yet another mass of gold and brown.

"Ewww, and where's his interior decorator when he needs one? Goodness me. He does need to know what majestic means. And boy, do gold and brown not compliment each other at all!" Isra remarked in disgust as yet again she was greeted with more vile colouring.

"Far be it from me to say, but what does my choice of decor have to do with you?" a deep male voice called out from what sounded like only a stone's throw away.

"What in the heathens?" Isra whispered to herself.

She paused to decipher exactly where the sound had come from. She was walking down a hallway, and as far as she could make out, there were no rooms to be seen, or at least as far as she could envision it. But this man was definitely talking to Isra from some place, else she wouldn't be able to hear his arrogant tone.

"Down here! Right beside the golden frame!" the man responded.

Again, Isra was perplexed. All she saw was the corridor she had been walking through, but she continued striding down the path while carefully looking around and behind her to make sure this person wasn't about to sneak up on her. That would be ghastly. Isra continued walking down the narrow hall, wondering if maybe she was imagining the voice, that maybe he was a figment of her imagination.

Not sure if I dreamed this whole thing up or there is a throne room around here somewhere! But damn, my eyes deceive me, for I do not see anything pertaining to such, Isra thought as she got to the end of what seemed like a never-ending path.

Something glinted at her from beyond the corner, something

glimmering in solid, hard gold. A large, ornate mirror stared back at her, showing her bewildered reflection. It was at least five feet in length and towered across the mediocre wall it hung from.

However, the most beguiling detail of all was that it was completely saturated in the finest twenty-four-carat gold and it was embellished with hundreds if not thousands of tiny rubies, sapphires, and emeralds. The reds glowed like ripe, plump apples while the royal blue and deep green shades added flavour to it, artistically speaking. Isra was so entranced by the beautifully ornate mirror that she barely paid heed to the large door next to it.

This door was equally elegant and enchanting, but it was much more plain in comparison to the encrusted mirror. While yes, it was still surrounded by that murky brown and tinged with glistening gold, the door was more theatrical. It looked as though it should have been outside but oddly enough was found within. Feeling an attraction that couldn't be explained, Isra tugged hard on the handle, pulling it open, and found herself staring face to face at a tall man with dark hair and round-rimmed spectacles.

"Oh, it's you!"

Isra glared at him as she allowed the door to slam behind her.

"Wait, do I know you?" she asked the man with intrigue. Pondering for a moment, Isra stared at him intently.

That jet-black hair. The round eyes meticulously framed by perfectly round spectacles, and lastly, that look of importance like he belonged solely in the world and everyone else should bow before him because they were meaningless. Now, where in the world had Isra witnessed that exact look before?

She tried going back in her mind to a time when she'd encountered someone just as pompous and ignorant to others, but the chances of it being the exact person were completely ridiculous.

No, it couldn't be? There is no actuality that it's him. I mean, he was never going to succeed in any place, never mind end up in a fantastical castle. But yet, that arrogant flare and deep voice strongly remind me of him. No, it's not him. That's an end to it. He was obliterated from civilisation aeons ago, and nobody would care to know him now. Still...

Isra went round and round in circles in her thoughts, agonising over the idea that this Prince Jonathan may have been the very same man she knew many moons ago. The same treacherous man that broke her heart when he engaged in a tryst with Everilda.

"I'm Prince Jonathan," he answered with a sharp glare.

His fierce-looking green-yellow eyes were all over Isra, scrupulous and painstakingly conscious of her entire being as he looked right into her emerald eyes. Naturally, they looked just as piercing as they usually were, but this sparked something else in Jonathan.

"Ah. I'm Lady Isra of the Dark, although some have worse names for me and many with acronyms," Isra replied pointedly.

She wasn't kidding about people having distasteful names for her. Many feared her and despite her being with Astrid for three solid years now, she was still someone that made people tremble without her moving a muscle.

"You know, I think I do recall you," Jonathan remarked. "But the possibility of us meeting again was rumoured to be never. I was told if I went near you, just an inch, I would be paralyzed inside my soul, although since no event has occurred, I'd be inclined to think that person was just spinning me a line. I mean, did you really go from being a sweet little witch to a full-blown queen of darkness?" Prince Jonathan asked with a little too much enthusiasm.

If he wasn't careful, Isra might have shot a fireball at him for being too intrusive or worse. But he wouldn't want to immerse himself too much in just what she might do if she didn't like his attitude. After all, he was still a man, and Isra rarely had any kind of tolerance for men.

Well, Astrid was a man, but alas, he was one she loved. Of course, it went without notice that he was the exception to the rule so she didn't endure Astrid. He was to be celebrated in her view, even when he did things that made her question why she allowed him to behave in such a manner that many would indeed frown upon.

"Oh, golly, it is you then!" Isra exclaimed in a cold voice. She pointed at the golden finery surrounding Jonathan before turning her attention back to him. "But how in all the laws of unrighteousness did you end up here? You were nothing. Just a pathetic boy that had barely come of age."

Isra spoke in such a way that Jonathan could only translate as maybe she still carried some lingering resentment towards him.

"I am afraid so," Jonathan said, confirming the grisly truth. "As to why I ended up in this not so humble abode, well, my brother Valien moved on to colder and more heavenly terrains, leaving my father no choice but to install me in this position. It's quite tragic, really."

Jonathan went on to explain, but Isra got the gist of how things had come to pass.

Fate always plays a part in some form or another, and sometimes where one person is doomed, another becomes rich and excels. It's just the way the cookie crumbles. You could get really lucky or you could perish in despair. You don't have a say in what plan the universe has for you because ultimately, it's not for you to know. Only when you find yourself in a certain time or place that brings you greatness or terrible despondency is when you are clear on where you fit in the scheme of things.

"Oh, how crushing to hear," Isra scoffed, but then she was sure that it wasn't as gruesome for Jonathan losing a brother so that he could claim a reign as prince.

Yes. It must have been tragic to have to rule a kingdom and finally have all the riches you ever wanted at your disposal. It must have been hardening to have gained so much through doing so very little. And therein lies the question of whether you actually deserve it! Isra considered resourcefully in her thoughts.

In any case, she didn't want to awaken any past shadows between her and Jonathan. She wasn't here to rile or judge him for his successes in life, as frivolous as they were.

"Yes, well, I still don't understand why I was threatened to be paralyzed deep in my soul if I ever set eyes on you again, but odd how it never happened," Jonathan articulated, a quizzical look on his face as though he had reasons to doubt it was ever true.

"Well, that depends," Isra began earnestly, "on a high number of factors. We could be here all day on the why and wherefore of something not happening. It's simply just science. Perhaps you were tricked into believing something so silly that you paid it mind by giving in to fear and therefore were sucked into the notion of such a thing coming to pass when really, it was just hearsay."

"Oh. You speak of such things as if you have experience in them. Maybe I was deluded by whimsical threats that tampered my way of seeing clearly. These threats made me terrified to even go near the fortress you eventually came to reside in," Jonathan conferred to Isra.

For once, he appeared unspeakably genuine, a marvellous conundrum, for sure, since Isra always believed him to be a pathological liar of sorts, a man so sick but unable to help himself or relieve his burden, for he couldn't help but continue to build falsified structures that simply lacked any substance of truth.

"Perhaps they were. But soul paralysation, as I hear, can only be enacted through the most resourceful dark magics, many of which are lost to the realm unless you know just how to tap into that energetic force," Isra explained in a harsh tone, although she was distracting herself from the reality lying at her feet, almost literally in this case.

"Well, it was Everilda who relayed this charming threat to me," Jonathan muttered, rearing his head at Isra.

Again, he seemed sincere, which was astounding for Isra to witness since she had him down as a compulsive philanderer who really couldn't help himself.

"Ah, well, she fairs well in her passing," Isra commented with a sly grin although she remained serious in her tone.

So, dear old Evie threatened him, did she? Well, I can't say I didn't see it coming, but I had no idea she was so determined to keep him from me. Not that it matters. It was simply a teenage crush. Not exactly a memorable one, either, Isra chided to herself as she thought back to the time when Jonathan was someone who truly rocked her world, at least if only for a moment.

"Evie always got the last word in, no matter what circumstance. That girl always poked her nose into places it didn't belong," Isra finished with a sharp tongue, though she meant what she said.

Everilda always had a way of throwing her weight about in things that had nothing to do with her. It didn't shock Isra at all that Jonathan had been entangled in Everilda's web, for he was dimwitted and weak. As far as Everilda saw it, he was her perfect target while she was at her worst. She always exploited the weaker ones because she didn't have the gusto to target someone mentally stronger than herself.

Jonathan looked taken aback. His eyes narrowed at Isra. For once, she saw he had real fear lurking within him, and it was evident he had no idea what Isra was referring to.

Time to put the poor chap out of his eternal misery. It is sad, truly, how these things emerge, but you know fate? It is never short-handed. Never discredit someone unless there is good reason. Poor old Jonathan doesn't even seem to know that dear old Everilda has left our earthly realm. It's time I gave this old fellow a good lashing of my famous truth concoction. Only it's not a potion as I'll be delivering it from my mouth, Isra thought, having concluded that Jonathan was none the wiser on Isra's meaning about Everilda, so she'd have to put him straight.

"Everilda left our earthly plane, dear. She cannot harm you anymore or make any more childish demands of you," Isra decreed.

It felt like there was an echo in the grand room. Jonathan felt Isra's voice travel across the walls and then bounce back towards her, although she had long finished her speech.

"Oh, well, that explains why it never came to pass," Jonathan retorted in a somewhat more relaxed fashion.

He seemed calmer at having received this information that Everilda's threats were simply that. There was no power lurking over him, waiting for him to trip up on himself because it and her were long gone out of the atmosphere.

"When a witch dies, so does her magic... even spells that she cast but didn't quite reach their full potential. So in short, if Evie decided you were to face some kind of torment if you had ever communicated with me, you would have been blocked from doing so but also severely punished if you pushed beyond the spell's boundaries. Basically, now that she's dead, there is nothing for you to breach. Do you understand my meaning, dear?" Isra explained, but it felt more like a lecture, like she was talking down to a child who had little knowledge of the lore of the land, not to mention the magics themselves.

It was also wise to note that Jonathan was mortal and therefore had no real understanding of magic or how it worked. And that was also probable as to why Everilda had chosen him to be her victim in the very cursed sense.

"I think I get it. Yes. Odd how she threatened me over something as trivial as wanting to see you, though. No offence intended, but after that showdown, I had no intention of going near either of you," Jonathan disclosed through gritted teeth.

His expression was more formal. He was trying to be polite because it was true that Everilda was vanquished but Isra was still alive and kicking.

"I am not easily offended these days, however, I didn't come here to discuss your little sordid affair. I came to speak about Ava, your handmaiden," Isra concurred, brushing Jonathan's weakly timed tangent completely out of the equation.

"Oh, her."

Jonathan seemed disinterested. He didn't have much in the way of high regard for his serving staff.

"Yes, well, you see, she rather dismally broke into my home, and while nothing was removed, I did find it got me quite cross. However, after taking a deep look into her predicament, she needs sympathy rather than a sharp telling off. The girl is not in a good way. She said she was seeking a decent meal and so my issue here is why could she not get that from you?"

Anything Jonathan said now could provoke Isra if he was not careful. Isra seemed to be intriguingly protective over Ava, which was baffling. Isra had no care at all for children. Or maybe there was something in Ava's personality that caused Isra to rethink her stance on the situation. Perhaps, in some way, Isra felt sorry for the girl, which was odd. Isra rarely had empathy for anyone. She did her utmost to block that stuff out as though it was something truly abhorrent that one didn't deserve to feel.

Ava was merely just a child herself, barely of childbearing age, and yet she was about to become a mother. That was if she was mature enough to succumb to the challenge. The way Isra viewed Ava was that the girl just about knew how to take care of herself, so goodness knows how a child would fare under her care. However, something called Isra to pay pity on this situation, and thus here she was, about to negotiate with Ava's not so kind employer.

"The servants always have access to the finest leftovers in the land," Jonathan retorted coldly.

Yes, it was evident Jonathan was not at all concerned for the wellbeing of his employees. Nonetheless, nourishment was a requirement for all life, and it was extremely off-putting to Isra how Jonathan so icily dismissed it as if it was nothing.

Isra pressed her arms across her chest while flashing him a glaring glance. The emerald in her eyes was extrusive as she showed him just how unimpressed she was with his actions. She was also rather impatient, and this was a quality that irked her.

"I have little care for that, but even as a servant girl, she should have decent food to replenish herself. She was nearly starved to death when my beau and I found her. And with the circumstance being the way it is, well, this is shoddy at best, Jonathan. Even for you," Isra finished with a sharp tone.

She was not amused with him at all. It didn't take long for Isra to be taken back to why she disliked him so much all those years ago. He was always such a callous and uncaring individual, and it did show in his mannerisms now.

Jonathan didn't have much tolerance for this lecture he was receiving from Isra but his ears pricked up at the most noticeable word that Isra spoke, which was circumstance. Of course, he knew the meaning, but he didn't quite fathom how it weaved its way into this conversation because to him, it was absolutely senseless. He obviously didn't have a single shred of a clue as to what went on with his staff at all.

"Circumstance? What do you mean by that? The poor girl has nothing within her but a rude mouth and little care for detail," Jonathan snapped, as if Ava displeased him greatly.

Oh, goodness. He doesn't know, does he? He can't know. How in the realm does he not know when his servant is with child?

Isra questioned the notion to herself. She felt like Jonathan walked around with his eyes half shut or something. Perhaps he just didn't take a keen interest in the lives of his workers, but surely it would pay to since Ava wouldn't be able to do much in due time.

"You haven't noticed the young adolescent's condition?" Isra probed.

"Well, how so?"

"The girl is clearly bulging at the belly," Isra remarked.

She was hoping Jonathan would have more of an inclination as to what she was referring to but maybe he was entirely clueless. Who knew? He certainly wasn't the smartest living soul in the hemisphere. That was undeniably known.

"Oh. I never paid her any mind. Well, in that case, I have to relieve her of her duties immediately," Jonathan responded in an irritated but yet extremely formal tone. He paused after saying "immediately," for he knew he would now be one servant short. It was no impasse for him as he'd soon be able to seek out someone much better suited for the role at hand, but the pressing matter was dismissing the girl.

"You are leaving a poor girl alone to fend for herself with no home and no suitable employment when she is about to become a mother?" Isra questioned with such a fierce stare that it made the mortal wonder if she'd make them implode at any moment.

He recalled Isra's reckless temper, especially when she deemed herself to be right and the other person immensely wrong. And in this case, Jonathan was that opposition, so he'd have to think fast to get himself away from her wrath as swiftly as possible.

A thought suddenly occurred to him. It was almost on a whim. Jonathan involuntarily pressed a finger to his lips while he fell silent for a minute. He needed to consider this thought carefully before proceeding as the impact of any such decision if made wrongly could be dire. And so, a thorough internal discussion was required before he made grace on said decision.

Aha. I have underestimated the problem to be far more troublesome than it has to be. With Isra standing in as the girl's benefactor, I see no other alternative but for Isra to take on the girl and her careless folly. After all, she has come preaching in sweet tempestuous little Ava's defence, and so it is the most perfect arrangement for all concerned. I won't have to deal with the little madam anymore and soon, Isra will realise just what she's dragged herself into. By that time, it will be of no consequence to me, he thought as he enacted this greatly endowed plan that only benefited him.

"Yes, she must take her leave right away. For she is no use to me with this impending condition but since you are so entranced by this haphazard little peasant, perhaps you should take the wench on?" Jonathan proposed in a very manipulative manner. He had his hands pressed together to signify how pleased he was with himself.

"You are suggesting that I take your servant?" Isra quizzed with much interest.

She was bewildered as to why he would ask such a thing. This was not a favour from one friend to another since Isra and Jonathan were in no way companions, but Isra felt that Jonathan was exploiting their connection in some form so he could cut Ava loose.

Oh, he was washing his hands of Ava, make no mistake. It was undoubtedly true that Ava was not Isra's miscreant for sure. Still, it was clear to Isra that the girl needed somewhere to hang her head if only for a short time.

"Yes, I feel she'd be better suited with you and your man. Sorry, I don't recall his name," Jonathan mustered with a low brow. "Nonetheless, you have vouched for her so it only makes sense that she goes away with you," he proclaimed in a deep voice as though he had decided and there was no way of beseeching him into changing his mind.

"I see. What do you mean, my man?" Isra responded while also querying how Jonathan knew she was occupied by the heart of another. Maybe Isra had let something slip and was so wrapped up in this situation with Ava she hadn't recognised that she'd made a faux pas.

"Why, you said your beau, so naturally I assumed that was a male companion that was also likely to align with you in more ways than one," Jonathan announced in a cheery voice. Yes, he sounded triumphant like he'd had one-upped Isra somehow, but Isra smelt a rat.

Never mind. He's always been one for games, so let him play it. It seems in almost fifteen years, our dear Jonathan has not matured in the slightest. Change seems to overlook people in the most bewildering ways, Isra thought. *Still, there is the small matter of the girl.*

"So, will you take my servant Ava or not? She is useful despite her untimely laziness and impeccable manner for turning anything into a catastrophic mess!" Jonathan exclaimed as though he'd seen this for himself and was glad to be rid of her.

Isra nodded as if she had an understanding of what had gone down here. It ultimately wouldn't serve her too greatly to leave with a new servant in tow, but then again, it wouldn't be so disastrous either? I mean, what is the worst thing that could emerge from engaging in this barter with her former karmic beloved?

"I suppose so, but it wasn't in my schedule," Isra retorted promptly.

She licked her lips in an irritated way but maintained that formal demeanour that she always carried so well despite whatever was going on around her.

"Aha. It is settled then," Jonathan declared in a sadistically happy voice.

Seemingly it gave off the impression that all of his dreams apparently had been made flesh at once. It was bizarre to Isra how she was somehow thrown into this conundrum. Perhaps Jonathan did have some resentment from that time although his exterior had succeeded over a great feat.

"You shall take that vile wench! Good luck. And be mindful of her kleptomaniac habit. She has quite the knack for it, and her explanations for it are beyond ludicrous," Jonathan added.

In any case, Isra had heard and seen enough. She'd come expecting some kind of peaceful resolution and perhaps an amicable decision concerning Ava; however, Ava was practically chucked in Isra's domain. Overall, Isra wasn't sure if the outcome pleased her but at least Ava would be in safe hands. Gaining a new housemaid was not on Isra's list of wondrous things to do. It was no matter though, as Isra was sure the girl could be put to work soon enough.

Without giving Jonathan a second glance, Isra clicked her index and middle fingers together furiously, which instantaneously manifested a puff of lime-green smoke all around her. This cleverly materialised green entity encircled Isra's form vigorously and with a moment's passing, she was gone.

11

───────────

It was just an ordinary early January morning. The snow was plundering down in a frenzy. The white frosty entity looked marvellous as it sparkled, enchanted by the rays of the warm, golden sun.

How peculiar it was when Astrid, who was deeply engrossed in a large tome, heard a loud rapping on the outside door. Of course, you couldn't mistake the sound the ornate door made when someone tapped on it hard enough. The door was made of pure oak and was rock-solid. This meant that anyone who dared disturb the peaceful silence sounded an alarm that travelled all the way to the sitting room at Shambre Fell.

Naturally, this was a much-needed armament, the way Astrid saw it. He wanted to know about every single knock that front door down in the grounds below had bestowed upon it. Isra didn't care for it, even with the recent intruder incident. She'd glare them to death anyhow if someone was stupid enough to let themselves into her premises! And nobody on this grand earth needed that displeasure. But she was out gallivanting amongst the pastures of nature, so Astrid needn't worry about her for the time being.

Astrid closed the volume he was reading and leapt off the couch, exiting the living room and proceeded to descend the large stone staircase, preparing to hone in on whoever was standing behind the grand door outside. And just as Astrid reached the bottom of the steps, the rapping commenced again.

For heathen's sake, I'm coming, Astrid cursed in his thoughts, unwittingly becoming irritated with the impatience of whoever he found himself accosted with when he opened the door.

Imagine how surprised Astrid was when he found himself face to face with an individual with recognisably jet-black, slicked-back hair. Oh, no! It could only be one. The legendary and absolute know-it-all of the universe himself.

"Oh, shit... Samuel!" Astrid gasped in shock before he jumped right into action, proceeding to close the door in Samuel's face.

With one great push, Astrid lunged forward, using all of his body weight in an attempt to force the heavy oak door shut; however, it was to no avail. The damn thing wouldn't budge. Not even an inch.

That is most peculiar. Why is it not shutting? I could have sworn I updated the spell that kept this thing locked from uninvited guests. And Samuel is an unwanted guest for sure! He always brings bad news. So no, we don't want to pay him any mind! Astrid blundered to himself. It was evident he was a little anxious; his plan to shut Samuel out literally was not going the way he envisioned.

To be fair, Astrid thought slamming the ornate oak door in Samuel's face would indicate that he wanted no part in whatever the light bringer was offering. However, Astrid should have known better, because Samuel was wise to all of Astrid's cunning little tricks. He could have outwitted Astrid with a mere click of his finger, but Samuel was refraining from being the smart one. For now, anyway.

The irony of it all was that Astrid had just fitted this solid steel lock and bolt mechanism and so he couldn't understand why it wasn't clicking together, especially with his extremely well-executed protection ritual that he had only just performed to ensure no pests got further than the beautiful grounds guarding Shambre Fell.

Perhaps Isra has dazzled us with another one of her enchantments. No, that can't be it. She pays no mind to security. No, it has to be something else, Astrid pondered.

However, before Astrid could rationalise further as to why the door wasn't locking, or even shutting, for that matter, the solid oak marvel flew open, leaving Astrid face to face with Samuel. It was funny; for someone who was almost five hundred years old, Samuel still had that youthful look about him. His sky-blue eyes glared at Astrid through silver moon framed spectacles.

"Well, that was rather rude, I must say!" Samuel remarked in a coarse tone. "Now, how nice, you not inviting me to your impending nuptials. Oh boy, where are your manners? Did they fly away and disappear along with your grey matter?"

He mockingly questioned Astrid, though some may have found it to be quite rhetorical.

"Ah, now then. Where is that charming individual James?" Samuel asked.

Again, Astrid wasn't sure if it was a flamboyant question or merely just a sardonic statement since James had only been here less than a fortnight ago.

"I am afraid I haven't seen him," Astrid sharply replied.

"No problem! I shall do a little of my own studious investigation…"

Samuel motioned, not paying any attention to Astrid as he closed his eyes. He whispered some very well chosen and hardly audible words under his breath, and before you knew it, James materialised in front of Samuel and Astrid in a flash.

This only left Astrid more concerned because now it was two against one. And lest he forgot, he and James had never really seen eye to eye. Well, until recently when James had come bearing a truce of sorts. Astrid, on the other hand, didn't take it at face value. As far as he was concerned, Samuel showing up spelt trouble. Now that James was added to the conundrum, who knew what was going to erupt as a result?

Both of them are on my doorstep. And goodness knows why. I couldn't care less to be quite frank, but they never come bearing something fortuitous!

James scratched his head in bewilderment, confused as to why he had been summoned in such an abrupt way, but instead laid the blame at Astrid's feet. But what else was new?

"What the hell am I doing here? I could have sworn I had only just left you?" James blundered at Astrid in an angry voice, only proceeding to display more of that by crossing his arms against his chest.

"You'll find out soon enough!" was all Samuel responded.

"Ha, why don't you both just vamoose already?" Astrid suggested derisively.

"Aww, I would, but we have business to discuss. Now, let us go inside and chat for a while unless you both want to be toads!"

Samuel jeered in Astrid's and James's direction, although he still sounded amicable when you considered the nature of his threat.

"Turn James into a toad. He'd love it. Now, I'm skedaddling before Isra finds out what's afoot. She'd have my guts for insoles if she suspected for one moment there was any trickery going on down here. And no offence, but you two never bring good news!" Astrid snapped.

"You can both be little horn toads at this rate and have your own cosy little lily pad to make merry fun on. Now let me into your divine palace, Astrid, or I'm going to get testy!" Samuel retorted.

"Fine!" Astrid relented. "But how the fuck am I supposed to explain this to Isra? Do tell me!"

Astrid fumbled, mad as hell, but there was no denying Samuel's immeasurable power. When that damn light bringer wanted something, you could bet your life he'd get it, even if he had to rile a few feathers in order to do so.

"I swear, if she gets fiery, I'm blaming the both of you!" Astrid countered back at Samuel.

Astrid was so pissed, he was almost yelling, spitting insults back and forth, but it was no use. He'd have to play along and entertain Samuel's presence even if it meant looking mighty conspicuous in front of Isra. But lucky for Astrid, the witch was on one of her many fine morning walks.

A few moments later, Astrid stood impatiently by the window as he watched Samuel and James stare at each other impetuously. It was apparent to Astrid that although Samuel had planned this event keenly, he hadn't discussed it with either James or himself. Still, if he looked across the dynamic views of the lands instead of giving the two his time, perhaps they'd just fade away.

No such luck was going to be presented to him on this not-so-joyous occasion.

"Oh, stop carrying on, and get a grip, boy. You know why I'm here!" Samuel instructed in a hoarse voice, making the light bringer sound tired and rather impatient.

"Actually, no. I don't. Perhaps you should enlighten me," Astrid returned to Samuel in a sarcastic tone, though he was doing his utmost to try to hold down some politeness.

Samuel gruffed as if he really was not impressed with Astrid's attitude. The light bringer sat upon the couch while James stood cautiously close towards the entrance of the living area, obviously making haste for a quick exit whenever he felt the need.

Yeah, he's planning a swift getaway. The cheeky bastard. I'm damned if I'm the only one that will be dealing with Samuel this morning, Astrid thought as he observed James standing motionlessly quiet in the corner with his arms folded across his chest. Clearly, he hadn't appreciated being summoned for this meeting.

"You know I am trying to enlist you both, so you are in the right domains here with the knowledge that will no doubt surpass you in the blink of an eye if you don't listen to my careful instructions, so it would please me immensely if you listened for once!"

Samuel grimaced as he responded, sounding annoyed with them both. But more so Astrid, for he was the one questioning Samuel's presence.

"Yes, I understand your need for thoroughness, Samuel. But Isra is off on one of her escapades, and I'd rather you two were gone before she gets back. After all, she has no inclination of who you both are. I want it to stay that way, too!" Astrid added in at the last second. Only it was too late, as he had already made a most terrible mistake.

"Oh, yes, it's always about the witch for him. Never about the impending importance of a great destruction that could tear apart this wondrous realm. No, that doesn't even come into his force field. He'd rather not rile his witch that he's so deeply obsessed with," James mocked in a callous voice.

"Oh, is that so? You'd better come over here and say that... or else, boy!" Astrid barked at James.

It was gut-wrenching as the raven-man's left eyebrow raised in disapproval of having to hear such things.

He always has to go for Isra. It never is anything else, is it? It always goes right back to my obsession with Isra, and how is that so when I'm in a commitment with her? Is he jealous or what? I don't understand why he has to constantly fuel the issue whenever he feels the need to do so.

Astrid cursed reverently in thought, having already found his long-standing annoyance for James raised even more so.

"I will then! Just drop the witch already, and then we won't be in the thick of it every time she engages in some dark trickery that pretty much guarantees we will get roped in whenever she does!" James shot back at Astrid with a stinging look.

For Astrid, this little outburst from James was just one too many.

"Oh, that does it! You really can't help yourself, can you? You just have to throw the nail down every single time, creating more bloodshed. Well, that's it. I'm not tolerating any more of your exasperating self. Off with your head!" Astrid boomed as he raised a pointed finger in James's direction.

It was only a matter of telling what Astrid would do. He was absolutely seething with rage. Nothing would be able to calm him this time. Not Isra, but she wasn't here, anyhow. And not some lovely motivational pep talk from Samuel that normally did the trick. No, there was no actual return from this one. Astrid was about to show just how mad he was. Someone would have to stop him before things got ugly.

"Whatever; do your worst!" James shouted.

He didn't care at all for what Astrid would or wouldn't do. James felt Astrid was bluffing as he took the usual tone for when he thought the former raven was bullshitting. In any case, Samuel was on hand to administer his form of discipline to remedy this extremely heated and on the verge of becoming toxic situation. He'd had his fill of both men for one morning, and if they weren't going to resolve their issues themselves then he would have to intervene.

"That's just about enough from the pair of you! So much child-like behaviour from supposedly grown men!" Samuel yelled from his position.

He raised his hand in the air as if to signal Astrid and James to stop their ruckus immediately. Whether they would or not was indeed another matter entirely. However, Samuel had an ulterior motive for his dignified hand gesture.

The light bringer paid Astrid and James no mind as he closed his eyes, focusing on both of their energies, zoning in on their auras respectively before he began concentrating. He sounded out some hard to decipher words that were presumably from another language as they sounded so indifferent. The words echoed as Samuel repeated them in succession.

"Ahhh wooooo. Ah wooooooo. Haddy ha. Ahhhh wooo."

Neither James nor Astrid bothered to notice the murky green energy surrounding them as though they were in the midst of a fiery vortex. This powerful green forcefulness circled around both men until it rooted itself in them. It carried on saturating James and Astrid inside their individual light bodies until each of them was in separate green cylinders of light.

Seriously, these two were so focused on fighting with one another that it was only when they had been smothered by the mysterious moss-green magic that they finally twigged onto the idea that something wasn't quite right. But it was far too late. Samuel's magic had begun its masterful work.

Astrid was going to stare out at James to give him yet another eyeful, only Astrid realised he was finding it incredibly difficult to see James or anything else for that matter. Astrid's vision had become so blurry that if he wasn't standing firmly against a wall, he might have fallen over right there and then. But this was so peculiar. Astrid couldn't figure out why he suddenly couldn't see a thing or why he felt so dizzy.

What the hell is going on? Why can't I see anything? Where did the room go? I can't understand why everything is so disorienting... and, oooh, I don't feel so good, Astrid thought as he became aware that something was most awry.

He felt off-balance. Astrid struggled to keep his footing as the green magic kept on working its will. And much to his displeasure, it had him entangled in its fierce grip before he was lowered down to the ground but far below anything Astrid could imagine.

James was experiencing something similar, but for some reason, he chose to remain calm. He had the idea that if he tried to find the logical cause for what was uninvitingly weaving a hell of a storm around him, he'd find the solution much quicker.

Surely it has to be better than Astrid's process of freaking out over what is occurring. I have to try to ascertain my whereabouts. If only I could get a grasp on what this energy is doing to me, maybe I can undo it, James retorted to himself in a flurry of thoughts.

It was a completely different perspective compared to Astrid's back and forth and wondering of what was happening to himself, but James was much more grounded in his knowledge. He was trying to dissect it and have it before him, piece by piece, so he could get to the bottom of whatever was trying to get the best of him.

It was interesting that both of these charming men, not too long out of their quarrel, had somehow been able to hear their inner thoughts without the ability to view what was happening to the other. There was a deep clarity though, of knowing exactly what the other was going through without being able to see or hear anything. The irony in that was priceless when you sat down and thought back on how much they detested each other. However, despite these superior thoughts of cunning and agility, Astrid and James would soon find out that their efforts were meaningless.

And while these two were doing their utmost to unravel this most bizarre mystery of sorts, Samuel sat back on the couch, awaiting the diligent outcome that would soon be greeting him, and, of course, James and Astrid. They would come colliding with reality, greenness and all.

Samuel eyed them carefully although he couldn't see them anymore; they were covered in the green mass, but Samuel knew instinctively they were under there somewhere. The green cylinders both lit up in unison before showering down more light energy. Only this time, it was a more putrid slime-green colour. Then the light began to fade as the magic tumbled onto the ground, leaving in its place two perfectly alike green toads.

"Ah, much better!" Samuel voiced as he admired his fine work.

Both of the little green toads stared at each other with wide, brown and green eyes with specks of yellow reflecting at them.

Samuel couldn't help but smile as he looked fondly upon his two most favourite men. Despite their new, green, amphibian forms, they still seemed to like glaring at each other. This was an amusing thought to Samuel as he had hoped as toads they might find some common ground. Or perhaps lily pad. Nevertheless, at least they'd be quiet for the time being, anyway.

Meanwhile, Samuel had no idea he was being eyeballed from the far end of the living room. The light bringer remained relaxed and in full composure as two glaring, piercing, emerald-green eyes were affixed on him. It was only when he caught sight of the fiery green flame heading his way that his vision catapulted right into the view of Lady Isra of the Dark.

Of course, Samuel knew exactly who she was... That long, flowing, almost white, shimmery hair travelled down past her shoulders and the small of her back. Those beseeching dark green eyes glinted back at him. And never mind the close-fitting, white, lace gown that clung to her fine slim frame, further displaying that eccentric hourglass figure...

Yes, it could only be one. There was no other.

12

Isra scowled at Samuel so intensely that he resisted the overpowering urge to turn away from her.

It was then that Isra made her way into the living area. She was nearly snarling at Samuel, but then she glanced down at the two toads sitting adjacent to one another on the floor. Both charming beings looked bemused concerning their predicament, but Isra suddenly stopped. She eyed the one on the right carefully, noting it had a golden colour in his eyes while the other was more green in nature.

Yes, she knew who this one was. It had to be Astrid, for sure.

Yep, that's him. But goodness, how did he get reduced to this despicable form? Isra murmured to herself in a pressing reverie.

Isra returned her attention to Samuel. She instantly started interrogating him as if he had enacted the most diabolical of feats in her presence.

"What the hell have you done here?" Isra demanded in a ferocious voice, only further sounding out her fury. She was so riled that she was screeching at the poor light bringer.

Isra didn't give Samuel much leeway to answer, but instead reached down, gently picking up the little toad on the right and whispered to it softly, "I know who you are. Stay calm now. I will see to it that you are relinquished from this vile commodity immediately."

"Ah, yes. That," Samuel responded.

Samuel appeared to be mighty cheery considering Isra was practically spitting feathers at him over this little debacle.

He watched as Isra slowly placed the green toad back on the stone floor before making haste in approaching her. Samuel had only taken a few steps toward Isra, witnessing the full glare she was giving off as she not so silently fumed in his direction.

Samuel was now in Isra's face, literally. He met her green glowing eyes with somewhat of a perplexed smile. As if that would diffuse the situation, but Samuel had already met Isra once, and he knew exactly how to handle her; however, this time around, he hadn't predicted she'd be here when he dished out his own form of discipline. Still, he thought he better try his hardest to win her over since she didn't seem best pleased with him.

He replied swiftly, "Ah yes, they were bickering so I took them down to a more ambient level!"

"Then I suggest you turn him back into his form immediately!" Isra instructed. She paused and then raged in a loud voice, "Or *else!*"

Isra closed her eyes for just a split second, deeply concentrating as she again whispered something to herself. Although it wasn't at an audible level for the light bringer to hear, he sensed trouble brewing. Especially since a green fireball materialised in the palm of Isra's hand in a flash. Clearly, the witch had no tolerance for Samuel. She then revealed the fireball that sat in the palm of her right hand. It glared back at the light bringer as he caught sight of the fiery lime-green flames it was made up of. It would only take one swift move from Lady Isra of the Dark, and that fireball would be right in his face.

Samuel smiled fondly as he recollected when he had last seen her so feisty. *It was such a shame that it had to end the way it did, but you can't go around unleashing your venom on people, dear. I did tell you I would disarm you, and that I did, but of course, you have no memory of such an event. It doesn't matter, really, but I will always remember you for having a flair for warm, glowing flames.*

He took care that he was not being listened to as he remembered this most poignant moment that he shared with Isra. Because even if her memory had been scrubbed clean, Isra was still a witch. She was able to hear thoughts clearly. If Lady Isra heard Samuel's recollection of her possessing such magics before, she may well have wondered how he came to know.

"Ah now, I think I know why I always referred to you as a little firecracker," Samuel joked in the midst of the situation. He was trying to be humorous despite Lady Isra still having that glowing sphere of fire just waiting to be propelled right at him.

No doubt, she wants to prove a point by launching that dynamic entity at me. Nonetheless, I am none too privy to her nonchalant threats, having dealt with them many times before. But I'll let her think she has one-upped me on this occasion, Samuel quipped to himself as he stood awaiting Isra's comeback. And with her being the scornful enchantress she was, it would be a peppy one at that.

"And how would you come to presume such things?" Isra questioned with a bewildered stare, instantly proving Samuel wrong in his assumption.

"Ah, my mistake. I must have misguidedly thought you were someone else. But let me guess, you are the famous Lady Isra of the Dark, am I wrong?" Samuel postulated with precise confidence, knowing he was exact in his meaning.

He didn't want to appear too certain. Isra might have some inkling that she and Samuel had made acquaintance before.

"Yes, I am," Isra answered with a profound glance.

Perhaps deep within, Isra suspected something wasn't quite right with this newcomer, but she decided to refrain from pursuing any line of enquiry on it. It was more important for Isra to stick firmly to the current situation that needed immediate resolution. Needless to say, she was none too pleased to see her beloved Astrid in his amphibian state.

"Nice to finally meet you. I have heard so many tales from your delightfully obtuse divine partner, Astrid. I am Samuel."

Of course, he was keeping things light-hearted while also maintaining that formal stance of his that made him so formidable to many. Isra folded her arms at the mere mention of Astrid, pointing down to the toads on the floor.

"Yes, and on the subject of Astrid, how about you change him back into the man he is *supposed* to be!"

"Of course, anything you say, firecracker," Samuel acknowledged, and before there was a need for Isra to say anything else, Samuel got to work.

With just one swift wave of his hand, a murky green light covered both toads, elongating them in its mesmerising power. And then by moving his hand downward, the spell was completed; both toads were suddenly wrapped in the purest white, shimmery light.

A second later, a very disapproving Astrid stood glaring at Samuel with disdain. You could bet your life Astrid wasn't rating Samuel too highly at this moment as he discarded soggy, mushed, green pond slime off his black silk shirt.

"That was not pleasant."

Astrid grimaced before he realised his Isra was in front of him, and his eyes lit up like fireflies. Immediately, Astrid reached over for Isra, pulling her into a passionate embrace as he did his utmost to deliberately ignore Samuel.

"Awww. I am sorry, dear. I told him to change you back as soon as I got here and witnessed what had gone on. Who the hell is he, anyway?" Isra questioned with much interest as she stared at his brown-golden eyes intently while locked her into his robust kiss.

James was equally annoyed as he too did his best to brush the cold pond slime away from him. Funny how both of them started this little shenanigan and yet they were as resentful as the other because Samuel had taken them down a notch.

"Yes, well, if he had behaved himself in the first instance, I wouldn't have had to do that, girl," Samuel cut in before either Isra or Astrid had the chance to respond. Presumably, Samuel was addressing Isra as he had affectionately given her the label "girl," although his meaning could only be decoded as sarcastic.

"Punishing me for speaking the forbidden truth in my own house! Goodness me, whatever next! Being banished for saying something that greatly offended that big fat ego of yours?!" Astrid retorted in disgust, though he wasn't kidding.

Samuel had taken things too far with his line of discipline on this occasion, according to Astrid's viewpoint.

"Yes, I know it was demeaning, love, but it is over now," Isra soothed as she tenderly stroked his neck before taking another scathing look at Samuel.

In an impulsive artifice, Isra turned away from Astrid to get a closer look at the light bringer. Isra's piercing emerald-green eyes scanned him from head to toe. She scrutinised him, taking him in piece by piece as she made a thorough examination of not only his physical exterior but also his metaphysical name tag. This was the energy that he carried around his non-corporeal self that truly defined who he was. And more precisely, just what he happened to be.

Isra began by gently honing in on the man's aura. She noticed the pearly white specks that sparkled around the shiny yellow interior before moving down to his under layers, which were an array of light blue and striking silver. It didn't take much investigation before Isra came to the dire conclusion with a painful gasp.

She grimaced as she eyed Samuel carefully with a wide eyed-stare. Samuel was methodical in his appearance, for he was dressed in a grand black tailored suit as though you'd find him at the most highly esteemed places. He also had perfectly slicked-back black hair.

Isra glared at Samuel with extreme contempt, realising very quickly exactly what he was.

Oh, no; he's one of those love and light disciples. Such a vile lot, they are. Those so-called spiritual folk who preach their narrow-minded beliefs, insisting we must all cooperate with their flimsy demands unless we want some grotesque consequence to be unleashed unto us. Disgusting, it is.

Absolutely abhorrent, Isra cursed to herself in a mass of thoughts. *But the question remains, how on earth Astrid got entangled with such a foe? One that he claims to be a friend, nonetheless! This is most perplexing to me, indeed.*

"Ha, you are one of those love and light types! How dreadfully tragic for you. There may be hope for you yet. Perhaps you can drink a plentiful concoction and that most beseeching ailment will go away," Isra affronted with a horrendous amount of hostility aimed in Samuel's direction.

Samuel resisted the urge to burst out into stupendous laughter as he chortled, "Oh, we can only hope, my dear."

Samuel couldn't help but find Isra's untimely insult most amusing because he was in quite the pinch of his life. If only Isra knew the terrifying truth of it, but alas, Samuel was not one to spill out his most cryptic secrets, especially to a creature who was enveloped in darkness such as Isra.

Ultimately, knew he had to be discreet, because who knew what Isra would enact if she knew Samuel was having difficulty finding his footing on his light path. The way the legends and lore told of it was that the light workers were always strong and defiant and never faltered. But in this instance, Samuel was falling by the wayside, and not a single soul around him noticed.

Or perhaps that wasn't strictly true; Astrid had already made the distinction that something was amiss with the light bringer, but he had taken it upon himself not to disclose that detail.

"Oh, she's a pistol, Astrid! You must be so proud!" Samuel giggled with a smirk on his face.

Conveniently, Astrid chose not to respond to the extremely sardonic comment. Even if it wasn't meant in an undermining fashion, it irked him, and so he maintained his silence.

Of course, I am proud of her. Why wouldn't I be? She's gone from the most torrential sorceress ever to exist on this wasted land to someone who's opened her heart. She's regained some of that essential light that she had forgotten for such a long and strenuous time. Samuel hasn't stuck with her as I have. He has no comprehension of the metamorphosis she's undergone, and so he remains sceptical that she could be anything but evil. Astrid felt like he was being dragged into some wild confrontation that Samuel still felt necessary regarding Isra.

Yes, Samuel had never been truly overjoyed to know of Astrid's alignment with Isra. Never mind the physical one that followed shortly after when he'd finally been able to get his hands on her in his humanised form.

"Come now, let's get to business. It was such a joyous event meeting you, Isra," Samuel addressed before turning his eyes towards Astrid, adding in, "But I am afraid I am going to have to detain your beloved; we have some business matters to discuss."

"I see now, and I suppose you expect me to leave after I caught you vandalising my precious one most disdainfully?" Isra quizzed with a furrowed brow.

She shot Samuel a harsh stare, giving him a good look at her glowing emerald eyes. Since Isra had her arms firmly pressed up against her chest, it was apparent she was not exiting the vicinity.

In order to conquer such a feat, it appeared that Samuel would have to force Lady Isra to leave. One could only imagine just what rocky path that would lead to, for Isra was not easily persuaded to do anything. Even more so in the circumstance where someone attempted to manipulate her into doing such an act.

Still, Samuel was not a stranger to Isra's disobedient tactics, and he had more than a few tricks up his sleeve. It was just a matter of unlocking the metaphorical Pandora's box that he had within him. Only he knew just how powerful that energy would be because it had been brewing inside of him for quite some time. He just had to take the plunge and pull the trigger.

Samuel smiled at Isra, although he suddenly got a much more harsh voice as he addressed her firmly, "It would be much better for you, my dear, if you went off on another one of your walks. I can make you, if necessary, but it would be more pleasing if you did so of your own accord."

Samuel didn't scowl and grunt like Isra. His attitude towards Isra was formal in nature. In this state, he was approachable whereas the witch was not. It was as though Samuel was an astounding authority figure in the community, one that Isra should undoubtedly acknowledge and show credence for, if she had any understanding of what mutual respect for her elders was. Samuel wasn't overly sure if Isra had truly ever given anybody that, but he was going to ensure she didn't throw one of her otherworldly tantrums on his watch. Oh, no. He wasn't going to have any of that diabolical nonsense.

"I see," Isra replied bluntly without any emotive feeling in her tone. "In that case, I shall be off before I have the urge to vomit. With all this light-hearted energy buzzing around the place, I feel rather dizzy. I shall willingly take my leave."

She turned her back to Astrid and Samuel, although neither of them was entirely convinced that she was going to actually exit the premises. Astrid threw a cold, harsh stare in Samuel's direction but proceeded to be silent, for he had nothing to say to the light bringer.

It was fair to say that after everything Samuel had done to both Astrid and Isra, Astrid had begun to have his fill of the usually enigmatic being. Samuel clearly felt it was okay to throw his weight around, coming here unannounced. Then he'd gone and bossed Astrid around as if Astrid was still his little feathered errand boy with two minor exceptions. Astrid wasn't under Samuel's employment anymore and neither was he a raven. Technically speaking, anyway.

Then there was the small matter of Samuel standing in the way of Astrid's blossoming romance with Isra every chance he got. Okay, so it had taken several years for Astrid to reclaim his position in Isra's life after Samuel had put the kibosh on everything with his mystical ruination that he'd enacted on Isra to make her forget her entire history with Astrid. But even after all that trouble Samuel had gone to, Astrid waited patiently and swooped in when the time was right.

Whatever Samuel has come out all this way for, I'm not going to have it. It doesn't bear any meaning. I will not pay it any mind. He can say it and then be gone, and that will be the end of it.

Or so Astrid was banking on.

Astrid's lingering thought was interrupted when he noticed

Samuel still giving Isra that undeniably charming, cheeky smile of his.

It was deliberate on Samuel's part because he knew better than anyone that it was much more proficient to engage a dark enchantress with sardonic humour than face their wrath by trying to dominate her with commands.

"Good. Now off with you, dear. This won't take long. In any case, I'd feel better if you didn't grace us with your darling presence while we old men discuss formalities. It would be so humdrum for a woman that holds so much prowess within such as yourself," Samuel cajoled, although he was being sincere.

He did feel that his damning announcement would bore Isra senseless, but since it also pertained to her, well, it was safer for her to not bear witness to it.

And with that, Isra proceeded to leave, turning her head around to face Astrid before she did. It always thrilled her how he kept his beady eyeballs affixed to her even when she was about to leave his line of vision. Something about it was just so entrancing. The way he never let her out of his sight for even a mere second was poignant in itself. Astrid possessed this quality in a man that not only made him domineering to the more feminine sex but was also extremely attractive.

Isra suddenly noticed James standing in the corner of the living area. He must have made off into the shallow dank corner when Samuel transformed him and Astrid back into their human selves. It was likely that James wanted to fade into the background since he evidently didn't want to stand next to Samuel and Astrid.

How funny, since they all seemed to know each other in some form or another, but Isra wasn't aware of how these connections had become so intertwined. They gave her the impression that they were carefully keeping that knowledge away from her. However, she was a witch attuned to the dark forces so she'd find out eventually, no matter how hard these men tried to conceal the truth from her.

Isra flashed her piercing emerald green eyes at James as she gently strode out of the room, taking one last look at Astrid before she departed. She noted he was eager for her to leave but that also he was greatly uncomfortable around these two men, so perhaps this little tryst wasn't quite as friendly as he made it out to be. Well, at the moment, it wasn't since Astrid was giving Samuel death stares, and Astrid didn't even acknowledge James's existence.

Oh, you hide so much from me, but it doesn't matter because I know what lies inside your heart. And that's the part you can never conceal from me, Isra mused with a smile on her face.

Samuel turned his head to make deathly sure Isra had taken her leave and then he muttered, "Ah, our young little witch has gone. How sad. Now, Astrid, old boy, do you happen to have any Irish whiskey in your pantry? I feel like I could use one after all the chaos that has occurred this morning."

Astrid rolled his eyes at Samuel immediately, as though the light bringer was out of character, but more so because the light bringer had caused the destruction. It was true. Not only had he shown up uninvited, but he'd turned Astrid and James into toads. And now here he was, acting as sweet as sin as though nothing had ever happened.

It begged the question if Samuel was feeling entirely himself; he seemed to have a rather short memory, according to Astrid. But in any event, Astrid knew it was best to be as hospitable as he could towards his former boss. The sooner Astrid saw to Samuel's needs, the quicker he'd be out of Astrid's hair and hopefully for good. Despite sounding harsh, Astrid desired peace more than anything, the quiet solitude of which to share with his beloved Isra and have nobody else rocking up and turning it upside down for him.

Still, Astrid voiced his concerns as he eagerly pressed Samuel, "It's a little early for getting intoxicated, surely? But I'll see what we have. Perhaps I can rustle up something."

"Good boy," Samuel acknowledged by tapping him warmly on the shoulder.

13

Samuel was greatly pleased with Astrid's ability to go ransacking about the pantry and find a perfectly unpolished bottle of Irish whiskey. The label was a bit faded and the bottle looked tarnished from the outside, but the gleaming brown liquid looked mesmerising.

"Ah. You found some, eh? Good on you, son. Now pour me a glass. And have one for yourself while you're at it," Samuel chirped in a merry tone before turning his attention to James, who, oddly enough, was still standing at the back of the room.

James's behaviour could only be described as avoidance, since he would soon have the responsibilities any well-respecting soul would have when taking the reins at Spirisity. It was obvious to all that James was not interested in the impromptu meeting of minds Samuel had elaborately set up. But he should have at least been intrigued, shouldn't he? I mean, was he not about to become the life and soul of the party? Well, spiritually speaking, anyhow.

"James, here now! Have yourself a glass of whiskey. Calm the racing mind, eh?" Samuel proposed from his spot on the couch.

"I'm fine, thank you kindly," was all that came from James.

Clearly, he wasn't privy to socialised drinking, even in a setting such as this.

Samuel was positioned on the settee next to a very awkward and bewildered Astrid, who still had no inclination as to what any of this entailed. All Astrid knew was that Samuel had rushed over, and as far as Astrid could see, Samuel was orchestrating a boatload of unnecessary chaos. There was no other rational explanation that Astrid could conceive. Still, at least with Samuel having his beloved whiskey, he'd be hushed for a little while.

Perhaps we will get to the bottom of all this mediocre theatre, and he will tell me what in damnation this is all about! Who knows what other tricks he has up his sleeve? All I know is that I am damn tired of it.

Astrid cursed to himself in a flurry of sardonic thoughts as he hastily poured a glass of whiskey for himself and Samuel. Well, the man had offered him one, so Astrid figured it would be rude not to accept the gracious gift. Besides, Astrid was irritated. So, one glass of the stomach-churning liquid really couldn't hurt. In the worst-case scenario, Astrid indulging in the beverage would give him indigestion.

Samuel grabbed his tumbler of whiskey without hesitation, proceeding to gulp it down.

"After all I have done, I truly needed that," Samuel mustered, slamming the glass on the cold stone floor.

Astrid folded his arms across his chest impatiently before chugging his tumbler of the rich concoction that slid down his throat like gasoline. Astrid grimaced as he felt the whiskey hit the pit of his stomach. The sensation made him feel queasy as it floated in there, swirling and waiting for the moment to come shooting back up. However, Astrid had a strong gut, and even the most stomach-turning entities rarely defeated him.

He paused before glaring at Samuel coldly. "So what in heaven's curses is this all about? You come here stomping your feet all over the place. You then turn my life upside down further by ordering me and Isra around as if we are your slaves. And woes betide you if she decides to come back before you decide she should because that one is gunning for you now," Astrid admonished, and clearly, he was disgusted with the light bringer.

But he wasn't done yet. Astrid continued by castigating Samuel.

"And you do all of this, including summoning James when he doesn't want to be involved in this any more than me. You have no right to come into my home and force me to be your loyal servant anymore, Samuel. Those days are long dead. I don't even know how you managed to conduct such a feat without Isra losing all restraint, resulting in her turning you into something most unfortunate, but instead, you transform me into a fucking toad! I mean, what in delirium's name is wrong with you?"

Astrid rebuked Samuel, although it was a question rather than a simple reprimand.

Samuel let out a long, drawn-out sigh as he shifted off the settee and moved over to the window ledge. For some reason, Samuel felt more comfortable looking out onto that glorious view. All those glowing green hills that stood out amongst the timeless Shambre Fell landmark suddenly seemed pointless now. Samuel watched a dark grey rain cloud descend upon the normally sea-blue serene skies. How poignant, considering he was about to reveal that darkness was afoot, descending the very foundations they stood upon.

"Astrid, I didn't come here to overrule you. It's just when you do not listen to my chain of command, I get frustrated, and—" Samuel cut himself off before turning to face Astrid with a look of melancholy.

You could see the years had taken a terrible toll on Samuel. With the whole chaos of Isra switching from goodness and purity to full-blown, torrential calamity all those years ago to then finding out Astrid was in union with her despite it all, it was no wonder Samuel's patience was wearing thin. He was tired of everything and everyone.

If he didn't hang up his hat, he may as well have been catapulted head-first into a nervous breakdown. The job just wasn't the same as it was when he was first assigned to it. The enthusiasm Samuel had for the role as light bringer had been placated into darkness over time, and now he had lost all interest in it. Perhaps he'd even sunk into despair, plummeting from a powerful and almighty light being to a terribly desolate man that was pale and withdrawn after having spent many years being ensnared by formidable foes.

And of course, needless to say, Isra had been his toughest customer, for she was already a witch of great force when Samuel had come to know of her. It only took a mere trigger to send her cascading into uncertainty, which was swiftly met with vast obscurity as she drifted further from all that was righteous and good in favour of the murkier path.

However, those times were long gone. Samuel took the matter into his hands when he learned that Isra's newly met companion Astrid had retrieved powerful magics before giving them over to Isra. These stalwart energies were the same ones that Samuel had originally confiscated from Isra's possession when he first laid eyes on her after she'd summoned a dragon.

In any case, Samuel snatched them back from Isra before conducting an influential spell that stripped her memory clean. She'd had no recollection of Astrid, himself, or James. Samuel had done a number on Isra's mind, and she didn't remember any of the events that were connected with any members of the light worker association. Of course, at this point, it was wise to estimate that Astrid was almost slipping out of the doorway as far as the light business was concerned.

Still, in any event, Samuel had dealt with it all, using the proper channels to do so, but even all these light years later, he felt tired and irked with himself over how that situation had played out.

Almost thirteen years later, Samuel had been compelled to swoop in when Astrid captured the vengeful mortal, Ronald O'Kutte. Naturally, it regarded Isra. I mean, who else could it have been? Astrid wouldn't have paid the human boy any mind if his delightfully enchanting witch had not been entangled somewhere.

Samuel came to speak with Astrid out of the blue when he'd witnessed Astrid's little torture session with the poor mortal. Astrid was not best pleased with Samuel's interruption; he had wanted to deal with Ronald in his way, but Samuel made a bargain with Astrid

—to release Ronald unto him and Samuel would give him Isra's whereabouts in exchange. That tough conundrum worked out well, considering the fatalities that could have occurred as a result.

But Samuel was back to visit Astrid yet again, and for a very similar reason, which the weary light bringer was about to disclose. Who knows how Astrid would react; he had already miserably attempted to make Samuel go away by trying to ignore the light bringer. However, Samuel was more than capable of sussing out every fragment of Astrid's mind, so he knew all the tricks the former raven would try to administer, because in Astrid's words, "Samuel always brought bad news."

And yes, in this set of not so dire circumstances, Astrid's assumption was exactly right. Samuel had arrived to dispatch the intelligence he had received from the heavenly masterful beings at "on high," and it was no surprise it pertained to Isra... yet again.

"I am not your enemy, old chap," Samuel began with a furrowed brow, and then paused mid-sentence to deliver a painfully eye-opening cognisance that no doubt would leave Astrid reeling. "But I must warn you, what I have to relay could have exuberant consequences if you don't heed my premonition." Samuel shot a worried glance at Astrid.

I am hoping for the first time in your mystical life that you take what I have to say at face value. I wish for you to only listen to me, and then perhaps we won't have a malefic pandemonium on our hands, Samuel thought, doing his utmost to minimise the damage that could be potentially damning if Astrid got the wrong idea regarding Samuel's revelation concerning Isra.

Astrid straightened. He still had his arms pressed against his chest as he shot Samuel a foreboding gaze. "Okay then, let's have it. What's up this time? As if I don't know, because yet again, you bring bad tidings to my domain." He scoffed quizzically.

"A not-so-divine charmer from Isra's darker past has caught the attention of 'on high' of late. In fact, this soul is here, not far from Shambre Fell," Samuel divulged in a low voice.

He was hoping with all his might that Astrid might handle this in a calm and dignified manner, but then again, the former raven did have a rather short fuse.

"A charmer from Isra's past? Errr, and who the hell might that be?" Astrid probed with a vicious, deathly stare as if he meant business.

There was virtually nothing in Astrid's eyes but coldness and a void that seemed to go on forever. Astrid didn't seem best pleased at what he was hearing with his very capable human ears.

"Oh, don't you know him? Jonathan something?" Samuel chirped as he rested his index finger upon his chin. "Yes, a former beau of hers. Surely to goodness you know of him?" Samuel pressed, finding it bewildering that Astrid would have most definitely laid eyes on the precarious mortal when he was spying on Isra on behalf of Samuel.

Oh, come on, boy; surely, the number I performed on Isra's mind didn't get you, either, did it? I mean, you have to know this pesky peasant because you castrated him verbally to me more times than I care to admit. You must have some kind of inkling who Jonathan is, Samuel mused away in thought as he considered the notion that Astrid may well have been so blissfully unaware of everything else since he was so wrapped up in Isra.

But stranger things have occurred in my midst, Samuel concurred in a follow-up thought before returning his focus to the reality around him.

Astrid's mouth dropped wide open at this revelation. His brown eyes with that golden yellow sheen were all over Samuel, encircling him, whirling and surging with vast intrigue over how Samuel came to know of such a circumstance, especially with Samuel supposedly coming out of the love and light business! Astrid was dumbfounded. It was unbelievable.

"How the hell is he back in the realm?" Astrid exclaimed.

Oh, he wasn't at all amused to have this detailed to him. But at least he finally remembered who Jonathan was.

"Well, funny enough, boy, he never truly left. No; he skedaddled for a while after being entangled with your Isra and her former partner in crime, Everilda, and then a few years ago, something most unfortunate happened," Samuel blurted out, but Astrid wasn't really giving Samuel the room to speak.

"And what was that, exactly? I thought he was long gone from our lands, forced to perish in the face of adversity after being humiliated by Everilda, as she had done some fancy witchery on him... or something of that sort," Astrid articulated in a sincere tone, although his manner seemed sardonic.

"The untimely death of Prince Valien resulted in this peasant rising the food chain, as far as the line of royalty goes. But this most mysterious occurrence didn't go unnoticed by 'on high,' if you remember correctly..." Samuel paused mid-thought because he also recalled the time where the dismal Jonathan lost all claims to his royal heritage.

"Jonathan had things all lined up for him, and it was a little too perfect, if you ask me. His brother, Valien, dies suddenly and then Jonathan goes from being cast out from society to abruptly levelling up? Don't even try to tell me that's not suspicious. You and I are drawn to the multi-faceted spectacle that is this dark, murky world, Astrid. You know as well as I do that was simply no coincidence," Samuel stated firmly.

The truth was, Jonathan was doomed to failure regarding inheriting the throne because of his selfish folly. After a lot of discussion and concern over the behaviour of the young teenage Prince Jonathan, his father King Marco put the kywash on Jonathan becoming king. He chose Valien, his more mature son, to succeed him instead of Jonathan. As far as Marco saw it, Jonathan wasn't worthy of the crown.

The old, withering king felt Jonathan didn't want it enough, or, more precisely, wasn't going the extra mile to put the work in to claim it. And so, he decided it was better for all that Valien got the ultimate prize, the succession of the crown. Of course, it was unorthodox for a parent to change the way the system worked pertaining to who became king, but Marco was mighty confident in his decision.

You can only imagine how difficult it was when Marco learned of poor Valien's death. The king couldn't cope with the news, and not long after, Marco's wretched carcass was found dismally lying on the cold floor. A noticeable element only adding further salt into the wound was the noose tied securely around his neck. It seemed King Marco had taken his own life because he couldn't bear to live having lost his favourite son, and being left with the other one was more torturous than he could bear. And so that was how Jonathan became a prince; Valien was completely knocked out of the running.

Samuel seemed to be in yet another train of thought as he reminisced to when "on high" first brought the matter of Jonathan to his attention...

It was a sad day for the residents of Bitterquel, but yet a most pleasant one for such a lowly peasant. Someone that was thrown out of his heritage by the very person that sowed him from his loins, and then suddenly he gets a miracle? Something that lays him the same very claim he was removed from? Don't think for one moment that it was simply a natural occurrence.

Jonathan had strong ties to witchcraft, having both known Isra and the fateful Everilda. He would have found ways to worm his way back in. I find it intriguing and yet deeply incriminating. But not one human soul suspected a damn thing? The peasants of this land are greatly stupid, but yet also very amusing.

"So Isra's former partner is lurking around in our neighbouring vicinity; now how in the hell does that incorporate Isra?" Astrid pumped Samuel; yet again, he was being evasive. The old, faithful light bringer was trying to conceal something.

But why give up the habit of a lifetime? Astrid thought.

"Karma is a funny thing, Astrid," Samuel proclaimed in a low voice before he turned his focus to James, who was still standing at the back of the room, not doing anything. He wasn't saying a word, but Samuel was old school and this was a private conversation between himself and his spirited son.

"Wait a moment. I just need to fix something up," Samuel muttered in Astrid's direction.

And with that, Samuel visualised a grand, silver wall at least ten feet wide and maybe even longer. It covered the entire living area of Shambre Fell. The metaphysical wall rose to the ceiling and blocked anything that was on either side of it from the couch Samuel and Astrid were sitting on and over to the wall James was resting against. It appeared to be sectioning off James from Samuel and Astrid. A most peculiar act, some would say, but Samuel was extremely fussy when it came to who knew what, and even one of his most trusted comrades was to be shut out.

"Karma is a conniving old dog. It softly creeps up on its designated victim. It doesn't matter how much time has passed. It will bite you right in the nuts. I've been waiting patiently over a hundred years for my revenge. And who knows, it's been so painfully endured that it may well be greater than that. I've been immortal for the most prolonged time that I may never even seize upon it. My point is, payback is a bitch. It will sit quietly in the shadows, just waiting for the right moment to claw you into its grasp, and when it does, watch out. Everybody has to pay the debt they incur sooner or later. Jonathan had a curse placed on him by that vengeful witch, Everilda. Now she paid the piper when your Isra killed her. And by the way, that was most resourceful. I can't help but admire the fact that she used the energy of your kinship to destroy Everilda. But it was due to Isra that Everilda managed to outsource some of the most forsaken magics in order to dominate Jonathan in the first place. And so the karmic price now befalls Isra because of that," Samuel explained cautiously.

"Nobody can ever know the true lineage of how you and I came to know each other. There is not one soul that knows how I got into the love and light business but you. Only you lay claim to the knowledge that I was thrust into this job because I was seeking revenge for something grossly taken from me many moons ago. But nobody can ever hear of that, Astrid. Not Isra. Not anyone. Ever," Samuel warned carefully before his voice became much lower.

"My immortality has always been a closely guarded enigma. I don't plan on ever releasing that sordid skeleton from where it dwells in my darkest moments. Do you understand?" Samuel finished his line of questioning abruptly so that Astrid could cut in, and that Astrid did so swiftly with very little tact.

"Yes, I get it. I won't blast your sordid past all over the stratosphere. So Jonathan and Isra are still connected in some form or another?"

Astrid quickly diverted the conversation from the rather callous remark he made only moments ago.

"That they are, my son. It's only a matter of time before their paths cross once more," Samuel articulated before glancing over at James, who, of course, still couldn't see or hear Astrid and Samuel. The elaborate, fancy silver wall of Samuel's was deliberately keeping James from eavesdropping. An interesting shift, as normally it was Astrid that was sheltered from these elaborate discussions.

"Of course, there is a significantly more dire consequence than karma working her will," Samuel retorted with a grim expression on his face.

It was one of sheer horror that offered very little in the way of comfort. It depicted sheer melancholy; something quite dramatic was about to emerge, leaping into the atmosphere and sucking the world dry of all of its purity.

"And what might that be?" Astrid asked with a wide-eyed expression.

Astrid waited patiently for a few moments with the belief that his query was purely meaningless and nothing of any sort of importance would come back as a result.

Oh, it's probably nothing to be overly concerned about. He's about to waffle on about the most trivial thing mankind could have conjured up. I bet it's just a mere fantasy of his whereby something bad might arise so he can feel slightly better about himself in this time of dismal reality.

Astrid coached himself before realising that Samuel was really taking an awfully long time to deliver an answer. Maybe the falsehood Astrid proclaimed this to be was not so.

Samuel simply lifted himself off of the couch before moving towards the window ledge again. There was something oddly comforting about looking out upon that wondrous view, those glowing green luscious hills with such poise and grace that stood perfectly elevated above everything else so effortlessly. They were the focal point of this grand stature of natural beauty. Of course, let us not forget the crystal clear, aquamarine waters that formed the stream guarding the land of Shambre Fell, masquerading it from any unwanted intruders. It really was a marvellous combination of Mother Nature's finest assets along with robust prominence that was pleasing to the eye.

For some reason beyond any inclination, the masterful sights set before Samuel provided him with both peace and clarity, as though he was in that most grounded state that one would be in as they performed their morning meditations. And with what he was about to detail to Astrid, Samuel needed to be in that level-headed mindset because it was only a matter of time before something or someone ran amok with the revelation that was about to be distributed unto them.

Samuel lost all notion of thought as he was sucked into the momentous beauty when he abruptly stopped and glared across at Astrid; corporeality was brought back into his focus.

"Sorry, I lost track for a moment there. Have you ever stared out at these stunning hills? I really do find them quite beguiling. Anyhow, back to the matter of importance..."

Samuel paused, trailing off. Yet again, he'd lost his footing in regards to what he was about to say before suddenly remembering only a second later. Samuel lowered his voice and took a huge, deep, cleansing breath, sighing on the exhale so that he released all that built-up tension inside him.

"Ah, yes. Our defiant organisation 'on high' have had it foretold that Everilda Daughtry will be resurrected from the peril she currently resides in," Samuel blurted out in Astrid's direction.

Astrid almost fell off the settee in complete shock as he took in those final words from Samuel's unadulterated lips. The words were unbecoming to him as he tried his utmost to make sense of what he'd just audibly witnessed. Slipping uncontrollably onto the cold stone floor, Astrid challenged Samuel's prediction without hesitation as he tried to regain his sense of calm, although it was unlikely that would be found right now since his world was colliding all around him.

Isra had murdered Everilda. And rightly so, since the poor tempestuous witch proved to be a menace to all who knew her. But Isra had acted in such a way that it was almost poetic. So it begged the question as to who could enact such a feat to bring back the most renounced failure of witches in history and restore her to her former self.

"What? You are joking, right? Everilda is dead. How in the demon's eyeballs can she ever be brought back from her passing?" Astrid probed as he sat in disbelief. His mouth was wide open from the severe shock unleashed upon him.

"There are ways," Samuel began hastily before stopping momentarily to gain some clarity on the situation. "It is said that a most powerful force hosts the ability to free Everilda from her desolate cessation, but that soul must undergo a most profound transformation, hereby tapping into the most damning magics that this world has ever known in order to be in possession of that which is needed to bring Everilda back from her grave."

Samuel explained in a dire continuance, of which he was beginning to bore himself, never mind anybody else that might be in his presence, such as Astrid, for example. But Astrid was taken aback. He wasn't sure how to absolve this information or whether there was a valid solution for it, but something Samuel said began to ring true for Astrid. But he didn't dare summon the courage to ask if it was that of which he believed.

"A source of power that has to darken themselves in order to reinstate this loathsome creature? I don't mean to be unkind, but why do I get the feeling you aren't telling me everything?" Astrid pried. He sounded riled, judging by how harsh his voice was becoming in this heated moment.

"That's because I am not. You know, even I have little access to these matters. It is classified and thereby restricted, even to somebody with as high esteem and regard such as me. But you know as well as I do, Astrid, just who has the qualification to conduct such an atrocity!"

Astrid was unable to comprehend what had just been bestowed

upon his ears. And with such adequate hearing, it was impossible to think that he'd simply misheard what Samuel said. No, it had to be true. There was no mistake in the words that slipped past Samuel's lips. Not a single question could be uttered that would change the entirety of what Samuel had spoken so very clearly.

Astrid shifted uncomfortably on the stone floor before turning to Samuel with a cold glare, but one that had much meaning. "So Isra is the being you proclaim to resurrect Everilda? And despite all she's done in bringing forth the light back into her domain, it's going to take one simple solitary action and she'll unleash darkness onto the world yet again?!"

Samuel gave Astrid a remarkably similar stare, although the light bringer's was far more relaxed. Samuel was relatively calm, unlike Astrid, who was bordering on the realms of panic, but yet Astrid remained adequately lucid enough so that he understood what was happening.

"Yes. I do feel Isra will bring back the cursed soul of Everilda Daughtry. Together, they will align as they form an alliance against the light. It wouldn't be terribly fallacious to suggest they'd unleash Armageddon together."

Samuel took a pause as Astrid soaked up this intense revelation. Samuel had concerns that Astrid would not handle this well. Astrid was not well equipped in dealing with the war of darkness at the most sodden of times, but now the person at the centre of it all was his Isra, the one he intended to wed. Well, it didn't bear thinking about what he'd do to protect her, and never mind attempting to stop her.

In Astrid's world, Isra would always remain supreme and he'd risk hell and high water to keep her safe. It didn't matter what she'd discharged onto the world in the meantime. He'd still make her the number one priority. And if that meant going against the light, so be it.

If Isra is to release Everilda back into this callous and dreary realm, maybe that is what she is going to do anyhow. I don't understand Samuel's obsession with these damn prophecies. And just exactly what does this do in reference to benefiting the existence we happen to reside in, anyway? Because if I remember rightly, it was only by Samuel intervening that Isra and I were stopped. He doesn't know if she would have done worse because he wasn't there with her in the heart of the moment. He has no comprehension whatsoever of what she may have conducted. Only Isra holds those vital answers, and Samuel's clever little memory spell safeguards her from regaining the clarity she once had, Astrid thought as he stood, glaring over at James, who was still frozen in time.

Ironically, Samuel excluded James from being present to this conversation, and now Astrid knew exactly why. If James was lucky enough to be able to grasp this sordid dossier, there would be no telling what he'd do. Unlike Samuel, James was still very much focused towards the light. It would be certain that James would perceive Isra as the enemy, and all notion of him having been her friend once upon a time would be tossed aside in favour of doing what was right and just. Let's face it, James was loyal to the cause, and anything else would likely be disregarded, no matter what or whom it happened to be.

It was now in this robust train of thought that Samuel suddenly piped up as he retorted softly, "And now you see why our interests are mutually aligned."

14

Astrid unpeeled himself from the cold floor, although he was suddenly plagued with dizziness. He felt a sharp sensation circulating around the back of his skull and a buzzing in his ears. Hearing this revelation was just too much.

He swiftly manoeuvred himself to the kitchenette in a bid to replenish his depleted energy stores. Quickly turning the cold tap, he reached for a crystalline glass hovering upside down in the cupboard before eagerly filling it with the freezing water. Without looking at Samuel, Astrid took a large gulp, hoping this stinging notion would somehow sink in that it would be possible to process this in a calm and diligent manner.

If she resurrects Everilda, it damns her. She's predestined to fall if she goes along with this mighty plot, but what if it goes awry? Prophecies never go down well, in my experience, Astrid hurriedly thought.

The idea of it made him feel frantic, especially since Isra was also karmically tied to her former beau in this inevitable conundrum.

"You cannot save her from this. Not this time," Samuel bluntly commented.

"The balance has to be restored. Back in their heyday, Isra and Everilda unleashed more chaos and bloodshed than you can imagine. Every damned soul has to pay the price eventually, even a mighty witch who may well have fallen prey to darkness. Jonathan is the key to all of this. He was the human that both witches fought over in a desperate bid to win over his affections. You know the story of Isra and Jonathan, of course. A sad one nonetheless. A beautiful innocent soul meets a handsome prince, and love beckons. But we all know how it ended. He broke her heart and chaos ensued. That's just the way it goes in these troubled times." Samuel finished with a sharp twang in his tone. He seemed bitter about it.

It's almost as though he wants Isra to get her comeuppance for that dalliance with that wretched Jonathan. In some strange way, he's hoping she'll fall prey to whatever grim fate the divine has in store. Meanwhile, I don't comprehend how Everilda factors in since she's perished. But if she is successfully brought back to life, that could make things complicated. Astrid felt deep concern regarding this impending predicament.

But what if I can get to her first before she has a chance? Samuel wouldn't suspect anything, not if I don't let him in on my plans...

Astrid cleverly engineered quietly to himself as he suddenly had a plan figured out to resolve the matter at hand.

"Perhaps, I cannot. It may well be the case that she is doomed to her fate," Astrid responded in a low voice.

"Yes, well, shocking as it may be, I must get on. Lots to get ready before the change commences," Samuel commented, excusing himself as he prepared to vacate.

"Onward you must go, Samuel. Hope it is a pleasant journey to enlightened fortitude," Astrid replied in a formal voice as he bade goodbye to the light bringer.

"Yes, may it be splendid," Samuel said as he turned away from the window, proceeding to exit the room.

Astrid's eyes narrowed, raising an eyebrow at Samuel as he noted that James was sitting perfectly still. *Samuel has clearly forgotten about James. I'll fight my strong inclination to laugh here, but he needs to be released.* Astrid's sly smirk appeared on the side of his face.

"Erm, Samuel?" Astrid piped up. "Aren't you missing something?"

Astrid pointed his index finger at James, indicating Samuel needed to remove the freezing spell.

"Ah, yes. You are quite right. How silly of me. I cannot take myself anywhere…"

Samuel chuckled as he swiftly got to work. He closed his eyes and envisioned the silver barrier coming down, instantaneously lifting James out of his stupor.

"Where have I been?" James stammered, feeling a little off colour, as though he'd been drinking a fair amount of alcohol, yet there was no visible evidence of such a thing happening.

"Doesn't matter," Samuel stated before impatiently folding his arms. "Come. We are going now, James. Don't dawdle."

James and Samuel exited the living room at once. Astrid heard the rapping sound as they descended the steps, which was shortly followed by the sound of the grand, ornate door closing.

"Okay, now that I have some peace, what should I do with this intriguing notion? I really have got quite a dilemma on my hands. Either way, Isra has been deemed to once again choose the callous darkness she's always been drawn towards. There must be a way of changing it," Astrid retorted to himself as he got busy filling a large pan with water and placing it on the stove.

Coffee would remedy the situation nicely, at least to give him some solidity in which to process his thoughts.

Isra sat idly on the grassy knoll just in front of the little stream that guarded Shambre Fell.

It wasn't in plain sight, though. The charming, babbling brook with cerulean-blue water raced downwards, adjacent to the clearing, where several large oak trees proudly stood. This was the land of Borahell, the very same location in which Isra had first met Romeo, the python.

In fact, his ceremonious oak tree still stood out amongst everything else. Even the tranquil stream looked small compared to

Romeo's former haven. Isra had always found this place comforting, like an old friend that never withered or changed in times of great uncertainty. She'd come here to dodge whatever was occurring at home. It was true the light bringer Samuel had irritated Isra somewhat, but she was used to the way those types behaved around those not in their dynamic club.

"Honestly, those love and light beings are so predictable. Do this. Do that. If you don't acknowledge my command, terrible repercussions will follow. I've heard it time and time again. It begins to pulverise one's mind after a time." Isra groaned under her breath as she watched the water drift downstream.

"It sure does," a male voice called out in reply.

Isra turned her head at once; that voice sounded strangely familiar. She just couldn't place it for some reason. Then she found her eyes laid on her pleasant observer.

Large, pointed black shoes and dark purple silk tights graced the man's bony legs while tightly fitted black trousers hung neatly at his waist. A forgiving white silk shirt loosely swayed across his stomach and was left open at the neckline. It was when she reached for his face that Isra recognised just absolutely who this was.

"No. It's not, is it? It cannot be true."

Isra gasped as she stared into the slightly baffled eyes of Jonathan, who was now Prince Jonathan, of course. Still, he had that dark hair that curled a tiny bit at the back, giving him the impression he was in severe need of a trim. Little ringlets could be seen at the base of his skull.

"Isra. How interesting to find you out here. I presumed I'd be alone," Jonathan whispered as he found himself staring into Isra's enchanting lime green eyes.

"One can never be friendless, it seems," Isra replied, although there was a pause.

This was HER place. How did Jonathan know to find her here?

Oh, maybe it's just a coincidence. His palace isn't that far away, after all. Bitterquel is a dreary, desolate town with very little life beyond those walls. I still find it intriguing that he somehow levelled up to be a prince. Of course, one's curiosity can get the better of them.

Isra conversed with herself as she eyed Jonathan with extreme scrutiny. She didn't trust him. No, there was something distinctly off here.

"You don't like me much, do you?" Jonathan probed, although he was smiling. It was more as though he was attempting to put on a brave face rather than submitting to the fact that Isra's invasive nature bothered him.

"Quite honestly? No, I don't particularly enjoy being near you, but somehow, we are in nature's splendour, so one must make adjustments," Isra muttered solemnly as she swiftly lifted herself from the forest floor, giving Jonathan the impression she was about to depart.

"I get the feeling you're still furious over what commenced between us," Jonathan bravely voiced.

It probably wasn't the best thing for him to say to Isra, but he seemed to be feeling penance.

"I'm long past you, dear. Times have evolved. We've all propelled on. Whether to immortality, dissolution, or retribution, we've all paid the price for our sins," Isra announced in a bold tone.

"Aha, yes. We have, but still; you peer at me as if I'm some spoiled piece of meat you'd long have disposed of from your cellar," Jonathan replied.

"Hahaha," Isra gushed with a smile before adding in, "but sometimes, I do that with everyone. However, I never placed a curse on you, unlike Everilda. She never really wanted you, anyway. Goodness only knows why she did that."

Jonathan frowned as he looked back upon his tryst with Everilda and her venomous, vindictive ways. "Strangely enough, I didn't feel as though there was any love there. I never quite got why she danced around the subject of us, but yet at every interval she tried to get me away from dormant females, such as you. Still, I guess it isn't much of a concern now that she has assuredly forgone our gloomy world," Jonathan returned in a dry tone.

It was noticeable that he was being moderately watchful; staring around, gently turning his head to explore the arena in front of him. It was as though he was inspecting his surroundings in case some commodity surged at him. Or feasibly, he felt as if he was being watched.

"This land is odd. I've not been here previously as far as I can recall, but at least I'm not being eyeballed by some death-inducing bird," he commented, sounding apprehensive.

Isra's eyes lit up at once. The striking lime-green in them was gleaming. It was clear Jonathan straightaway had Isra's attention but he seemed rather confused by it all.

"A bird? Dear, please report to me. What classification?" Isra asked quizzically.

She prepared to contemplate the sentiment. Idly turning her awareness to the crystalline stream, she watched her reflection delicately as she paused in front of it. For a second, it seemed so surreal, but something stirred in her memory.

This vacant likeness of a man...

It was blurred so Isra couldn't impeccably manufacture every last detail, but it was ever-present in her mind. He'd perpetually been there. Right from the start. Whoever he was.

"I think it may have been a raven," Jonathan resolved sharply. "One of those onyx, mystifying creatures of the night with foreboding jet black feathers and ardent eyes that watch your every step."

"Yes, I know what ravens are," Isra moaned soberly.

She endured reticence for the next few seconds as she deemed the prospect of what may have been.

"Actually, I think I can recall a particularly threatening black raven. I tried hard to ignore it. The fickle fellow was always glaring at me, flashing its luminous golden yellow eyes wherever I turned. It was always around, especially when I was courting you. Well, at least for the limited-term, anyway," Jonathan abruptly added in.

Isra gasped in shock, clasping her hand to her mouth. She'd suddenly connected the events from the past and realized they led straight back to him. For some reason, everything was connected. No matter what event had gone down in Isra's life, he'd always been there, even from the very first moment he'd laid eyes on her.

"Astrid!" Isra exclaimed calmly, although perhaps she should have whispered since she still happened to be standing next to Jonathan.

He was there. The whole damn time. But how to goodness did I not ever know of this back then? One must dig deeper, for there is some great investigation to do. Would Astrid lie to me about how we came to meet? Isra hurriedly perused in thought.

She didn't have any clarity, but clearly, something was amiss. And while she hated to think such grotesque things, it appeared Astrid was probably not quite as honest with her as she presumed him to be.

"Sorry, who? I don't recall anyone of that name," Jonathan quizzed her.

"Ah, not to worry; it was long ago, in darker times. I must get back."

Isra excused herself without apology, and she darted around the grassy clearing and out of sight before Jonathan could say goodbye.

"Peculiar as ever," Jonathan muttered under his breath as he had a bemused look on his face regarding Isra's vanishing act.

15

Samuel sighed with annoyance whilst grasping a clear glass of Irish whiskey. The light bringer had to admit the sticky golden nectar was soothing right now, as he hadn't had a satisfying day. Samuel looked down at the tumbler and leaned his back against his jet-black leather settee. It was lavish for a man of his stature since it was a four-seater; he could lie on it if he wished.

However, this evening, Samuel was tense after having practically lost his temper with both James and Astrid. Actually, things hadn't been going the way he had envisioned. Samuel felt out of sorts with himself, but then again, he was retiring from the light versus dark business. And if he didn't have a stratagem fathomed out, he likely soon would have one devised.

Of course, Isra was proving to be quite a thorny obstacle. Samuel had dealt with Isra on many occasions. Her turbulent nature of doing what she felt habitual was beginning to aggravate him but nonetheless, Samuel wasn't giving up. He recognized Isra would be a challenge.

She was a genuine non-conformist at heart. There wasn't a single time that Samuel could recall whereby Isra had acted with decorum. No, she'd always go forth with her practice. And that was just something he'd have to admit, but maybe there was still a means of persuading her.

Samuel panted as he downed the syrupy amber whiskey without hesitation. It felt satisfactory as it reached the pit of his devoid abdomen, although there was a burbling sensation as it surged inside his gut. Samuel's digestive system was frothing at the bit and the swallowed whiskey permeating his unprotected stomach lining wasn't helping. A silly move on his part; he neglected to eat beforehand. In any event, the rampage ensuing in his belly was essentially relieving as Samuel sat haphazardly, thinking about how to address his quagmire.

"I knew she'd be relentless. She's hard to convince. It's not like we haven't been through this before, but if she doesn't renew her darker self, I'm in real jeopardy."

Isra unleashing the more shadowed part of herself was crucial to his plan. As far as elaborate schemes go, this one had been arranged to the very last detail.

Now, it was worth noting that Samuel never really planned anything. It went against everything he stood for. It was a bloody ridiculous folly as far as he saw it. Only peasants tried to plan every moment in their lives to the absolute detail. And why would he want to stoop to the level of some fumbling dim-witted moron?

No, and thank you kindly, but Samuel was far more refined than to allow such low, vibrational behaviours to enter into his sphere, although there was the question of how he was going to handle this Isra matter. For yet again, the witch was proving troublesome at best, but she was deemed to play a major role in Samuel's agenda.

But let us not forget, Samuel still maintained that he was calm and collected being in the light. Yes, there had been signs he was falling at the wayside, but so far, only Astrid had detected it. James wasn't clued up on the subject and thought Samuel had just grown tired of the job. It happened to the best of folk. They'd put in arduous amounts of determination for many years and eventually, it wore them down. Their patience grew thin and they'd end up losing their flair for the role and when that occurred, the only real thing to be done was to swiftly move on to new pastures.

Not every person went dark just for the sake of it. No, there was always some vile atrocity that made them loathe what they'd signed up for, and in Samuel's case, it was Lady Isra.

"Yes, of course, it had to be her, didn't it? I'm starting to think that villainous creature was created on this earth to wear me down to my very last nerve," Samuel grunted in a callous tone.

The light bringer was rambling in such a way that he didn't consider the idea that someone could be listening to him discuss his obtuse conundrum. That someone poked its luminous purple head out, revealing two perfectly formed inquisitive and brightly coloured lime-green eyes before shifting his vision towards Samuel, having a look of disdain on his animated face.

"Must you mumble so loudly? I am trying to spin myself up a nice little sweet treat up here!" Ronald cursed in an annoyed voice.

"Oh, do be quiet," Samuel answered swiftly before countering his remark as he explained, "I am trying to figure out how to deal with our lovely witch in question, for now she proves unpredictable and stands in my way yet again."

"You could just off the little bitch and throw her body into a ditch and get on with it already," Ronald suggested in a disgruntled tone.

He sounded annoyed at having to hear Samuel rant about Isra when he was doing his utmost to concentrate. Having spider hearing didn't exactly help things when Samuel oohed and ahhed about every last fragment of the situation, and very loudly, I might add.

"Damn! If only she wasn't immortal! Well, fuck me... why didn't I think of that one? Oh, I know. I'm not an imbecile. Deary me, I must think of something better. Besides, that's a really intelligent way to rile Astrid even more. Killing his venomous enchantress! Goodness me, where in the heavens do you attain your grey matter from? It is absolutely imperative that you seek out a new one this instant, dumdum," Samuel countered in a sarcastic tone.

It was ambiguous enough that Ronald could detect just how

furious Samuel was despite the light-hearted spin he attempted to placate onto it.

In a fiery rage, Samuel slammed his hand down on the coffee table. Clearly, the light bringer felt defeated, although maybe that term wasn't the best one since Samuel was hardly acting like a unicorn drenched in glittering, shimmery technicolor lights at this moment in time.

Maybe it was more accurate to say that Samuel was slowly evaporating into something much worse. Something dark. A repulsive entity. One that manipulated every soul around them to get their wicked way or else there would be something much more sinister lying in wait. Yes, Samuel was turning out to be quite the questionable character, but the biggest mystery of this most unorthodox transgression was *why*?

"There must be a way. Something that can distract her other than that silly little peasant slave girl who's knocked up in Isra and Astrid's not-so-humble abode. Although she's not doing her job to the highest potential," Samuel muttered away to himself.

Obviously, he was neglecting the fact that was more to his little pun than he had intended.

"Oh, you put her there? I got the impression it was the weasel-boy," Ronald quizzed with a bewildering stare.

"Yes, they think it's Jonathan, but honestly, could he have set up something as elaborate as a slave girl in need of a more stable accommodation and she just so happens to land in Isra's lap? Come on, boy, where is your head? Before we made acquaintance, you were quite the attentive scholar with magics and so forth. I mean, you of all people should know these things don't just manifest into thin air," Samuel declared before he went back on himself as he suddenly had a thought jump into his head.

"Well, in some cases, they do indeed manifest out of nowhere, but one must remember there is always an action undertaken in order for that entity to be brought forth into reality. I planted the seeds, old chap. I also inclined that she was in a most undesirable situation, and so I forced my hand. I made it possible so that Isra and Ava would interact, using that squealer of a man, Jonathan, as my third party. And so there you have it, my friend. That is how this wonderful web was woven," Samuel said with a most peculiar grin affixed to his face.

Nonetheless, the ever-so-nosy Ronald was sceptical over how Samuel had managed to wrangle this gross affair without the most formidable of witches in the land having any knowledge of it. Surely, one must be risking life and limb to perform such an act with the belief that she'd never hear of it? It was dumbfounded at best.

"Hmm, but how did you *really* get Ava to be there? Breaking into Isra's domain when the poor girl wouldn't have any knowledge of Isra or her fine establishment? You must have enacted some fine feat. To be frank, how on earth did you get so obsessed with Isra? You being involved in her growth in such a way should be frowned upon. I say you're a little too concerned over her, and especially her alignment with that Astrid fellow."

Ronald quizzed Samuel in a serious tone, although he wasn't clear as to what kind of a response he'd get, or if he would even receive one, to begin with.

Samuel straightened, getting more comfortable against that plush magenta throw that was glaring against everything in Samuel's bachelor pad. Strictly speaking, Samuel was not one of those singleton types that relished the single life. He hadn't gone into this by choice. It was forced upon him, and now with him being so set in the ways he had become accustomed to, he had no time or care for anything so trivial such as love.

"You know, boy, that is a most intriguing story. It started around thirty years ago. Well, around that. I encountered a young couple of whom the woman had just given birth. They were desperate and had no other alternative but to come to me. And this is where Isra comes in," Samuel articulated with a smile, beginning his cautionary tale.

"It is worth noting that the young woman was in a most grim scenario. Although she was a mortal and pure of heart, she had become increasingly concerned over her daughter.

The poor wee thing had only been born a few months prior, but the couple came to me because the young infant was demonstrating unique powers that the couple did not understand. And so one night, they came to me hoping I could give a solution to their 'problem' so they could finally rest their weary souls, knowing they had done the best they could for their child. That child was Isra.

It was a dark and cold lonely October night. Soggy, discolored orange and red leaves were scattered all over the place. I still remember the moon serenely shimmering brightly among the blackened, murky skies.

It was just after midnight and the loud chiming of the clock striking twelve echoed throughout the wastelands of the mystical Glamvein where this charming couple rented a quaint little cottage only a few yards away. At least, Gwendolyn had, anyhow, because Isra's father refused to be seen anywhere near Gwendolyn and his illegitimate offspring.

The irony of it was fascinating. Young Gwendolyn was indeed a mortal. But she had fallen head over heels for a very respectable warlock who was already married, so they had to conduct their affair in secret. And so when Gwendolyn fell pregnant, her beau did all he could to discourage her from having the baby. However, she was a woman with very old-fashioned values and didn't believe it was fair to kill the child.

She tolerated the long, arduous pregnancy, and when the time came for the child to emerge into this tainted world, Gwendolyn found that not only was her partner unsupportive of her, but he was almost urging her to flee, leaving behind young Isra. Of course, this did not happen. Gwendolyn tried her hardest to be patient with the infant Isra, but found that the baby had the most profound of skills no mortal child could ever possess.

But let us forget that Isra's father was a warlock, and one of great lineage at that, so it was no surprise that young Isra had the gift of magics.

It was harrowing for Gwendolyn, who had been cooking up a mighty feast of the most succulent beef stew with finely harvested vegetables of the autumnal season. Among them were pumpkin and swede as well as delicate sweet carrots she had picked from a neighbouring farm. So, dear old Gwendolyn had been steaming the pumpkin, swede, and carrots when she suddenly caught a whiff of smoke out of nowhere as she was washing the floors.

Completely shocked beyond comprehension, the dainty and weak-minded Gwendolyn looked up in fear at the sight that befallen her. The entire kitchenette was drenched in thick, grey smoke, and the mischievous Isra sat up in her high chair, completely amused by it all.

Immediately, Gwendolyn freaked out and turned Isra's chair around so she could not see anything else, but the infant outwitted Gwendolyn by spinning her head around to the point Gwendolyn feared it may have come clean off. Only it didn't.

Isra was smiling and giggling the entire time. She had a joyful expression plastered across her face and it was then that Isra stared right at her mother, and then the child took one look at the stove. It only took a mere flash of her eyes, and the entire place went up in blazing orange flames.

Gwendolyn couldn't believe her eyes and although she had been swift in throwing a bucket of water over the stove, sending freezing water into her cooking that she had slaved over for hours, she was greatly concerned, not only for the safety of her child, but more so for herself. So, in a panic, she contacted Isra's father, who could only advise her to seek help from me.

It was then at the gasp of midnight that I met them both. Gwendolyn was tired and desolate, having felt like she had no other choice but to take drastic action, whereas the father was more dignified in his stance; but still, he looked concerned for the child's welfare as he stood eagerly awaiting me in a long, jet-black, thick coat. An equally cold and forlorn face greeted me as he peeped his flaming orange eyes out of a mass of over-combed onyx hair.

I looked dumbstruck at the man. I knew without hesitation exactly what he was. It was no shock to me that he was urging the damned peasant Gwendolyn to abort the pregnancy, for this man was none other than the rugged warlock, Damien Daughtry.

Anyhow, Damien had underestimated Gwendolyn, for not only had he engaged in an affair with her but now there was a child to think about. If this sordid liaison ever became public knowledge, it would be scandalous. He didn't want to put too much into the idea that he'd get out of this with his reputation intact. Not that it was squeaky clean, you understand, but Damien was slowly rising the ranks. People were starting to fear him since he had been accosted from the famous Wingdom's Academy. This was thanks to a lustrously brief interaction with a demoness, Rhinannon, who had been plunged into hell by the good and plentiful souls at Wingdom's who had seen to it that not only was she taken care of, but in turn, Damien was expelled from the academy.

But Damien was now beginning to climb up the social ladder as far as the occult went, and he was quite the respectable warlock. This little child being in his midst could jeopardise that for sure.

Damien was the first one to open his mouth when he uttered, "I know you and I aren't on the same side, but I believe you can assist us here in getting rid of this wretched child, or at least freeing her from her torment."

Now, it was dumbfounding for Damien to say that, as surely for a man well-versed in the magics, it was evident that this sort of thing didn't frighten him. But Isra was conceived in grossly dishonourable circumstances, and so Damien was perplexed at exactly how he was going to absolve himself.

I gave Damien an inquisitive stare and replied honestly, "Well, she's just a wee girl. A baby. She cannot be taken care of as you wish it. Believe me, that's a much kinder and tactful way than you described it..."

I paused in thought, mulling over the situation in which Damien and Gwendolyn were very much in dire straits.

Perhaps there is a more unlikely elucidation to this botheration of sorts. Maybe I can assist in a much greater way than already planned, but first, I must consult 'on high,' as they may be able to give me some commentary on exactly who this child is and her future, if there is one written in the heavenly realms pertaining to her.

I turned to Damien, who was getting more flustered and impatient by the second, and retorted earnestly, "Please, allow me some time to get the clarification we all need to sufficiently resolve this matter."

It was then that I walked off to a nearby mountain peak, leaving Damien Daughtry and his illicit beau baffled as to why I had left. Nonetheless, as Gwendolyn was a mortal woman with no magic in her blood, she looked slightly more fazed than her counterpart. However, I paid neither of them any mind as I looked ahead to seek out the perfect contemplation spot.

I found a beautiful location. Remote in nature but astounding in visual imagery that beckoned. Among the grand splendour of the accurately named Glamvein was a mass of pure green land that stood out for miles surrounding the monumental mountain peak.

Aha, the perfect place to gain some momentum, I thought to myself, and without giving either Damien or his awkward beau a second thought, I walked over to the landmark. And taking great heed to be cautious of a huge, gaping hole around twenty feet downwards so that I was not foolish and slipped off, I situated myself on the ledge of the cliff. Immediately centering myself, I quietly ruminated about the dilemma that had been placed into my hand.

Of course, you have to ascertain that these difficult hitches are often not easy to find a solution for, but I was determined that if I went within hard enough, I'd come up with something that would suit everyone's best interests.

I closed my eyes and called on the superficial folk that I often refer to as 'on high,' the spiritual ambassadors that not only guard the sacred realms but also pass on insightful guidance to those flitting between the two worlds. Now, as I was at the forefront of the metaphysical realm, I had a direct hotline to these folks in power. Think of it as a telephone connection, only the cord could never be dismantled nor tampered with. I could also connect with them whenever I saw fit. Day or night. It didn't matter. I would always get through to those with the highest inner knowledge.

After what seemed like several never-ending seconds, which I thought I may well have completely lost myself in a stream of nothingness, something began to shift into my consciousness. A white sea of pure light spontaneously appeared in my midst, but before long, it revealed itself to be much brighter than I originally pictured.

It was expanding. The incandescent light grew larger, and it showcased flashes of gold swirling all around the fading white shimmer. I normally would have become discontent at seeing the discernible symbolism growing dimmer as time passed, but for some inclination beyond my notion, I suspected there was a much greater reasoning behind it, a more profound inner purpose residing in all of this that had yet to be revealed.

And then it was given to me in full technicolour. I saw Lady Isra in her prime, at around age eighteen. Her shimmery fair hair billowed out of a midnight-blue velvet cloak while she stood out against the ferocious aquamarine waves of the watery wasteland, Seclera. And yes, it was the same timeline that she met Astrid in his humanized form, where he had gone to extreme lengths to have Damien's demoness transform him so that he could be up close and personal with the witch.

It was no surprise that I saw Astrid standing next to her; however, the most extraordinary thing happened. I suddenly saw two golden flames surging inside their hearts. I could *see* inside Isra and Astrid's bodies. Their hearts were illuminated by the most passionate orange flame. I then heard tediously, over and over again, the strangest conundrum. It was very astute, but yet also slightly repetitive in the way it was relayed to me.

If I wasn't in the spiritual position I was, I might have been terribly pissed off with the repetition of it, but the message was loud and clear as it coursed inside my eardrums.

'Twinflame. Twinflame. These two souls are twin flames. They are destined to unite in the physical realm, but be cautious because their coming together is also fated by great darkness. It can either be one or the other. Ultimately, they will choose their paths, but Lady Isra is set to become a prominent figure in the future. She will usher the precursor that unlocks the forbidden magics many only dream of possessing.'

At last, the self-sacrificing noise dimmed, the visual imagery was discarded, and I awoke from my mental slumber. I now had the knowledge of exactly what to propose to Damien and his squeeze, Gwendolyn. And no doubt, he'd cast her aside for something more favourable in due time, but never mind—back onto more important matters.

Of course, it went without saying that I had no inkling of who Astrid was or who he would be at that time. 'On high' never showed us anything unless they truly felt we needed to know. So Astrid was just a mere blur in the spectrum of nothingness. Isra was far more influential; however, I didn't have much knowledge surrounding her either. All I knew was that she was fated to unleash great darkness unto the world. In that situation, I had to do what I saw fit for the greater good.

Taking myself away from the clifftop, returning to normality in a flash, I walked over to the disgruntled couple. Both of them had an extremely unrestrained look etched upon their faces. Evidently, they had grown impatient despite me only being gone a few minutes.

I acknowledged Gwendolyn with a half-smile, but I was just being formal, trying to keep in line with the scrupulous task; however, I didn't dare mention what I had foreseen.

Sometimes being in this line of work, you keep things close to your chest. You never know what someone might do with the truth if they cannot comprehend it. I'm not saying Damien Daughtry and Gwendolyn were unstable by any means, but if they had any understanding of who Isra was condemned to be, they might have had second thoughts.

"I might have a solution to your little problem," I began in an earnest voice, although I paused to give the newly made parents some time to fully digest what I was proposing. "I shall take on young Isra. I will ensure she gets the best esoteric education the realm can offer. I will undertake the task to ensure she is sent to the finest supernatural establishment—Wingdom's Academy. Nonetheless, there are some fine print conditions to my offer,"

Gwendolyn said nothing; she didn't want the tainted child anyhow. That was obvious. Damien Daughtry, although astonished, petitioned me in a low voice. "All right, what are they?"

I smiled again, only this time, the warmth had gone. I was deadly serious. When it came to matters of great importance, I knew exactly what face to give.

"She will have no idea who you are. As far as she will be concerned, her parents are nonexistent. I will keep an eye on her from time to time, dropping into her life when she doesn't expect it, just like any father would for his child. The only difference is I will be more like a guide of sorts, to keep her from treading upon the immortal path of darkness and fortitude in the hope she may have a better outcome than what has been prophesied for her."

Damien Daughtry eyed me up closely, having heard my request and considered it with keen interest. It was clear the master warlock had nothing more to say when all that came out of his mouth was, "Fine, she will never know who we are. You shall take the child. And let us never speak of this again."

"Good. I shall draw up the paperwork soon enough. You will bring Isra to me, without delay, exactly one hour from now. It is then we will complete this deal, and then you two shall part ways from her and never see her again," I retorted, instilling a pause just in case either of them changed their mind.

It was agreed that Isra would be brought to me sometime later and I would draw a contract up so that it was binding that my conditions were met imperatively with the highest regard. I was very funny when it came to legalities. I had to make deathly sure they would indeed keep to their side of the agreement. It was imperative for Isra's future that she have no contact with her biological parents, and I had to enforce that upon them.

I made it clear, written in fairly legible writing:

'Here I decree Isra Daughtry is now placed in the care of myself, Samuel Reynaldi, Chief Light Bringer, Heralded of Spirisity, so that the infant can be raised in an intellectually whimsical environment. Thus the only consequence of this arrangement is that Gwendolyn Passe and Damien Daughtry hold no rights over the child and will never see her again. This contract is legally binding and cannot be broken, and so it is.'

The time came for Damien Daughtry to meet me again in the very same spot we first met. Ironically, he was early and had Isra cradled in his arms as though she was some pestilent being he couldn't wait to be rid of. It was interesting how Gwendolyn was not present, but perhaps Damien had coached her beforehand, thereby making the decision it was best she not attend.

He handed Isra over to me without a care. The child was swaddled in a mass of soft, cream-coloured blankets. As her father passed her to me, Isra immediately smiled at me, flashing those famous piercing green lime-green eyes that made her the distinctive creature she is. They were wide with curiosity, and she reached over her tiny delicate hand that softly tugged my black suit jacket.

It was a moment I will always remember. And sweet it was, too. Alas, I doubt Isra will ever remember such a time, but she always has the chance to go deep within herself and seek it out."

At last, Samuel had finished his tale, and Ronald looked back at Samuel in amazement. He took a moment to soak in this cluster of revelations that had been so expertly delivered.

Ronald gasped spontaneously as he cajoled in disbelief. "No way! That's the same father as—"

Ronald didn't even finish his thought, but Samuel knew exactly what the spider meant.

"Yes," Samuel continued, "the very same father as her arch-nemesis, Everilda Daughtry." Samuel took a pause, gently allowing some much needed air into his lungs before subtly adding, "If only Isra knew how connected she and Everilda Daughtry are, or were... the damsel may just throw a fit; that is, depending on how you read this very complicated matter. And most complex of all, I am Isra's benefactor and she has no clue just how tied together she, me, and our estranged Astrid really are. It's only a matter of time, my friend, before this climatic entanglement is unravelled without some metaphysical force holding it in."

Ronald had been very keen on listening to all of this. It was a captivating story, even though he didn't favour Isra or Astrid a great deal, but there was a pressing question—one that had so far not been fully answered. Ronald understood that, yes, in the spiritual realms, people and situations had a habit of being drawn to each other, but it still begged the query as to how Samuel managed to place Ava in Isra's path?

Ronald felt like Samuel was dancing around it, making himself look like the big hero, the proud light bringer that had so kindly saved a witch—fated for darkness, no less—from being an orphan by doing his utmost to ensure she was safely taken care of, watching every step she made from his comfortable seat at Spirisity. But since Samuel was going through quite the mid-life crisis, even for an eccentric like himself, it was baffling he would not want to detail this one thing because surely, like the rest of the wonderful things he had undertaken on Isra's behalf, it was for her highest good?

Or perhaps he didn't want the limelight shining down on him, showing just how much he had been in the thick of it from day one...

"So I see," Ronald came back at Samuel with a raised eyebrow before jumping straight in with, "but *how* on the earth's graciousness did you manage to place such a distraction like Ava in Isra's way if you are, more or less, her spiritual father?"

"Hmm. That is a funny story," Samuel quipped. "Poor old Jonathan needed a slave girl. He was pathetically needy and couldn't manage himself, never mind the grand place of Bitterquel, so I managed to find dear old naive Ava, who was in quite the issue with some gentlemen whom she'd been briefly involved with. However, it turned sour and the man rejected her but the girl was with child. This placated her in the most desperate of scenarios. She needed to think up a solution and fast. The world is very hard on someone like Ava. She believes she deserves all the riches without giving one scrap of appreciation in return. All I did was offer her what she needed most. I mean, what other charming offers were going to land in her lap other than the treat of working for a snob prince? As soon as I got her there, I planted some spells in her way. Poor girl is as dumb as a post and wouldn't know magic if it banged her poor sodden head. These little whimsical trails were designed to lead right to Isra's fortress, which, of course, I did some trickery to make certain Ava could get in without any enchantments blocking her way, and everyone still thinks that sweet little Ava broke in, needing a morsel to satisfy her bulging belly."

"Oh, my!" Ronald exclaimed. He didn't know what else to say, so he decided to shut up.

"As for me and Isra, I may just have to entertain her wildly curious ways myself. She is in my way right now, but perhaps if I reason with her—if I tame that heart of darkness that lies inside her—we can both come off smelling like roses. And maybe she will start to see things from my perspective," Samuel mused with a cheeky half-smile as he gave Ronald a thoughtful gaze.

It was one of those where it was almost as though Samuel was hinting he wasn't just going to dissuade her but maybe he had another aspiration in mind, one he wasn't going to entail what that was until he had the fiery little witch in his tight grasp.

Ronald was sure it was an action that would vex Astrid and further inflame the lingering hatred between him and Samuel.

16

Isra was headed towards the stone path leading directly to Shambre Fell.

Jonathan's revelation about a raven lurking around her had startled her. Isra had been led to believe Astrid's first appearance was made back when she'd had that irritating slave boy Kane in her grasp. She couldn't even begin to imagine she and Astrid had met before that.

"No. It's ridiculous at best. If I had met Astrid, then surely I would have known? It's maddening," she muttered as she approached the grand oak ornate door before taking one last look at the world around her.

The crystalline stream that ran around Shambre Fell seemed to glisten a little brighter, which was ironic for late December.

"One would think if he had met me, he would have told me about it. Oh, it doesn't matter. Best get on. There is much to do before the wedding," Isra countered to herself as she strode up the gray stone staircase, still moving over the pressing notion on her mind.

After a decent rest, this may reach a conclusion. I have been awake throughout the twilight. Yes, after sleep, I shall ponder this again.

It was just around ten o'clock in the morning. Astrid had risen early as he'd heard Isra come in at the crack of dawn. He figured she must have been up all night and needed to slumber so he'd made himself a large coffee before settling into the deep red velvet armchair. Astrid knew it was still fairly early, so he was perusing through a large tome as he heard the snow pummelling down outside. It was hammering at such a speed that a thick carpet of it gathered outside the entrance to Shambre Fell. The turrets of Lady Isra's and Astrid's tower were just about visible among all the white deluge.

Astrid paused. He detected a whiff of sweet strawberry. Judging from the fragrant fruity scent wafting out from the kitchen, Isra must have been in the kitchenette before she'd tottered off to bed. Lady Isra was quite the tea connoisseur, so perhaps she was conjuring some up before bedtime.

"Why she feels the need to accumulate such a variety of leaf teas, I will never know," Astrid chortled, feeling quite amused, turning his attention back to his book.

However, seconds after, the door burst open, leaving Astrid bemused as Contessia strode in. Her normally bright purple hair had faded into an ombre lilac. She seemed to have lost a significant amount of weight; her white dress billowed out around her like a sheet. Unfortunately, Contessia had not been the same since Lady Isra had come back from the grave, and since she'd recently been dragged back from the hellish realm, Contessia's mental state had declined even more so.

In truth, the purple-haired girl had not been herself for the last few months. She was withdrawn and rarely came out of her bedroom, and if she did, it was out of some piquing curiosity.

Astrid couldn't stand to be around Contessia, but even he noted she was not well in her mind. He tried to have compassion for the girl but honestly, he found her rather aggravating so he preferred her when she chose to be elsewhere—out of his sight and out of his way. And most of the time, Contessia seldom chose to seek solace in her sanctuary but this was one of the rare occasions when she decided to roam the chateau.

That dumb slave girl Ava had been bringing things to Contessia, but alas, it was too early for the wee thing to be up and about. And Contessia was ravenous, barely having touched her roasted duck draped in rich orange oil sauce, served with sweet grilled potatoes and finely chopped vegetables also cooked in the fatty extravagant sauce.

If only I could find something to satisfy me. Perhaps I shall take myself back to my bedroom before that ghastly Astrid makes an appearance, Contessia murmured to herself as she considered the idea that she could just rustle herself up something and then skedaddle before the raven-turned-man awoke for his morning hit of caffeine. Little did Contessia know that Astrid's glowing eyeballs were all over her.

Contessia was about to open the large cupboard door when she suddenly glanced across to the shelf above, seeing the sea-blue glass jar gleaming brightly. Contessia recognised the weary individual trapped inside. Cora had been encased in the jar for almost two years now, but still she had that sappy, woe-is-me glance about her. It was as though the world owed her a favour, but alas, she wasn't going to get any of those anytime soon.

The hardcore truth was that the universe owed you nothing. You had to earn the respect and the power, because let's face it, someone bigger and brasher than you would soon be along to lay their greedy paws on it, wanting to snatch it up without lying a finger to have rightfully gained it.

Cora was one of these self-righteous folk. She solely believed in the godliness and cleanliness of the world and still hoped with all of her might that justice might prevail and she'd be released from her eternal prison, but Lady Isra was not somebody easily swayed.

Astrid quietly lifted himself from his comfortable armchair and proceeded to walk to the kitchenette. He approached her slowly and with caution, carefully noting her interest in the glowing blue jar. As a matter of a fact, Astrid was right behind Contessia. And boy, would she be disgusted at the raven-man being in such close proximity to her.

Contessia reached over, clasping her hands around the jar. It felt cool and icy as she held it. In fact, it was so cold; she couldn't keep a tight grip on it.

"I wouldn't be touching that if I were you," Astrid called out in a gruff voice from behind her.

Contessia was so startled at hearing Astrid's voice she gasped involuntarily, "Oh, goodness!"

Before she knew what was happening, her hands lost their grip on the jar and it slid right out of her hands as though they were made of butter. And with a clatter, it shattered onto the ground in a million pieces. Tiny turquoise shards of sparkling glass glittered wildly as they lay scattered across the cold grey stone floor. Cora was terrified as she stood in the middle of the massacre of glass, but all Contessia could do was weep at the sight of it.

"Oh no, whatever shall I do? Lady Isra shall have my guts for insoles!" Contessia babbled helplessly as tears streamed down her porcelain face.

"Never mind that. What the hell are you doing touching her possessions? You should know better!" Astrid growled at her sharply before he pointed his finger at the mess glistening back at him on the floor. "Isra shall be furious with you when she discovers this. Get out of here before you cause any more trouble!"

He huffed as he bent to examine the chaos shimmering brightly on the floor. Only Astrid wasn't the only one angry with Contessia. Cora stood in the midst of all the gleaming shards of glass, unable to fully comprehend what had happened. You'd think she might have been overcome with joy at finally being set free, but alas, she was not.

Contessia backed away two paces, turning her eyes to the door in a panic. She knew the best thing she could do now was skedaddle out of harm's way, but Astrid was still very nearby. This made Contessia deeply uncomfortable, but just when she considered exiting out of the doorway, Cora shrieked hysterically at Contessia.

"Look at what you've done! I'm in the midst of chaos and all you can do is weep? Girl, can't you see the sheer atrocity? If Lady Isra finds me now, I'm done for."

All at once, the kitchen door burst open and Isra strode in, adorned in a long, flowing, white lace nightgown. Clearly still half-asleep, Isra had heard the commotion from her chamber upstairs and had come to see for herself just what in the heathens was going on.

Isra was absolutely seething with rage as she spat out fiercely, "SILENCE! What is the meaning of this?! Explain yourselves this instant! All of you!" Isra reached for her midnight-blue velvet cloak. "And you, Astrid? Just what in the hell is going on here? Hmm?"

She questioned him furiously, although her tone was slightly less aggressive towards Astrid than it was with the entire congregation; but still, she was pretty mad. Astrid ignored his counterpart, for he was fixated on tiny Cora, who was still shouting her tiny mouth off despite the dire predicament she was in.

"Now, you'll let me go right now or else!" Cora threatened angrily.

For a little tiny thing, she had a lot of gusto inside her. It was very ballsy, and this was a quality Astrid found deeply intriguing. It was as though he'd suddenly found a new plaything.

His eyes lit up dramatically as he cooed, "Well now, what a pretty mess this is!"

The poor helpless Cora had her arms folded as she stood amongst all the glass that had been smashed to smithereens from Contessia's mishap.

"Oh, please, Sir Astrid, don't hurt dear Cora. It is not her fault. I'm the one who ought to be chastised. I was the blundering fool who was snooping around, after all," Contessia pleaded with Astrid. A look of fear was residing all over her face. Shame tinged in her eyes as the raven-man simply smirked at her.

"Now, now. Don't be a spoilsport." Astrid glowered at Contessia as he turned his attention to Cora once more. "But what is this. Do my eyes deceive me? A little creature that was once protected by round glass walls, and now that is no more. What a tragedy!" Astrid sniggered as he bent, grabbing Cora who was suddenly mortified at what the ghastly raven-man would do next.

Isra was still standing by the doorway, bemused at the situation unfolding before her, though she had comprehension of what was occurring now. Her piercing green eyes affixed to the scene, she slowly moved towards Astrid before she glared at the culprit, Contessia. The way Isra flashed a dead stare over at Contessia was penetrating enough to make the girl think she was in a lot of hot water but yet the witch remained outstandingly calm. It was shocking when you considered that Contessia had just obliterated one of Lady Isra's favourite toys that she had admired frequently whenever her eyes happened to catch sight of it.

"What is this?" Isra questioned Contessia with a raised eyebrow. "Why were you playing with my possessions?"

Only it was Astrid who diverted the attention from Contessia back to himself. Perhaps in a way he was assisting Contessia, keeping her safe from the witch's wrath, but Astrid had his own vile agenda as it was soon to be known.

"Oh, this little sweet thing is no longer encased in its jar," Astrid retorted with a grin. "Now, what shall we do with it?" he mouthed in Isra's direction but loud enough for the terrified Cora to hear.

"I always wondered what your fascination with putting people in glass jars was, my love. But nevertheless, we must ensure this habit is truly decimated for the good of all," Astrid commented although he was being most sincere.

"Well, I was keeping her as a nice ornament. But her smart mouth spoils the attractiveness of the thing, you see," Lady Isra commented with a snarl.

"I don't like her. She irks me, so!" Astrid remarked, smiling over to Isra. "I don't think she serves any purpose being in our home any longer, dear. Don't you agree? In fact... "

The raven-man paused between his words; however, he didn't have time to finish as he was distracted by the miniature girl in his hand beating him, or at least doing her utmost to, anyway. But she was so small that she barely even bumped against the raven-man's robustly strong fingers.

Although he hadn't reckoned on Cora being the feisty, well-endowed being that she was, the tiny girl kicked Astrid's thumb as he held her tightly in between his fingers.

"Let me go, this instant! You horrid man! Or I'll bite you senseless!" Cora threatened.

"How cute! It even talks!" he murmured. "Well, no matter, the most noisy things are soon silenced when they are no more."

Astrid clenched his fist, suffocating the life out of poor, desperate Cora, and before you knew it, all that was left was silvery-blue dust that he discarded without a care onto the cold stone floor.

"There, that is much better. Now I don't have to tolerate that wretched noise," he replied happily before turning his attention to Contessia. His eyes narrowed at her as she fell haphazardly against the wall in terror.

"Now, if I catch you in here again, similar will befall you. Don't misunderstand me. I am not one to be toyed with," Astrid barked at Contessia.

The raven-man was in good spirits when you took into account that he had just disintegrated tiny Cora into fine sparkling silver and blue dust, closely resembling glitter as it lay glistening on the floor.

"Trust you to be in a good mood after you vanquished my delicate little plaything," Isra commented, still in the middle of a death stare directed at Contessia.

"Why don't you be off now, love? Astrid wants to consume his caffeinated beverage in silence," Isra suggested to the terrified girl who had backed herself away in the corner.

She was almost leaning against the window ledge; she had been so frightened by Astrid's tone towards her. Her purple hair was practically standing on end with the shock of it all. But she had also seen firsthand Astrid's fiery temper to boot.

Isra also seemed like she was ready to vacate the vicinity as she eagerly threw her midnight-blue cloak over her rather enticing white lace nightgown that barely covered her. Nonetheless, as she pulled the luscious velvet hood over her head, she was completely saturated in the generously rich fabric.

"I think I'll position myself elsewhere for a while. I still feel disorientated due to being awoken in that hellish realm," Isra muttered firmly to Astrid.

"Aww, who said you could go?" Astrid called over to his counterpart. "There's plenty for two."

He winked as he fiddled meticulously with the iron kettle that would soon be overflowing with that delightful dark chocolate-coloured liquid that he loved to devour so much.

"Sorry, dear. I must go. After what's just commenced, I feel like a morning stroll," Isra mouthed.

She sounded antsy and slightly agitated. This was revealed in her body language as she attempted to casually walk past Astrid.

"Oh, how disappointing. I was hoping to detain you for some early morning revelry," Astrid announced with a cheeky grin. Excitement was plastered all over his face as though he was a child that had experienced far too much excursion.

Isra's eyes lowered dramatically in a subtle wink just at the thought of it. *Oh, yes, I can only imagine where he's heading with that little escapade. As sweet as that may be, I shall pass on this occasion*, Isra chuckled wildly to herself in thought before returning her attention to Astrid to politely decline.

"Aww, sorry love, as frightfully enchanting as that sounds, I must decline," Isra answered hurriedly as she really wanted to get going. Being here was just tiresome, especially after what she had witnessed so early in the day.

Some fine morning sun rays will be just the ticket, although they are a rare commodity indeed in this winter season, Isra comforted herself as she thought of the warmth they would have on her tired, withered bones.

"Charming..." Astrid passed comment as he eyeballed Isra sternly following her rebuff. However, the raven-man wasn't going to be easily swayed by Isra's avoidance.

Why is she even heading out in the first place? It's hammering down with miniature snow bombs laced with ice out in that broken-hearted wilderness. Why is she so keen to get away from me? Hmm, Astrid articulated to himself in a careful expression, for he knew Isra was anxious to depart, but the real question that was harbouring in the ether was why?

Of course, Isra was a recluse at heart, so she'd never admit the true reason for her incessant gallivanting. But still, Astrid was none too privy to her endless excuses of needing to get a breath of air.

I mean, there is plenty of air all around us. All she has to do is open the wretched window. What is so treacherous about doing that? But no, she must be present in nature's glory and defilement and most importantly away from me. Honestly, sometimes I wonder why I ever got myself entangled with this repressive occultist. But alas, that blame can only be laid at my own domain. I fell in love with her so-called repulsive beauty that lay underneath all the darkness and vengeance that danced around her imperfect soul, Astrid accursed himself as he found himself yet again frustrated over Isra's forbearance regarding him.

"Well, perhaps later we can resume this discussion over a late morning brunch followed by a delightfully hot caffeinated beverage and just maybe," Astrid paused, careful to select the right word, for he wanted his meaning to be absolute, "I shall hand-select a fine spanking for your tardiness."

He finished in a low but stern voice; however, it was apparent he wasn't being completely firm, as a wide-eyed smirk manifested itself as he curled his lips with pleasure at the anticipation of it.

"That does indeed sound enthralling so yes, later," Isra answered, not showing that cold and solemn stare she had affixed to her as she left without delay.

It is worth acknowledging that Isra wasn't angry with Astrid, nor had he triggered her, but there were many occasions just like this where she needed her space to reflect and be in the sanctity of her thoughts.

17

Isra had been wandering around in a daze for about ten minutes. Her aim was not to stray too far from Shambre Fell, but as usual, her curiosity led her elsewhere.

It was blissful strolling through the forest, not having a care. The sheer joy of hearing the trees sway back and forth in the late December wind was reassuring. However, it did seem eerily quiet as Isra headed towards the north; something she didn't usually do. Normally, she'd wander through the forest into the clearing and then retreat towards more familiar boundaries. But today, in what was a spontaneous action, Isra ventured away from the woodland terrain, finding herself face to face with a gigantic, wide-open ocean when she came out the other side.

Isra was greeted with sparkling aquamarine waves that could be heard crashing against the land as she stood in wonder, but yet she still felt the serenity of it all just by being present, standing there and soaking in the tranquil fluctuations surging all around this pristine district. Little did Isra know that she was in the borders of Seclera. Naturally, she had been here just over fifteen years ago, but her memory had been stolen away by Samuel Reynaldi.

All Isra knew of Samuel was that he was part of that callous love and light brigade she had grown to loathe so much, and she didn't care to know much else. She'd already had her suspicions of Samuel when she'd caught him shortly after he'd unleashed his pent-up fury onto Astrid and James by transforming them into slimy green toads. In any case, she had not latched onto the fact that there was far more about the illustrious light bringer than she cared to take heed of. If she'd been more conscientious of the world around her, Isra would have realised that there were many coincidental events, and they were all connected to Samuel.

Isra took in the bounty of the extremely lavish deep sapphire ocean that lay before her. Opalescent waves glimmered as dusk slowly made its appearance among the gray cloudy stratosphere. Isra didn't pay attention as a tall man with slicked-back, jet-black hair materialised beside her, for she was so transfixed by the giant briny.

Isra took her gaze away from the striking fascination only to find her piercing green eyes fall on the larger than life Samuel, who was poised before her in a long, black suit jacket and his usual attire, those unmistakable black trousers that classically coordinated his ensemble.

Not even taking a breath, Isra vociferously glared at the light bringer. Her eyes glowed that bright lime-green that she was famous for as she wasted no time in declaring her fury.

"What in the damnation's massacre are you doing here?" Isra snarled at him.

Samuel waved a forewarning hand in Isra's direction before he began addressing her in a formal tone. "Now, now. I was hoping for pleasantries. I only came to speak with you as I felt we should have a more personal talk. So how about you desist and allow me to relay what I have to tell you? Hmm? Or have you been staring at this wondrous spectacle so long that you've forgotten the art of civility?"

Samuel questioned her in a sardonic manner although he was actually hinting at the fact Isra was so influenced by the blueness of it all that he was implying in some form or another that she'd lost her way... a little.

"I don't really have much care for you *light* folk," Isra grimaced with a sly remark.

Samuel chuckled with a small half-smile and pressed his arms across his chest, once more giving Isra that very rigid attitude he was known for.

"Ah, yes; you call us the love and light brigade. Dear girl, I've heard this from you so many times that my sides may start to split in half from laughing merrily about it. Now onto the business at hand. Ah, that's it. Our young Isra has found herself in remoteness beyond her comprehension, whatever shall we do?"

Samuel motioned to Isra with a quizzical look, once again raising his finger in her trajectory.

"What is that supposed to mean?" Isra snapped, although she wondered just what Samuel was referring to.

Who is this so-called light soul? He appears out of nowhere and starts waffling on about nonsense I've never heard of. I suppose he thinks I'm supposed to just humour him? I thought he was a companion of Astrid's but now he gives me the feeling like he is a trickster or magician, one that manifests into being with no warning whatsoever. And what exactly does he mean by he's heard it from me before? I only met him for the first occasion yesterday and even then he irked me beyond words. Now he's badgering me, and it is most irritating, to say the least.

Isra pressed the intriguing questions to herself but yet again, she had no inclination of the answers.

"Ha, look out around you!" Samuel called out to Isra in a melancholic voice. "Examine your surroundings in fine fervour and tell me what you see!" Samuel instructed. Of course, he had reasoning for his detailing, but really, he wanted to decipher if she could actually come back with the conclusion he already knew.

"I don't quite fathom your meaning. It's a wide-open ocean, guarded by acres of land. A quaint scene where one would come to collect one's thoughts if they were in times of danger or desolation," Isra returned, once again surveying the seascape that captured her imagination.

"How observant of you. That is very astute," Samuel

complimented sweetly. "However," he paused as he hurried onto a brand new tangent, "I am a little disappointed you haven't noticed that you are not in one of your usual haunts. A witch of your expertise should know when she is in borders that are not her own. But never mind; there is always room for improvement."

Samuel spoke in a low voice as though he was trying to hint to Isra exactly what he wasn't saying in a roundabout way.

"Who *are* you?" Isra probed. She had the strangest recollection she'd experienced this before.

Samuel straightened his stance, again flashing Isra that charming smile of his as he let both of his arms fall effortlessly to his side.

"I am the light bringer, Samuel Reynaldi, lord and chief of the realm Spirisity and the former employer of your beau, Astrid," Samuel announced matter of factly.

Isra threw Samuel a perplexed glance as she pried earnestly, "So why aren't you castrating him instead of me?"

"Oh, girl." Samuel sighed with impatience. "I'm not here for Astrid. My enthusiasm in this matter most certainly pertains to you. Besides, Astrid is not really one for this type of discussion. I mean, even before you transfigured his feathers into flesh, he still wasn't as invested in this as you and I,"

He furrowed his brow as Isra gave Samuel a bewildering stare.

"You and I? We are not aligned. I am a powerful entity. I am the darkness. I delight in the wretched majesty of it all. I understand and breathe in the mystery that is the occult world. I am connected to everything around me whereas you, you just prance around like some pretty boy with unicorns and sunshine and all that fluffy love and light lark. I shall violently pass, if you don't mind."

Isra sneered at him. Her eyes rolled as she resisted the faltering urge to turn away from the eccentric stranger standing in her presence.

"Yes, you are a creature that has dived head-first into despondency and desolation, returning from the brink of death and still being in incredibly fine form. I know exactly what you are. You've exceeded every expectation we had! We are more affiliated than you think, you and I!" Samuel pronounced with enthusiasm. "But I do sense your lack of interest in this matter, so perhaps you shall allow me to convince you?"

Samuel was able to detect instantly that Isra was far from impressed at his little admission there. Such a big gesture of trying to envelop her into his tainted realm but he'd have to do much better than that if he was going to even get close to making headway with her.

Isra was stubborn. Samuel knew this. She wasn't going to see his reasoning straightaway. He'd have to keep hammering away at all her principles, her misguided ethics and bold manner of not wanting to do something she felt was abhorrent. If he was going to succeed in winning Isra over, he'd have to give her something far more appetizing.

You can drench the most callous and cruel things in a spectrum of colours to make them appealing. You can shower everything in the most splendid incandescent glitter even though it's shrouded in blackened drudgery. It's even possible to shine a light on the darkest of souls to give them some artificial feeling that not only makes them interesting but also virtually inanimate if they've lost their edge. But what you absolutely can rarely do is make the light sound like it is the most wondrous thing to a creature whose heart is drenched in the torrential rain of despondency.

There were no truer words; Isra would have known far more than anyone else just what a foul lie that entailed. And so there was no point whatsoever in Samuel trying to paint the realm of those who walked in the higher realms as something enticing when he knew full well that Isra wouldn't engage with an impossibility such as that. Ever.

"As you wish, my dear. However, I would like to correct you on your perception..." Samuel paused in mid speech, rather irked by Isra's comment, but then also quite joyous about it. She really did come out with the most obscene things, but nevertheless, what did one expect for a dark soul?

Ah, she is a feisty one indeed. Ha, assuming the light beings dance around the mortals in this ridiculous operative she's conjured up. Yes, I suppose she thinks we wear little funny hats and tiny golden halos to boot. No, my pet! The folk up here don't entertain any of that nonsensical chicanery. The things 'on high' do are more behind the scenes, and so the eyes down below rarely get a front-row seat, although you may perceive it in any way you see fit. Nonetheless, I have a little reality check in store for you, my girl.

"It's not as cut and dry as your foresight leads you to believe, my girl," Samuel remarked immediately, leading on to a more dominant attitude as he let slip, "but it is your choice to remain in that line of thinking. We light bringers don't impose our beliefs and ways onto anyone. It is not that way. I'd never approve of anybody attempting such feats, neither would I condone it. Every being on this earth has to find justification for their morals. We cannot influence them."

Isra scoffed, but this time, she was a little more gracious. "Be that as it may, I have no business with the light. They don't have any with me. So forgive me for my impending question, but why seek me in this venturesome expedient?"

"I am someone very intrigued by your presence. I understand that you've undergone quite the transgression in order to become the remarkable entity you are today. I know you've been defeated in years gone by and you've risen despite the adversity you faced."

Samuel continued in a fond-sounding tone that gave Isra the distinct impression he didn't only admire her ballsy attitude but rather relished in it. However, Isra was not easily moved. She wanted to interrogate the light bringer, grilling him with her every query. She didn't know him from Adam, but yet he had such knowledge pertaining to her. It befuddled her incessantly, but yet also piqued her ever-wandering curiosity.

Isra yearned to know just how this man claimed to know her so when she couldn't even recall her ever becoming acquainted with him. It caused her great mystique for she was sure she'd never share such an integral part of herself without having trusted a soul, first and foremost.

"And Astrid? Just how does he fit into this complicated interest that you have in my rather fetching personality?" Isra inquired in a low voice.

This was a futile act on her part—Samuel would see right through it. But in any event, Isra was showing that despite all the secrecy, she would be open to knowing Samuel's reasoning, even if she did still have him under high suspicion.

Samuel paused before moving slightly closer to Isra. His shiny blue eyes flashed upon her green beauties that dazzled in the morning sun, another reminder of why Samuel had grown so attached to Isra in a roundabout way. Yes, she was a formidable foe. Yes, she had her faults and her whimsies. That sharp, coarse mouth of hers echoed her truth so beautifully that Samuel couldn't help but swoon just a bit.

"I have no intention of informing Astrid of our dalliance. It's strictly between you and me. You are of the utmost importance to the world and to me, that is enough to indicate that I don't need to share," Samuel elaborated curtly; although, he still had that sincere smile of his that profoundly displayed he was being true.

Isra was taken aback. Her bold green eyes glimmered slightly as the late December winds howled furiously with gusto. She wasn't one to keep secrets from Astrid. Just the thought unsettled her. Even if Samuel's agenda was innocent, Isra doubted Astrid would be amused at the idea of Samuel alone with her in some secluded wilderness.

There was no doubt about it, Astrid would come charging in and then these two men would have something a damn sight more than an eloquent sit-down. No, it would be more accurate to say Astrid would be seething with anger and deal with Samuel in his own unique way. That is when—and if he—became aware of the misleading light bringer's creepy mannerism of which he was grooming Astrid's beloved Isra right now.

"I am important? I've never heard of such absurdity. It is reckless for you to even presume I could be a mighty force in your battle of forcing goodness upon those who don't wish to seek it. They are comfortable where they are, in that place where they are buried, down in the dismal dark. It is all they have ever known. It may not seem appealing to you, but to many, it is better than the gross alternative of facing themselves and all their internal fears," Isra scolded.

Isra turned her head away in such a ferocious way that if she'd spun around any faster, her head would have come clean off.

She pulled her midnight-blue cloak up to her neck, allowing the warmth of the thick, luscious fabric to conceal her from the icy winds that were coming. It was soon to be January. A new dawn. And yes, winter would be far from over but soon, there would be a reprieve when spring made her courageous entrance.

However, for now, Isra would have to endure the bitter cold that rained down on the lands. As much as she detested it, she knew better than to criticize nature's magnificence. If Isra had been blessed with more flesh on her weary bones, perhaps she would have found it easier to adapt to the harsh, frosty temperament. Alas, that was not to be.

Isra turned her back towards Samuel. Her golden-white hair softly poked out of the hooded cloak. The strong winds weren't showing any signs of calming, although this was Seclera, a place surrounded by water, so blustery gales in these parts were to be expected.

"I have very little time for your words," Isra announced, turning on her heel.

It was obvious that at any second now, she'd be making her departure, and it was clear to all and sundry that she had no interest whatsoever in hearing any more of what Samuel had to bring to her disposal. But Samuel was not so easily thwarted.

"STOP at once!" he ordered.

Samuel flashed his fierce gaze at her. Those cold foreboding blue eyes of his were fixated on all of her personage. He then raised his hand in her direction, indicating that no matter what her reservations, she must listen to him or else...

Not that he could do much. Samuel Reynaldi versus Lady Isra of the Dark—he'd be asking for it, right? But he was determined she'd hear what he had to bestow unto her and if she didn't care for it, well, that was her prerogative.

"You really do amuse me, Isra. Honestly, I came down here and perhaps it was foolish of me to think such things, but I was under the premise that we could have an amicable conversation. Although maybe that is beyond your vast array of talents," Samuel surmised in a low voice. "However, you must be forewarned that I am not your enemy. Yes, you have your suspicions, but who wouldn't? But I am actually fighting your corner, girl, and have been since the very millennia."

"I barely know you and yet you proclaim to know me so well. What are you?" Isra probed.

"I am your benefactor," Samuel announced with a grin.

He wasn't even being remotely comical at this point. The man was deadly serious. You could tell by the way that Samuel's stare bore into Isra. It was so intense that anyone might have thought his eyeballs would burst out of their sockets if he wasn't careful.

Isra gave Samuel a sceptical sideways glance as though she didn't believe what he was saying, but when she looked right at him, he didn't move an inch. He didn't even twitch. Isra folded her arms in a bold notion and pressed them against her chest before eyeballing the light bringer again with great curiosity.

"If this is so, why don't I recall us ever making acquaintances?" Isra quizzed with a wide stare.

No, I don't believe him. I haven't got the slightest idea who this man is, and until now, I thought he was Astrid's friend. Perhaps there is more to this cautionary tale than I gave him credit for. Doesn't he have dear old Ronald O'Kutte holed up in his lair? Just what might he be cooking up? Hmm.

Isra quietly pursued the idea in solitude before she was distracted by Samuel giving her the most beguiling answer.

"We have, girl. I met you when you were about this high." He pointed to just below Isra's knees. "We became lost from each other for a while, but circumstances overruled me. But my, have you blossomed since then. You've lost love but gained something even more miraculous. Slain a dragon. Defeated your most formidable of foes and, may I add, with such finesse. Then you were awakened from a curse, and, I don't mean to poke at the irony here, but you've dished out a fair few of those in your time. And here we are, standing face to face, when so much more is about to commence," Samuel recited with a cheerful look on his face, although his tone was melancholic.

"Interesting, and yet how come I have no memory of this?" Isra glared at Samuel with a deathlike rivet.

Samuel softened his ogle on Isra before replying in a stern voice, "This world is a perilous realm, full of enchantment and danger. Both are equally matched to make a whole. Sometimes the thing that must be done in order to prevent casualties is the unpopular one. I took away your precious memories many moons ago. I am more than happy to restore what is rightfully yours, but first, you must declare your assurance to me that this conversation does not get relayed to Astrid."

Isra's face dropped as he uttered those words. *He wiped my memory clean so that I wouldn't recall knowing him? But why? What in damnation could be so torturous that I wasn't deemed fit to have known of it?* Isra questioned seriously, as she had very few answers here.

Samuel's idiosyncrasy was both callous and cunning, but it posed a very important query. Why all the secrecy? And more significantly, why was he demanding that Isra not breathe a word of this to Astrid?

"Oh, now, that does fill in quite a few blanks for me. One of your comrades showed up yesterday. His name is James, is it not? Quite the slender fellow. Smelling of all that good, righteous crap. I didn't care for him much, but he and Astrid seemed to have a pre-existing acquaintance," Isra explained.

Her eyes narrowed at Samuel cautiously. She was beginning to put the puzzle pieces together. Why didn't she find James appealing? She really couldn't get a grasp on why but something about it felt so wrong. At least now she had a credible notion of why, but the rancid deception was still pungent.

It didn't bear much thought as to what the convincing light

bringer might be planning So he was offering to return her memories to their rightful place. It was almost as though he was bargaining with Isra. Like he'd said to her, *All right you give me this tiny piece of insurance and I'll give you what was once believed to have never existed.*

It almost sounded too good to be true. And more precisely, what if Samuel was playing Isra? She didn't trust him. Not an inch.

"And just what will you do if I decide to enlighten him on this enthralling chat?" Isra sniggered, although she was wildly inquisitive to know just what Samuel would do if she happened to disobey him.

"Now, now, let's not go towards anything that might be unpleasant. You are a fine creature. We wouldn't want to tarnish your vengeful spirit now!" Samuel remarked in an eager tone but there was a sudden pause.

He seemed as though he had been caught off guard. Isra was a tough cookie despite how young she was, but she knew exactly what cards she was going to play. Anyone looking in on the outside would have assumed Isra was trying to one-up Samuel by goading him into revealing why he wanted Astrid none the wiser on this little shenanigan.

"Hmm, I am not sure I can take any of this as gospel. After all, I am someone whose every whim is rooted in darkness. More importantly, why on earth would I care for your pathetic morals?" Isra probed. "According to your version of events, you wielded the power to manipulate my mind enough to ensure I'd have no memory of it. I find it impeccably interesting how I never got the chance to best you there and then. I mean, if you know me as well as you claim, you know for certain that I'd have done my utmost to shake you down."

It was true. Isra still didn't believe that Samuel could do anything to her.

Come on, she was the mighty sorceress. He was a light bringer, although something told Isra he was barely hanging on by a thread. There was something remarkable in his demeanour. A dark shadow clung to him, ferociously lying dormant in his soul. Isra could smell it. He wasn't as good and pompous as he'd been making out to be, but he was putting on quite the engaging performance.

"Maybe. That could have been the case. But even us light beings have means to disarm those who fall prey to the realm of the wicked. I had no desire to rip away your memory, Isra, but as you'll soon be able to recall, you'd gone too far. You were present in a forbidden hell dimension, one that I wouldn't normally dare tread upon, and there you were, about to unleash chaos onto the earth. No, I couldn't have that. Not in my realm, honey." Samuel finished with a lick of his lips.

"I see. But I still don't understand. If I was so bad, why not kill me there and then? We could have been done with this petulant mess. I'd have been none the wiser and you light folk wouldn't be continuously getting on my last nerve," Isra retorted sardonically.

Puh-lease, like he ever possessed the power to destroy a witch! Ha, chance would be a fine thing. No. There's more to his little tragic tale than meets the eye. None of this adds up to anything of rationality. And you're telling me these people are supposed to be civilised? Isra joked merrily to herself.

Oh, Samuel's game was more than pathetic. It was embarrassing. Who the hell did he think he was dealing with anyhow? No, none of this was making any kind of sense.

"I never wanted to harm you, Isra. But as fiery confrontations go, this one was unprecedented. I couldn't let you get away with that. I dealt with the issue as I deemed wholly necessary. Something you've done many times, only you've done it to satisfy your own will. I stopped you simply because the world would benefit from my actions. Can you actually say that's irrational now? Taking your wretched memories away, well, I thought that would soften the blow. You see, it wasn't just you that was going to burn the cosmic realm to embers. You were not alone," Samuel revealed. "Now, I really shouldn't have to elaborate further. I did what I had to. I was hoping you would show some sort of cooperation, but maybe I am being too reasonable. Hmm?"

"Well, it seems you know a lot more than you give credit for but I was alone, wasn't I?" Isra quizzed with a wide-eyed stare. "I mean, if you knew me so well, you'd have been fully aware that I had no contact with humans for years. No civil conversation to speak of. I had no close companions. *Nada.* None," Isra announced bluntly, although there was a bittersweet edge to her words.

"Yes. That is all true. But you were with Astrid. He was right there with you... right from the beginning," Samuel blurted out.

"But that's impossible. Astrid and I have only known each other for three years?! I remember the exact moment he came to me. He came pecking away at the window sill of that ghastly Lillian. I know when it was. I happened to be there."

Isra stammered as suddenly something struck her memory. She recalled the moment in technicolor... It was that very fateful night she'd managed to stow herself away in Lillian's beautiful quaint cottage. Isra remembered the unmistakable words as Astrid's voice echoed, "Isra, Lady of the Dark. Come here, for I seek you."

I remember it so clearly. He was there. There's no way in damnation he could ever have met me before? He knew who I was. He called me by name. But wait... How would he have known to address me by my name if we hadn't already met? Oh, my goodness, I hate to admit this, but what if this old Samuel chap is right? I don't trust him, but he may well be telling the truth. But why the hell would Astrid lie to me about it?

Isra mulled it over in her thoughts, even though such an occurrence seemed abhorrent to her. Astrid was her counterpart, surely she'd have known the accurate details of their relationship? No, it really was impossible.

Samuel could see Isra wasn't taking to his reasoning. Perhaps it was her high sense of rebellion. Oh, how that grated on him.

No matter what I say, she really couldn't give a crap. She's all about the darkness and wielding her majestic power. Well, sweetie, once upon a time, I GAVE you that power. I gave you a stately home. And you thought you just happened to come by it? That sob story of a former witch dying there was actually convincing? Please, girl. I expected better from you than this, but I suppose it is my fault, really. These years have taken their toll on me. I've slipped into despondency and stupidly assumed I could take away your memories, banish Astrid from the realm, and neither of you would cross paths again, but how reckless was I? He was always going to reappear in your life. Sooner or later.

"Perhaps, if I lay claim to that prestigious life of yours at that grand palace? Or is it a chateau? Honestly, sometimes I forget myself. Shambre Fell, is it? Yes, now, one might wonder how I came to be so knowledgeable about that. Girl, I created the life you have now. The union with Astrid? I facilitated it. Well, not the romance coming together, but I'm the reason you've got that eccentric mansion. And so a little bit of respect wouldn't go amiss since I could snatch it back at any given time!"

Isra's glowing green eyes froze at once upon hearing this. It was yet another revelation that made no sense to her whatsoever. That her entire life almost had been fabricated by magic by the sounds of it.

"No. I remember it. It was old and unoccupied. Nobody had cared to dwell there for aeons," Isra recalled.

Samuel chuckled. "Ha, Isra. That was exactly what we wanted you to think. It was easier that way. I set you up real nice. I was able to keep watch on you this entire time, but I guess as time escaped me, I stopped watching you. I never knew you and Astrid were together until he kidnapped that Ronald O'Kutte chap."

Samuel's tone softened and Isra seemed slightly more reasonable. Her fierce gaze dimmed to a shocked expression. Her eyes fixated on Samuel as if he was some kind of a god. But yet she barely knew the man, although he did have this unbelievably charming exterior about him.

"I see things are not what I once thought them to be. So come now, what is it you want of me? Let's get it over and done with so I can be on my way!" Isra inquired in a low voice.

Samuel smiled, relishing this moment, as he could finally deliver what had been promised for so long. "Ha, I thought you would never ask. Now, do an old chap a favour and close your eyes, just for a moment," Samuel instructed.

Isra slowly let her eyelids shadow her eyes until they were shut. *I can't comprehend this man seriously. He claims to know me so well. Oh, let's just go along with his silly charade. Maybe I can teach him a thing or two. These light bringers are all the same. He's going to seduce me with some fancy pants, 'do good or be punished' nonsense, no doubt. I have little time for that tomfoolery. But whatever. Needs must,* Isra thought.

Samuel looked dead-on at Isra standing before him. He was being precise, as he wanted to ensure her eyes were definitely closed. The last thing the light bringer wanted was for Isra to catch a glimpse of what he was envisaging. That would be a most reckless mistake in Samuel's eyes. Nevertheless, there was no time for pondering. Isra's eyes were shut so Samuel proceeded in circling himself around her slender form before muttering something softly under his breath.

"What was once crushed to oblivion now may be restored. In thy name, I give you your sacred reprieve. I resurrect the long lost magics rightfully to thee. Unbreak my friend and solidify because now the end is nigh... I command you to return to thy creator!"

And with this, all of a sudden, bright lime-green fragments flew around Samuel's head, hovering around his personage as they fluttered about, mindlessly lingering in the blustery skies. However, their destination was a much different one than originally presumed; the beautiful shattered pieces of lime-green were now making their way towards Isra.

In a magnificent moment, Isra's eyes immediately opened and she saw the precious glass-like entities coming straight for her. One might have thought to make a run for it, but Isra was deathly calm. It was intriguing; before Isra could even blink, the shattered pieces made a dash for it and swiftly realigned themselves before materialising as a solid green orb in the palm of Isra's hand.

There was a strong sense of familiarity as Isra felt the weight of the round orb but before she could begin to ponder just exactly how she had this inner knowing, Isra was abruptly struck with a pounding sensation in the centre of her forehead, located in between her eyes. Isra's forehead was stinging ferociously all over with the vile, pervasive vigour that wasn't subsiding. After only a few seconds, Isra felt an overwhelming sensation of burning pain travel down to the base of her skull.

Although the entire event had first been subtle in nature, it was soon evident that more was to commence as the surging pain grew in magnitude. With her forehead feeling as though it had been set alight, tiny beads of sweat cascaded downward and Isra had insight descend upon her. Mesmerising imagery floated inside her mind. The swift influx of entrancing pictures began circling back and forth inside the deep pits of Isra's subconscious. Although nothing was astute at this point, some of them that emerged painted a very vivid picture.

Oh, my! Hell! Now I see it. Goodness. It was exactly how he said it was. Oh my, do I feel dizzy! This is almost unbearable.

Isra grimaced as the mediocre reality slapped her right at the centre of her third eye. It was bewildering, to say the least. But Isra saw herself sitting on the steps of Wingdom's Academy all those years ago, weeping over that poor sap Jonathan. And right next to her was a black raven! Those yellow eyes of his were unmistakable. It could be no other!

No, it cannot be! There's no possible way! It's insane to think about— but there he is, right by my side. Again! Astrid really did know me all this time. But look deeper, as the plot does indeed thicken and boil over with unimaginable mystery.

First of all, Isra had a clear glimpse of herself and Astrid stood opposite one another that fateful day when he introduced himself as a humble traveller of the realms, insisting that Isra had nothing to fear. But how bemusing; she was able to recall this distant memory when she'd had no notion of it until now. Ha, and then she remembered scolding him ever so harshly by emitting, "Then don't address me as if I'm some regimental empress of the realms" in that cold, icy voice.

More depictions actualised and she had it clear as day. It was that auspicious time that Astrid had taken her to Nefaria Sands, the infamous land that was dominated by frosty turquoise seas blended together exquisitely with lemon-yellow sandy shores that you might only find in a subliminal dream. There he stood proudly as he presented to her that green, glowing spectacle of beauty. The very same green orb she now held in her hand. Only now, everything had come back to her with a vengeance.

Just when I thought it couldn't get any more complicated, Astrid was joining me on a renegade against the light. We were going to destroy the world together with this mystical orb. Wow. One can only presume the frolics we'd have unleashed if we'd had the chance to show this sorry world a thing or two. But then this Samuel character came along. Yes, he'd visited me from the start, trying to reprimand me for my dark ways. Oh, how predictable. But then I met that James fellow because they had both engineered it to be so. But somehow, Astrid came along. Smack bang in the midst of everything, ruining Samuel and James's elaborate plan.

"Oh my!" Isra gasped, as she resisted the temptation to place her free hand across her mouth, for it would no doubt lead to her dropping the precious green entity.

I have to leave this place and take this glittering spectacle with me. I've got to get to Astrid NOW before this Samuel fellow conducts any more chaos in our wake. If I can get away clean, maybe I can change whatever he's attempting to accomplish here.

Isra knew she had to go. Astrid would have to be told everything and sure he'd lied to her, but he'd had good reasoning for it. He always had her best interests at heart. Perhaps the pain of knowing Isra, not being able to tell her for so many years, cruelly stung him at the core of his heart. That it was easier than acting like he'd only met her three years ago. But so many questions lay unanswered.

"I knew I had met you before, but I had indeed forgotten. Why, it's true. You certainly did bewitch me!" Isra exclaimed in amazement.

"What I once stole from you I have now returned. I trust that you'll use these forbidden magics well," Samuel retorted curtly, flashing Isra a soft, warm smile.

The shock had very evidently overtaken Isra, but there now lay a very bewildering question dormant in Isra's mind.

Why would Samuel give Isra the very conduit that would not only restore her memory but also give her the ultimate power over him? What was his end game?

18

Astrid glanced up at the antique bronze clock that sat opposite the bizarre meshing of plain white walls and gold interior. The clock's large hand pointed to the number twelve, indicating it was noon. Astrid found it very peculiar, for Isra had been gone almost two hours. This was way beyond her usual outings, whereby she would have made an appearance by now. And so, Astrid's suspicions were reaching their peak.

Just where could she have gone off to? It's not like her to just vanish for hours at a time. But, oh, wait a moment! Didn't this happen before? When she found herself in Ronald O'Kutte's trap? In all fairness, that was when she ran out on me after we'd had that unfortunate event that was Onyx/ Kane's death.

Hmm, one can only ponder just what frightful sights could be in store. Perhaps I should go off into the forest. Maybe I can bring her home. After all, I'd like to prevent a most unsettling occasion if I can, Astrid conversed to himself in a concerned train of thought.

He had a rather twitchy finger pressed against his lips with a most perplexed expression upon his face that only contributed to his apprehension. The raven-man was rather restless, having only executed Cora as the sun came up, but nevertheless, Astrid was certain his reasons for gallivanting about were sure to bring him peace. His desire to seek out Isra was rational, so he'd pursue this quest.

Let us not be crude, but Astrid had wanted to detain Isra earlier for some frisky shenanigans in their humble abode. And so, by finding her, he could certainly kill two birds with one stone.

Samuel and Isra were still facing each other, although Isra was displaying a rather guarded expression, all while still holding that charming lime-green orb in the palm of her hand. It was intriguing how the gleaming spheroid united itself so precisely face-down inside Isra's dominant hand.

I remember holding this before; I am sure of it. Yes, that is it. Astrid presented this very same curiosity to me when he snatched me away with him to that wondrous place. Now, where was it? I remember the turquoise waves brushing against the lemon-yellow sand, like something out of a dream. And then that big old man appeared, throwing his weight about. Of course, that's it. He demanded Astrid and I stop what we were enacting immediately, and then everything went dark. But I can still feel his hands across my forehead and that odd tickling sensation—then I was able to remember nothing more. The most peculiar thing is how he's manifested himself to me after all this time. I mean, why does he feel the need to be in my presence now?

Isra pondered this intriguing notion thoroughly. Samuel's sudden reappearance did give her food for thought. It had been fifteen years since the light bringer swiftly brought Isra and Astrid's grand rebellion to a halt. And yes, Isra was right in her questioning on why he'd taken so many years to get back in contact. There must have been some kind of event that triggered Samuel's return, but of course, Isra didn't have a single clue on what that was.

Isra was highly suspicious of people at the best of times, but now her head was swirling with all the probable notions of why Samuel may have made his presence known in her realm.

Let's face it—Astrid didn't give a damn about the light versus dark saga. He'd done that shit to death more times than he cared to count. Towards the end, it had become something he'd begun to loathe with a passion, as it had cost him Isra for the longest time. But Isra was invested in the knowledge of these things so her prickly personality and her scrutinising mind were sure to notice something was off in Samuel's supposedly light-hearted demeanour. The reality of the situation was that Samuel wasn't being transparent with not only Isra but himself too... and oh boy, was she catching on.

Samuel turned to Isra solemnly, although he maintained his light-hearted stance as he articulated softly to her in a chipper voice, "I understand you have your reservations about me, but my reasons for why I came to you are genuine. I do appreciate that you may feel as though you have to be cautious of me, but I want to assure you I only have the best intentions."

Isra resisted the urge to scoff as she currently had in her possession the most vigorously powerful magics. It would be considered extremely impolite if she sneered at the infamous Samuel, but still, she wondered why he'd throw this fantastical feat at her when he'd once confiscated it.

"Ha, and yet you felt the need to wipe my memory clean. One can only regard your intentions with the highest suspicion." Isra lowered her voice, giving her a calmer tone. "That may be true indeed, but the thing that is most puzzling to me is why would you hand this prized entity to me? Because I remember it now. You came down to the beguiling land Astrid had expeditiously transported us to. One moment we were alone, him having already handed the dynamic orb to me, and then you appeared before we knew it. There you were, arms folded across your chest, and you were furious with the pair of us. You glared at him like a father would do when scolding a delinquent child. It was no surprise when he responded in kind to you, and then I recall the lecture you elegantly tried to bestow upon me."

Isra muttered in earnest, knowing full well Samuel couldn't dispute a single word, as it was completely bona fide.

Samuel relented a little, loosening his stance as he realised there was little point in arguing. *The little witch is indeed unfeigned, but I had hoped she would have dropped her guard by now. Perhaps there is still time for her to be slightly more agreeable with my way of things. Ah, only time will tell,* Samuel concurred to himself in thought.

To be truthful, Isra was giving him more than he'd prepared for. She was a resilient soul, to say the least.

"That I did. Yes, my dear, you are completely right, but what you don't comprehend is that I was acting under the orders of the light beings. Now those from 'on high' are a very forceful organisation indeed, and even I have very little control over what actually inaugurates into being. But let me call attention to the fact you were about to unleash Armageddon. Not in my realm, honey. So yes, I apprehended you," Samuel recalled with a fierce fashion, although there was a slow pause as the light bringer put a well-positioned finger to his lips in thought.

He then quickly admonished, "But I gave you several warnings whereby I stated I would disarm you if you went too far down the dark, trodden path."

"Yes, well, perhaps you shouldn't have kept such precarious secrets from me when we first met. Maybe I'd have been more trusting. But no, you had to go on with your merry light ways in your most high form while having me down as this wicked conjurer that would have ripped out all of your hearts," Isra bit back in a sombre tone.

Samuel glanced at her before smiling wildly. He grinned from ear to ear as if Isra had just said something highly amusing. "Oh, girl! We both know you'd never have placed your utmost confidence in me. You were far too despondent for that. Nevertheless, I understand your meaning and while I enjoy this trail blaze into the past, I do feel we should get onto the correct footing," Samuel advised.

"Be that as it may, there are far greater aspects of trepidation than you could ever comprehend. While you may suspect me to be something that is not at all apparent, I must remind you of the code that still grounds you. You may indeed consider yourself exempt with recent dalliances with the dark side," Samuel warned in a well-meaning tone before giving her the side-eye as he reprimanded her, "but I know of recent events whereby you took it upon yourself to snatch away the soul of some poor wretched peasant girl."

Oh, dear! I was wondering when he was going to bring that up. These love and light types are so frigging predictable. You know exactly what they are aiming towards despite their ridiculously fluffy light-hearted exterior. Oh, I bet he knows all about me. Now I seem to recall he wanted me to flip back towards the light. Ha, well there's no chance of that, Isra amused herself, having worked out Samuel's exact agenda. *Yes, it is the light bringer's job to reprimand those drawn to the dark of every little sordid thing they've done, but while doing so, they put on this pretend facade of 'oh, it's still not too late to repent.' How about no to that revolting idealism.*

Isra laughed so loudly she thought she could have burst at any moment as she recited, "Ah, sweet old Contessia. She is darling and yes, I did take her soul, but you pathetic light folk have no power over me. So do yourself a favour and vamoose before I'm forced to show you what else I can accomplish. Trust me; I don't take kindly to someone who patronises me... whether they be light or dark."

Isra chuckled with fierce enthusiasm. It was evident Isra wasn't taking any of Samuel's bullshit. Samuel paused as yet again he wasn't getting anywhere with the witch, but still, he had an ace up his sleeve.

"Now, now, don't be so quick to rebuff me as some putrid human. We both know how much you despise those types, but I must reveal to you a most endearing secret, my dear..." He grinned mischievously. Samuel knew this was the absolute tidbit that would be vital if he was to gain Isra's full attention.

"And what is that?" Isra asked in a somewhat cutting tone.

Yes, it was true that Isra didn't care for Samuel's elaborately drawn-out theatrics but she'd humour him. Samuel laughed again, but this time, he had a tiny glimmer in his sky-blue eyes like he'd discovered something quite dynamic but yet futile if it happened to weave its way into the wrong hands. Only now, Samuel was very astute over his occultist knowledge.

He summarised carefully, "Oh, girl, haven't you learned anything? You're the one! The one destined to taint her heart with the darkest and most foul of magics and thus resurrect the wretched being you detested so much! But perhaps it's not clear enough for you yet. Oh well, let's break it down further, shall we?"

Samuel muttered in his usual sardonic tone but he was deadly serious. In any event, he'd soon be disgracing the light realm by giving every single facet of the prophecy to Isra, but wasn't this limited to "on high"? Why in the actual fuck would Samuel have the guts to grace Isra with such a vital piece of informative spill? He had to be playing a different side of the field for sure. But Samuel was a dominant yet reserved soul. He wouldn't give away every piece to the puzzle now, would he?

Samuel cleared his throat, breathing in deeply before he carefully recited those words he'd already verbally demonstrated to Astrid not that long ago. "Yes, well," he began, "these things are not easy to relay, but one must maintain their sense of ethereal knowledge in these parts, for not everything is how it appears to be, you understand?"

He motioned to Isra, although Samuel was clear in his mannerisms, hoping she'd grasp the concept he was posing a question to her. However, the witch had a blank expression on her face, so evidently, she'd missed Samuel's nudging point.

Well, it's no matter. We'll just continue. Perhaps elaborate a tiny bit on what exactly is at stake here and how this deliciously dark plan is integrated as one, Samuel thought as he started to speak in a slightly more modest tone. He was also communicating a little louder than before this and so the emphasis was on his tone now more than anything.

"It is said that a most powerful force hosts the ability to free a destructive, wretched being from its hellfire, therefore causing desolate cessation when that one returns to the earth. However,"

Samuel paused, allowing a few moments to pass before he continued, only now he was staring right into Isra's lime-green glinting eyes, as he had to catch her attention with the next chunk of engrossing material, "it is very important to heed this; that soul delves into the most putrid depths of the netherworld, undergoing a terrifying transformation. And let me advise you, it won't be pretty. Not by a long shot. But, this is necessary, as the chosen one will tap into the most damning magics there are. This is crucial because the ultimate destruction of one's goodness and cleanliness is the absolute ritual needed to release the demonic one from its hellish and watery grave."

Isra proceeded to look at him blankly. She had no comprehension of what the pompous light bringer was talking about. If she had to stare at him any longer, she knew damn well she'd call him out on his tomfoolery because honestly, the witch was befuddled as to what his meaning was.

Does he really do this for an occupation? Dashing around as though the devil may care while he's harassing strangers and talking in riddles. He's making himself out to be a buffoon. Nobody has any idea of what he is referring to. He really is quite the baffling character; however, one must humour even the most eccentric of species, Isra quipped to herself in a mind ramble before turning her focus back to this not so endearing charmer who was still standing in her midst, reverently enchanting her by responding with a subtle eye gaze.

Isra was still muddled at Samuel's poetic speech. In any event, she'd ask for clarification. "You know I don't have the faintest idea of what you are talking about, so perhaps you should enlighten me. My brain is a little overwhelmed. It probably needs a good old spring cleaning," Isra explained, resisting the urge to roll her eyes.

"Oh, dear girl." Samuel chuckled with a ferocious grin. "Have you forgotten your dearly departed Everilda? Why, it's *you* that is destined to bring her back from the ashes."

"Come again? I am not sure I heard you clearly," Isra piped up.

She did have some recollection of the Everilda part, but she wanted to be certain she'd heard the whole "resurrection from the ashes" statement properly.

"Isra, you are the one that will tarnish your already confounded soul when you restore the callous Everilda Daughtry from her ghastly resting place," Samuel professed in a low voice.

And now, his connotation was undoubtedly known.

19

"And now do you see why I would be involved? It's a deeply sensitive matter of the highest importance, but you have to understand that only I can lead you to your destiny," Samuel queried, although he might want to rethink the destiny part. Perhaps prophetic cascading down into darkness might have been more appropriate.

He was hoping by now that she'd grasped the concept, but he'd let his little revelation sink in before he attempted to further push the matter. After all, he'd just revealed that Isra was the one who would be doing the deed of resurrecting dear old Everilda, but the trouble is, would the rebellious witch do it?

She barely listened to reason at the best of times and now was no different—but on the other hand, Isra had access to her long-lost magic that Samuel had once confiscated from her.

And one of the most remarkable approaches of coaxing a witch was to throw something bewitching in their way, and sure enough, they'd be attracted to it like a moth to a flame. Not to mention Samuel had known Isra for a very long time and even though she had surrendered most of her despicable ways, Samuel had the hindsight that she could still be tempted by the enigmatic and wondrous of feats, even if they happened to be deadly necromancy, which, Isra herself would be perpetrating in the name of obscurity.

Isra stood back in amazement, although she took due diligence in keeping that enthralling green orb in the palm of her hand. Perhaps she feared Samuel would snatch it from her but nonetheless, she calmly humoured him, having listened to his indulgently sinister proposal.

"You indeed present to me such precarious things, but I don't quite fathom why you wish for ME to bring back Everilda. I do feel it would be considered safer for the realm if she stays dead and buried," Isra muttered before she went into a somewhat delicate pause as she perused the entrancing notion for a second.

"I do believe the sacred creed is true. It is not ethical to revive somebody when they are expired because it is said that when they are regenerated, regardless of what force was used in doing so, the soul, even when returned to its former host, sometimes does not remain the same as it would have been in its fleshly coating," Isra pointed out, although she did have some cautious reservation, which Samuel could evidently sense.

"Oh, you are quite the rigid one when it comes to disagreeing, Isra." Samuel chuckled. "But in any case, I shall give you some time to mull over my engaging offer. Of course, it goes without saying that you must not replay any of this to Astrid. No matter what the circumstance may be," Samuel instructed sternly.

He did have a faint knowing that Isra may not be as cooperative here, so he relaxed his normally sombre tone.

"Hmm, I don't know whether time is going to make any difference. What's done is done. What would bringing back Evie do for the utopian realm, other than welcoming in fright, dissonance, and chaos?" Isra pressed, for she was not convinced in the slightest that restoring Everilda to her former glory was a wise choice.

Samuel resisted the urge to snigger but instead maintained his common sense of formality, for in this expeditionary feat, he was the wise one and Isra was his unlikely protégé.

"Oh, Isra! Haven't you heard? The universe is conspiring against us all. There isn't one creature that roams upon this earth that hasn't had some form of chaos, relentlessly attacking it in some form or another. It's about how you rise to the challenge. Discord will always be a factor in the greater scheme of things, but you can change the course of events in one climatic swoop," Samuel elaborated diligently.

He then retorted in a sinister voice, "It's those that try to relinquish the fates that have been laid out in front of them and go against the authority of the divine. They are the ones that will pay the penultimate price sooner or later."

"I cannot say I AM overly concerned with what the love and light brigade proclaim as gospel. I am a free spirit. It doesn't matter what they believe or what they state I must enact. They have no control over me whatsoever," Isra announced; she didn't care for that bouncy, fluffy, love and illumination crap.

"Ha, don't disregard it just because you have no time for it. We light beings—the keepers of all the souls—have more power than you care to acknowledge. You just don't have the foresight of it. I could quite easily rip that glowing spectacle from your palm, smash into it into smithereens, and there would be nothing more said about it. But I'm willing to allow you to make amends. Even for someone cloaked in darkness, you still have your Achilles heel, girl. I might be a sly, elusive bastard when it comes to it, but I'm still aware of how things are beyond the veil of uncertainty. Why, you forget yourself so flippantly, Isra. You of all people know there is a karmic consequence for every action undertaken in this celestial paradise," Samuel remarked callously, not caring he'd likely offended Isra.

"Ultimately, that is your opinion of me, but I have very little care for it."

Isra shrugged while she gave Samuel a solemn gaze. Her crystalline green eyes glistened in the sunlight as she felt the warm rays coating her back whilst also having the additional heat rise from the fabric of her velvet cloak. She was feeling the heat so intensely that she shed the midnight-blue artifice, revealing her delicate white lace nightgown. Even the well-adjusted light bringer found himself distracted for a moment and had to compose himself.

"If Astrid was here, he'd rip your eyeballs right from their designated sockets," Isra uttered boldly as she caught Samuel completely fixated upon her slender frame.

"Yes, well, as beautiful as that sounds to your rich, twisted mind, he's not here. Tragically. It's just me and you, baby!" Samuel articulated evilly.

It was fair to say he had been distracted by the fallacious temptations of Isra's beguiling beauty. Taking a breath, he calmly conducted himself as he articulated formally, "Well, before I get sidetracked, I must warn you that if you don't go back to that burnt-out grassy knoll where you executed dear old Everilda, ungracious ramifications may follow."

Isra guffawed wildly as she burst into an unexpected fit of laughter. It was way past hysterical as she clutched her chest upon feeling a sharp painful sensation underneath her left rib.

Quite honestly, Isra couldn't believe what she was hearing. It was ludicrous. This so-called enlightened man apparently must be floating around on a white fluffy had the sheer audacity to suggest that SHE, Lady Isra of the Dark, go off on a fruitless escapade where she'd make her way back to that infamous clearing located in the scorched land of Rainfur before then unleashing some disastrously potent magic. Then, in due time, Isra would wait around like a sour lemon while Everilda made her fateful appearance? It was insane. Never in all her tenure had Isra been witness to such nonsensical chatter, but these love and light folk did chat some real shit, right?

Isra neglected to remember that when Samuel had first come to her, he'd calmly given her the suggestion that the light would be there for her if she so chose to slide over to that lark. But Isra declined; it didn't satisfy her thirsty need for exploration in the darker terrains, and then that charming Astrid popped up out of nowhere and laid on an elegant banquet in her honour.

Suddenly, a memory of Samuel introducing himself to Isra for the very first time struck Isra in her temple. The feeling of it was painful as it re-emerged in her subconscious. The imagery was faint, but just about visible as Isra recollected within her mind's eye Samuel Reynaldi dressed from head to toe in jet-black. His slicked-back hair was also black as night. And there he was, lecturing her in a weird sort of way that could also be considered as him negotiating with her as he explained to Isra about her path being the "wrong" one for her.

Yes, that was it. He'd materialised out of nothingness and started babbling on about how I could change my destiny. Oh, my goodness, I see it so clearly. He tried to sway me back by inviting me to his realm for a steaming cup of coffee. I remember myself dismissing his fine offer, and he replied, 'I could endeavour to make it sweeter for you.' He was trying to win me over but I had sadly forgotten this until now. But why in hell's knowing would he want me to bring Evie back from the dead? Surely she's better off where she is! Well, I imagine the realm is, anyhow, but he's so determined on me performing this unsightly task.

Isra realised the full-blown reality of how Samuel came to her before was replayed right in front of her eyes.

Samuel didn't find Isra's reaction terribly funny,   as his probing startled her somewhat. "Is something amusing you, girl? Because I cannot fathom how you'd find karmic payback entertaining," he muttered in a sardonic tone.

"Oh, it's not that. It's just you're this enlightened soul and you tell me I must restore my dead friend back to life. Not to mention that she's my ex-nemesis and I destroyed her with the energy of love itself. It's really quite endearing. I thought you light bringers would have come up with something far more elaborate than this." Isra shrugged candidly.

Samuel held himself back as he considered the situation fully for a moment. *She's a freaking complex cookie to crack. I thought I'd have had her at my level by now. Oh, dear, what is one to do when one must convince another that the wrongdoing is actually right? Darn it. Why is this so difficult? More importantly, why is Isra being so stubborn? She is more resilient than I estimated.*

He had to convince Isra that this was what she needed to do. More than that, Samuel had to reach Isra deep down at her core so that she'd fully understand the implications of not committing such an action. She had to know just exactly what she'd be undertaking, and for her to learn that, Samuel would have to make it personal. Yes, it would have to resonate with the darkest depths of Isra's rotten soul; otherwise, she wouldn't care. Samuel would have to fabricate his elaborately formed rationale so that it ravaged Isra's non-compliance.

"Hmm, now you were resurrected, were you not?" Samuel questioned with a look of inquisition.

"I was, yes," Isra promptly answered.

"Therefore, you know the law of mortality better than anyone. Girl, you were eviscerated by the shards of a glacier. You were pronounced dead. That should have been the final curtain for you. But alas, it was not to be. WHY? Because some poor forsaken soul loved and respected you enough to go against the code and bring you back from the brinks of oblivion. So now, all I am asking is for you to breach the very same ethics," Samuel petitioned to her.

"Since the very beginning, you infamously proclaimed to be drawn to the darkness. Not only that, but you were deemed to be the very fine spectacle that would orchestrate some of the most sinister feats in this cosmos and so far, you've played out your destiny spectacularly. You've come a long way, princess! You were just a young sweet thing, barely having any comprehension of what was laid before you, and here you are. You've fought against rotten love. Become immortal. Conquered death. Do you need me to elaborate further? Because if I do, we could very well be here forever," Samuel muttered curtly. He was getting rather irritated with Isra.

"You should not be standing before me in my presence now. You know that. I know it, and even more so, the bloody universe knows it, too. But you've overcome every single thing that has come up against you! There is no better entity to fulfil this special purpose!" Samuel uttered, making his point distinctly clear.

Isra swallowed. He had her bang to rights here. She'd have

nothing to fight against him with now. She knew, even though she was immortal, that by laws of nature, she should have died that day, but Romeo redeemed himself by restoring her life.

"If that is truly so, why would you want this? You are a light bringer after all, are you not? I thought the light folk were all kind and good. Surely they'd never want to be part of something so vile like this," Isra asked sullenly, as she still wasn't comprehending Samuel's reasoning or why this was so damn important to him.

"I am. There is no light bringer but me, dear girl!" Samuel answered. "But even I have my vices. There are good and bad in the world. You know that. Light and dark. It's all just a big charade because only one can ever win. And it's up to us truly which one that is. I'm betting on the shadowy terrain being stronger right now."

Oh, my! There really is something ghastly wallowing away inside him. Well, one best not hang around too long, or it will surely fester, Isra conversed with herself hurriedly, as she knew she needed to skedaddle out of here or he'd be lecturing her all day.

Isra straightened herself, getting hot on her heels as she proceeded to leave. She figured if she left now, she could prevent any further debauchery because goodness knows what the entrancing light bringer had up his sleeve next.

"All right. Your demands are tough but reasonable. I will mull over it and come back to you with my response in due time," Isra uttered. She then paused, quickly noting it was past one in the afternoon. "I must go. Astrid will be concerned about my departure. Good day to you, Mr. Samuel."

Isra clicked her left thumb and index finger together abruptly while still clasping the glowing green orb in her other hand as she prepared to make an expeditious exit. Giving the hypnotising serene ocean of Seclera one last look before she vamoosed, Isra was thinking of illustrating something particular to Samuel regarding his shrewd plan but faltered as she thought better of it.

It is wiser to let sleeping dogs lie. After all, he's letting me vacate with my magic when he could have stopped me, she thought, although she had neglected to remember Samuel was much too cunning for the likes of her.

Little did Isra know that Samuel Reynaldi was standing there with a grin plastered across his face, his shiny blue eyes almost glowing as he retorted softly, "Oh, girl... we'll be seeing each other again. I can guarantee it."

20

Astrid had everything assembled in preparation for his jolly jaunt. In his inventory was a fresh flask of scalding black coffee, dark as his soul and bitter enough to tantalise his mature taste buds. It was just the way he liked it.

He also had taken with him a well-polished silver steel sword. It had a gold etched handle that was saturated with the deepest red rubies. It was more an antiquity than anything else as he'd likely not have to use it. But prevention was always better than having to seek out a cure.

Isra had been gone for a few hours. Astrid was getting fidgety upon not knowing her whereabouts. As time passed on, he grew tenser.

All Astrid needed to do now was make his way towards the vastly renowned clearing in Borahell, where he'd no doubt lay his eyes upon Isra. It was one of her many special haunts and the very same place she had met the wise python Romeo three years previously and was also where the dank, dark pit of snakes was located that Isra had also haphazardly fallen into at the time.

It made the most sense that Isra could be there as it was a stone's throw away from Shambre Fell. And despite Romeo's passing, Isra still often visited Borahell as it proved to be a tranquil place where she could console herself when the drudgery of the cruel world became too much of a burden.

Astrid was finally about to vacate the premises when suddenly he heard a loud clattering coming from downstairs. It sounded like a harsh shattering, so since he had already dealt with one pressing incident today, Astrid took it upon himself to investigate.

He raced down those grey stone steps in seconds. He quickly reached the landing, where Astrid stood motionless, preparing to confront whoever had the sheer audacity to enter his home. He listened carefully while perched outside the living room door, considering whether to blast it open. Although no noise had occurred for a few precious seconds, Astrid was not going to take this lightly. It was unlikely he'd scared the intruder off. They were still in the lounge, although everything had gone dead quiet.

Astrid was not going to let this deter him from his investigation, so he called out in a stern voice, "I know you're in there. Whoever you are, reveal yourself and your shenanigans now!"

He wasn't messing about. Astrid was grave in his demeanour, but oddly enough, no answer came. And so Astrid still wasn't satisfied as the mystery had not yet been unlocked but it would take more than a bit of resolute silence to put him off the trail. He gently pushed his nose past the door, wedging it open with his left leg. Astrid patiently waited before he pressed his weight against it, making it fly open at once.

Astrid didn't know what to expect as he keenly surveyed the living room, first scanning his eyeballs across the red couch. Then they drifted over to the back of the room, where Isra's blood-red armchair sat elegantly unoccupied. Feeling bemused, he took his eyes away, focusing on the windowsill again, and it was then that he caught sight of the intruder. That sullen-faced peasant girl!

That chocolate-brown hair of hers hung unkempt across the side of her face as she looked at Astrid in trepidation of just what he might do. Ava was mortified. Those bewildering brown eyes fell to the floor but Astrid had no time for pleasantries. He was going to get to the bottom of this chicanery.

"Just what do you presume you are doing in my house?" he probed.

At first, he didn't raise his voice, but Astrid was furious and found it increasingly difficult to maintain his composure.

Ava kept her eyes firmly on the ground. She felt incredibly intimidated by him already, never mind allowing Astrid's fiery eyes glaring into hers. Ava got the distinct feeling that Astrid was a rather dark and mysterious character, so she didn't wish to show her weakness as that would lead to trouble. This girl was well known for getting herself into sticky situations she couldn't get herself out of. She had always been ruled by her fear, but the impending anxiety as her heart pumped ferociously inside her chest was too much to bear.

"Please, sir. I didn't mean no harm," Ava squealed. She threw her hands in front of her face in a defensive motion as she emitted words in a hysterical tone.

It was then that Astrid observed a bright, violet liquid gleaming at him. The vivid purple was almost glaring at him as it lay spilt on the stone floor. Evidently, Ava had been rummaging around in Isra's kitchenette cupboard, where she kept all her magical components such as herbs, candles, and harsh potent oils. But Ava was just the slave girl that had been compassionately employed by Isra, so what was the young thing doing playing around with Isra's potions and tonics?

When Astrid looked closer, he noticed the fragments of crystalline glass glistening in the dimly lit lounge. Surveying the scene carefully, then glancing back to Ava, Astrid yanked her by the ends of her hair and vociferously tossed her onto the couch.

"Please, do not hurt me!" Ava pleaded with him.

Astrid flashed her a curt smile, although he was menacing indeed as he spoke, "Oh, I won't hurt you just yet. But believe me when I say you're going to tell me what's going on here. And why is there fluorescent violet goop all over the place? Hmm?!"

"I was..." Ava started, although Astrid's hollow brown eyes

blazing over at her caused her to tremble so she stopped mid-flow. But alas, the raven-man wasn't easily thwarted.

"Yes, you were doing what exactly in my beau's kitchenette of all domains to carry out your quaint expedition of foraging?" Astrid quizzed her.

She better have a jolly good reason for creating this disarray in Isra's little cupboard. I am not willing to tolerate any more tomfoolery in this house. So if this girl has got any sense of humility, she'll get down on her knees and confess her debauchery or else, Astrid cursed to himself as he pursued the idea that Ava might be a little spy. The question that flashed to the forefront of his mind was for what or who?

"I was looking for evidence for him. You see, my employer is very strict, and he will most certainly punish me if I don't deliver on what he is asking," Ava confessed, although she was reckless enough to let it slip so foolishly. Clearly, Ava hadn't taken heed of the implications this would cause.

Astrid glared at Ava solemnly. He pressed his arms against his chest. He didn't believe a word of what she was saying, but she was behaving suspiciously enough to convince Astrid something was awry.

I don't know what part of her tale is more ludicrous. Perhaps she's falling so short that she had to conjure up more bullshit to impress me. Well, damn; she's failed spectacularly on that little conundrum. But there could be something interlinking in this. And why do I get the distinct impression it involves Isra? Hmm. Astrid muttered away to himself while still eyeing the girl with severe scrutiny.

Eurgh. It always comes down to Isra. There's always some foe out there, lying in wait to get a glimpse into Isra's world. Always so envious of her power, but they can't do it the old-fashioned way; oh, no. They've got to play dirty. But playing the sweet and cool game doesn't wash with us immortals. We're not immune to the patheticness of their weak games. No, so they'll always get rumbled, even if they believe they are invincible.

Astrid knew how this shit went down. He'd been through it so many times now that it was damn predictable. They always drifted towards Isra. She was the reason folk often strayed from their terrain but their deceptive energy often gave them away.

It was proving difficult for Astrid to decipher what exactly was occurring. On one hand, he was certain Ava was being dishonest about the whole charade, but on the other, he believed she was scared enough to blurt out the truth. He'd have to dig deep into the abyss of prevarication to get to the root of it.

Astrid took it upon himself to take a somewhat sinister approach with Ava. He figured if he was menacing enough, her lies would come to the surface pronto because nobody messed about with Astrid when he got mad.

He moved towards the terrified maid, towering over her as he got right in her face and probed her. "And just who is he? Your employer, I mean. It's that old stalwart, Prince Jonathan, is it not?" Astrid inquired with a wide-eyed stare. He was certain Ava was referring to that pathetic, slimy, little weasel that had entangled with both Isra and Everilda when they were young and naïve.

If it wasn't him, who else could it be? *It has to be Jonathan. Otherwise, I'm stumped beyond my knowledge,* Astrid muttered to himself, carelessly forgetting that Ava was there as he wandered into his thoughts.

"Erm, no," Ava answered promptly. "It's that old chap; oh, golly. Now I cannot remember his name," Ava stuttered as she proceeded to delve into her memory. She'd heard him say it so many times in that formal tone. Surely, she should have been able to recall it.

Astrid listened as Ava continued with her drawling on. He was beginning to wonder if she'd ever get to the point. It was irritating for Astrid to stand there awaiting some gratifying answer to his impending question.

"Oh, fiddlesticks! Why can't I recall it? It was something like Renand or Ronald. No, that's not it. Oh, darn. I feel so stupid; he's told me his name many times. I've known him for a while!"

Ava chattered hurriedly. It was clear she was in a fluster as she muttered away to herself. Her fast-paced ranting was barely audible. None of what she was saying made any sense whatsoever.

Astrid felt annoyed. Surely, she'd know who it was if she was searching around so keenly to find something in Isra and Astrid's home for the old fellow. *Maybe she's stalling. The girl is only merely satisfied by wasting my time, now she has the goat to infuriate me as well. Oh, just hurry up with it! Save us all a headache!* Astrid ranted to himself impatiently in thought.

Ava, however, now had the brightest glimmer in her sullen hazel eyes. Something had evidently piqued her curiosity but it was her mouth that did the demonstrating of exactly what was going on in that little mind of hers.

"Mr. Reynaldi!" she exclaimed at once.

No, it can't be. No way. No. Not him.

Astrid's right eyebrow rose sharply as his entire body shuddered. His mouth dropped. If it hadn't been firmly attached to his body, it just might have fallen onto the floor. Astrid's brown eyes swiftly flashed bright red. Oh, how he glared at Ava in that split second where she'd spilt her guts.

"You have to be kidding me? No way in damnation could it be him!" Astrid quizzed her with anger.

Yes, he was furious. Not only had Samuel played his part in causing absolute mayhem for him and Isra before, but now he had a spy in the vicinity, one who was innocent enough to do his shady dealings for him.

Ava gulped back the urge to vomit as anxiety sent her stomach into mass chaos. The acidic juices swirled inside her abdomen ferociously. It probably didn't settle matters that she was also carrying a sprite inside of her. Being with child at the best of times was not an easy task.

"Mr. Reynaldi was very clear. I am to keep watch on Lady Isra, the witch of whom you have a union with, or face his wrath," Ava blurted out, shedding a tear.

For now that she had confessed, she was done for. There was no possible way on earth Lady Isra and Astrid would keep the girl in their domain, not after this treachery that had occurred right in their midst. There was more chance of Samuel becoming extremely acquainted with the ghastly old iron chains in Astrid and Isra's infamous basement that had played home to many before him.

Alas, Ava was young and without a keen sense of judgement, so perhaps Astrid would adopt a shred of compassion and take pity on the poor girl. But the way Ava stared at him only made her feel as though that was a lost cause.

Astrid was understandably furious, but he needed to know the actuality of it. If he prodded Ava in the right places by being ruthless and also methodical at the same time, he'd get to his destination. And that meant Astrid would have to simmer down his temper in order to make Ava feel slightly more comfortable to expose Samuel.

Astrid promptly clicked his thumb and index fingers together, conjuring up a reddish-brown mahogany chair. It had beautiful detail down the legs, only adding to the natural elegance of the wood. There was a metallic gold bolster, which he added for support, as he agilely situated himself on the chair but facing the back end of it so that he was resting against the cushioning. He then muttered something barely audible under his breath. A deliberate act perhaps; Ava wasn't sure what on earth he was gibbering on about, but in the next instance, a steaming hot mug of black coffee materialised in his right hand.

"Ah, there's nothing like a fresh cup of my favourite caffeinated beverage to awaken the old noggin," Astrid articulated as he took a huge swig of the black velvety liquid before turning his attention back to Ava.

She still looked incredibly intimidated, but considering Astrid had changed his demeanour a great deal, Ava now felt less rigid although still uncomfortable with the situation at hand.

"Now, why don't you tell me all about Samuel and how this originated? And how myself and Isra became entangled in this abhorrent mess?!" Astrid proposed to her gently.

He was trying his best not to be forceful. He needed to maintain some kind of human decency, although this was not his forte. He wasn't equipped with the enigma of human emotions and behaviours. Having said that, Astrid had witnessed more than his fair share of disgraceful actions coming from those that wore a flesh suit. He often felt that the world would be better off if everyone developed the gift of kindness, but most failed to do so, in his opinion.

Ava felt an incredible tightness in her chest. Just below her breastbone was the pounding sensation that echoed from beneath her heart. It was merely the thought of telling all and sundry that gave her chills. She knew from the conversations that occurred less than a month ago that Samuel would quite possibly decapitate her if he was given the opportunity.

"It began around the last full moon. About a month ago, perhaps longer. I was staying in a barnyard. I had literally nowhere to go, my options having been limited, and so there was this strange man that appeared out of nowhere. I thought he may have been the devil at first. He was so formal but yet talked in intricate riddles so I never really was able to grasp onto what he was saying. But he told me if I came to your home and gained the trust of Lady Isra, he'd set me up good and proper in one of the most renowned establishments in the land of Bitterquel, but only if I did EXACTLY what he had laid out in his instructions."

Astrid's eyes narrowed at Ava; he had the sinking feeling he'd heard this tale before, but he put his judgements aside as he urged her to continue. "Please, go on. I'm sure this is about to get more insightful indeed," he uttered in a presumptuous way, as he expected where this might be headed.

"Mr. Reynaldi was extremely clear when he explained Lady Isra had fallen under some ghastly curse. He believed it had been designed that way because of how many she had mistreated in her time, but actually, little did he know that an enemy of hers had gained entry into her dominion. Now he believed that this was the precise time in which to strike. I remember his words all so well," Ava recalled as her mind wandered to that cloudy day whereby she had made her destiny.

～

SAMUEL ARRIVED at the scene promptly, having already made sure he was to be at his finest since the day's festivities were only just beginning.

The fortuitous witch Lady Isra of the Dark had fallen prey to a curse where she now lay dormant in a slumber-like state. Samuel couldn't be more prepared for this most gratifying day. He'd ironed his jet-black trouser suit to perfection. Not only that, but he'd also made the extra effort of combing his jet-black hair so that it was impeccably slicked back.

The peasant girl Ava was already there, awaiting his arrival. The poor, weak, little thing was standing on her tippy toes, as she wasn't quite tall enough to see the glorious scene from where she stood. Samuel Reynaldi towered over the forlorn girl. He was a remarkable six foot and three inches. And it went without saying that Ava was greatly intimidated by the faithful light bringer.

Samuel saw that Ava was ready and waiting and so he made his approach. It was evident that she was undoubtedly terrified of him, but she'd ultimately made her bed and quite literally since she'd soon be residing amongst royalty. Samuel couldn't help but notice Ava's bulging belly, as she was soon to be giving birth to a child.

Aww, our young one has been indulging in sweet fantasies. Well, there will soon be more to satisfy her tastes when she's incarnated in Jonathan's charming manor. But I imagine she'll be having more than her share of delectable, mouth-watering treats, Samuel remarked with some mild amusement to himself.

Oh, yes; he couldn't have picked a better specimen to have some rampant fun with. She'd do anything to save herself from a terrible fate.

"Ah, young Ava," Samuel piped up. "I'm so glad we could meet on this joyous occasion... "

Samuel trailed off, as his tone changed dramatically. When he began speaking again, it was much more sombre.

"As it stands, Lady Isra is now transfixed by a very dark spell. It's quite interesting, as one of her long-standing enemies' relatives caught up with her three years later. Still, you have to appreciate the irony of it, as she's dished out a few ghastly curses herself in her time. Anyway, she's out of the picture for the foreseeable future so I can get up close and personal with her beau, Astrid. You must understand he was once a raven, one that is very much in love with her, and he's done the most reckless of things by kidnapping the mortal whom he believes is solely responsible for her not-so-earthly departure. Anyhow, 'on high' has sent me to reason with him and perhaps make him see how this unjust matter can be resolved. But before I can assist in that, we must attend to you as you play an important role here," Samuel imparted in Ava's direction.

Ava looked slightly unnerved as Samuel flashed her his trademark grin. He was quite the charmer. He could sweet talk anyone into doing just about anything with his flattery and extensive occult knowledge.

Primarily, Samuel was a light bringer. He knew all about the arduous battle between the light and dark, having been submerged in it shortly after vacating the earthly plane. After he ascended into the heavenly realm he now resided in, the sacred beings known as "on high" gave Samuel the fortuitous task of bringing those back from darkness, dragging them by the strands of their hair if he had to, crashing down into the light. Now sometimes, this method worked swimmingly and others, not so much. Sometimes souls plunged so far into their own obscurity that they refused to see any other way but the darkness, and this was often frustrating to Samuel but he always gave fair warnings before he intervened.

It hadn't gone down so well with Lady Isra. Ha. She rebuffed my efforts more times than I care to acknowledge. She was impenetrable. She justified her wicked ways, saying the universe had done her wrong. She was immovable. And then later, she and Astrid joined forces, of whom was just as wretched as her. Their personalities meshed together and before you knew what was occurring, I had a potential Armageddon on my hands. Suffice to say, I had no choice but to disarm Lady Isra, transferring her to a domicile where she'd be out of harm's way while retaining no memory of the entire affair. Astrid was given a severe dressing down before being banished from my realm. And that put paid to that.

Now, the witch lives in the nether realm, where she is slipping down to the cursed sanctification, but yet doesn't qualify to be considered truly dead. Her earthly form is still breathing. It's in this state that I can interrupt whatever is about to be executed on her behalf. My old boy Astrid knows far more than he cares to divulge, but little Ava here is going to present a fine distraction when it is deemed right.

What he was about to request Ava to enact was going to be crucial if he was going to succeed in infiltrating the close bond of Lady Isra of the Dark and Astrid the Raven. Or at least Astrid used to exhibit the majestic form of black feathers and glistening wings.

"And what is it that you ask of me, Mr. Reynaldi?" Ava piped up in a brave voice.

The girl seemed to be beaming full of self-confidence or maybe it was an impetuous ego, as she felt she had a tiny glimmer of power. Who knows?

"Now, now, let's not be formal. My name is Samuel," Samuel paused for a second before admonishing solemnly, "as you already know. Now, let's get to business, shall we? With our dear old soul Lady Isra out of action, I'm going down to speak with Astrid. When the time is right, Ava, I shall place you in their midst. And go you will, child."

Samuel instructed her, although judging by the hoarse tone of voice, he wasn't asking. Yes, this whole thing might have seemed a little thorough to some, but Samuel was trying to make sure his plan would be a success.

You see, Samuel had been a very patient man. He'd found Ava sleeping rough in some barnyard. She was a victim of despondency, never having anywhere she could call home. Neither did she have the greatest supply of food, as she'd been feasting on berries and nuts that grew wild nearby. But Samuel stumbled upon the poor girl unwittingly and was prepared to make her a surprising offer. He knew she'd practically snap his hand off and it was because of this that he knew she'd make the perfect scapegoat to infiltrate Lady Isra and Astrid.

Having already had many dealings with them around fifteen

years ago, Samuel was ready for round two in the proceedings. He'd already banished Astrid from his realm because of his relentless succumbing desire for the witch Isra. But Samuel was aware that even him doing his utmost to tear them apart wouldn't be the end of it.

One must remember if two souls are drawn to one another, nothing, not even a forced separation from the almighty can keep them apart. Samuel knew better than anybody that if Astrid and Isra got within an inch of each other, it would strengthen the magnetic ethereal cord between them, and that could spell disaster for the land.

There would be no telling what catastrophic events could occur as a result of such a mesmerising energy. In Samuel's eyes, he believed he was justified in spreading Isra and Astrid across the lands.

Samuel had significant knowledge of Isra. For instance, that she was the illegitimate child of a warlock, Damien Daughtry. As for Astrid, well, he had his inauguration in the occult world. It didn't really matter that he was a raven. Everybody has the ability to shift into another form. It just so happened that Astrid inhabited a different skin than what he had been created with.

And so that was where Ava came in. Samuel was going to exploit her in the best way he knew how—by promising her salvation from her wretched existence IF she did everything he said.

Samuel sensed the sheer desperation in Ava. Never mind the raw stench of horse manure that went along with it. But she fit brilliantly into Samuel's elaborate plan whereby he'd set her up in Bitterquel palace almost overnight. Of course, it went without saying Samuel would engineer this by magic. He'd place an overwhelming spell on dear old Prince Jonathan, his courtiers, and anyone else that wasn't aware of Ava's not so humble beginnings. It would be foolproof.

Samuel didn't want to drawl on and with time escaping them; he explained his clever plan to Ava as she stood on, looking impatient. It was as though she wanted to depart but Samuel wasn't done yet.

"You are to go to Lady Isra and Astrid with this, er, sob story, whereby you're holed up in that eccentric fool Jonathan's palace with no food or water. And you'll lay it on thick how he's treating you so undesirably with you being with child and all. Then you will beg and plead with our charming foe Isra on how you could be severely punished if you return to dear Jonathan. After all, he's a womaniser, a greedy man that wants nothing but his riches. He cares little for his servants, and if you don't make a terrific mess of it, they'll be reluctant at first, but take you into their home, no trouble at all. And then, you'll begin to play your part in this enterprise."

Samuel drew a breath in, pausing before his tone changed yet again. Now he sounded more unmelodious. He was not only formal but incredibly stern to boot. But all he said was, "Just be mindful... if you fail to conduct ANY of which you have been asked, I will see to it personally that you never see the light of day again. It was pleasant conversing with you."

And he left it at that, not even letting a single second pass before he departed in a puff of smoke. Ava looked dumbstruck at Samuel's threat, but he had vacated so there was nothing she could do but follow through.

"AND THAT WAS when Mr. Reynaldi instructed me to go to you and Isra, but mainly her. He's not really interested in you," Ava remarked at Astrid with caution, as she still feared he could fly off the handle if she wasn't diligent enough.

"But for him, it was all about the witch. I don't know what your origins are with him or how his beguiling interest began, but he's all about Isra."

Ava noted Astrid's reaction to what she was relaying to him, as she saw red in Astrid's eyes. It startled her more than she cared to admit. The normally calm and controlled raven-man looked absolutely furious. Those normally brown eyes of his glowed ferociously back at Ava, showing nothing but bright blood-red in their centres.

21

———

Astrid held in his impending anger as Ava made a deliberate attempt to deflect from the conversation at hand. It was evident Ava was deeply fearful of Samuel, and who wouldn't be after what Astrid knew now?

It was always about Isra. In fact, in some weird way, Astrid already knew this to be the truth. Even back in Isra's teenage years, Samuel had some odd fixation towards Isra. At first, Astrid suspected it to be some exuberant fascination about the witch, as Samuel always seemed ready to jump right in when it came to her. And everybody had proclaimed Astrid as the obsessive one, eh?

Okay, so Samuel was a light bringer. It was more or less Samuel's job to try and stop Astrid and Isra from running around with potentially dangerous dark magics in their possession, because who knows what they'd have managed to accomplish if Samuel hadn't halted them when he did. But even Astrid felt like Samuel had been obsessed with her from the very beginning.

He didn't have to go down and pay her a personal visit when she'd first turned over to the darkness. Samuel didn't have to magically whisk Isra over to Spirisity against her free will. No, he'd gone and done that anyway so he could get close to her. Oh, my; how it was all coming together. Everything suddenly made sense.

"It all revolved around Isra. From the very start…" Astrid exclaimed with a shocked expression as he cautiously eyed Ava.

The girl was still on his favourite red settee, the one he most frequently occupied with Isra. For now, there was a strong probability that the poor girl should stay. At least to keep out of Samuel's way, as no doubt when Astrid confronted the astonished light bringer, sparks would fly.

"Yes. He's most intrigued by her, although I can't fathom how, as I've never really seen the interest in witches myself," Ava admitted honestly.

"Hmm. Well, I am afraid I am going to have to leave for a while, but after what you told me today, I think it is a wise choice that you stay within these walls," Astrid advised with an emotionless stare.

He paused and considered the situation fully and what he had originally intended to do. If Ava hadn't spilt the beans on Samuel's shenanigans, then this could have gone in a different direction. But needs must, as the old saying goes.

Now that Ava had revealed to Astrid what was going on, he'd found it would be more compassionate to let her stay—for the time being. When Isra discovered just how connected they all were, she might be inclined to do something rash herself.

"I was going to ask you to vamoose earlier today. I had all kinds of scenarios playing out in my mind, but now I fully understand the way of things. I feel it is going to be a safer move if you stay put," Astrid explained carefully before he was quick to change his tone to a more formal one as he uttered, "However, I cannot guarantee you'll be given the same grace when Isra finds out about all of this. But for now, I will prevail."

Ava said nothing. She merely nodded. That was enough to indicate to Astrid that what he'd just said to her had sunk into her peasant brain. Now he could attend to more important matters.

~

ASTRID WAS BACK UP in the bedroom again, finishing off the job he had meant to take care of earlier before he was interrupted. Since he'd already gathered most of what he felt he needed, it was a simple task of running down to the kitchenette. He quickly replenished his flask with more steaming coffee, as the previous one had gone cold.

Astrid then made his way down the long, winding staircase and out of that grand ornate door. There was no time to lose. Astrid had no idea of Isra's whereabouts and so initially, he was going to investigate all of her old haunts. It was like one of those needle in the haystack searches, but at least he had something tangible to go on. Who knew more locations that Isra could be hiding out at but Astrid?

Just as Astrid pushed open the oak door, he caught sight of a familiar face staring back at him. They gave a somewhat forlorn expression as mousey brown hair dangled over a worrisome forehead. It was the strangest unnerved expression that one gave when they desperately wanted to say something but yet didn't know how. Interestingly enough, two light brown hazel eyes peeped out from under that unkempt hair. It was uncanny how they gawked at Astrid in a most skittish manner.

"Oh, how delightful. It's the jolly one," Astrid remarked in a callous tone, as he wasn't best pleased to see James.

James didn't seem amused. He appeared to be quite irritated with Astrid, but then again, what was new? Astrid always managed to get under James's skin in one form or another.

James piped up in a shrill voice, "Oh, I can't even begin to tell you how I've so dearly missed your sardonic commentary. It really brightens my soul."

"Ha, so anyway, what are you doing in these parts? I thought you'd be long gone after Samuel's dramatic transfiguration of us," Astrid uttered in a low voice, although he wasn't certain as to why he was being so quiet.

James straightened, relaxing his facial expression a little as he replied, "It's funny; I'm here to discuss that with you. I've noticed some things recently that irk me."

Astrid resisted the urge to choke with pure unadulterated

laughter at this one. *Oh, golly! This peasant isn't as stupid as he seems at first glance. Perhaps he is finally awakening to the fact that all is not well. Ha, more bewildering things have been given premise in times gone by.* Astrid chuckled away to himself silently in thought.

"Well, that's quite endearing and all, but I am afraid other things have my attention. Isra has gone walkabouts, and so I'm off to find her," Astrid calmly mustered.

He needed to keep his head if he was going to be successful in his quest. Having a cool and collected mindset was just the ticket to getting to where he needed to be.

"Jolly, I will come with you!" James announced with a wide grin; however, this was met with discord from Astrid, who didn't approve.

The raven-turned-man eyed James with close suspicion, giving him an eagle glare before he emitted solemnly, "No. I'm going alone. You will only be a hindrance. Besides, you still carry around that sword like a sissy girl," Astrid interjected in a hurried voice, emitting much pent up frustration as he didn't want James coming along.

"Charming, but you're always losing that sorceress of yours. Don't you think it's time you placed her under duress?" James suggested quizzically with no emotion whatsoever.

It was true—James didn't really gravitate towards Isra. Well, there had been one occasion where they could have made a proper acquaintance but Astrid had put paid to that with his meddling. And thank goodness too because maybe they wouldn't have been together without that interference courtesy of Astrid.

Astrid shot James with a vexed glare. *He's just as bad as fucking Samuel. Neither of them is fond of her, so why the hell does he want to come along, anyway? Unless it's to gloat, which I'm not prepared to tolerate in this lifetime or any other. He's going to have to get over his impetuous self!* Astrid ranted away to himself as he turned his focus away from James to slam that grand ornate door shut.

It was quite symbolic in a way. The way Astrid thrust his fist upon that door so that it firmly closed behind him, a very non-verbal way of articulating to James that this was not negotiable.

It was a few seconds before Astrid replaced his focus onto James, telling him bluntly, "Yes. I am well aware of you disliking Isra, but it doesn't change anything. You cannot fucking well come, boy! You'll just get in the way. You'll make a bloody arse of yourself in the process, too. I'm not having it."

"Oh, how the times have changed since I've known you! I would have thought by now you'd have loosened up a little. I never understood your fixation with this witch. I always thought of her as a creature of malefic darkness. But yet here you are, all these years later, having not only won the girl over but you're holed up in this elaborate promised land with her as your queen." James finished curtly, giving Astrid a somewhat friendly half-smile.

"I was just doing what the 'on high' intended. I never meant to cause you any malice. Maybe we can let the past go for once and all, eh? What do you say, old fellow?" James imparted in a convincing tone. "We're both too old for this crap. Let's just put it to bed already. I've had a few strange occurrences brought to my attention lately, and while I don't know the ins and outs of it, I'd like to pursue this further. So how about me and you just drop this quarrel to the wayside, hmm?"

James pressed the issue eagerly, as he seemed keen for some type of resolution to be found underneath all the drama, hatred, and resentment he and Astrid had shared over the many years they had known each other.

Astrid lowered his stance, releasing the tension that was widely apparent in his body language. He unclenched his fists, dropping his arms by his sides softly as he proceeded to follow on with a new area of enquiry. "What do you mean by strange occurrences?"

James lowered his voice slightly so that it was just about audible to any being that happened to be lurking around the vicinity. "I've heard whispers. And some suggest that all is not well in certain quarters."

Astrid's eyes narrowed at James once more. Something struck a chord with the raven-man. Astrid's brown eyes with that golden yellow sheen froze right there on the spot. It was hard for him to comprehend, but there was something unmistakable in those fateful words. It was so striking the way James had slowly recited every syllable that it echoed in Astrid's head.

Yes, Astrid had his reservations concerning James. Truthfully, they'd never got off on the right foot but in this case, Astrid couldn't help but think that they might be on the same page here. It was miraculous. For the first time in years, Astrid and James might well have been able to agree on something.

James was not talking as he usually would. There was something distinctive in the way he voiced his concerns. *He's got to be talking about the old devil, Samuel. Why else would he show up here, practically begging my forgiveness? Hmm. Peculiar as it is, I have more important matters to attend to. Isra is still off wandering somewhere. I need to find her. James would only get in the way of that. He's always managed to get in the middle of things in some form.* Astrid realised he'd gone off on a tangent while James was still standing in front of him.

"If you're pertaining to Samuel, trust me, I already know," Astrid muttered in a hurried tone, as he wanted to set off as soon as humanly possible.

James was astounded. It was apparent in his eyes that he was not best pleased. There was even the slight possibility that the angelic agent was offended at such a thing.

He immediately crossed his arms across his chest in an impatient and irritated stance as he probed bluntly, "What do you mean, you already know? How? You're not even bloody connected to 'on high.' How the hell is it that I'm the guy about to take over Spirisity as head light bringer and I'm the last fucker to uncover it?!" James stammered furiously as yet again he felt as though he was being kept in the dark.

Astrid couldn't help but respond sardonically as he articulated, "Well, perhaps 'on high' are just as discombobulated as you are. And why would I need to be connected to the light beings to discover such gripping insights, hmm? You think because I am not affiliated with those wishy-washy types that I'm not going to detect when something is awry? Please, like I need such high-ranking connections such as yourself to pick up on Samuel's erratic decadence. No. I discerned quite some time ago that things weren't as favourable as he'd made them out to be."

James resisted the overwhelming urge to curse Astrid's name. Oh, golly! How that raven-man could vex him with hardly any effort whatsoever.

Well, I suppose he was more preoccupied with the deathly condition of his enchantress. Why would matters concerning light versus dark concern him? We all know he's always supported the other side, but Samuel may also be journeying down that path. Well, it's just too much to bear. I am the one that is deemed to be upholding all that is gracious and unsoiled. It is I that will bear witness to the greater good and all its benefits. James blustered to himself, quietly vociferating his disgruntlement.

"And you never said a damn word to me? You've known all this time that he was going through a transmutation and it never occurred to you that maybe I should have been told about it?" James exclaimed.

He was furious. How dare Astrid have possession of this knowledge and not relay it to him. It was typical of the raven-man, though, to keep something to himself and not share with others.

"It was on a need-to-know basis. After undertaking it upon myself to visit Samuel personally and witnessing what he'd said to me first-hand, I decided nobody else needed to know," Astrid explained coarsely.

Of course, he didn't have much tolerance for James's aggression and pent-up anger but naturally, the boy would be inclined to express an emotional reaction. When you took stock of the awkward position James was about to be thrust into, it came as no surprise he was agitated.

"This is just typical of you. It's always about you. It's never about others or how they might be affected, is it? Always you," James muttered in an annoyed tone before pausing. He remembered a significant part he'd neglected to consider during his rant. "Or if it isn't about you, it's you doing your utmost to piss everyone else off by protecting that damned enchantress of the nether realm," James shot at Astrid.

"Leave Isra out of it," Astrid warned in a stern voice.

Astrid angrily twitched his fingers, not knowing whether he should scrunch his fists or leave his hands swaying by his sides. He was aggravated that James was still here in his presence when he could have buggered off by now.

"Fine," James countered. "Anyway, shouldn't you be going to seek out your little witch?"

He quizzed Astrid in a somewhat friendly tone although it was very much evident that James had a lot of tension still residing in himself. But perhaps, for now, he thought better of it as there were more important matters to attend to.

Astrid swiftly moved away from the grand ornate oak door in an attempt to end this unproductive conversation. As he stepped forward, he noticed the violet rose bush that he fondly remembered Isra tending to when he'd had a conversation with her all those years ago. Next to it was the bright red apple tree Isra had instructed Astrid to plant after they had defeated Everilda. Or she had, in a manner of speaking, but alas, Isra wasn't here to enjoy her beloved plants.

How Isra had laughed when she said, 'Plant an apple tree right in that corner. I want apples as rosy red as Everilda's face.'

Astrid stopped himself amid his train of thought, realising this reminiscing wasn't assisting him in finding Isra.

"That is indeed the desired course of action, but I'd like you to get lost first," he snapped at James without thinking.

Well, actually, James was grating on Astrid's patience, so it wasn't exactly shocking he'd said that.

"Again, you are so endearing with friendliness," James mocked just as sarcastically.

"Well, I'm sorry. You ain't coming with me, boy. You're a nuisance at the best of times," Astrid mouthed callously. He didn't care much for offending James. The boy was really beginning to get on Astrid's nerves.

"Why can't I come?" James pressed yet again. "Have you not considered that perhaps I can help?"

"I am sure you could," Astrid rebuffed calmly. "But after

information that has been relayed to me today, I feel it better serves if I go alone. I appreciate the sentiment but it's just not so."

"I understand. Look, I know things are rough in your dominion right now, but if I can help in any way, would you please have the decency to call upon me?" James asked, although he did seem confused by Astrid rejecting his kind offer.

"I presume you know where she goes walkabouts better than any other soul," James acknowledged as he contemplated where he'd encountered Isra before, so Astrid would most certainly know where she could be found better than anyone.

HOWEVER, something lay undiscovered by Astrid and James, as the two men walked side by side down the long, unwinding, grey gravel path. A shadow crept out from behind the majestic apple tree. A mysterious silhouette in twilight-black lifted a velour hood, revealing a well combed-back head of jet-black hair.

"Aww, how pleasant. They are off gallivanting to find the little sorceress. Well, I'm going to visit our dear old friend, Ava, as it seems she's been naughty."

Samuel sniggered with a devastatingly cruel smile.

22

James turned as he and Astrid made it around the stream together. Astrid was headed towards Borahell and James was going to turn around the bend leading to Seclera, where Spirisity was located. After all, it was soon to be James's newly occupied place of residency.

"I guess I'll be off then. I hope it's not rude of me to say this, but if you do successfully find her, could you find some means of letting me know? I'd like to be aware of the goings-on before the fall-out commences," James recited in an eager tone, but he was somewhat anxious.

"*When* I find her," Astrid responded boldly before he took a pause. "I am not sure there will be time to prepare you for what comes next. My main focus will be getting to her before he does. He's obsessed with her, James. He has been from the very beginning. I can't even describe to you how swiftly I need to get to her before this gets dire... for ALL of us."

He was almost snapping at James, as he knew he needed to get going. Having an intimate chat was the last thing on Astrid's mind.

"Samuel?" James questioned. "But that makes no sense. I know

214

he's lost his way over the years with battling you and Isra, but that's nonsensical at best."

It was true he didn't think Samuel was the one who was "obsessed," as Astrid had put it.

"You know, once upon a time, I might have come to the same conclusion, but think of it. Samuel turns up just as I propose unholy matrimony to Isra. And then she absconds from my sight? You can't say that's all just a mere coincidence. As I said, I have had knowledge related to me and while I am not at liberty to reveal it, I know there are greater things at hand than the love and light versus dark side debacle."

Astrid feared James wasn't going to be wholly understanding. After all, James was on the light side and therefore not awakened to the deception of it all yet.

"I understand," James muttered, although there was a hint of disappointment in his voice that Astrid wasn't going to elaborate further. "I don't understand why you're being so secretive about it all, though. One could assist if you opened your eyes to the realm of possibilities."

Astrid gave James a solemn death stare, emitting pure disbelief in James's lack of understanding of just how dire things really were becoming.

"My eyes are open. Believe me, that's just the problem. You guys in the love and light lands have no clue. I'm the one in the thick of it. I've seen more darkness emitted from the light than I ever have from the likes of Isra," Astrid articulated calmly. After all, he'd been back in this from the beginning.

"I'll see what I can dig up on my end. Maybe Samuel has been so engulfed in himself and this thing he has with Isra that's he's left a tidbit of a clue somewhere. We might get lucky, you never know," James calmly announced, although he seemed sarcastic in his demeanour.

Astrid motioned back towards James with a serious stare, but his hardness loosened as he muttered distinctly, "You know there is something you can do for me, James."

~

SAMUEL REYNALDI carefully noted that Astrid and James had gone their separate ways. Astrid was headed towards the naturalistic Borahell while James was moving towards Seclera. Both were in search of Lady Isra. But Samuel wasn't here outside Lady Isra and Astrid's château for that. Oh, no. He was merely observing that situation closely. He'd come for another matter entirely.

"That silly little peasant girl, dear old Ava. Now one might question just how I could pay my respects? Ah, of course. Give her a good old talking-to for her wretched absurdities. Ah, opening her big fat gob. Yes, that's enough reason for my visit. Come to think of it, I have more than one. I warned that sodden girl more times than I care to count, and off she went, giving away the goods to Astrid and Isra. Well, we must rectify her behaviour at once!" Samuel chortled to himself as he softly manoeuvred from his ample hiding place behind the apple tree.

Samuel took great care ambling up towards the ornate door, pushing it open with ease as he let himself into Isra and Astrid's eccentric abode.

Of course, Samuel was pondering the notion of how Isra was getting to grips with her newly reacquainted memories and magic, not to mention his ingenious proposal he'd bestowed to her only less than an hour ago.

One would hope she'd come to her senses. That's if Astrid doesn't get to her before I do. But oh well, I have to attend to little Ava first and foremost. Ah, our sweet-tempered little spring chicken. Just where would I find the pathetic, simpering girl who resisted my most generous offer? Hmm...

Samuel made his way up the elegant grey stone staircase at once, practically running up those steps. He didn't care if he was discovered; he already knew Astrid and Isra were off the premises. However, Samuel couldn't help but notice the deathly quiet that emitted throughout Shambre Fell. Not a soul was to be heard. Even as he pushed the door to the living room open, it was still eerily silent.

"Well, I'll be damned. Nobody is here. How very peculiar," Samuel uttered loudly.

Samuel looked taken aback as he stared around him. Isra's kitchenette was modestly tidy. No empty coffee cups to be seen anywhere. However, there was a rather intriguing spill of bright purple luminous liquid, followed by splintered shards of glass that lay glowing on the cold stone floor.

"Ah, this looks like our girl. Isra wouldn't smash potion bottles aimlessly. No, she'd know better than to waste whatever magical trickery she's got cooked up in these. Hmmm, but before I give up completely, I'd best check upstairs. One never knows where the mortal may have been smuggled in."

Samuel idly picked up one of the shattered potion bottles, placing it back on the mantelpiece before he turned on his heels. He exited the living room promptly, shutting the ornate door behind him.

He was quick in climbing up the staircase that led to the second floor that would lead to Isra's bedroom, which she shared with Astrid, but Samuel wasn't going to let that distract him. It was predominantly Isra that he was invested in.

Samuel took care not to be blinded by the deep violet and pillar box red that saturated the walls of Isra and Astrid's bedroom. Even the bed was drowned in blood-red velvet covering that elegantly complimented the icy-white sheets; perfect setting whereby one would most definitely be seduced before retiring for the night in soft, silky white satin.

"Well, she's not here either. Hmm. So much glorious, colourful, splendour, but yet it's distracting. This is a boudoir for lovers. How could I be so foolish? Thinking she'd be here. No. Astrid has had time to do away with the little miscreant. The trouble is where would he have placed her for safekeeping?" Samuel muttered in annoyance.

The reality dawned on him that he had indeed been led on a wild goose chase.

"Unless that pesky little raven has had help in whisking her off somewhere... Well, in any case, I'm wasting my time. The child isn't here. More to the pity, as I had quite the showdown anticipated. It's no matter. Isra is still out wandering around. And I think I have an idea of where she's headed."

And with that, he simply clicked his thumb and forefinger together before disappearing in the blink of an eye.

"Perhaps a hot coffee will stimulate my senses. Give me a return to normality, even if just for a time," Samuel muttered solemnly as his voice trailed off along with him.

The light bringer was rather miffed. He'd come to grab a moment with that poor girl Ava but alas, she was nowhere to be seen. Samuel didn't have the slightest idea of where she was. Perhaps the little peasant had indeed been cloaked so that she was out of harm's way, but there was no trace of her.

In any case, only one thing was certain. Astrid had been given help, and Samuel had firm suspicions on who that person may be, as much as it had pained him so.

23

James was rummaging around in Samuel's eloquent office, frantically looking for something that might be of some use. The terrified peasant girl Ava sat perplexed by the old man's desk as she watched James empty Samuel's desk drawers one by one. Each of them lay idly heaped on the floor as he continued searching for whatever he was seeking.

"There has to be something. He must have left a trail. It can't just be hearsay; not he said, she said," James countered loudly.

He sounded rather vexed. After all, he'd been working for Samuel for fifteen years and never suspected a thing. He'd always been a model employer. *Do this, boy. You'll be fine. You've exceeded beyond my expectations*—always praise emitted from Samuel's mouth. James never felt that Samuel was treading the path to obscurity. But after speaking with Astrid at length, it was very much apparent that was indeed the case.

"I've always thought that light beings were good people, trying to do what is right despite it all. Perhaps he has a secret stash somewhere that not even those closest to him know of," Ava piped up reluctantly.

She had to admit she felt awkward, but this kind gentleman had whisked her away at the drop of a hat. She was in his debt, truthfully.

~

ONE HOUR EARLIER

AVA FOUND herself staring vacantly out of the window, sipping warm, rich cinnamon tea from her seat on the red couch.

She was unable to relax since Astrid had left so suddenly. She was afraid that Mr. Samuel Reynaldi might materialise at any moment. But Astrid warned her to stay put, for he had business to attend to. Ava had been left to her own devices in Astrid and Isra's living room/kitchenette and had found herself thirsty, so she'd made herself something to drink. It was a rarity for the girl, who had never been privileged enough to savour something so fine in her entire life.

The kitchenette was stocked with the most pungent and satisfying loose-leaf teas, so Ava had helped herself. Astrid had been gone a while now, and so she was a sitting duck. She aimlessly stared out into the vacant world around her.

The gardens of Shambre Fell were exquisite. Just outside the entrance to the refined chateau were beautiful, deep red and mystical violet rose bushes that grew wild along the front of the manor, whereas in the corner, the magnificent apple tree stood on its own, boasting a fine crop of ripe blood-red apples, which was unusual to be seen in winter.

At that moment, just as Ava wanted to touch one of those yummy ruby-red apples so badly, a fleeting notion of being able to handpick one for herself and take a bite, right amid her deep fantasy of snatching one of those ruby-red apples, a bright emerald-green energy began to fill the quaint kitchen of Shambre Fell. It saturated the room as shimmery silver smoke emerged from the centre, whereby a soft shadow materialised. Two shiny forest green eyes shrouded under a mass of mousy brown hair came into view as James emerged from the smoke.

Ava gasped in horror when she laid eyes on the soon-to-be light bringer, who stared back at her. "Oh, my! Are you connected to him? Oh, golly. I know I'm in trouble, but the raven-man made me tell! I couldn't help it. I swear," Ava pleaded desperately. It was as though she thought she was about to be killed.

"Calm yourself. I'm not here to harm you. I'm here on behalf of Astrid. I am an associate of his," James announced warmly.

It was evident Ava was very fearful, so Samuel had done quite the number on her. The girl was borderline paranoid, judging by her begging and whimpering.

"Oh. I thought he'd sent somebody to make mincemeat of me. I did disobey Mr. Reynaldi so terribly, but I never planned for it to happen!" Ava squealed helplessly.

She cowered on the red settee so much that she was clinging to the damn thing as though her life depended on it. A foolish act indeed, as James's intentions were only to escort Ava from the vicinity.

"Yes, well, I understand there are misconceptions, but I am not Samuel. My name is James. I'm here to retrieve you from this humble abode. But come on now, there's no time to lose. We don't know how long it will be before Samuel comes looking for you again," James explained quietly. He lowered his tone of voice so that it was barely audible.

"The raven-man? He asked you to come fetch me?" Ava asked pleadingly. She had no comprehension of what was happening to her.

"He sure as hell did, child. I'm not sure what's going to occur after Lady Isra returns from her period of absence, so we must go right away!"

"All right," Ava agreed. "It's a good job I never brought anything with me."

"That it is," James muttered.

Time was passing fast. They needed to get back to Spirisity immediately so that Ava was not here by the time Samuel came to find the juvenile.

She gently lifted herself from the elegant red settee and walked to James. She did feel awkward standing next to him, but there was no time to worry. James simply clicked his forefinger and thumb together, conjuring up a mass of lime-green smoke, and they were gone in a flash.

⁓

JAMES CONTINUED FORAGING in Samuel's desk drawers, hoping he might find something of interest, but Ava had a good point, and he couldn't help but agree with her.

"Yes, those that reside in the light are foretold to be good people indeed, but sometimes they lose their way. Just because somebody proclaims to be good doesn't mean they are."

He slammed the final drawer back into Samuel's desk, feeling exasperated that he'd found nothing.

"Well, perhaps he has hidden it somehow, the evidence of whatever you desire to know so badly," Ava muttered sullenly.

She was tired of being holed up with no real notion of what her future was. Ava was still with child and had no idea where she was headed. Obviously, she couldn't stay with Astrid and Isra. And she doubted Prince Jonathan wanted her back at his palace anytime soon. Things were very uncertain for her.

"Hmm. Or maybe there is something we've neglected to notice. If he does indeed have an obsession with the witch Isra, perhaps I've been searching in all the wrong places," James retorted with sheer dismay.

He thought that at least maybe that there would be some shred of a clue somewhere. Even Samuel wasn't known to be an implicitly tidy person.

I've not even got started on my search yet and already I'm coming up with nothing. If Samuel has been in this fine stature for a time, he could have stowed away exactly what we need anywhere. Oh, it's hopeless. He's probably been far too clever than any of us could comprehend.

James huffed impatiently. He was almost ready to abandon his search.

"Or perhaps you could just look where nobody told you to!" a sharp voice piped up from out of nowhere. It sounded shrill, but strangely, it appeared to be coming from the living room.

"Who said that?" James called out. He stopped fumbling around at once and swiftly exited the office, ensuring he reached Ava and took her tagging along with him. "Come; let's see what this is all about."

James and Ava entered Samuel's living room and were astounded at what they saw. It wasn't like anything neither of them had ever seen before. It was more like a bachelor pad than a humble abode of a modest light bringer. As soon as they walked in, they were greeted by a neon pink blanket draped across the middle of a black leather couch. Then, just to the right, was the gilded gold fireplace, burning coal embers, sizzling away that you could hear it amongst the intangible silence. And then there was a perfectly positioned window whereby you could look out onto the wonderful scenery of Spirisity.

There was so much splendour to see. The view was breathtaking. If you looked closely, the glorious green hills of Shambre Fell could be spotted far ahead with that spindling tower sticking out. But the most predominant view was the charming yellow crocuses and violets that carpeted the land so majestically.

"Why, it was me!" the voice chuckled.

James looked around him, bemused, as he couldn't see anyone.

"Hello, you! Over here!" the voice chided loudly.

It was then that James's wandering eyes fell into the shiny, bright purple and black spider. He was adjacent to the left, sitting idly by the window and hanging from a silken silvery web in mid-air.

"Oh, my!" James gasped.

He was shocked to see the creature being so animated. The fellow looked very distinctive in that deep purple colouring with matching purple boots on all of his little spidery legs. James hadn't realised Samuel owned a pet, let alone a quirky arachnid.

"I am sorry. I truly didn't see you," James apologised.

He felt stupid, as Ronald had been desperately trying to catch his attention and James hadn't even batted an eyelid. He didn't think he'd be laying his eyes on a creepy little critter.

"Hey, don't worry about it. I get that all the time," Ronald muttered candidly. "I couldn't help but overhear your predicament. Is it true that the light bringer has become somewhat despondent? See, I know things that in normal circumstances I wouldn't ever hear of..."

Ronald seemed concerned. Maybe he'd observed more of Samuel's digression than he'd cared to.

"He has indeed. It turns out Lady Isra of the Dark has absconded yet again. Samuel apparently had an interest in her, but since nobody can find Isra, we have yet to discover what it is," James explained cautiously, for he didn't know who this critter was. "However, there are concerns that it isn't exactly love and light, if you get my drift... Samuel's been in the business too long. If you ask me, he should have hung up his hat when the whole Astrid and Isra debacle kicked off years ago."

"Oh, dear. Lady Isra of the Dark. Yes, I know of her. She kidnapped my brother three years ago. She made him her slave. He was compelled to live in her wretched basement, until one day, she decided to let him go. I tried avenging him, and now I reside in this disfigured state because Astrid made a deal with the devil, so to speak," Ronald responded awkwardly.

James glanced up at Ronald sheepishly, as he realised just who he was speaking with.

"Uh-huh. I did hear of such. Unfortunately, I am not completely aware of all the details."

James excused himself momentarily. He was being diligent in what he said now, knowing he was in a delicate situation.

Samuel hadn't actually gone into it with James. But it occurred around a month ago that Samuel unearthed the details from "on high" about Astrid capturing a mortal man—Ronald O'Kutte. Alas, Samuel had likewise gained the knowledge that Isra had fallen prey to a curse, thereby fulfilling a prognostication made about her sixteen years earlier. Astrid concluded that Ronald O'Kutte was responsible for Isra exiting after they'd quarrelled.

Little did they both know there was more than this tale originally entailed. Samuel made his latency known to Astrid, giving the men an opportunity to talk for the first time in aeons. Samuel bartered with Astrid, reiterating that if he let Ronald go, he'd be given Isra's location. But in compensation, Samuel ensured Ronald atoned for his impish deed.

And here Ronald was, in this rather frightful new form, created by Samuel. It wasn't thoroughly known what Samuel intended to do with Ronald in the long run, but for now, he'd saved that meagre man's life. Undoubtedly, with James soon to seize control of Spirisity, Ronald's future could well hang in the balance, unless Samuel proposed to take Ronald with him, which was improbable.

"Astrid, the raven-man, was planning to kill me. He concluded I was the cause of his witch vacating. Yes, I placed her under a painstaking spell under the impression she'd executed my brother. Astrid divulged that Isra had freed my brother Kane. Isra had nothing to do with it, and she did not know of it either. It was his closely guarded secret, one that might jeopardise their relationship. As Astrid went on, I learned that Kane had been irrational enough to show up at Shambre Fell after Isra let him go. Isra wasn't there, but that raven-man brutally transformed my brother into their little black cat. I'd killed Kane not knowing who he was. But then this Samuel chap showed up, stating he'd unveil Isra's whereabouts, but only if Astrid spared me and granted him the leeway to deal with me. And he did that, all right. Now I'll feast on flies for the rest of my days, listening to that blithering idiot ramble to himself."

"But Astrid was the bloody reason she disappeared in the first place, or so I've been told..." Ronald trailed off, realising he'd disclosed far more than he initially wanted to. "Yes, but never mind that. It's past. Now, you said Samuel rambles to himself! Just what has he told you? Let me explain who I am. I'm James. I'm soon to be made the new lord and chief of Spirisity."

"Well, he witters on about Isra. How she's a thorn in his side. A prickly foe that won't budge to his will. He's trying to act charismatic one moment and then the next, he's practically spitting his dummy out," Ronald divulged, although there was a short pause as he remembered the most important part of all.

"But the most intriguing part is he wants Lady Isra of the Dark to resurrect a friend of hers. There was some tantalising tidbit about a dark curse, but only if Lady Isra darkened her heart by engaging in an act of true evil; someone who Isra considered more an enemy than a companion, but there was history between the two women. Samuel knows more than he cares to admit, as he told me a most fascinating story, that they both descend from the same father."

"All right now, I know back in the day, there was quite a ruckus between Isra and an old school friend. Oh, now, what is her name? Ellis? No, that's not it. Elena. Nope. Oh, how I am confuzzled. Now, what the hell is it?" James stopped abruptly in a vain attempt to recall Isra's long-time feud with her former partner in crime.

They were both at Wingdom's. Yes, that's correct. Oh, and they had both fallen for that Jonathan fellow... but what was her freaking name? Oh, this is going to irk me so much! Come on. Remember. Wait—not Everilda Daughtry? Because if it's true, that means... Oh, my!!!

"Everilda!" Ronald responded without delay.

"Right, yes. Everilda Daughtry; but you said they have the same father? Isra and Everilda, I mean? How could that possibly be?" James probed with a vexed tone.

He didn't understand how something so huge could have been concealed for so long.

Meanwhile, why didn't anyone tell us? I was involved with Isra back when she was a young thing, preparing to unleash all manner of her shadow side unto those she deemed to have wronged her. Including Everilda. This could have been catastrophic if she'd ever become aware of her paternal lineage. It still could be! How freaking stupendous of Samuel to keep it from us all. Do 'on high' even know? I'll go out on a limb and say not. Goodness gracious, James ranted callously to himself, knowing full well things could get dire if they got back to Isra.

"Samuel said Isra's parents were Damien Daughtry and some

woman living in a lack of finery named Gwendolyn. Damien and Gwendolyn came to Samuel for help when the poor lass couldn't handle infant Isra. Samuel is the only one who knows Isra's true heritage," Ronald admonished.

"That's terrific. Nobody knew! Not a blooming soul? And he kept it all to himself this entire time! Do those 'on high' even know about this?" James quizzed Ronald, although truthfully, he already knew the answer.

"Strangely enough, 'on high' does know. There was a contract drawn up stating Isra's true paternity and that Samuel was to be her guardian. That might be the vital source of information you didn't seek to find. For how can you search for something that you have no awareness of?" Ronald responded curtly.

He was beginning to feel like a sitting duck. He'd just broadcast a most vital clue that James had failed to properly acknowledge, and here the man was, still asking silly questions. Of course, it could have been a simple notion that James refused to believe, but Ronald knew better.

Before he'd been transformed into this hideous creature, he had done a fair bit of studying on the occult. While he hadn't known of this secret regarding Isra, he did know there was quite a lack of understanding on what she was really about. He'd tried quizzing her on how she came to earn the title of Lady Isra of the Dark and naturally, she'd rebuffed him, dismissing it as nothing. But because darkness was deeply rooted in Ronald's family, he knew a thing or two about someone who concealed their true nature. And yes, now he comprehended that Isra didn't murder his brother but still, she remained quite the mystery to him... one that angered him considerably.

"All right." James composed himself. He lowered the tone of his voice as he became calmer. "I know this might come across as an imbecilic question, but where is that contract now?"

James knew there wasn't any purpose in getting riled over it. What was done had already been finalised. Vilifying something because it happened in your absence was most unproductive indeed.

It was a much better stature to be an adult about it rather than throwing a tantrum over something you couldn't have any control over.

"Hmm. That's an excellent question because I do not know," Ronald quickly uttered.

"Yes, well, we need to make an attempt to destroy it, or at least hide it. Keep it well preserved somewhere away from Lady Isra's wandering eyes. And not to mention Astrid, as he is sure to tell her if he finds out. One must ensure that every possible action is taken to prevent chaos from ensuing," James announced matter-of-factly.

He was already acting like the light bringer he was deemed to be. A fantastical approach for somebody to possess when you consider the severity of the situation.

"He might have simply lost it," Ava muttered, sounding quite annoyed.

She'd been lumbered with James back in Spirisity for a while now, and she was wondering when she'd get a reprieve to depart on her lonesome. None of this light versus dark stuff was of any great importance to her.

"No, that's not probable," James muttered softly. "He knows exactly wherein the truth lies. We just have to dig deeper. Where would Samuel place an intricate object that is connected to Isra?" James questioned while Ronald looked back at the soon-to-be light being, absolutely baffled.

"Erm, may I beg your attention, but who gives a fig where the contract is? Likely, you won't ever find it. If Mr. Reynaldi kept it a secret for this long, do you honestly think he'd leave a trail just so somebody could discover this? Have you not learned anything? This is just one of the reasons why it was so easy for Samuel to get away with this charade. He's a mastermind at it, you see. He's not going to pave a pathway saturated in gilded gold, shimmering and glittering the way to what you seek. He's far more calculated than that," Ronald lamented.

"I don't quite fathom your meaning!"

James sounded slightly taken aback. He'd never been spoken down to by a spider before, but this one had a lot to say.

"Well, it's simple enough. You either want the witch back, or you don't. I'd forgo this pandemonium for a moment and concentrate on where she might be. After all, it doesn't matter whether you have the evidence or not at this point, for isn't she the main instrument in Samuel's plan?" Ronald elaborated.

"That she is," James agreed at once.

"Well, screw the formalities, and find the sorceress! That Astrid chap sure wants her back in their sheltered fortress, does he not?"

Ronald continued to pester James with his line of questioning. You'd have thought by now that James was getting irritated by Ronald being so pressing, but one would hate to admit that the arachnid had a point.

"Right you are there, old boy. The thing is, to retrieve Isra, we must find out exactly why she's vanished. It's a very complex matter indeed," James continued dryly.

"Aha, but yet you continue to be distracted by something that won't aid your search, no matter what you do. I've given you the answer you need. She's not here, so I'm rather perplexed as to why you are. All you're doing is delaying the inevitable. Stalling won't get you any further than where you are now. Jeez, if you're the next light bringer, start thinking like one. Take action!" Ronald urged.

"Well, actually, I didn't specifically come here for Isra. I came to deposit Ava while I took the opportunity to ransack Samuel's office. Astrid is the one who's doing the legwork in seeking her out!" James conceded.

"Ah, the young peasant girl who found herself trapped in Samuel's enigmatic web! Why am I not surprised that he wants her head after she backtracked on their deal, if it can even be called that?" Ronald insinuated as a mischievous half-smile appeared on his face.

"I didn't want to back out, but the raven-man, he's frightening, and he scared the freaking life out of me! If I wasn't staying in that awful fortress, things might have been different. He pulled it out of me, you see. The truth. And, well, after I told the Astrid fellow, he said I should stay there until something can be finalised, but I had no idea Mr. Reynaldi would come after me," Ava explained sheepishly, clutching her stomach tenderly.

Ronald observed the girl's bulging belly and remarked, "Oh, I see you have more than your fair share of trouble on your hands. Well, if I was you, I'd stay out of his way. If he's not afraid to go after a most renowned witch known for her wicked power then I'd say you're in very real danger, my girl."

"That's what we are engineering to do," James muttered angrily. "It remains to be seen as to where we can place her. It's normally not the light's responsibility to deal with teenage miscreants, but since Samuel will very literally want her head served on a gilded gold platter..."

James paused as the realisation hit him deeply. *Samuel won't stop until Ava is found. She won't be safe anywhere. Not in Spirisity. Certainly not in Shambre Fell. We can't find a location for her that would be deemed concealed enough in the ethereal realms unless action is taken to prevent such an attack.*

A plan was beginning to emerge in his mind.

"We must do all we can to ensure she is safe. I may have to converse with 'on high,' as none of us expected this. I could see to it that an arrangement is made whereby she can live solely and raise her unborn child. But time is our enemy!" James continued; he'd already made up his mind on how to proceed.

James turned to Ronald with a serious stare. His arms were folded across his chest as he solemnly commanded, "I feel it is best if we do not allow the information of Lady Isra of the Dark's lineage to become public domain. It must remain a mystery to her. You must not ever relay to anyone what you know. Do you hear me, young chap? You will not tell a soul. Astrid cannot ever be allowed to hear of this. He is Lady Isra's counterpart. Trust me when I say he would reveal it to her in a heartbeat. The implications of her knowing would be cataclysmic for us all. I'm telling you that efforts must be doubled if this is to remain a secret for all eternity—"

James stopped midway as he glanced over at Ronald, who was, for once, as quiet as a mouse. His dangly, short, purple legs stirred slightly as wind crept in from the open window that had haphazardly blown into his web.

"If I hear that you may be at risk of divulging this to any personage whether living or dead, I will be forced to extinguish your life immediately," James declared gravely. "I know the love and light business is a comical matter for some, but I take my calling seriously. All jokes aside, I don't think you'll fare terribly well either way."

Ronald was speechless.

James grabbed Ava without hesitation and mouthed solemnly, "Come. I think I know how to move forward from here on. I can't promise that times won't be tough, but at least you'll survive intact."

He departed with Ava in tow, leaving Ronald to contemplate what might become of him now that things were most definitely changing in the realm of Spirisity.

24

"Darkness, my old friend. We meet again. It's been such a long time since I visited, but here we are," Isra softly uttered.

She had fond feelings towards the eloquent mountain peak. She gently placed her hand against the cold grey stone, wondering if it would still emit the same magic frequency she'd felt so long ago.

"To think I had forgotten this place."

Isra marvelled as she carefully held the green glowing orb in her dominant hand while she pulled her left from the mountain. It still stood remarkably well, considering the years had weathered it away. Many chaotic storms had collided with it over time, but it had that enviable character that stood out amongst the deterioration.

Isra continued admiring the grey stone mountain from where she stood. Ironically, the narrow crevice she'd once sheltered in from the torturous rain had now almost completely closed, and there was just a thin slit in which the gaping hole once was. Isra recalled the fateful night in which she'd ripped her heart out, exchanging it for the immortal power with which darkness rewarded her...

The skies were alight like fire. They collided with the night as luminous golden-yellow lightning danced across the melancholic dark-blue skies. Rain hammered down ferociously upon the wretched land while I stood on the edge of that peak, contemplating the biggest decision of my tenure.

Then, the moment came. I let my hand hover against my heart. And with one swift tug, I ripped that entity out of me, offering it up to the darkness.

The rest is a little hazy; I woke up in a daze, but I do remember being interrupted by that rather irksome light bringer, reprimanding me for summoning dragons. Oh, how he got under my skin! Annoying, irritating, pompous little man. The very same fellow NOW expects me to resurrect my arch-nemesis from the darkest depths of the netherworld. One would indeed question his sanity and assume this love and light crap isn't all it's made out to be.

Glamvein was a truly eminent sight to behold. Tempting luscious green grass surrounded it like an island, and it seemed to go on forever while the most dignified part of it stood out amongst the grandeur. Many regarded Glamvein as an eyesore because of the hazardous magics that had been misused by pretentious folk who assumed the power was theirs to wield for their selfish gratifications. Nobody knew its true lineage, but it was abandoned for several years. Isra had infamously reawakened the darkness locked within it only fifteen years ago.

Isra's head shifted, and her glistening green eyes clashed with a sparkling auspicious yellow gleam. The distinct hazel captured her awareness immediately as she sank deep into the enticing void of those warm brown eyes.

"Astrid," Isra purred.

She made sure to show that bright lime-green glowing spectacle as she made her way towards Astrid while clasping the entity in her dominant hand.

"I see you've reclaimed an old friend, eh? I don't have to fathom too hard where that glorious conduit came from, now do I? I guess Samuel outdid himself this time, but I never expected to witness such a feat," Astrid admonished diligently, as he laid sight on the wondrous gleaming green commodity he'd once presented to Isra when they stood together on the famous Neferia Sands.

I had indeed assumed that thing had been destroyed. I watched him shatter that shimmering ball of dark energy into a million glittering pieces. Why in damnation would he bestow it to her after all this time? There's something amiss here. Not once would the Samuel Reynaldi I know ever conduct such an atrocity in the name of love and light. No, the man I knew would have incarcerated it and Isra's sacrimonous magic to boot. He's taken the liberty to not only resurrect that bewitching doohickey but give Isra the power to wield it for whatever reason, of which he's not disclosing, Astrid retorted to himself, pondering on why Samuel might have bestowed such a gracious gift unto Isra.

"Your former employer returned to me what he once stole. It was a nice offering, but he's a rather formidable man. I don't like him much," Isra confessed meekly. "He has some bizarre ideas. I don't agree with his plan for me. It seems quite unorthodox for a light bringer to suggest such a thing to a creature such as myself."

That's a relief. For a second, I thought she might be wholly tempted into engaging his pragmatic belief system, Astrid conferred to himself.

"Well, Samuel hasn't ever been normal, per se. You could say he's quite troubled. I witnessed things back then. A synchronistic string of events made me suspicious of his true calling. He makes all the right noises and even says the right words, but in reality, it's not all it appears to be."

There was a strong hint of hesitation in Astrid's voice. He was in full comprehension now of exactly what was occurring. Astrid realised Samuel was creating this entire show to feature Isra. She was the golden centrepiece in his plan. She was his end game.

Isra was obviously in full awareness of what was expected of her. That was evident. Astrid wasted no time whatsoever as he grasped Isra tightly, pulling her against his chest as he whispered into her ear gingerly, "Dare I ask? Are you going to commit the most ghastly action he demanded that you enact?"

"Oh, so you know about the whole debacle? Death, bloodshed, terror. It's pretty straightforward from there." Isra blushed apologetically, as she suddenly got a glimpse into the mechanics of

Samuel's mind. *So Samuel filled Astrid in on his sordid plan, but let's see if he got the scoop in the same format it was delivered unto me.*

"Don't be naïve. Of course, I know. Samuel made a big ruckus about a prophecy whereby you were foretold to darken your heart by resurrecting someone from the depths of hell. He even insisted that both of these wretched souls will wreak havoc upon the land, and if not stopped, it would be dangerous to the realm and all who reside in it. We both know that's you and Everilda. But I think I know you better than he does. I don't believe you'd enter into such an agreement, as you know what that would entail," Astrid mustered in a low voice.

"If Everilda and I were to be in the same locality, it would be torturous for all concerned! Sure, we buried the hatchet of times gone by, but both she and I possess the same nature at heart. My soul has already been drenched in the blackest of evils. If Evie was to be brought back into this cosmos, she too would be saturated in that darkness. That power is bigger than me. Stronger than her. We'd be able to conduct atrocities that the light beings couldn't even fathom in their worst drawn-out nightmares."

Isra scoffed with melancholy in her voice. Astrid could tell she was being deadly serious, although she ensured humour was placated into the situation.

"I know. I'm not sure if you'd still want me if such a magnetic force was placed in your domain," Astrid conceded with a furrowed brow. "Still, I can't help but find it entertaining for James. There's no way he can handle you. Never mind freaking Everilda as well."

Astrid chuckled with a hint of resentment. Yes, it was no secret he still loved to one-up James, even if they had agreed to pause their vendetta of sorts.

Isra's face lit up at once. Her lime-green piercing eyes glowed ferociously back at him as the sun shimmered a little brighter on this fine afternoon. It was ironic, considering this fortress was dominated by shadows. Very rarely did the sun make an appearance in Glamvein.

Isra's eyes narrowed at Astrid sceptically as she flashed him a wicked half-smile.

"Don't be preposterous. Please, like I'd ever consider such a thing. I was quite impressed at how you handled sweet little Cora this morning. I bet the poor tempestuous thing is in a better place now," Isra cooed sweetly.

"You liked that, huh? Me destroying your little plaything with one fatal swoop. Interesting," Astrid marvelled comically. "Do tell me, what is your fascination with putting people into glass jars? I certainly find it intriguing."

Astrid eagerly awaited her candid response.

"It is true. I preferred her to be in the glass jar I incarcerated her into. I guess one can adapt to the nature of things. But I think you saw me do vile things over the long tenure we've known each other, and so naturally, you wanted to unleash your devilish virility unto the world. My dear, sweet Astrid wanted to play," Isra retorted playfully, her voice sounding as sweet as honey.

Astrid smirked. He said nothing. A crude smile materialised on his face that told Isra all she needed to know.

"Oh, so that's it?" Astrid quizzed in a seductive tone. He got up close to Isra so that his nose was touching hers intimately as he whispered into her ear, "Are you worried I'll take your place as head villain?"

"Never," Isra responded. She lifted her midnight-blue cloak over her head as she proceeded to walk away from him.

So why run then, huh? Astrid thought.

He was blown away at how Isra was reacting. Samuel must have done a number on her for sure! Astrid darted straight after Isra as she was contemplating vanishing from the mountain peak.

"Come back here! We've got this small matter of discussing how we're going to deal with Samuel," he called out after her.

"I'm sure whatever you'll come up with will fit him mighty fine," Isra responded; completely dismissing Astrid.

Astrid couldn't believe the sheer nerve of her. *Oh, my lord. She's pressing my buttons today. Can it get any more predictable at this point?*

The light versus dark charade has reached its peak, and she's right at the centre of it all. One can only imagine just what he offered her in exchange for enacting subterfuge on his behalf!

He was completely bewildered as to why Isra was behaving in this strange manner. She was his counterpart, for goodness sake. They were soon to be wed in unholy matrimony. The thought of Samuel having succeeded in getting to her at the core made Astrid feel very uneasy indeed.

Astrid darted after Isra, reaching for her left hand as he forced it to collide with his own. His grip was rigid; there was no way Isra was going to be able to vamoose like she usually would in awkward situations.

"Hey. I'm not done with you yet. It appears I've upset you. That plagues me greatly," he mustered calmly, lowering his voice so that it was just audible.

The light breeze that fluttered about in the January winds made Isra's golden hair blow haphazardly, making her shimmery green eyes stand out even more in the grandeur.

"Oh, it's not that. It's all of this. This Samuel chap showed up out of nowhere, greeting me like I'm some queen of the realms. He's almost freaking lying at my feet, worshipping me. It's unfathomable. Then I remember it all, just like it was yesterday, and suddenly, I realised I know exactly who he is. He was right by my side the entire sodding time... and so were *you*. But why in blazes didn't you ever tell me?"

Isra questioned Astrid with a furrowed brow. Her glowing green eyes stared him dead in the face, but she was so perfectly silent in her stance that she didn't even blink. Not for a second.

Astrid swallowed. Isra had a point. He'd been invested in her life for many years. They'd shared one adventure after another. They'd almost unleashed Armageddon upon the world. There were downcast moments where she'd been in the deepest despair and yet he'd never said two words to her about it until three years ago, where he'd carefully engineered his return into her dominion.

"Without your memories, I seriously doubted you'd ever believe me. Supposing I had come back right after Nefaria Sands? What would you have done? And what if Samuel took matters further, castrating me into one of his hideously contorted forms whereby I'd have no opportunity whatsoever to escape his clutches? I had no choice but to lurk in the shadows, eagerly awaiting the moment I could make my entrance," Astrid blurted out awkwardly.

That's it. The cat is out of the bag. Only time will tell if she is receptive to my most dignified reverie.

Astrid breathed a sigh of relief. He'd finally discharged the most revealing notion he'd wanted to bring to Isra for the longest time. Isra said nothing. She was deep in her thoughts, processing all that Astrid had relayed to her as she stood sullenly on the edge of the cliff's peak.

Astrid loosened his grip on Isra's hand, thus releasing it from his grasp. "I'm sorry," he mustered rawly. "I never, ever expected Samuel would be the one we'd be fighting. I always thought he'd hang on to the goodness of it all until the very end, that his demise would be due to being caught in the crossfire of mystical warfare. I was mistaken."

This seemed to alleviate Isra's unyielding demeanour, encouraging her to relax somewhat as she came to her own conclusions about everything. "I suppose that we will never know," she said in a pensive tone.

"Still, one appreciates the sentiment. I've experienced betrayals that were far more sinister. Well, as thrilling as this was, I must depart," Isra muttered sombrely.

She had a lot to consider. However, Astrid didn't appreciate the gesture. As Isra proceeded to exit the vicinity, she turned her back on her counterpart much to his sheer annoyance.

"Hey. We're not finished here. You'd best get back here now, or I'll—"

Astrid had his arms folded neatly across his chest while he flashed Isra a deathly sober riveting glance. Isra spun around at once. She had the biggest grin on her face.

She quizzed sweetly, "You'll do what exactly, sweetness?"

Oh, that does it. She's pushed it way beyond the parameters this time.

I'm not tolerating this. She was once a rebellious witch who will remain one until the end of time. We've got much to do at this juncture, and she's trading near venomous rancour with me. Darn it. No more Mr. Nice Astrid. No, sir! Astrid retorted to himself gravely as he contemplated why on earth Isra was yet again acting in this offbeat manner.

Astrid detected in the heat of the moment that the sun was gradually fading away. Sundown would soon be upon them. They would have to get a move on if his vigorous plan was going to be a victory.

He looked at Isra for a split second, staring into her eyes while carefully examining all there was to see. Those piercing green beings valiantly glowed back at him like shining emeralds as the daylight withered away. And it was in that precious, sacred moment between them that Astrid knew exactly what to say.

"You cast spells! Mesmerising sorceries designed to enrapture their designated martyr. Well, I will start casting my little array of enchantments," he paused, lowering his voice, "with my lips."

Isra lowered her firmness as she marvelled, "Well, I'd like to see that one in action."

"Oh, I believe you soon will."

Astrid chuckled. He slyly moved in for a kiss as Isra's piercing lime-green eyes dazzled back at him. It was sneaky of him, as he had his hands swaddled around Isra's waist while holding his body strenuously against Isra's right hand, which was still laboriously latched onto that glistening green orb. He was shrewdly thwarting Isra from making a quick getaway, although with that shiny, radiant spectacle he sure as hell didn't want her flying off without him, as, no doubt, Samuel was waiting for the chance to snatch it back from her.

Astrid took his focus off Isra and the glimmering entity for a moment as he changed his tone to one of propriety. He was still fixated on her, but anyone could see the raven-turned-man was tense.

"I know this isn't of the most immense importance to you, but we must discuss the impending matter at hand. I know you've been the main fixture in Samuel's plan, but I have a means of blighting his little avaricious mirage in the bud. Not only that, but it may well send him packing to the murkiest plains of extinction. Nonetheless, I do need you to cooperate with me. Don't flake on me now, girl. Not when we've accomplished so much thus far. Things are about to get far more serious than you've ever imagined, and so I need you with me. All the way," Astrid instructed Isra as he devised his plan.

Isra's eyes softened as Astrid veered in, lustfully kissing her once more. Her eyes met his as she found she was unrestrainedly impertinent as to what he had in mind.

"Your former boss has some very unusual ideas in affiliation to darkness. He's supposed to be one of those prim and proper, love and light types, but, alas, he is not. His approach flabbergasts me as to why he'd want me to rouse Everilda from her slumber, but I suppose his end game is one that will delight himself and not the macrocosm he presumes to be so important," Isra said guardedly as her eyes narrowed at Astrid once again. "All right, dear heart. I'm listening. So what are your intentions?"

"We're both indestructible. Nothing can take us away from this hideous cosmos. I have a scheme that will shift the face of things infinitely. But those good and charitable folks at Spirisity may well be tottering in their boots at the probability of it," Astrid disclosed lightly as he pointed at Isra's chest.

"You ripped your heart out once. You sold it to the darkness. What I propose is in lieu of offering it up on a plate to the most atrocious of hells; on this opportunity, we reform the stratagem. I'll tear my heart out of my chest, but rather than seducing the indomitable authorities, we consolidate our hearts simultaneously, as one, so that they collide with that same undeniable force you used once before. But we're not handing over our souls to the seclusion here. No; we're forming a steadfast alliance with it. Uniting our hearts as one. Neither one of us will ever be able to be surmounted. Together, with our connected energies, we will have everyone at Spirisity and 'on high' running for sanctuary. We will be impervious," Astrid forebode with a grin.

Isra's eyes lowered at once. *He wants us to merge. He is suggesting that he too pull his heart out, but this time, it will accompany my own.*

We'll be connected in ways the others can't even dare envision. Two immortals; a force to be reckoned with. This Samuel lad may well be running for the hills, though time will tell if he's got the stomach for what he's about to behold because, boy, is it about to get heated, Isra thought.

Oh, dear Samuel Reynaldi was about to get a lot more than he'd bargained for.

"It's not what I expected you to say, but one must admit, it is ingenious. Of course, I am indeed wondering just how we might enact this devilish feat?" Isra questioned with a sly half-smile. Evidently, she was impressed with his efforts in vanquishing the estranged light bringer.

Astrid laughed before breathing softly on Isra's neck as he whispered once more, "Well, I hear that two magically inclined folk are about to get hitched, so what better occasion to make it official, eh? Hey, hear me out on this one. It's the ultimate marriage. We weld our two hearts together, proclaiming our esteemed desire to one another, and then we make our intentions known to the universe. Samuel will never see it coming, and James, well, he won't be best pleased either, but once it's done, girl, that's it. It's game over. And then I'll bring you with me to the kingdom of Spirisity. The world will know just who we truly are," Astrid announced proudly.

He was thrilled to present Isra to the lands as his high priestess to govern them all, and with him perfectly positioned by her side, they'd be unstoppable.

"Aha. The plot does indeed simmer and come to a grinding halt," Isra stated wickedly.

"That it does, my love. Anyhow, we need to conduct this ceremony of ours, and while I'd have desired nothing more than to do it in the sacred spot where you first made that grand gesture..." Astrid trailed off mid-thought, realising he had a small flaw in his plan.

Wait, we can perform the tearing out of our hearts in this prestigious land and then go to Nefaria. Samuel wouldn't be smart enough to presume we'd revisit that location after being caught unawares by him before. No. He'd be off gallivanting everywhere but Nefaria Sands. Yes, that's how we'll play this. Sometimes, to have the upper hand, one has to think strategically beyond the parallels one has become accustomed to.

Astrid chuckled away in thought before realising he'd left Isra standing in front of him, still completely unaware of his plan.

"You know? I think I've got this in the bag. We do our little endearing heart ceremony here, and then we shall journey to Nefaria Sands. Do you remember it? The serene island coated in buttery-lemon sand. As you recall, it's so bright that it almost shimmers white in the glossy sunlight. With those tranquil cerulean-blue waters that idly surround it, cleverly secluding it from all else, nobody will ever think we'd be having a quaint rendezvous there," Astrid recited with confidence.

"I love how your mind works. All the fuckery in the macrocosm still cannot belittle your intelligence," Isra gushed with a wide-eyed grin as she swallowed while glancing back at Astrid. "So, I guess we'll be freeing the black furies in a moment or two, huh? It's been a while for me."

"Hmm, and for me," Astrid answered, unanticipated.

This provoked Isra to have a steadfast twinkle in her lime-green florid eyes as she found this news somewhat alluring.

"But I was the one who completely handed over my heart up to the infernal faction on that momentous stormy night. I still recall the deluge striking against my skin. As every drop battered my head at such an accelerated speed, it ricocheted off me as though I was unadulterated electricity, an essence that could not be tinkered with."

Astrid's gaze became seriously foreboding as he looked Isra straight in the eye, uttering, "Oh, you were that, all right. Within seconds of you holding that broken, tattered heart of yours up to the pitch-black midnight skies, vast amounts of golden-yellow lightning danced across the hemisphere. I was bold enough to watch the illumination show you had put on. Eventually, the rain stopped. The lightning dissipated, and you were so exhausted when you returned to consciousness that you almost collapsed. When I looked in on you afterwards, you were sound asleep in that enigmatic little mountain crevice. And then, when I came back to check in, you stood eloquently with that charming creature you'd magicked out of nowhere. Franco, yes; that was his name. And then, of course, Samuel materialised, so I had to make myself scarce while he attempted to talk you 'round to his way of thinking," Astrid explained cautiously.

"Aha, so you were spying on me then?" Isra probed sarcastically, although Astrid detected a tinge of humour in her mannerism; evidently, she wasn't cross with him.

"Technically," Astrid admitted with a sly laugh. "Samuel originally asked me to keep watch on you, but after you'd turned the tide, he had no bloody clue as to what shenanigans you were conducting anyway, even though he'd asked me to stay away. He tried enlisting James, although he was a rookie, and a shoddy one at that. If it wasn't for me, they'd have never been able to discover anything about you. For a bunch of almighty love and lighters, they were incredibly stupid," Astrid joked.

The thought occurred to him that he'd been Samuel's little messenger from day one.

"Ha. Well, I always knew I was being watched. Even in the blackest of nights, somebody out there was carefully eyeballing me from the shadows. Just answer me one question. How the hell did I never catch you?"

Isra probed him with a wide-eyed stare. She was deadly serious. If Astrid had been so thorough in his work, keeping tabs on her ever-changing movements, surely he must have struggled to keep his beady eye on her one at least one occasion.

"Pffft. I was more worried about being caught by Samuel. After a time, he warned me to steer clear of you at all costs. He even threatened to banish me, which he eventually followed through on. But damn, there were times when your gleaming eyes almost witnessed me and I flew off. I guess none of that is any concern of ours now," Astrid admonished with a furrowed brow as he looked upwards at the dreary grey skies.

"It's time," Astrid urged Isra gently.

He pointed up at the melancholic skies; now, the sun had clearly disappeared from view.

"That's an immense piece of avoidance, baby, but all right; here we go."

Isra motioned, sounding slightly irritated that Astrid hadn't elaborated further on his stalking of her, although she had an inkling that there was way more he could divulge on the subject.

"Come on now. Let's not dilly dally. I haven't got the tolerance for any messing about," Astrid reprimanded Isra sharply.

"Right. I guess it's time to welcome back the ye olde black magic," Isra mustered with a sly half-smile as she stood awkwardly.

Astrid wasted no time in extending his hand before he linked Isra's with his own. Grasping it tightly, he closed his eyes as he responded sarcastically, "Oh, please, girl. Don't expect me to believe for one moment that you discarded the forbidden arts for something light and fluffy. We both know it's a load of bollocks…" He trailed off as he felt something surging at the base of his chest. A tight pressure generously encircled his heart. It was increasing by the second, but Astrid still had a sense of humour despite the seriously dark event occurring as he recited, "Anyway, white magic is no fun."

"Ha! Coming from you, dear, that is indeed a riveting notion. You should know better than to toy with the forces in such a way." Isra scoffed with melancholy as she too closed her eyes in rapturous delight.

"Enough already, or it won't just be Samuel getting a magical bitch-slapping," Astrid rebutted in an austere tone, although since he had an enormous grin plastered on his face, it was wholly challenging for Isra to decipher whether he was being deliberate or not.

However, before Isra could ruminate further, she heard a sharp crackling sound that distracted her, a thunderclap rumbling vociferously from above. Blackness began descending from the downtrodden, overcast skies. The sky was completely saturated in pure obsidian. Nonetheless, neither Isra nor Astrid could see it, as both had their eyes closed.

Isra immediately thought of some sardonic come-back to throw over to Astrid. *A mystical spanking, eh? Wonders will truly never cease. I'd love to see you try, dear!*

But she was soon thwarted as her chest began to pound incessantly as the vociferous pressure intensified around her heart. Her heart momentarily stopped for a few seconds, although it felt like forever as it slowed to a grinding halt. Now there was this buzzing sound echoing around her chest as it began to irritate her greatly. The urge was immeasurable as the annoying sensation became too much. Isra reached deep inside the walls of her chest, desperately searching as she moved her fingers inside her internal organs.

Instantaneously, she felt her finger catch upon the precious entity. Isra didn't hesitate in snatching the darling commodity inside her. The pain that ensued was excruciating as it surged inside Isra's body. The back of her head burned as the vast pressure continued working its way through her body. For a moment, the dizziness alone was enough to make her want to blackout, but somewhat reluctantly, Isra latched on to her heart and pulled it out triumphantly and held it in the palm of her hand.

Silently holding it, she awaited the moment when everything would come full circle.

Astrid was barely paying a scrap of attention as the world surged above him. The blackness continued to multiply as harsh, dense clouds infiltrated the illustrious midnight-blue skies. He had a firm handle on the situation, eagerly focused on the chaos being enacted upon his heart.

The pain hardly phased him as he felt his heart tightening inside his chest. The never-ending expansion of it was so swift and increasing vastly by the second that there was no other alternative. He'd have to dig deep, reach inside, and remove that doohickey from his body before it agitated his nervous system anymore.

Taking his entire hand, he rummaged around before he reached his destination, clutching onto that ever-bulging being as he tugged it out of his body. He held it in his hand as it vibrated away, cleverly matching his pulse, which was in overdrive.

"It's showtime," Astrid retorted candidly with a smug grin. "The love and light brigade won't stand a chance after this."

Isra couldn't help but find amusement despite her calamity as she responded swiftly, "Why, Astrid. It's just like you to one-up those poor souls! All right, let's be having you, dear!"

"You first," Astrid urged in a low voice.

He stood holding his beating heart as he awaited Isra to tempt the dark forces above. The sky was saturated in pure black. There wasn't a single star to be seen amongst the unwavering amount of clouds that had materialised while Isra and Astrid were conducting their ritual.

"Good golly. Here we go again..." Isra muttered.

She wasn't sure whether she should be entertained or irritated by Astrid's sardonic commentary. Gently taking a deep breath, Isra raised her dominant hand with her heart enclosed in her fist up to the murky skies. Slowly, she lifted it higher, offering it the mystical platitude above as she recited cautiously, "Darkness, my old friend. Here we meet again. Take my heart. Covered in darkness. Unleash your wretched power, but first of all, allow it to merge with my beloved's at this timely hour."

This was Astrid's cue. He carefully raised his right hand, clutching his heart, to the skies in symmetrical alignment with Isra's so both of their hearts were directly parallel to one another as they waited to be accepted.

It was only a fleeting moment of reticence before the celestial spheres acknowledged this dark desire. An excessive rumbling of thunder could be heard from above. It was vastly echoing throughout the land as it shook every living being down to its core. Black lightning glittered across the weary, darkened skies before torrential rain began plummeting onto Isra and Astrid's heads, saturating them in its cleansing power, before a shimmery gold light peaked through amongst the dense blackness.

At the centre of Isra and Astrid's hearts, this gold light began to get brighter while the black lighting continued to collide upon the acreage. There were barely any stars to be seen as all was blanketed in the black fury.

The speck of gold that had risen from within their hearts had now absolutely illuminated them so that the skies were alight with a blazing gold gleam. It was at this juncture that the deluge had slowly begun to dissipate to a trickle. The thunder came to a grandiose halt. The lightning simmered from glittering obsidian indignation pummelling the skies to just a tiny flare, gleaming in the celestial spheres.

Astrid was the first to open his eyes as he realised he now had Isra's heart in the palm of his hand. He reached for her, squeezing her heart inside her carcass, which caused her to jolt with ferocity, bringing her back to life as her senses rekindled inside her body. Isra's piercing green eyes blinked open at once, and she realised she was now holding her beloved's heart whereby her own should have been awaiting her.

You see, this was the most wondrous thing about the powerful merge they'd just performed with the cosmos. They'd both gifted one another with the endowment of trusting the other with their most cherished possession... knowing how fragile that precious commodity was if for any reason they were to break their bond.

Isra held his heart ardently before jabbing it into Astrid's chest. This caused him to convulse temporarily as his alertness returned.

"Well, wasn't that an exciting jaunt?'" he spouted. "Hey now, who wouldn't feel empathy for the love and light army after this, eh? I practically feel contrite for the deplorable dumbasses."

Astrid beamed evilly. Isra smirked at Astrid's discourteous assertion. Both she and Astrid were already imperishable but now they'd incorporated their benevolence, interweaving it with one heinous aptitude. They'd be altogether unstoppable. And unkillable. No matter what hoodwinks the love and lighters endeavoured to fire at them.

Almost, dear. Relatively so, Isra chuckled to herself as she speculated just how those forlorn dimwits would proceed when she and Astrid happened to emerge in their promised lands.

Oh, dear! This certainly wasn't going to be favourable for Samuel; and his apprentice, soon-to-be light bringer, James. You'd be hazarding your life that he'd rapidly be deprecating his ill-timed decision to use Lady Isra of the Dark in his loathsome stratagem.

"Well, we'd best get a move on. It's a fair way to dear old Nefaria. The sands of sin await you, my lady," Astrid announced warmly, holding out his vacant hand for Isra to join him in anticipation of their journey.

25

Isra held Astrid's hand as tightly as she could muster. Squeezing it, she kept her eyes shut. Now that her memories had come back to her, Isra tried to picture Nefaria Sands from before, although it appeared to be somewhat of a blur. The real thing would indeed have to suffice.

I wish I could remember. There was nothing but pale yellow surrounded by those icy-blue hues as the waters rushed upon us. It was a beautifully sunlit day, where the glowing entity was so bright I was almost blinded by its brilliance. Oh, my! Isra gasped abruptly as one of her memories had returned to her as clear as day.

"All right. We're here," Astrid muttered calmly as he recited, "so feast your eyes on this spectacular landmark!"

Isra's piercing green eyes lit up at once as she marvelled at the shimmery yellow sand dominated by rich blue hues and gentle waves crashing against the shore. Nefaria hadn't changed in the slightest. It was still the same beautiful location that once made Astrid announce it was something out of a subliminal dream.

"Well, I must say. It's prettier than ever," Isra gushed. "Although I recall it more vividly now. You and I stood here. You handed me that glowing orb of wicked energy, and then that Samuel man appeared.

Isn't it funny how that stands out amongst the rest of the memories that were lost for aeons?" Isra asked with curiosity as she flashed him her trademark wide-eyed stare.

"It doesn't surprise me at all. But truthfully, we're not here to reminisce. Not in the greater scheme of things anyhow," Astrid admonished in a gruff voice. "In fact, the last time I checked, I'm attempting to marry a witch. One would presume to question whether she wants the same thing as yet again, she's stalling the beautiful process."

He eyed her slim figure carefully, noting the delicate white lace nightgown that clung to Isra's small frame while being majestically covered by her midnight-blue velvet cloak. He waved a finger at Isra in a disapproving manner.

"No, this just won't suffice at all. We must do better. Hmm..."

He trailed off as he began thinking of what would be suitable to fit his fine preferences.

"This charming ensemble, as much as I like it, well, it lacks flair, and I want something more refined, so let's see," Astrid mumbled to himself as he closed his eyes, imagining a gleaming white light encircling Isra, starting from the top of her head.

It slowly descended her body, saturating her in its white brilliance before she was revealed in a low-cut bandeau wedding gown. It was tight on the waist, showcasing her slender frame, and completely adorned in sparkling opals down the skirt that dragged beautifully on the sandy floor. Isra's golden-white hair was half tied up with a diamond clasp while the rest flowed effortlessly in the breezy sea winds. Her glowing green eyes looked mesmerising as she shimmered perfectly in the sun's light.

"Damn. Don't you look splendid? But wait, one must fit the bill if one is truly going to match your rich splendour," Astrid exclaimed.

He couldn't believe just how amazing Isra looked. She stood there so eloquently; it was almost as if she was a mirage rather than his fortuitous bride to be. Astrid clicked his fingers, and before you knew it, he was standing there, very dapper in a black suit jacket and matching trousers that were perfectly tucked into a tight-fitting, crisp, white silk shirt.

"Well, finally, we match. So now I think it's time we strengthen the bonds of unholy matrimony, hmm? Hey, I'm a traditionalist, but both you and I are one of the same. Violently oppressed by the vileness of the light. We've been seduced by the compelling fantasies of the dark. There's no escaping that, no matter what conniving tricks they attempt to play. It's futile, baby."

"That we are, my love, but what is one to do when one is held down within the stronghold that many of these wretched folk call life?" Isra asked inquisitively, wondering why he was so peppy on this subject matter.

"Create a new one. Master the illusions of your mind. Transcend your destiny. Go farther than anyone has ever expected you to propel beyond their expectations. Throw them the biggest curveball the universe has in store when they realise you've not only succeeded but done far better than they ever imagined!" Astrid elaborated in a low voice.

He seemed proud of himself. It was as though there was something inside him that was just beaming, ready to unleash unto the world, and now he was simply preparing for it.

Isra gasped unexpectedly, lowering her gaze for a second as she perused deep into Astrid's bewildering eyes. "I think I understand you more than I dare to admit. Your body is entwined with my own. Your heart aligned with mine. It's no coincidence that we are where we stand right now. And in many ways, dear heart; you facilitated it. In your way, you saw what fate was going to bestow, and you intervened. It's admirable that someone such as yourself risked everything just to get to me."

Isra gently strode forward, bringing her mouth to Astrid's ear as she whispered, "I remember, love. I've seen it. You were there with me all along."

Astrid reached for Isra's hands, grabbing tightly to them as he held them inside his own. "I did many things pertaining to you that went against the code of not only the light but Samuel's ruling. I don't regret it for a moment. If given the opportunity, I'd enact the very same in a heartbeat. Lady Isra, my one true counterpart and life partner, will you please do me the honour of synthesising our hearts and minds as one? Consolidating our union to the highest order?" Astrid asked Isra proudly.

"That, I will," she answered quickly.

Isra was very much drawn by every word that rolled off Astrid's tongue. It was as though she was under a trance. She found herself deeply transfixed by all he had to say.

"And will you promise to be faithful and true eternally until the very time when immortality ceases to exist between us?" Astrid pressed Isra again as he enunciated his meaning.

"I solemnly shall as long as we both shall reign together in these current forms we inhabit," Isra responded softly, not taking her eyes off Astrid for a moment.

"Do you decree to be forever bonded to me? Merging our hearts into one whole and staying true to our connection no matter what damage or peril comes our way? Do you swear to be mine, no matter what the circumstance? No matter what hell or earth deems to throw unto us to cascade us into chaos?" Astrid asked finally as he took an unexpected glance at the scenery around him.

An orange gleam stared him in the face. It illuminated Isra, contrasting brilliantly with her white gown as she stood out against the sunset that had magically appeared out of nothingness. The serene yellow glow of the sun's rays that descended upon the beautiful land of Nefaria shone wondrously against the yellow sand.

Isra stood triumphantly and said, "That, I shall do. Until the end of eternity, whenever that may be, but one would deem it to be never."

Isra noticed the warm, illuminated glow dissipate as clouds began to form above her and Astrid.

"I now declare you, Isra, as my wife. My divine confidant. My eternal lover. The ties that bind us are now entwined, and so shall you kiss me." He breathed into her ear as their hands were still locked together in an embrace. "I mean, quite frankly, I'd be extremely disappointed in you if you didn't."

Her lips fell upon his. His arms clung to her waist and they sank into each other in a passionate embrace. Astrid then thoughtfully glanced over at Isra's bare fingers while he was still holding them tightly.

"Ah, I knew I missed something. Wait," he said imperviously as he zoned in on her tiny, delicate hand, paying close attention to her forefinger as he imagined a dark, shimmery emerald energy dropping onto Isra's hand.

She could only look on in amazement as the vibrant magnitude collided into her skin, causing a tingling sensation. A small heart shape slowly materialised on her wedding finger. The powerful surge of energy intensified as it solidified. It then came to a halt as a sparkling heart-shaped emerald ring with a gold band was left on her finger.

"Oh, my! Now that is something to be envious of," Isra marvelled as she admired the beautiful heart-cut emerald by moving her hand closer to the sunlight.

"I'm glad you think so. There could only be one dynamic green stone suitable for you. I trust you approve of my choice of precious materials?" he asked as he pulled her in close so that her body rested comfortably against his chest.

Isra locked eyes with her newly wedded husband. Her mind was awash with the tantalising feeling of joy. She allowed herself to be sucked into it even though it wasn't her forte. Astrid pulled her closer to him so that there was no room for her to escape his warm-blooded body. It was then that Isra suddenly made the move of looking deeper into Astrid's eyes, only to find that familiar slicked-back black hair and sky-blue eyes staring back at her...

Goodness gracious, she couldn't believe it. She clasped a hand to her mouth as she uttered, "Oh, my. He really is everywhere, isn't he?"

The vision of Samuel swiftly dissipated, but Astrid was left looking perturbed, undoubtedly questioning why his wife was being so off-colour.

"Who is?" Astrid questioned.

"I looked into your eyes for a moment, and there he was, smug and smiling as he stared back at me relentlessly," Isra admitted as she looked rather perplexed.

She reluctantly allowed herself to be held by Astrid as he lovingly held her while also thinking of some diligent way to proceed further.

"Oh." Astrid paused with a look of concern and then abruptly pressed her further. "Wait. I don't need to ask, do I? I guess he really does need to feel included in every last thing pertaining to you."

"That, he does, my love. The real question is, how does one deal with someone that continues to persist this line of inquiry whereby the subject is uninterested in anything he has to say?" Isra asked, as she too flashed a worried glance.

"Then maybe it's time you and I make an appearance in the realm of Spirisity because he needs a good talking to," Astrid muttered crossly before pulling Isra against him tightly. "I think this little obsession of his needs to end once and for all."

26

Newly married and ready to cause all manner of havoc, Isra stood a few inches behind Astrid as he concentrated on the heavily cagey blockade between Spirisity and the non-metaphysical lands. The head light bringer and chief Samuel Reynaldi had enamoured it so that no one could penetrate unless they had a concession from the light lands. Of course, Isra was stained with immorality so the only way she was getting past Samuel's contriving bolt was by having Astrid inaugurate it on her behalf.

Isra was getting frustrated as Astrid murmured some words stumblingly while checking out the locality. He looked like a bundle of nerves, as he kept glancing across his shoulder. Notably, this was to assure that nobody was observing while he executed his feat. After all, he was about to slip Isra into the divine land of Spirisity.

She's forbidden to enter. I'm just unlocking the door, but you can bet your life they won't be best pleased when we make our admittance. It will be something that remains in their minds for centuries to come, how the dark infiltrated the shiny holier-than thou-lands so scrupulously guarded, and did so right under their noses, Astrid chorused away in logical thought.

"Could you please hurry up, love? I'm getting antsy," Isra called out from behind him.

She was shuddering in a distinguished black tight-fitting lace gown that exquisitely clung to her angular body. The dress was quite the apparel, deftly cut off the shoulder, augmenting her bust and her derriere, as the long black sleeves went all the way down to her hands.

"I'm doing the best I can muster here. How about you give me a moment so I can bust open the damn gateway?!" Astrid snarkily responded.

He was still carefully reciting some hushed words under his breath, taking care that he was not heard, for that would inevitably be reprehensible if the wrong ears happened to be nosing about.

"Well, the way you are progressing, we'll still be here in the adjoining century," Isra uttered in a distasteful tone.

She corrugated her arms, frowning at him rashly. For some reason, Astrid seemed to find great delight in this. He snorted laughter amidst his gruelling task.

"Yes, dear. Patience," he chortled. It always made him howl with laughter at how eager she got in such little time. "Besides, we will still be around in a hundred years. We're unsinkable, you silly fool."

He turned to take a peek at Isra's facial expressions, but he saw she was still remarkably ticked off.

"No doubt of that, my love. Get a move on," she ordered.

She tapped her right foot onto the hallowed ground that ferociously defended the entrance to Spirisity. Astrid attempted to block out his wife's peevishness for a moment and fixated on the gleaming archway that stood before him. Closing his eyes, he returned to his buried concentration as he depicted the borders opening up for him as they always had before.

The serene verdant green archway brightened with neon green flames. The heat coming off them was enough to alarm someone who wasn't wholly experienced in what they were conducting, but Astrid was well-seasoned in these matters.

Astrid appreciated better than anybody that the aggressive eerie green flashes were there to avert any abject individual that might have assumed themselves desirable enough to come in. Astrid had executed this detailed ritual more times than he cared to realise. It was less than a second afterwards that they gingerly stretched back so that a confined crack could be seen among the flames. Astrid snatched the opportunity, jerking Isra by the arm, and he hurriedly ambled through with her in tow.

"Oh, we're going in, huh? I thought you'd be dilly-dallying a moment longer," Isra precipitously acknowledged, as she was displeased at being wrenched by her arm without admonition.

"Yes. We're going in. Come on!"

He moaned at her impatiently as the glistening green archway at Spirisity's entrance all at once became awash with pure, blazing, white incandescent energy as Astrid and Isra stepped through.

"Well, isn't this whimsical?"

Isra gasped in astonishment as she aroused the memory of her earlier visit to Spirisity approximately fifteen years ago. The golden crocus heads were wavering in the chilly air among the green pasture that circulated across the acreage. Tiny violets were sprinkled far and wide, but the most momentous of all was the tall grey citadel that was a condominium to the light bringer, Samuel Reynaldi. Not dismissing from mind were the egregious grey stone steps that led up to the door. However, Isra was centred on the exquisite bluebells that integrated the exceptional harmony of abundant green and affluent yellow.

"It is. Anyway, we don't have time. Let's go."

Astrid hauled her away from her dawdling. He didn't want anyone to witness their outlandish entrance.

Samuel sat idly on his doorstep, whiskey tumbler in hand, admiring the charming scene around him.

For an early January evening, the sunset was illuminating. Orange hues dominated the serene blue skies. The greenery of Spirisity had never looked more magical. Bright, sunny, yellow crocus heads stuck out amongst all the deep violets that beautifully blended in with the green grass ever so effortlessly, then to the left of Samuel, beyond the pasture, delicate bluebells swayed ever so gently in the gracious winter wind.

You'll soon be done here, old chap. It's a pity Isra wasn't more lenient, but one cannot be responsible for a witch's rebellious desire to go against what they deem right. I have no idea if she'll do it or not. If she does go all the way and resurrect Everilda Daughtry from the gut-wrenching netherworld, well, let's just say it would be a spectacle for all concerned. James has no idea what he's volunteered himself into. Sure, he was going to be called the next light bringer, but if the boy had any brains, he'd be skedaddling as far as his skinny legs could carry him. Never mind, eh? Peasants will be peasants, after all, Samuel thought as he swigged a huge gulp of whiskey, sighing reluctantly.

Still, won't it be amusing, as no doubt Astrid has no inclination whatsoever of my rendezvous with the witch in question. I feel he was truly wasted on us. He spent so many years fighting the good fight in my gracious hospitality, and then kaboom. WITCH! And then it's all gone to pot, and practically overnight. Oh, dear. What a calamity. I bet he's not wanting to see Everilda's smug face. Ha. Lady Isra of the Dark and her arch-nemesis together again. More beautifully brutal than ever. It's almost fucking poetic.

Samuel scoffed ardently.

To think that he'd soon be leaving this place didn't seem right. Spirisity had been Samuel's home for many years. He'd been the law and order of the infamous mystical realm for decades but James was taking over, and he'd have to vacate the premises. It was somewhat of a sour note as he looked out onto the majesty of the land, but ultimately, Samuel had made his decision.

Samuel was sore over the fact he'd not managed to catch up with Isra, so he had no idea whatsoever if she'd fulfilled the prophecy. Isra was a rebellious soul at heart, so who knew if she'd gone for it; but he didn't have much time left.

Samuel necked the rest of his whisky eagerly before placing the tumbler by his side. It was beautiful out there, and he admired the view before him. However, he became distracted when he heard something rustling. Samuel looked directly ahead, and there she was.

Those two lime-green eyes glowed back at him unmistakably. Yes, the unthinkable had happened. Lady Isra of the Dark had managed to get past Samuel's enigmatic barriers, and here she was in Spirisity.

"Oh, my. Well, aren't you a vision, indeed, my girl!"

Samuel gasped awkwardly. He didn't know how to conduct himself. Isra, having made her way to Spirisity, caught him off guard. It was completely unplanned where mystical law was decreed; it was absolutely forbidden.

No dark souls could enter unless they had permission from the light bringer himself. Of course, Astrid would always be able to pop back whenever he deemed fit. But in recent times, he hadn't come by much at all, so Samuel never felt the need to revoke his key. But Isra, on the other hand, was dark and therefore forbidden from entering such a prestigious land.

Isra revealed herself, pulling back the hood of her midnight-blue cloak. She stood on the edge of the yellow crocus and violet carpet that dominated Spirisity. It was the fluorescent green of her bewildering eyes that had immediately caught Samuel's eye. Isra was dressed from head to toe in her usual jet-black. She had on a wonderfully forgiving tight black bandeau gown with long black sleeves that were beautifully detailed with lace embroidery at the bottom.

It was worth noting that Isra was poised, still holding that shimmering bright green orb in her right hand. And one could only imagine what she was going to do with that spectacle if she had deemed it wholly necessary.

Uh-oh. It looks like she and Astrid have had time to chew the fat. Damn. Is she going to agree to my proposal? One would question why she looks so ravishing. Oh, my! Samuel thought.

"Isra. How unexpected of you. Why, I never expected to find you here in my neck of the woods," Samuel mouthed in a shocked tone.

"Neither did I. But apparently, we have some unfinished business to discuss. A small matter of your dire plan pertaining to myself. I'm afraid I don't bring good tidings, old man!" Isra mocked sullenly.

She cared very little whether Samuel Reynaldi was offended. His ghastly plan had been blown wide open.

"I do apologise for my confusion, but goodness knows, girl. You're not supposed to be among us. How in damnation did you manage to get yourself here?" Samuel exclaimed. He was exasperated, having little control.

Isra chuckled. A huge grin appeared as she announced softly, "I have friends in very high places. But if you must know, I used the back door," she articulated sarcastically. *I'm sure he knows my meaning. He's just too dim-witted to comprehend the notion that Astrid, his former and faithful servant, went against the code in the name of love. But it must be heartbreaking for Samuel to see, one must admit. Oh, well. I care not for this man's impetuousness.*

"I see. I wonder if I could fathom a guess as to whom, but I know better, don't I? Oh, dear..." Samuel paused, feeling rather conflicted within himself.

He had no comprehension of what to do next. He put his forefinger to his lips hurriedly as if some passing thought would come to him, giving him a fast solution on how to remedy this before anything could fester. And let's face it, Samuel hated when things came to a head.

She's defied the pure laws of nature. A witch of her calibre in my peaceful land; how in the name of malice was she able to accomplish such a feat? Well, it doesn't bear thinking about. Somehow, she's managed to slip through my elaborate net. Oh, golly! We're really all in for it now. I should have taken that fucking shimmering green spectacle from her when I had the chance. Now everything I've worked for in my long life could be destroyed right in my midst. Collateral damage indeed, Samuel murmured to himself in candid thought, knowing Isra's extreme rule-breaking must have been enacted for a reason.

Before Samuel could react, however, he was distracted by a rustling amongst the delicate bluebells. A shadowy figure emerged from them. They were also adorned in a velvet cloak, only this one was jet-black.

The onlooker slowly pulled down the hood to reveal a pair of brown eyes tinged with that familiar yellow sheen. He glared ferociously at the other participants except for Isra, with whom he simply smirked at warmly—a gesture of affection since he cared very little for anyone else that happened to be present.

"Astrid!" Samuel gasped. "Well, now, isn't this intriguing. You and your ladyship, in my lands, of all places. May I kindly remind you that Spirisity is a sanctuary for those who choose to dwell in the light?" Samuel uttered crossly.

He stood awkwardly outside his dominion, not entirely certain on what his next move should be.

"Samuel," Astrid calmly responded. "It distresses me that you thought you could use Isra to satisfy your selfish needs. As for how she gained entry into Spirisity... well, my dear old man, I simply escorted her here. Under my name, she can enter any of your light lands as she pleases. And may I remind you, it's all about to be transferred into James's name soon enough, so that card will not be revoked. Much to your disappointment, I imagine."

Astrid scoffed sardonically and strode forward so he could take his position, right by Isra's side. The fact that both of them had come together could only mean one thing. Trouble was soon to be afoot.

"Yet again, boy, Spirisity is a sanctuary. Those who abscond into darkness are strictly prohibited," Samuel admonished angrily. *Astrid let her in. Of course, he did. She could have conducted any malefic spell of her knowledge, but with him by her side, she did not need to. He just handed her the keys to the kingdom without hesitating. The real tragedy here is that our downfall is his willingness to sweetly gift his witch whatever he deems she should have. He's always been overzealous with presenting her gifts. Such gracious offerings nearly always come with great subterfuge,* Samuel blundered in thought.

Oh, how he cringed at the mere thought of Astrid's brash rebellion. However, he was a hypocrite, for he, too, had engaged in some severe rule-breaking lately. Samuel was for sure making Astrid's rebellious nature seem sweet and clandestine in comparison. But still, he had to keep up the pretence.

"Goodness boy, you really don't give two hoots about Spirisity, do you? You know, I remember once upon a time when you were in full agreement with the regulations protecting our supreme land," Samuel countered furiously. "But then came along our little firecracker and all notions about Spirisity being a divine sanctuary were soon forgotten. And me along with it."

Samuel huffed. His impatience was becoming very evident now. His frustration was getting the better of him. Soon, that well-dignified exterior of his would crumble into nothingness.

"Or at least it should be!" James addressed in a loud voice as he emerged from the far end of the bluebell thicket.

Nobody had noticed he was there. Perhaps the soon-to-be-announced light bringer was hiding. One might say he had been preparing his enigmatic speech, for it was sure to offend.

James had his arms pressed firmly against his chest. His green eyes glared at Samuel angrily while he simply nodded in Astrid's direction, a signal of sorts. Finally, for the first time in millennia, there was a calmness between the two of them.

Astrid hadn't even been aware of James's presence, but perhaps he was more preoccupied with keeping his eyes on Samuel, especially since the wayward fellow was standing in very close proximity to Isra. *I don't think he can do anything in the here and now. Not with myself and Isra's combined efforts, but I'll keep my beady eyeballs on him just in case he tries anything. Not that he would if he values his fucking life,* Astrid calmly instructed himself in thought.

He and Isra had done the unthinkable to get to this point, and now they were about to reveal that glorious enchantment unto the world, thus not only safeguarding their union but being a united front against the light for the first time since, well... forever.

James was about to say his piece for all to hear. Now, this was going to be exciting, as Astrid had always had James down as a goody-two-shoes type, but the shoe was on the other foot. Samuel was the bastard who had been caught red-handed breaching the light decree. Astrid was sure to listen with keen ears to this one despite the misgivings he'd harboured towards James.

James began his preaching aimed in Samuel's direction. He recited loudly for all participants to hear, "It might have failed to come to your attention, but this is deemed to be a peaceful land. It's not a place for old vendettas that have yet to be cast aside. It's NOT here for your sad agendas that seriously lack finesse. No, Samuel. It seems in all my years of fighting the obscurity by your side as your right-hand man that you've neglected to inform me of your wayward ways."

"Is this it? The sacred moment of my life that you all gang up on me? Well, I guess this is where you show me what you got, boy. Come on," Samuel goaded James before adding, "But it's only a matter of time, boy. You think you know everything, huh? You're about to become the chief light bringer of Spirisity, but SHE," Samuel pointed at Isra, "is a bloody abomination. She's brought more bloodshed and chaos to this land than I could ever begin to fathom. Don't think for one second that she's going to be anything other than that. We cannot change who people are deep in their wretched souls. It's human nature. And believe me, boy, she WON'T change!"

"That's seldom the point here, now is it?" Isra derided him.

She eyeballed James with fascination as she whispered something under her breath, taking care to concentrate as she acted. It only took a second, and a quaint violet recliner materialised by the bluebell thicket. It was beautified in the most elegant plush velvet with gold gilding on the arms while the legs had a comparable finish. Isra ambled over to the chair thoughtfully, planting herself on it so that she had a precise view of Samuel.

"Ah, now, that is much better. Where was I? Ah, that's it. I'm the bad girl. I'm the one that has repudiated herself to the devil. Oh, my goodness. Doesn't this ever get old for the likes of you? Now, tell me; don't you think aiming to get me to rejuvenate my mortal adversary to release chaos unto the realm goes against your fancy-ass light bringer code? Because I was led to conclude you were holier than thou. However, appearances are most deceiving, aren't they?" Isra interrogated Samuel with a wide-eyed stare.

"And you," Isra turned to confront James, inspecting him carefully. "You are to be the next light bringer? You've continued to be at loggerheads with Astrid as long as you both can recognise, and yet you haven't acknowledged what's declining with your dear old boss here! One would even assume you have no idea what you're truly in for. But it doesn't matter..."

She hesitated briefly, turning to flash Astrid a mischievous smile, as he remained quietly next to her by the bluebells as she rested harmoniously upon her throne.

Isra caressed her lips viciously in James's direction as she beamed, "For you are about to explore all you'll need to know about me, love."

James looked taken aback at Isra's cold response. It was enough to make the hairs on the back of his neck stand up. She wasn't the sweet girl he'd once met when he was showing her around Shambre Fell. No, she'd matured astonishingly. Now she was the scoundrel everybody had anticipated she'd be. She'd exceeded everybody's expectations.

"Well, I don't mean to be foolhardy, but we were at no time enemies. Once upon a time, you and I enjoyed a very amicable conversation, but evidently, you don't recall it," James mustered apologetically.

He was esteeming that perhaps he could be on some good footing with Isra. They needn't oppose one another. All of that was so superfluous, as far as he was concerned.

"Ah yes, you showed me around the distinguished calibre that is now my home. It's just a pity you had to play this deplorable travesty to make me lodge there. As for my memories, dear boy, they have come back. I know exactly who you are. I know the crest you are about to acquire, and let's have none of that 'Oh, let us be civilised balderdash. No, dear; light and dark do not synchronise. Forget it. That's just a dingy fairytale all of you hopelessly anticipate becoming a reality. Well, let us not be aggravated by the attitude of hicks. Onto more agreeable matters," Isra dismissed him candidly.

"It was nice of you to go running to 'on high' so that I'd have no memory of the awful events that took place. Now, however will I repay you? Mmm," Isra contemplated while she held a critical finger to her lips.

"We must honour the fact that you did aid Astrid in his time of need. I will give you commendation for that, albeit, only just. You stole my maid, although quite forthrightly. I won't miss the foul stench of horse manure," she concluded curtly, twitching her nose at the bare thought of Ava and her indecency.

"I didn't abduct her. I merely brought her to a safe place of residency," James piped up. He sounded defensive.

It was at this stage that Samuel's ears pricked up. *So James preserved our dear little Ava, eh? Well, isn't that amusing. He's taking his role far too vigorously and he's not even light bringer yet. My, my, someone certainly wants my assignment, don't they? Well, when the chips are down, let's see if he can deal with our little spitfire because I don't feel like she's going to churn down at any time soon!* Samuel snickered to himself, although he was astonished by James's actions.

"That you did. It doesn't matter. I suppose you think with you becoming the next light bringer that I'm going to tone down my deplorable darkened ways?" Isra grilled him in an astringent voice.

"No, but I was counting on—" James closed mid-sentence, as he understood it was ineffectual; a reckless excursion.

"Ah, you were hoping we'd be allies? Light and dark dancing simultaneously under the stars. Flitting around charmingly like butterflies and cherubs, and all of that other baloney! I think not, boy. Conceivably, I've been too forgiving. After all, Samuel did try to persuade me to bring back my old friend Everilda from her premature grave. Namely, the one I installed her in. Maybe what we need here is a little demonstration. A battle of wits, maybe? Let's see what you light folk are really composed of. Will your strengths pull you over, or will you fall by the wayside? Either way, it's going to be a jolly good show."

Isra licked her lips wickedly as both James and Samuel looked exceedingly uncomfortable.

James was deviating apprehensively from where he stood. His sword dangled by his side, flapping in mid-air as it hung from his belt loop. James's fingers calmly advanced towards his sword as though he was tempted to clinch it in his hand at any second. But all he could do was gawk weakly at Isra. Her green ignited eyes glowered back at him ferociously. She looked as though she was enamoured as she sat so regally upon that velveteen chair.

Samuel, on the other hand, had changed white as a ghost. He had an agitated expression adhered to his face. Beads of sweat crossed his temple. Samuel appeared as though he was heading towards another Irish whiskey but yet he didn't flounder. Not an inch.

He was most decidedly conceding the urge to remove himself

from his location on those grey steps where he'd so deftly placated himself. In any event, you could tell by the disturbing expression all over his face that he was gravely uneasy about what Isra was about to do. There was certainly no stiff upper lip now to encounter the once daunting light bringer.

28

Samuel conveyed a worrisome glance of unease as he checked out Isra with scrutiny.

"If I may implore you, dear girl, what are you intending to do?" Samuel asked keenly.

He fearlessly deployed himself in front of James. It was as though he assumed that might have detracted Isra.

It was at this point that Astrid declared, "Well, this doesn't look good for our light bringer, does it now?"

"She's going to launch an attack on Spirisity," James exhorted with a critically troubled glance back at Samuel.

This caused the light bringer to bolt into action.

"Well, you don't say!" Samuel came apart at James. He then moved to Isra with a hard-nosed stare. "No. That is against all of our guidelines. How dare you come here, brandishing your dark, putrid magic around, tormenting the good and benevolent souls of Spirisity. Get out of here this minute!" Samuel ordered Isra as he rashly waved his hands, exhibiting his displeasure.

"Ha, but I thought you wanted me to be this way, old man! Am I not to your liking now? Oh, dear; that is disappointing. Oh, well. Needs must!" Isra countered in Samuel's direction.

James glanced around as if he checking for an exit. Of course, he wasn't quite as adapted as Samuel was for these types of circumstances, so he wanted to dart out of there. However, Isra's piercing green eyes tightened on the future light bringer with a snarl as she growled, "Going somewhere, my boy? I think not. Why, my little party is just commencing!"

"Oh, great. Now we're done for!" James squawked at the top of his lungs.

"Sshhhh now!" Isra muted him in a low voice as she softly closed her eyes.

In euphoric concentration, Isra began noiselessly mouthing some chosen words under her breath. Isra lightly lifted her hand to the sky and then it was displayed that encased inside it was the burnished lime-green orb.

The monstrosity glistened with such acumen as it pummelled the jet-black skies, sparking ferociously until it hit the expanse. At once, the bright, scintillating energy radiating out from the orb began to accumulate as luminous green light designated itself all around Spirisity, discharging a blazing green light show as it completely circulated the once harmonious land. Within a few seconds, gloom commenced on Spirisity. Serenity evaporated.

James and Samuel solemnly looked on at the carnage that was about to befall them. Astrid was still coolly by the bluebells as he beheld the show being acquitted from above. Of course, he was erected inches away from where Isra was, captivated in an introspective state, constructing mayhem.

Samuel was furious. He couldn't accept how deliberately Astrid had metamorphosed, for he was once Samuel's most considerable ally in the battle against the dark. Astrid had been associated in many locales where some poor soul had decamped from the light into the perilous confines of the dark.

How can he be so cool about all of this while she's up there unleashing calamity unto us all? He's got the severe audaciousness to stand there while this is developing in our midst! Oh, I'm not having that. Not in my fucking realm. How dare they infiltrate in, uninvited like this, waving their tarnished magic around like excrement. Samuel fumed inherently to himself as he gave Astrid a death stare.

"How dare you, Astrid. You have got some nerve, standing there unflinchingly as chaos is being discharged as we speak!" Samuel raged at Astrid.

"Now that is funny. You seem rather distressed. Isn't it interesting how you were altogether fine as you strategically materialised to Isra on our wedding day? How the tables have turned." Astrid giggled, seeming to be thoroughly amused. "Well, we'll launch enough dark torrential hell at you, and we shall see if something sticks. I must admit, I have been entertained already."

Astrid chuckled merrily. He then went quiet as he saw a bolt of lightning strike the grass. Astrid looked skyward, expeditiously seeing that several bolts of lightning were nose-diving down from the forlorn skies, shaking Spirisity to its core.

Isra wasn't done. The black fulmination had effectively bestridden the grey rain clouds that were detonating with a vicious downpour. Rain gushed down onto the entirety of Spirisity as thunder bellowed from above, echoing its displeasure throughout the acreage as it surged onto everything in sight.

The gleaming green energy from the florid orb began to disembark back down from the surface, lighting up the skies as it did so, hastily making its way back to Isra's hand. Rain continued to batter down hard, clobbering the grassland so savagely that all the violets and crocuses dipped into the earth, knocked down. Their stems were contorted and mushy and they feebly sank into the soil. However, the lightning came to a standstill, which gave for a moment's pause.

For a second, James and Samuel exhibited relief. The worst was over. A ceasefire had culminated. Or so they estimated, because Isra opened her eyes... but Samuel gasped—she was staring right at him. Her eyes shone, glistening more than he'd ever seen.

Isra ardently felt the orb pulsate as it sat upon her skin. Its depth was beautiful and yet bewildering. She was rather enthralled by it all. This one charming commodity that had been lost to her for so long was now enjoined with her in reality. It was a poignant moment.

Isra peeked up at the cloudy cobalt skies and babbled sullenly. Anticipating something, she beamed mindlessly at the sky. Samuel and James were just as engrossed; however, both men were more troubled of what aversion was about to emerge rather than beguiled at the wonders of creation. It only took a second, and all at once, a colossal jet-black thing appeared.

At first, it was burdensome to analyse just what it was, but then it became abundantly clear. It was beyond anything James had ever witnessed. This larger-than-life, onyx abnormality with silver flecks drifted above the realm of Spirisity. As it got closer, large, charcoal, shimmery wings were exposed.

Samuel placed a hand to his mouth in awe. He also caught sight of the ginormous claws. Isra looked on contemptuously as she watched James and Samuel cower in dread as the dragon surged straight at them. Samuel instantly raced right away for his humble abode and dashed up the steps. James grasped his sword at once, assembling for battle, as the dragon came up close to him.

"I'm ready for you," he called out as he braced himself for combat.

Samuel had come to the entrance to his property, teetering on the steps, so he held onto the wall for support. It was when he spun around that he noticed Isra was no longer installed on her throne. In fact, the chair she'd magically adjured out of nowhere had also dissipated. She was nowhere to be seen.

"Isra has gone! Where the hell is she?" Samuel called out hurriedly.

Astrid was aghast as he'd realised what Samuel was saying was true. Isra had completely hightailed. There was no trace of her. Astrid didn't make any approach to sound the alarm, but he looked exceptionally puzzled. His wife had dispersed out of nowhere. The colour depleted from Astrid's skin at once. He was now enormously concerned for her welfare.

"Yes, she has," he advised carefully.

Now he was alone with Samuel and James. He and Isra had descended into Spirisity to cause this gigantic ascendancy, and Isra was no longer under Astrid's attentive eye. To say he was perturbed was an understatement.

The scaled critter had possibly heard Astrid's fearful words; it abruptly withdrew from the immobilised James and glided away at once, supposedly to follow Isra. Nonetheless, his harbour was unknown.

"Thank fuck for that. Let's hope that is the end of it!" Samuel yelled as he ran his fingers through his hair anxiously, quickly readjusting his silver half-moon frame spectacles, as they'd become dislodged during all the commotion.

"Actually, it's not," James declared. "You fractured protocol. You tried to overshadow one of the most fragmented souls for your own gain. Isra may already be in the dark, but trying to sway her to rejuvenate someone dangerous to herself and the realm itself—Well, it's absurd."

James drew a huge sigh, feeling aggrieved about what was ahead, but he knew it was imminent no matter how he felt. "I'm afraid I have no choice but to hereby decree that you, Samuel Reynaldi, are ejected from Spirisity. Effective immediately. Any and all celestial agreements, connections, and contracts are now terminated. 'On high' is no longer at your beck and call. This is not something I get any amusement from, but you must go. Now," James advised Samuel. "For 'on high' have never taken too kindly to a betrayer of the light."

Samuel absorbed those words, but conclusively, he wasn't terribly phased. Over his tenure, he'd seen more dissatisfaction, deception, and desolation than he cared to count. Although he was a well-seasoned man, having the background to administer the role he'd been in for so long made him acutely tired of it all. He had hoped that Isra would have followed through on his request, but honestly, being dispelled was the least of his dilemmas.

Samuel bent his head apologetically. "Well, if that is to be the way of it, then farewell, old chap. Good tidings and all! May you always be blessed by the sanctity of that which you uphold. As for me, I am tired of this shit."

Samuel turned to leave. He waved his hand clumsily and then after a moment, he was gone, scattered into nothingness.

Astrid was still present. He had to admit, it felt surreal. Never did he ever imagine he'd get to see this. But it was happening.

Samuel had been given the heave-ho. James was taking his role as the new light-bringer sincerely. Although he had not yet been appointed, it was what was in his heart that counted. Astrid couldn't help but find buried affection in what he'd witnessed.

With Samuel gone, it was the end of an era. He could confidently rest assured that nothing more was to transpire pertaining to his union with Isra now that Samuel Reynaldi had finally been relegated.

It turned out to be a truly good day, although that assumption probably wasn't ringing true for Samuel, who'd had a disheartening one indeed. But even those that have been forsaken live to fight another day.

THE CHARRED LAND of Rainfur hadn't seen much movement of late. The old cabin that sat quaintly by the burnt-out grass bank hadn't been occupied since the last occupant.

It seemed like a typical evening. The barrages had desisted and the epic thunder and firebolt show had also been brought to a close. However, there was something far more alluring that would soon have the Wiccans that dwelled here running for their lives.

Just as everything looked to be returning to its usual bleak calm, a black dragon with silver-scaled wings touched down from the heavens. Although he was a brutish fellow, he appeared to be positively fascinated with the bright lime-green energy that carried him here. He very plainly had no importance in harming anyone as he sat mesmerised by this shimmery green energy that had overshadowed the burnt-out clearing of Rainfur.

Within moments, the all-powerful force accelerated up, surging in brutality. The earth began to shake forcibly. The incinerated grass shook in the wind as the bright, glazed life force began to resemble the shape of a person. Green flames besieged the figure as lime-green became more dazzling, so bright, it was almost blinding. The heat from the fire was becoming so excessive that if the land wasn't already blackened to a crisp, it might have been totally cremated.

At last, the character appeared from the green, glowing, serene light and floundered across the charred grassland as they sought to find their footing. The disorientation took over as a pair of sapphire-blue eyes met the dragon's silver ones in a cumbersome glance.

"Well, I've not seen this place for a long time. I never once thought I'd happen to lay my eyes on a dragon. My goodness! Is it me, or is Rainfur truly be-damned? I can smell the stench of a farmhand from over here," a woman with fair, shoulder-length hair said in a low voice.

"I've not been here long. But one thing is clear; my return can only mean disorder is on the compass," she guffawed with a sly laugh.

ASTRID BELATEDLY CAPTURED sight of Isra's long, flowing, golden-white hair as he dashed towards Shambre Fell from the bottom of the gardens. He'd been combing the area far and wide since she'd absconded from his view.

"Oh, there you are. I've been searching for you everywhere," he gushed in a bothered tone as he buckled Isra into his heated embrace, snagging her tightly as she allowed herself to be held by him.

"Yes, well, after all of the theatrics, I chose to go outside for a walk. I needed to appease the voices," Isra asserted meekly.

Astrid was relieved to see that Isra still had the emerald ring on her finger, and he once again engaged her into his grip, but even he couldn't discern what she meant by "voices."

"The voices?" He squeezed her lightly. "You've been hearing something?"

"Yes. They won't stop humming. I can't physically shake them. I thought at first it might have been some after-effect of the alchemies I used. Sorry—*we* used. But it appears something else may well be ensuing," she complained mysteriously.

"Well, let's not concern ourselves with any of it," Astrid disciplined Isra calmly. He turned to face her as they stood outside the ornate wooden door of Shambre Fell. "It's been a long day and night. You are beaten. We should get you inside. I'll make you some tea to help you sleep."

Astrid tried enticing her, as he felt the deficiency in Isra's body. She was losing her balance as she adhered to his strong arms for dear life.

Isra disregarded him. "I don't think I can sleep, Astrid, not for a moment. But tea does sound elating after all this."

She gazed up at the sky for a moment. She hadn't even realised it had got dark. The midnight-blue skies spotlighted Shambre Fell as silvery-white stars sparkled in the scope. Just beyond some fluffy off-white clouds, Isra discovered the luminous glowing white new moon shining gleamingly.

"Well, after the excitement you've had today, I insist," Astrid argued. He hesitated for a moment, deliberating just how to explain to Isra why rest was a necessity. "Samuel has been dispelled from the lands. James made the order," he admitted. "It's over. After everything they've thrown at us, finally, we can both pause."

He took great care to enunciate with a wide-eyed grin as he held her close to him once more.

"Oh, I wouldn't be so sure of that," a voice derided in the distance.

A barefoot woman with her face and head buried in a scarf ambled towards Astrid and Isra.

"In fact, I wouldn't be sure of anything. But I would like some tea, if it's not too much trouble. I am rather parched. You know, from being dead and all," Everilda warbled as she pulled back her scarf to reveal her shimmery golden hair. She smiled excitedly as her blue eyes met Isra's bewildered, piercing green ones with an impertinent glance.

"Everilda? Is it really you?"

Isra examined her as she pulled away from Astrid to ensure her eyes were not playing tricks on her.

"That it is. I don't know how the hell I am back. But hey, needs must!" Everilda crowed as she eyed her former foe.

And there it was. Everilda Daughtry had advanced from the grave.

Despite Isra not fulfilling Samuel's self-gratifying prophecy, somehow Everilda had been aroused from her peril. The only inquiry was whether the two women could co-exist with one another. Because when you put two all-powerful witches back in each other's bosom, it only added up to chaos.

THE END.

DARK SPELLS READING ORDER

1. Her Dark Love
2. Kissing Darkness
3. Seducing Darkness
4. Queen of Darkness
5. Her Dark Soul
6. Her Dark Heart
7. Her Dark Rose
8. Darkness Reborn

ABOUT THE AUTHOR

USA Today Best Seller Isra Sravenheart resides in the UK. She is an avid reader, particularly in the fantasy and paranormal genres, and very much into all things fairytale and dark in nature. She is also a witty wordsmith.

Isra is known for being obsessed with coffee and very particular towards cats of which she owns four of the buggers.

You can follow Isra through her blog, or any of these social media platforms:

facebook.com/IsraSravenheart

twitter.com/ISravenheart

instagram.com/israsravenheartauthor_

bookbub.com/authors/isra-sravenheart

goodreads.com/Isra_Sravenheart

ALSO BY ISRA SRAVENHEART